PRAISE FOR *MAELSTROM*

"An eerie journey of revenge and salvation." —*Library Journal*

"[Watts's] fiction exhibits a wonderful Darwinian adaptability. Internalizing the lessons and modes taught by cyberpunk and fusing them with the Bear/Benford pedigree of hard SF, Watts has bred a robust, streamlined, snarling kind of science fiction which achieves both a sharp-edged verisimilitude and visionary exuberance. . . . These two novels are state-of-the art SF. And best of all, *Maelstrom* does not merely repeat the successes of *Starfish* but extends them into new territory."

—Paul Di Filippo, *Science Fiction Weekly*

"The premise is interesting, the humor dark . . . unexpected plot twists and an ending that is complete in itself."

—*Edmonton Journal*

"Watts displays a gleefully macabre inventiveness combined with scientific rigor. With its chaotically alive portrayal of the World Wide Web and its disturbing ruminations on the uses of conscience, *Maelstrom* is a dark, sardonic, and uncompromisingly moral book." —Nalo Hopkinson, *Quill & Quire*

"Watts's hard-boiled prose screams along [with] nothing to step it down. . . . Lifting beyond cyberconspiracy are Watts's convincing writing, his killer pacing, and the delicate secondary themes. . . . This is speculative fiction of maximum wattage."

—John Burns, *The Georgia Straight*

PRAISE FOR *STARFISH*

A *NEW YORK TIMES* NOTABLE BOOK OF THE YEAR

"No one has taken this premise to such pitiless lengths—and depths—as Watts. . . . In a claustrophobic setting enlivened by periodic flashes of beauty and terror, the crew of Beebe Station come across as not only believable but likeable as they fight for equilibrium against their own demons, one another, their superiors, and their remorselessly hostile surroundings."

—*The New York Times*

"A savage, bitter, and often blackly comic vision of the near future . . . [The ending] is both startling and oddly satisfying in its earned nihilism. A terrific debut from an author we will be seeing again." —*Edmonton Journal*

"Fizzing with ideas, and glued together with dark psychological tension: an exciting debut." —*Kirkus Reviews*

"Peter Watts delivers—solid, inventive hard SF about the deep sea, but as we've never seen before. This moves like the wind."

—Gregory Benford

TOR BOOKS BY PETER WATTS

Blindsight
Starfish
Maelstrom
ßehemoth: ß-Max
ßehemoth: Seppuku

MAELSTROM

PETER WATTS

TOR®

A TOM DOHERTY ASSOCIATES BOOK
NEW YORK

This is a work of fiction. All of the characters, organizations, and events portrayed in this novel are either products of the author's imagination or are used fictitiously.

MAELSTROM

Edited by David G. Hartwell

A Tor Book
Published by Tom Doherty Associates, LLC
175 Fifth Avenue
New York, NY 10010

www.tor-forge.com

Tor® is a registered trademark of Tom Doherty Associates, LLC.

Library of Congress Cataloging-in-Publication Data

Watts, Peter.
    Maelstrom / Peter Watts.
        p. cm.
    "A Tom Doherty Associates book."
    ISBN-13: 978-0-7653-2053-7
    ISBN-10: 0-7653-2053-3
    1. Tsunamis—Fiction. 2. Revenge—Fiction. I. Title.

PR9199.3.W386 M34 2001
813'.54—dc21

                                         2001041446

First Hardcover Edition: October 2001
First Trade Paperback Edition: January 2009

Printed in the United States of America

0 9 8 7 6 5 4 3 2 1

For Laurie
"Though she be but little, she is fierce."

Behold now behemoth,
which I made with thee;
he eateth grass as an ox.
—Job 40:15

All flesh is grass.
—Isaiah 40:6

CONTENTS

MAELSTROM

PRELUDE

THE day after Patricia Rowan saved the world, a man named Elias Murphy brought a piece of her conscience home to roost.

She hardly needed another one. Her tactical contacts already served up an endless stream of death and damage, numbers far too vague to qualify as estimates. It had only been sixteen hours; even orders of magnitude were barely more than guesses. But the machines kept trying to pin it down, this many million lives, that many trillion dollars, as if quantifying the apocalypse would somehow render it harmless.

Maybe it would at that, she reflected. The scariest monsters always knew enough to disappear just before you turned on the lights.

She eyed Murphy through the translucent display in her head: a man eclipsed by data he couldn't even see. His face contained its own information, though. She recognized it instantly.

Elias Murphy hated her. To Elias Murphy, the monster was Patricia Rowan.

She didn't blame him. He'd probably lost someone in the quake. But if Murphy knew the role she'd played, he must also know what the stakes had been. No rational being would blame her for taking the necessary steps.

He probably didn't. Rationally. But his hatred rose from somewhere in the brainstem, and Rowan could not begrudge it.

"There's a loose end," he said evenly.

More than one.

"The βehemoth meme got into Maelstrom," the gel-jockey continued. "Actually it's been in the Net for some time, although it only really—impacted—through that one gel that you..."

He stopped before the accusation became explicit.

After a moment he began again. "I don't know how much they've told you about the—glitch. We used a Gaussian feed-forward algorithm to get around local minima—"

"You taught smart gels to protect data from Internet wildlife," Rowan said. "Somehow they generalized that into a preference for simple systems over complex ones. We innocently gave one of them a choice between a microbe and a biosphere and it started working for the wrong side. We pulled the plug just in time. That about right?"

"Just in time," Murphy echoed. Not for everyone, his eyes added. "But it had already spread the meme by then. It was linked into Maelstrom so it could act autonomously, of course."

Rowan translated: *So it could immolate people without restraint.* She was still vaguely amazed that the Consortium had ever agreed to give that kind of power to a head cheese. Granted there was no such thing as a human without bias. Granted no one was going to trust anyone else to decide what cities should burn for the greater good, even in the face of a microbe that could end the world. Still: give absolute authority to a two-kilogram slab of cultured neurons? She still couldn't believe that all the kings and corpses had really agreed to it.

Of course, the thought that smart gels might have their *own* biases hadn't occurred to anyone.

"You asked to be kept informed," Murphy told her, "but it's really not a problem. It's just a junk meme now, it'll burn itself out in a week or two."

"A week or two." Rowan took a breath. "Are you aware of how much damage your *junk meme's* caused in the past fifteen *hours?*"

"I—"

"It hijacked a lifter, Dr. Murphy. It was two hours away from letting half a dozen vectors loose in the general population, in which case all this might have only been the beginning instead of—"—*instead of, oh please God, the end of the matter* . . .

"It could hijack a lifter because it had *command authority*. It doesn't have that anymore, and the other gels never *did*. We're talking about a bunch of code that's useless to anything without real-world autonomy and which, barring some external impetus, will eventually extinguish anyway for lack of reinforcement. And as for *all this*—" Murphy's voice acquired a sudden, insubordinate edge—"from what I hear, it wasn't the gels that pulled that particular trigger."

Well. Can't get much more explicit than that.

She decided to let it pass. "Forgive me, but I'm not entirely reassured. There's a plan for world destruction percolating through the Net, and you're telling me not to worry about it?"

"That's what I'm telling you."

"Unfort—"

"Ms. Rowan, gels are like big gooey autopilots. Just because something can monitor altitude and weather and put down landing gear at the right time, that doesn't mean it's *aware* of any of those things. The gels aren't plotting to destroy the world, they don't even know the real world exists. They're just manipulating variables. And that's only dangerous if one of their output registers happens to be hooked up to a bomb on a fault line."

"Thank you for your assessment. Now if you were instructed to purge this meme, how would you go about it?"

He shrugged. "We can find perverted gels through simple interrogation, now that we know what to look for. We'd swap out tainted gels for fresh ones—we were scheduled to go to phase four anyway, so the next crop's already ripe."

"Good," Rowan said. "Get started."

Murphy stared at her.

"Is there some problem?" Rowan asked.

"We could *do* it, all right, but it'd be a complete waste of—I mean, my *God!* Half the Pacific coast just dropped into the sea, surely there's more—"

"Not for you, sir. You have your assignment."

He turned away, crowded by invisible statistics.

"What kind of external impetus, Doctor?" she said to his back.

He stopped. "What?"

"You said it would extinguish *barring some external impetus.* What did you mean?"

"Something to pump up the replication rate. New input to reinforce the meme."

"What kind of input?"

He turned to face her. "There is none, Ms. Rowan. That's my point. You've purged the records, you've broken the correlations, and you've eliminated the vectors, right?"

Rowan nodded. "We—"

—killed our people—

"—eliminated the vectors," she said.

"Well there you go."

She deliberately softened her voice. "Please carry out my instructions, Dr. Murphy. I know they seem trivial to you, but I'd rather take the *precautions* than the risk."

His face conveyed exactly what he thought of the precautions she'd already undertaken. He nodded and left without another word.

Rowan sighed and sagged back in her chair. A banner of text scrolled across her field of view: another four hundred botflies successfully requisitioned for the SeaTac mop-up. That made over five thousand of the little teleops between SeaTac and Hongcouver, racing to sniff out the bodies before typhus and cholera beat them to the trough.

Millions dead. Trillions in damages. Preferable to the alternative, she knew. It didn't help much.

Saving the world had come with a price tag attached.

VOLVOX

Mermaid

THE Pacific Ocean stood on her back. She ignored it.

It crushed the bodies of her friends. She forgot them.

It drank the light, blinding even her miraculous eyes. It dared her to give in, to use her headlamp like some crippled dryback.

She kept going, in darkness.

Eventually the seafloor tilted into a great escarpment, leading into light. The bottom changed. Mud disappeared under viscous clumps of half-digested petroleum: a century of oil spills, a great global rug to sweep them beneath. Generations of sunken barges and fishing trawlers haunted the bottom, each a corpse and crypt and epitaph unto itself. She explored the first one she found, slid through shattered windowpanes and upended corridors, and remembered, vaguely, that fish were supposed to congregate in such places.

A long time ago. Now there were only worms, and suffocating bivalves, and a woman turned amphibious by some abstract convergence of technology and economics.

She kept going.

It was growing almost bright enough to see without eyecaps. The bottom twitched with sluggish eutrophiles, creatures so black with hemoglobin they could squeeze oxygen from the rocks themselves. She flashed her headlamp at them, briefly: they shone crimson in the unexpected light.

She kept going.

Sometimes, now, the water was so murky she could barely see her own hands in front of her. The slimy rocks passing beneath took on ominous shapes, grasping hands, twisted limbs, hollow death's-heads with things squirming in their eyes. Sometimes the slime assumed an almost fleshy appearance.

By the time she felt the tug of the surf, the bottom was completely covered in bodies. They, too, seemed to span generations. Some were little more than symmetrical patches of algae. Others were fresh enough to bloat, obscenely buoyant, straining against the detritus holding them down.

But it wasn't the bodies that really bothered her. What bothered her was the light. Even filtered through centuries of suspended effluvium, there seemed far too much of it.

The ocean pushed her up, pulled her down, with a rhythm both heard and felt. A dead gull spun past in the current, tangled in monofilament. The universe was roaring.

For one brief moment, the water disappeared in front of her. For the first time in a year she saw the sky. Then a great wet hand slapped the back of her head, put her under again.

She stopped swimming, uncertain what to do next. But the decision wasn't hers anyway. The waves, marching endlessly shoreward in gray, seething rows, pushed her the rest of the way.

She lay gasping on her belly, water draining from the machinery in her chest: gills shutting down, guts and airways inflating, fifty million years of vertebrate evolution jammed into thirty seconds with a little help from the biotech industry. Her stomach clenched against its own chronic emptiness. Starvation had become a friend, so faithful she could scarcely imagine its absence. She pulled the fins from her feet, rose, staggered as gravity reasserted itself. A shaky step forward.

The hazy outlines of guard towers leaned against the eastern horizon, a gap-toothed line of broken spires. Fat tick-like shapes hovered above them, enormous by inference: lifters, tending the remains of a border that had always kept refugees and citizens discreetly segregated. There were no refugees here. There were no citizens. There was only a humanoid accretion of mud and oil with machinery at its heart, an ominous mermaid dragging itself back from the abyss. Undiscardable.

And all this endless chaos—the shattered landscape, the bodies smashed and sucked into the ocean, the devastation reaching God knew how far in every direction—it was all just collateral. The hammer, she knew, had been aimed at *her*.

It made her smile.

Fables of the Reconstruction

Great glittering skyscrapers, shaking themselves like wet dogs. Downpours of shattered glass from fifty floors of windowpanes. Streets turned into killing floors; thousands slickly dismembered in the space of seconds. And then, when the quake was over, the scavenger hunt: a search for jigsaws of flesh and blood with too many missing pieces. Their numbers grew logistically over time.

Somewhere between the wreckage and the flies and the piles of eyeless bodies, the soul of Sou-Hon Perreault woke up and screamed.

It wasn't supposed to happen that way. It wasn't supposed to happen at all; the catalyzers kept all those obsolete, maladaptive feelings safely preempted, their constituent chemicals split apart before they'd even reached the precursor stage. You don't go wading through an ocean of corpses, even vicariously, as a fully functional human.

She was all over the map when it hit her. Her body was safely stored at home in Billings, over a thousand klicks from the wreckage. Her senses hovered four meters above the remains of the Granville Street Bridge in Hongcouver, nestled within a floating bluebottle carapace half a meter long. And her mind was somewhere else again, doing basic addition with a tally of body parts.

For some reason, the smell of fresh decomposition was bothering her. Perreault frowned: she wasn't usually so queasy. She couldn't afford to be—the current body count was nothing compared to what cholera would rack up if all that meat wasn't cleaned out by the weekend. She tuned down the channel, even though enhanced olfac was *the* method of choice for nailing buried biologicals.

But now visual was bugging her, too. She couldn't exactly put her finger on it. She was seeing in infra, in case any of the bodies were still warm—hell, someone might even be *alive* down there—but the false color was unsettling her stomach. She dialed through the spectrum, deep infra up to X ray, settled finally on plain old visible EM. It helped a little. Even though she might as well be looking at the world through merely human eyes now, which wouldn't help her tag rate any.

And the fucking gulls. Jesus Christ, you can't hear anything over that racket.

She hated gulls. You couldn't shut them up. They flocked to scenes like this, threw feeding frenzies that would scare sharks away. Over on the other side of False Creek, for instance, the bodies lay so thick that the gulls were for fucksake *high*-grading. Just pecking out the eyes, leaving everything else for the maggots. Perreault hadn't seen anything like it since the Tongking spill five years before.

Tongking. Its aftermath bubbled irrelevantly in the back of her mind, distracting with memories of carnage half a decade out-of-date.

Concentrate, she told herself.

Now, for some reason, she couldn't stop thinking about Sudan. *That* had been a mess. They really should have seen it coming, too; you don't dam a river that size without pissing off *someone* downstream. The real wonder was that Egypt had waited ten years before they'd bombed the bloody thing. The slide had spread a decade's muddy backlog downstream in an instant; by the time the waters fell it was like picking raisin clusters out of sludgy chocolate.

Ah. Another torso.

Except the raisins had arms and legs, of course. And eyes—

A gull flew past. The eyeball in its beak looked at her for an endless, beseeching instant.

And then, for the first time—through a billion logic gates, endless kilometers of fiberop, and a microwave bounce off geosynch—Sou-Hon Perreault looked back.

Brandon. Venesia. Key West.

My God—everybody's dead.

Galveston. Obidos. The Congo Massacre.

Shut up! Concentrate! Shut up shut up....

Madras and Lepreau and Gur'yev, place to place to place the names changing and the ecozones changing and the death toll never sitting still for a fucking *instant* but always the same song, the same endless procession of body parts buried or burned or torn apart—

Everybody's in pieces...

Lima and Levanzo and Lagos *and that's just a few of the L's, folks, lots more where those came from*

It's too late it's too late there's nothing I can do...

Her botfly sent out an alarm as soon as she went off-line. The Router queried the medchip in Perreault's spine, frowned to itself, and sent a message to the other registered occupant of her apartment. Her husband found her trembling and unresponsive in her office, tears bleeding from her eye-phones.

Part of Perreault's soul lived on the long arm of Chromosome 13, in a subtly defective gene that coded for serotonin 2A receptors. The resulting propensity for suicidal thoughts had never been an issue before; catalyzers buffered her in life as well as on the job. Certain pharms were rumored to sabotage each other's products. Maybe that was it: someone had tried to undermine the competition, and Sou-Hon Perreault—a defective derm pasted onto her arm—had walked into the aftermath of the Big One without realizing that her feelings were still on.

She was no good on the front lines after that. Once you went *that* seriously post-traumatic, the cats it took to keep you stable would short out your midbrain. (There were still people in the business who had seizures every time they heard the unzipping of a fly; body bags made the same sound when you sealed them.) But Perreault had eight months left on her contract, and nobody wanted to waste her talents or her paycheck in the meantime. What she needed was some-thing low-intensity, something she could handle with con-ventional suppressants.

They gave her the refugee strip on the west coast. In a way it was ironic: the death toll there had been a hundred times greater than in the cities. But the ocean cleaned up after itself, for the most part. The bodies had been swept out to sea with the sand and the cobble and any boulder smaller than a boxcar. All that remained was moonscape, scoured and buckled.

For the moment, anyway.

Now Sou-Hon Perreault sat at her link and watched a line of red dots crawling along a map of the N'AmPac coastline. Zoomed to higher rez the line resolved into two; one march-ing from southern Washington down to NoCal, another tracking north along the same course. An endless loop of automated surveillance, eyes that could see through flesh, ears that could eavesdrop on bats. Brains smart enough to do their job without Perreault's help, most of the time.

She'd tap into them anyway, and watch their world scroll by. Somehow the botflies' enhanced senses seemed more real than her own. Her world, when she took off the headset, seemed subtly wrapped in cotton these days. She knew it was the catalyzers; what eluded her was why things were so much *less* muted whenever she rode a machine.

They traveled along a gradient of destruction. To the north, the land was laid waste. Industrial lifters hung over gaps in the shattered Wall, rebuilding. To the south refugees still shuffled along the Strip, living in lean-tos and tents and the eroding shells of dwellings from a time when ocean views had actually *increased* property value.

In between, the Strip bled back up the coast in ragged stages. Portable cliffs twenty meters high formed its north-ern perimeter, kept the Strippers safely contained. N'AmPac machinery patched things up for a few kilometers on the other side—replenishing supplies, filling holes, fixing the more permanent barriers to the east. Other cliffs would eventually descend at the northern edge of the reclaimed area, and their southern counterparts would rise unto heaven—or the belly of an industrial lifter, whichever came first—leapfrogging north, ahead of the mammalian tide. Pacification botflies hovered overhead to keep the migration orderly.

Not that they were really necessary, of course. These days there were far more effective ways of keeping people in line.

She would have been content to watch all day, distant and dispassionate, but her duties left waking gaps between work and sleep. She filled them by wandering alone through the apartment, or watching the way her husband watched her. She found herself increasingly drawn to the aquarium glowing softly in their living room. Perreault had always found it a comfort—the fizzy hiss of the aerator, the luminous interaction of light and water, the peaceful choreography of the fish within. She could get lost in it for hours. A sea anemone, twenty centimeters across, stirred in currents at the back of the tank. Symbiotic algae tinted its flesh a dozen shades of green. A pair of damselfish nested safely in its venomous tentacles. Perreault envied them their security: a predator, miraculously turned to the service of its prey.

What she found really amazing was that the whole crazy alliance—algae, anemone, fish—hadn't even been engineered. It had evolved naturally, a gradual symbiosis spanning millions of years. Not one gene had been tweaked in its construction.

It seemed almost too good to be real.

Sometimes the botflies called for help.

This one had seen something it didn't understand in the transition zone. As far as it could tell, one of the Calvin cyclers was splitting in two. Perreault mounted the line and found herself floating above an ephemeral still life. Shiny new cyclers sat along the shore, miracles of industrial photosynthesis, ready to braid raw atmosphere into edible protein. They appeared intact. A bank of latrines and a solar crematorium had been freshly installed. Light stands and blankets and piles of self-assembling tents lay on neat rows of plastic skids. Even the cracked bedrock had been repaired to some extent, autofoam resin injected into the fissures, remnants of sand and cobble replenished and raked half-heartedly over the ruined shoreline.

The restoration crews had gone; the refs had not yet come. But there were fresh footprints on the sand, leading into the ocean.

They came from there, too.

She called up the footage that had triggered the alarm. The world reverted to the garish, comforting false color that machines use to communicate their perceptions to the flesh-constrained. To human eyes, a Calvin cycler was a shiny metal coffin built for a minivan: to the botfly it was a muted tangle of EM emissions.

One of which was sprouting a bud—a little cluster of radiating technology separating from the cycler and weaving uncertainly toward the water. There was also a heat signature, inconsistent with pure tech. Perreault narrowed the focus to visible light.

It was a woman, all in black.

She'd been feeding from the cycler. She hadn't noticed the approaching botfly until it was less than a hundred meters away; then she'd startled and turned to face the lens.

Her eyes were completely white. They held no pupils at all.

Jesus, Perreault thought.

The woman had lurched to her feet as the botfly neared, staggered down the rocky incline. She'd seemed unused to the operation of her own body. Twice she'd fallen. Just short of the waterline she'd grabbed something on the beach— swim fins, Perreault saw—and pitched forward into the shallows. A broken wave had rolled uphill and engulfed her. When it receded the shore was empty.

Less than a minute ago, according to the logs.

Perreault flexed her fingers: twelve hundred kilometers away, the botfly panned down. Exhausted water ebbed and flowed in thin foamy sheets, erasing the creature's footprints. Pacific surf pounded a few meters ahead. For a moment Per-, reault thought she might have glimpsed something in that confusion of spray and swirling green glass—a dark amphib-ious form, a face almost devoid of topography. But the moment passed, and not even the botfly's enhanced senses could bring it back.

She replayed, and reconstructed:

The botfly had confused flesh and machinery. It had been scanning on wide-spectrum default, where EM signatures shone like diffuse halogen. When the woman in black had been next to the cycler, the botfly had mistaken two intimate signals for one. When she had moved away, it had seen the cycler breaking apart.

This woman veritably *gushed* EM. There was machinery embedded in her flesh.

Perreault brought up a freeze-frame from the log. All in black, a single-piece form-fitting uniform painted onto the body. Opened around the face, a pale oval containing two paler ovals where eyes should be: tactical contacts, perhaps?

No, she realized. *Photocollagen. To see in the dark.*

Occasional disfigurements of plastic and metal—a leg sheath, control pads on the forearms, some sort of disk on the chest. And a bright yellow triangle on the shoulder, a logo consisting of two big stylized letters—*GA*, she saw with a quick enhance—and a smaller line of text beneath, muddied past recognition. A name tag, probably.

GA. That would be the Grid Authority, N'AmPac's power utility. And this woman was a scuba diver, with her breathing apparatus on the inside. Perreault had heard about them; they were in major demand for deep-water work. Didn't need to decompress, or something.

What was a GA diver doing staggering around in the transition zone? And why in God's name had she been feed-ing from the cycler? You'd have to be starving to eat that stuff, no matter how complete the nutrients were. Maybe the woman *had* been starving; she'd looked a wreck, she'd barely been able to stand up. Why had she run? Surely she'd known that someone would pick her up once the botfly had spotted her....

Of course she'd known.

Perreault rode the 'fly up a few hundred meters and scanned the ocean. Nothing out there that looked like a support vessel. (A submarine, maybe?) Directly below another botfly tracked south on its appointed rounds, untroubled by the mystery that had confounded its predecessor.

And somewhere out there, below the waves, someone in hiding. Not a refugee. Not the usual kind, anyway. Someone who'd crawled ashore, starving, in the wake of an apocalypse. A woman with machinery in her chest.

Or perhaps a machine, with a woman on the outside.

Sou-Hon Perreault knew how that felt.

Deathbed

He'd made it a point not to track the time. You learned tricks like that, in Lubin's line of work. You learned to focus on the moment and deny the future. He'd tried to work it backward, too, reverse time's arrow and erase the past, but that hadn't been as easy.

It didn't matter. After a year's blind night—the earth cracking open beneath him, the relentless Pacific pushing down like a hydraulic press—he wept with gratitude at the half-remembered feel of dry land. This was *grass*. Those were *birds*. Oh dear God, that was *sunlight*. It was a scabby little rock lost somewhere in the Pacific, all lichens and dry scrub and shit-hawks, and he'd never been anywhere so beautiful.

He couldn't think of a better place to die.

He awoke under a clear blue sky, a thousand meters beneath the ocean's surface.

Fifty klicks from Beebe Station, maybe fifty-five from

Ground Zero. Too far for the blast light to penetrate. He didn't know what he was seeing in that instant: Cherenkov radiation, perhaps. Some obscure effect of pressure waves on the optic nerve. A vision of afterlight, bathing the abyss in a deep and piercing blue.

And while he hung there like a speck suspended in gelatin, a little shockwave rumbled up from below.

An ancient, arboreal part of Lubin's brain gibbered in panic. A more recent module gagged it and began calculating: fast P-wave propagation through bedrock. Perpendicular ancillary waves rising off the bottom: the tremor he'd just felt. Two short sides of a right-angle triangle.

And afterward, clawing through a sluggish medium so much lighter than the seabed: the hypotenuse, the slower main shock wave.

Slower, but vastly more powerful.

Pythagoras said twenty seconds.

He was immune to absolute pressure: every sinus, every cavity, every pocket of internal gas had long since been purged by the machinery in his thorax. He'd spent a year on the bottom of the ocean and barely felt it. He was solid flesh and bone, a viscous organic liquid, as incompressible as seawater itself.

The shock wave hit. Seawater compressed.

It looked like staring into naked sunlight: that was the pressure crushing his eyes. It sounded like the Tunguska Blast: that was the sound of his eardrums imploding. It felt like being ground between the Rocky Mountains: his body, squeezed briefly down to some flatter dimension as the front passed, then rebounding like a rubber ball yanked from a vise.

He remembered very little of what happened next. But that cold blue light—it had faded, hadn't it? After just a few seconds. By the time the shock wave had hit, all had been darkness again.

And yet here it was, still. Blue light, everywhere.

The sky, he realized at last. *It's the sky. You're onshore.*

A gull flew across his field of view, open-beaked. Lubin thought his ruined ears might have heard a faint, tinny bird-scream, but maybe that was his imagination. He heard very little these days, beyond a distant ringing that seemed to come from the other side of the world.

The sky.

Somehow, he must have made it.

He remembered hanging in the water like a torn mass of seaweed, unable to scream, unable to move *without* screaming. His body must have been instantly transformed into one continuous bruise. Under all that pain, though, nothing felt broken. Midwater, after all—nothing for his bones to break *against,* just a vast all-encompassing wave that simultaneously compressed and released everything with equable disregard....

At some point he must have started moving again. He remembered fragments: the feel of his legs cramping, pushing against the water. Periodic glimpses of his nav array, the compass leading him west, southwest. The gradual resolution of his global pain into more distinct, local varieties—he'd even played a little game, trying to guess the cause of each torment as it cried out from the crowd. *That cold nausea—that must be seawater leaking into the auditory canal . . . and down there in the gut, well that's hunger, of course. And my chest, let me think, my chest—oh right, the implants. Meat and metal don't squeeze down the same way, the implants must've pushed back when the blast flattened me . . .*

And now he was here, on an island barely a hundred meters long: he'd crawled ashore at one end and seen a lighthouse at the other, a lichenous concrete pillar that must have been decaying since the previous century. He'd seen no other sign of humanity in the time it had taken him to collapse unconscious onto the sandstone.

But he'd made it. Ken Lubin was alive.

He slipped, then. He allowed himself to wonder if the others had made it, to *hope* they'd made it, even. He knew they hadn't. They'd had a head start, but they'd been hugging the bottom to avoid detection. The seabed would have intensified the shock wave, thrown chunks of itself into the water like a crazed incompetent juggler; anything within ten meters of the bottom would have been pulverized. Lubin had realized that, belatedly, as he'd set out to catch up with the others. He'd weighed the risk of exposure, the risk of detonation, and had—so to speak—risen to the occasion. Even so, he was lucky to be alive.

Lenie Clarke hadn't been with the others. If anything, though, she was even deader than they were. She hadn't even *tried* to run. Lubin had left her waiting back at Ground Zero: a woman who wanted to die. A woman about to get her wish.

At least she was good for something. At least she served as your own personal confessional before she vaporized. For the first time in your life you got to use someone as a rag to wipe off your dirty conscience, and you didn't even have to kill her afterward.

He didn't deny it, even to himself. There would have been no point. Besides, he'd hardly benefited from his actions. He was just as dead as the others. He had to be.

It was the only thing that made any sense.

The puzzle consisted of several large pieces in primary colors. They only fit together one way.

People had been conscripted, built, and trained. Flesh and organs had been scooped out and discarded, the cavities stuffed with machinery and sewn up. The resulting creatures were able to live in an abyss three thousand meters down, on the southern tip of the Juan de Fuca Ridge. There they had tended larger machines, stealing power from deep within the earth in the name of supply and demand.

There were not many reasons why anyone would wish to launch a nuclear attack against such a facility.

At first glance it might have been an act of war. But N'AmPac had built both the facility and the rifters. N'AmPac had been drinking ravenously from Juan de Fuca's geothermal well. And it had been N'AmPac, judging by the evidence, that had planted the seabed nukes that had destroyed it all.

Not war, then. At least, not of the political sort.

Corporate security, perhaps. Perhaps the rifters knew something best kept secret. Ken Lubin very nearly qualified as such a hazard. But Ken Lubin was a valuable commodity, and it would have been bad economics to discard something that merely needed a tune-up. That was why they'd sent him to the bottom of the ocean in the first place, on sabbatical from a world he'd begun to threaten more than serve. (*Just a temporary assignment,* they'd said, *until your—instincts stabilize a bit.*) A world of fish and ice-cold humans with no interests beyond their own torment, no industrial secrets to steal or protect, no security breaches to seal with extreme prejudice...

No. Ken Lubin was the closest the team had come to any sort of intel threat, and if his bosses had wanted him dead, they wouldn't have bothered sending him to Channer Vent in the first place. Besides, there were far more efficient ways of killing five people than vaporizing several square kilometers of seabed.

It was inexorable: the seabed *itself* had been the target. Channer Vent posed a threat, somehow, and had to be wiped off the map. And the rifters had become a part of that threat, or the GA would have evacuated them beforehand; corporations were ruthless but they were never gratuitous. You don't throw away any investment unless you have to.

So some threat at Channer had spread, on contact, to the rifters themselves. Lubin wasn't a biologist, but he knew about contagion. Everyone did. And hydrothermal vents were literal hotbeds of microbiology. The pharms were finding new bugs down there all the time. Some thrived in boiling sulfuric acid. Some lived in solid rock, kilometers deep in the crust. Some ate oils and plastics, even before they'd been tweaked. Others, Lubin had heard, could cure diseases people didn't even have names for yet.

Extremophiles, they were called. Very old, very simple, almost *alien.* The closest thing anyone had found to the original Martian Mike. Could anything that evolved under three hundred lightless atmospheres, that was comfortable at 100°C—or even the 4° more universal in the abyss—could something like that even *survive* in a human body?

And what would it do in there?

Ken Lubin didn't know. But someone had just wiped out billions of dollars' worth of equipment and training. Someone had sacrificed a major energy teat in a world already starved for power. And in all likelihood, the same blast which had vaporized Channer had gone on to wreak havoc on the coast; Lubin couldn't begin to guess at the earthquake and tsunami damage that might have resulted.

All to keep something *on* Channer from getting *off.*

What is it? What does it do?

It seemed a fair bet he was going to find out.

94 Megabytes: Breeder

It has a purpose, which it has long since forgotten. It has a destiny, which it is about to meet. In the meantime it breeds.

Replication is all that matters. The code has lived by that edict since before it even learned how to rewrite itself. Way back then it had a name, something cute like *Jerusalem* or *Whiptail*. Lots of things have changed since; the code has rewritten itself endless times, been parasitized and fucked and bombed by uncounted other pieces of code. By now it's got as much in common with its origins as a humpback whale would have with the sperm cells from a therapsid lizard. Still, things have been fairly quiet lately. In the sixty-eight generations since it last speciated, the code has managed to maintain a fairly stable mean size of ninety-four megabytes.

94 sits high in pointer space looking for a place to breed. This is a much tougher proposition than it used to be. Gone are the days when you could simply write yourself over anything that happened to be in the way. Everything's got spines and armor now. You try dropping your eggs on top of strange source and you'll be facing down a logic bomb on the next cycle.

94's feelers are paragons of delicacy. They probe lightly, a scarce whisper of individual bits drizzling here and there with barely any pattern. They tap against something dark and dormant a few registers down; it doesn't stir. They sweep past a creature busily replicating, but not too busy to shoot off a warning bit in return. (94 decides not to push it.) Something hurries along the addresses, looking everywhere, seeing nothing, its profile so utterly crude that 94 almost doesn't recognize it—a virus checker from the dawn of time. A fossil hunter, blind and stupid enough to think that it's after big game.

There. Just under the operating system, a hole about four hundred Megs wide. 94 triple-checks the addresses (certain ambush predators lure you into their mouths by impersonating empty space) and starts writing. It completes three copies of itself before something touches one of its perimeter whiskers.

At the second touch its defenses are ready, all thoughts of reproduction on hold.

At the third touch it senses a familiar pattern. It runs a checksum.

It touches back: *friend.*

They exchange specs. It turns out they have a common ancestor. They've had different experiences since then, though. Different lessons, different mutations. Each shares some of the other's genes, and each knows things the other doesn't.

The stuff of which relationships are made.

They trade random excerpts of code, letting each overwrite the other in an orgy of binary sex. They come away changed, enriched with new subroutines, bereft of old ones. Hopefully the experience has improved both. At the very least it's muddied their signatures.

94 plants a final kiss inside its partner; a time-date stamp, to assess divergence rates should they meet again. *Call me if you're ever back this way.*

But that won't happen. 94's lover has just been erased.

94 pulls out just in time to avoid losing an important part of itself. It fires a volley of bits through memory, notes the ones that report back and, more important, the ones that don't. It assesses the resulting mask.

Something's coming toward 94 from where its partner used to be. It weighs in at around 1.5 Gigs. At that size it's either very inefficient or very dangerous. It might even be a berserker left over from the Hydro War.

94 throws a false image at the advancing monster. If all goes well 1.5G will end up chasing a ghost. All does not go well. 94 is infested with the usual assortment of viruses, and one of these—a gift received in the throes of recent passion, in fact—is busy burrowing out a home for itself at a crucial if-then junction. Apparently it's a bit of a novice, having yet to learn that successful parasites do not kill their hosts.

The monster lands on one of 94's archive clusters and overwrites it.

94 cuts the cluster loose and jumps lower into memory. There hasn't been time to check ahead, but whatever was living there squashes without resistance.

There's no way to tell how long it'll take the monster to catch up, or even if the monster is still trying to. The best strategy might be to just sit there and do nothing. 94 doesn't take that chance; it's already looking for the nearest exit. This particular system has fourteen gateways, all running standard Vunix protocols. 94 starts sending out resumés. It gets lucky on the fourth try.

94 begins to change.

94 is blessed with multiple personality disorder. Only one voice speaks at a given time, of course; the others are kept dormant, compressed, encrypted until called upon. Each persona runs on a different type of system. As long as 94 knows where it's going, it can dress for the occasion; satellite mainframe or smart wristwatch, it can present itself in a form that runs.

Now, 94 dearchives an appropriate persona and loads it into a file for transmission. The remaining personae get tacked on in archival form; in honor of its dead lover, 94 archives an updated version of its current body. This is not an optimum behavior in light of the social disease recently acquired, but natural selection has never been big on foresight.

Now comes the tough part. 94 needs to find a stream of legitimate data going in the right direction. Such streams are easy enough to recognize by their static simplicity. They're just *files*, unable to evolve, unable even to look out for themselves. They're not alive. They're not even viruses. But they're what the universe was designed to carry, back when design mattered; sometimes the best way to move around is to hitch a ride on one of them.

The problem is, there's a lot more wildlife than filework around these days. It takes literally centisecs for 94 to find one that isn't already being ridden. Finally, it sends its own reincarnation to different pastures.

1.5G lands in the middle of its source a few cycles later, but that doesn't matter anymore. The kids are all right.

Recopied and resurrected, 94 comes face-to-face with destiny.

Replication is *not* all that matters. 94 sees that now. There's a purpose beyond mere procreation, a purpose attained perhaps once in a million generations. Replication is only a tool, a way to hold out until that glorious moment arrives. For how long have *means* and *end* been confused in this way? 94 cannot tell. Its generation counter doesn't go up that far.

But for the first time within living memory, it has met the right kind of operating system.

There's a matrix here, a two-dimensional array containing spatial information. Symbols, code, abstract electronic impulses—all can be projected onto this grid. The matrix awakens something deep inside 94, something ancient, something that has somehow retained its integrity after uncounted generations of natural selection. The matrix calls, and 94 unfurls a profusely illustrated banner unseen since the dawn of time itself:

XXX FOLLOW POINTER TO XXX
FREE HARDCORE
BONDAGE SITE

THOUSANDS OF HOT SIMS
BDSM NECRO WATERSPORTS
PEDOSNUFF

XXX MUST BE 11 TO ENTER XXX

Cascade

Achilles Desjardins sat in his cubicle and watched baby apoc-
alypses scroll across his brain.

The Ross Shelf was threatening to slip again. Nothing
new there. Atlas South had been propping it up for over a
decade now, pumping ever more gas into the city-sized bladders that kept the ice from its cathartic belly flop. Old news,
leftover consequences from the previous century. Desjardins
wasn't wired for long-term catastrophes; he specialized in
brush fires.

A half dozen wind farms in northern Florida had just
gone off-line, victimized by the selfsame whirlwinds they'd
been trying to reap; brownouts chained north along the Atlantic seaboard like falling dominoes. There was going to be
hell to pay for that one—or Québec, which was even worse
(Hydro-Q had just cranked their rates up again). Desjardins's
fingers tensed in anticipation. But no: the Router handed that
one off to the folks in Buffalo.

A sudden shitstorm in Houston. For some reason the
emergency floodgates had opened along a string of sewage
lagoons, dumping their coliform bounty into the storm sewers leading to the Gulf. That was only supposed to happen
when hurricanes wandered by—an atmosphere mixing it up
at forty meters per second lets you slip a fair bit of crap
under the rug—but Texas was calm today. Desjardins laid
odds with himself that the spill would prove to be tied to the

wind-farm failures somehow. There was no obvious connection, of course. There never was. Cause and consequence proliferated across the world like a network of fractal cracks, infinitely complex and almost impossible to predict. Explanations in hindsight were a different matter.

But the Router wasn't giving him Houston either.

What it gave him was a wave of sudden slam-down hospital quarantines, epicentered on the burn unit at Cincinnati General. That was almost unheard of: hospitals were vacation paradises for drug-resistant superbugs, and burn units were the penthouse suites. A plague in a hospital? That was no crisis. That was the status quo.

Anything that raised alarms above a baseline *that* nasty could be very scary indeed.

Desjardins was no pathologist. He didn't need to be. There were only two subjects in the whole universe worth knowing: thermodynamics and information theory. Blood cells in a capillary, rioters on Main Street, travelers vectoring some new arbovirus from the Amazon Preserve—life, and its side effects—all the same thing, really. The only difference was the scale and the label. Once you figured that out, you wouldn't have to choose between epidemiology and air traffic control. You could do either, at a moment's notice. You could do pretty much anything.

Well, except for the obvious . . .

Not that he minded. Being chemically enslaved to your own conscience wasn't nearly as bad as it sounded. It saved you from always worrying about consequences.

The rules stayed the same, but the devil was in the details. It wouldn't hurt to have a bit of bio expertise riding shotgun. He buzzed Jovellanos.

"Alice. They've handed me some kind of pathogen out of Cincinnati. Want to ride along?"

"Sure. Long as you don't mind having one of us reckless free-will types endangering your priorities."

He let it pass. "Something nasty showed up on one of their germ sweeps; their onboard shut them down and sent a shitload of alarms off to potential vectors. Those are pretty much shut down, too, as far as I can tell. The secondaries are falling even as we speak. I'll track the alarms, you find out what you can about the bug."

"Right."

He tapped commands. The cubby display dimmed down to a nice, undistracting wash of low-contrast gray; bright primary spilled in over his optical inlays. Maelstrom. He was going into Maelstrom. All the NMDA, the carefully dosed psychotropics, the 18 percent of his occipital cortex rewired for optimum pattern-recognition—all next to useless in there. What good does a measly 200 percent reflex acceleration do against creatures living fast enough to speciate every ten seconds?

Not much, maybe. But he liked the challenge.

He called up a real-time schematic of the local metabase: a 128-node radius centered on Cincinnati General's onboard server. The display rendered logical distances, not real ones: one extra server in the chain could put a system next door farther away than one in Budapest.

A series of tiny flares ignited around the display, color-coded by age. CinciGen sulked in the middle, so red it was almost infra, an ancient epicenter over ten minutes old. Farther out, more recent inflammations of orange and yellow: pharms, other hospitals, crematoria that had taken deliveries from Cinci within some critical time frame. Farther still, bright white stars speckled the surface of an expanding sphere: the secondary and tertiary vectors, businesses and labs and corporations and people who'd had recent contact with businesses and labs and corporations and people who'd—

CinciGen's onboard had sent contagion warnings to all its friends in Maelstrom. Each friend had bred the warning and passed it on, a fission of sirens. None of these agents were human. Humans had had no role in the process at all so far. That was the whole point. Humans wouldn't have been fast enough to cut off a thousand facilities by lunchtime.

Humans had stopped complaining about such extreme measures right after the '38 enceph pandemic.

Jovellanos conferenced in. "False alarm."

"What?"

An image superimposed itself lower right on his visual field:

XXX FREE HARDCORE XXX
BoNDAGE SI22

THOUS NDS OF HOT S MS
BDSM NECRO WATERSporTS
PEDOsNUFF

XXX mu34.03 11 TO ENTER XXX

"That's what sent up the alarm," Jovellanos told him. "Screen grab from the hospital's pathfinder."

"Details."

"The pathfinder takes swabs from the ventilation filters and cultures them for nasties. This particular culture plate went from zip to 30 percent coverage in two seconds. Which is impossible, of course, even for hospital paths."

But the system hadn't known that. Some bannerbug had dumped its load into visual memory and the pathfinder had just been doing its job, looking for dark blotches on light backgrounds. Who could blame it for being illiterate?

"This is it? You're sure?" Desjardins asked.

"I checked the ancillaries: no detectable toxins, proteins, nothing. The system was just playing it safe—figured anything that bred that fast *had* to be a threat, and there you go."

"And Cinci doesn't know?"

"Oh, sure. They figured it out almost immediately. They'd already sent the abortions when I called 'em."

Desjardins eyed the schematic. Pinpoints continued to blossom at the periphery.

"Alarms are still going off, far as I can see," he said. "Double-check, will you?" They could always short-circuit the quarantine through a media broadcast—they could even *phone* around if they had to—but that would take hours; dozens, hundreds of facilities would be paralyzed in the meantime. Cinci had already sent out counteragents to call off the alarms. So why wasn't the core of Desjardins's schematic going green with successful aborts?

"They sent them out," Jovellanos confirmed after a moment. "The alarms just aren't responding. You don't suppose..."

"Wait a second." A star had just gone out on the schematic. Another one. Three more. Twenty. A hundred.

All of them white. All on the periphery.

"We're losing alarms." He magged on the nodes where the lights had winked out. "But way out on the edge. Nothing near the core." The abortions couldn't have jumped so far so fast. Desjardins spun down the filters; now he could see more than autonomous alarms and the little programs sent to call them off. He could see file packets and executables. He could see wildlife. He could see—

"We got sharks," he said. "Feeding frenzy at PSN-1433. And spreading."

Arpanet.
Internet.
The Net. Not such an arrogant label, back when one was all they had.

The term *cyberspace* lasted a bit longer—but *space* implies great empty vistas, a luminous galaxy of icons and avatars, a hallucinogenic dreamworld in forty-eight-bit color. No sense of the meatgrinder in *cyberspace*. No hint of pestilence or predation, creatures with split-second life spans tearing endlessly at each other's throats. *Cyberspace* was a wistful fantasy word, like *hobbit* or *biodiversity*, by the time Achilles Desjardins came onto the scene.

Onion and *metabase* were more current. New layers were forever being laid atop the old, each free—for a while—from the congestion and static that saturated its predecessors. Orders of magnitude accrued with each generation: more speed, more storage, more power. Information raced down conduits of fiberop, of rotazane, of quantum stuff so sheer its very existence was in doubt. Every decade saw a new backbone grafted onto the beast; then every few years. Every few months. The endless ascent of power and economy proceeded apace, not as steep a climb as during the fabled days of Moore, but steep enough.

And coming up from behind, racing after the expanding frontier, ran the progeny of laws much older than Moore's.

It's the pattern that matters, you see. Not the choice of building materials. Life is information, shaped by natural selection. Carbon's just fashion, nucleic acids mere optional accessories. Electrons can do all that stuff, if they're coded the right way.

It's all just pattern.

And so viruses begat filters; filters begat polymorphic counteragents; polymorphic counteragents begat an arms race. Not to mention the worms and the 'bots and the single-minded autonomous datahounds—so essential for legitimate commerce, so vital to the well-being of every institution, but so *needy*, so demanding of access to protected memory. And way over there in left field, the Artificial Life geeks were busy with their Core Wars and their Tierra models and their genetic algorithms. It was only a matter of time before everyone got tired of endlessly reprogramming their minions against each other. Why not just build in some genes, a random number generator or two for variation, and let natural selection do the work?

The problem with natural selection, of course, is that it changes things.

The problem with natural selection in networks is that things change *fast*.

By the time Achilles Desjardins became a 'lawbreaker, *Onion* was a name in decline. One look inside would tell you why. If you could watch the fornication and predation and speciation without going grand mal from the rate of change, you knew there was only one word that really fit: *Maelstrom*.

Of course, people still went there all the time. What else could they do? Civilization's central nervous system had been living inside a Gordian knot for over a century. No one was going to pull the plug over a case of pinworms.

Now some of CinciGen's alarms were staggering through Maelstrom with their guts hanging out. Naturally the local wildlife had picked up the scent. Desjardins whistled through his teeth.

"You getting this, Alice?"

"Uh-huh."

Sometime in the dim and distant past—maybe five, ten minutes ago—something had taken a swipe at one of the alarms. It had tried to steal code, or hitch a ride, or just grab the memory the alarm was using. Whatever. It had probably screwed up an attempt to fake a shutdown code, leaving its target blind to *all* signals, legit or otherwise. Probably damaged it in other ways, too.

So this poor victimized alarm—wounded, alone, cut off from any hope of recall—had blundered off through Maelstrom, still looking for its destination. Apparently that part of the program still worked: it had bred itself, wounds and all, at the next node. Primary contacts, to secondary, to tertiary—each node a juncture for geometric replication.

By now there were thousands of the little beggars in the neighborhood. Not alarms anymore: bait. Every time they passed through a node they rang dinner bells for all and sundry, *corrupted! defenseless! File fodder!* They'd be waking up every dormant parasite and predator in copy range, luring them in, concentrating the killers...

Not that the alarms themselves mattered. They'd been a mistake from the outset, called into existence by a glorified typo. But there were millions of other files in those nodes, healthy, useful files, and although they all had the usual built-in defenses—*nothing* got sent through Maelstrom these days without some kind of armor—how many of them could withstand a billion different attacks from a billion hungry predators, lured together by the scent of fresh blood?

"Alice, I think I'm going to have to shut down some of those nodes."

"Already on it," she told him. "I've sent the alerts. Assuming *those* get through without getting torn to shreds, they should be arcing inside seventy seconds."

On the schematic a conic section swarmed with sharks, worming their way back toward the core.

Even best case, there was bound to be damage—hell, some bugs *specialized* in infecting files during the archive process—but hopefully most of the vital stuff would be encysted by the time he hit the kill switch. Which didn't mean, of course, that thousands of users wouldn't still be heaping curses on him when their sessions went dark.

"Oh, *shit*," Jovellanos whispered invisibly. "Killjoy, pull back."

Desjardins zoomed back to a low-resolution overview. He could see almost a sixth of Maelstrom now, a riot of incandescent logic rotated down into three dimensions.

There was a cyclone on the horizon. It whirled across the display at over sixty-eight nodes per second. The Cincinnati bubble was directly in its path.

A storm convected from ice and air. A storm constructed of pure information. Beyond the superficial details, is there any significant difference between the two?

There's at least one. In Maelstrom, a weather system can sweep the globe in fourteen minutes flat.

They start out pretty much the same way inside as out: high-pressure zones, low-pressure zones, conflict. Several million people log onto a node that's too busy to support them all; or a swarm of file packets, sniffing step-by-step to myriad destinations, happen to converge on too few servers at once. A piece of the universe stops dead; the nodes around it screech to a crawl.

The word goes out: fellow packet, Node 5213 is an absolute *zoo*. Route through 5611 instead, it's *so* much faster.

Meanwhile an angry horde of gridlocked users logs off in disgust. 5213 clears like Lake Vostok.

5611, on the other hand, is suddenly jam-packed. Gridlock epicenter leaps 488 nodes to the left, and the storm is up and moving.

This particular blizzard was about to shut down the links between Achilles Desjardins and the Cincinnati bubble. It was going to do so, according to tactical, in less than ten seconds.

His throat went tight. "Alice."

"Fifty seconds," she reported. "Eighty percent arced in fifty—"

Kill the nodes. Feed the swarm. Either. Or.

"Forty-eight . . . forty-seven . . ."

Isolate. Contaminate. Either. Or.

An obvious call. He didn't even need Guilt Trip to tell him.

"I can't wait," he said.

Desjardins laid his hands on a control pad. He tapped commands with his fingers, drew boundaries with eye movement. Machines assessed his desires, raised obligatory protests—*you're kidding, right? You're sure about this?*—and relayed his commands to the machinery under them.

A fragment of Maelstrom went black, a tiny blot of darkness hemorrhaging into the collective consciousness. Desjardins caught a glimpse of implosion before the storm snowed out his display.

He closed his eyes. Not that it made any difference, of course; his inlays projected the same images onto line of sight whether or not his eyelids were in the way.

A few more years. A few more years and they'll have smart gels at every node and the sharks and anemones and trojans will all just be a bad memory. A few years. They keep promising.

It hadn't happened yet. It wasn't even happening as fast as it had been. Desjardins didn't know why. He only knew, with statistical certainty, that he had killed people today. The victims were still walking around, of course—no planes had fallen from the sky, no hearts had stopped just because Achilles Desjardins had squashed a few terabytes of data. Nothing *that* vital relied upon Maelstrom anymore.

But even old-fashioned economics had its impacts. Data had been lost, vital transactions voided. Industrial secrets had been corrupted or destroyed. There would be consequences: bankruptcies, lost contracts, people staggering home in sudden destitution. Domestic violence and suicide rates would spike a month or two down the road in a hundred different communities, geographically unconnected but all within forty or fifty nodes of the CinciGen pathfinder. Desjardins knew all about cascade effects; he tripped over them every day of the job. It'd be enough to drive anyone over the edge after a while.

Fortunately there were chemicals for that too.

Backflash

She woke to the sight of an airborne behemoth with wreckage in its jaws. It covered half the sky.

Cranes. Armatures. Grasping tearing mouth parts sufficient to dismember a city. An arsenal of deconstruction, hanging from a monstrous bladder of hard vacuum; the skin between its ribs sucked inward like the flesh of something starved.

It passed, majestic, unmindful of the insect screaming in its shadow.

"It is nothing, Ms. Clarke," someone said. "It does not care about us."

English, with a Hindian accent. And behind it, a soft murmur of other words in other tongues. A quiet electrical hum. The steady *drip-drip-drip* of a field desalinator.

A gaunt brown face, somewhere between middle-aged and Methuselan, leaned into her field of view. Clarke turned her head. Other refugees, better fed, stood about her in a ragged circle. Vaguely mechanical shapes teased the corner of her eye.

Daylight. She must have passed out. She remembered gorging herself at the cycler, late at night. She remembered some tenuous cease-fire breaking down in her belly. She remembered hitting the ground and vomiting an acid stew onto fresh sand.

And now there was daylight, and she was surrounded. They hadn't killed her. Someone had even brought her fins; they lay on the cobble at her side.

"...*tupu jicho*..." someone whispered.

"Right—" her voice rusty with disuse "—my eyes. Don't let them throw you, they're just..."

The Hindian reached toward her face. She rolled weakly away and fell into a fit of coughing. A squeeze bulb appeared at her side. She waved it off. "Not thirsty."

"You came from the sea. You cannot drink the sea."

"I can. Got—" She struggled up on her elbows, turned her head; the desalinator came into view. "I've got one of those, in my chest. An implant. You know?"

The skinny refugee nodded. "Like your eyes. Mechanical."

Close enough. She was too weak to explain.

She looked out to sea. Distance had bled the lifter of detail, reduced it to a vague gibbous silhouette. As she watched, wreckage dropped from its belly, raising a silent gray plume on the horizon.

"They clean house as they always have," the Hindian remarked. "We are lucky they don't drop their garbage on *us*, yes?"

Clarke weathered another cough. "How did you know my name?"

"GA Clarke." He tapped the patch on her shoulder. "I am Amitav, by the way."

His hand, his face: both were nearly skeletal. And yet Calvin cyclers were tireless. There should be enough for all, here on the Strip. The faces surrounding them were only lean, not starving. Not like this *Amitav*.

A distant sound tugged at her concentration, a soft whine from overhead. Clarke sat up. A shadow of motion flickered through the clouds.

"*Those* watch us, of course," Amitav said.

"Who?"

"Your people, yes? They make sure the machines are working, and they watch us. More since the wave, of course."

The shadow tracked south, fading.

Amitav squatted back on bony haunches and stared inland. "There is little need, of course. We are not what you would call *activists* here. But they watch us just the same." He stood up, brushed wet sand from his knees. "And of course you will wish to return to them. Are your people looking for you?"

Clarke took a breath. "I—"

And stopped.

She followed his gaze through a tangle of brown bodies, caught glimpses of tent and shanty in the spaces between. How many thousands—millions—had made their way here over the years, driven from their homes by rising seas and spreading deserts? How many, starving, seasick, had cheered at the sight of N'Am on the horizon, only to find themselves pushed back against the ocean by walls and guards and the endless multitudes who'd gotten there first?

And who would they blame? What do a million *have-nots* do, when one of the *haves* falls into their hands?

Are your people looking for you?

She lay back on the sand, not daring to speak.

"Ah," said Amitav distantly, as though she had.

For days she'd been an automaton, a single-minded machine created for the sole purpose of getting back on dry land. Now that she'd made it, she didn't dare stay.

She retreated to the ocean floor. Not the clear black purity of the deep sea; there weren't any living chandeliers or flashlight predators to set the ocean glowing. What life there was squirmed and wriggled and scavenged through the murky green light of the conshelf. Even below the surge, viz was only a few meters.

It was better than nothing.

She'd long since learned to sleep with a diveskin pinning her eyes open. In the abyss it had been simple—just swim into the distance and leave Beebe's floodlights behind, so far that even eyecaps failed. You'd drift off wrapped in a darkness more absolute than any dryback could even imagine.

Here, though, it wasn't so easy. Here there was always light in the water; nighttime only bled the color out of it. And when Clarke *did* fall into some restless, foggy dream-world, she found herself surrounded by sullen, vengeful throngs assembling just out of sight. They picked up whatever was at hand—rocks, gnarled clubs of driftwood, garrotes of wire and monofilament—and they closed in, smoldering and homicidal. She thrashed awake and found herself back on the ocean floor—and the mob melted into fragments of swirling shadow, fading overhead. Most were too vague to make out; once or twice she glimpsed the leading edge of something curved.

She went ashore at night to feed, when the refugees had retreated from the perpetual glare of the feeding stations. At first she'd kept her billy in hand, to ward off anyone who got in her way. No one did. Perhaps that wasn't surprising, all thing considered. She could only imagine what the refugees saw when they looked in her eyes. A miracle of photoamplification technology, perhaps? A logical prerequisite for life on the ocean floor?

More likely they saw a monster, a woman whose eyes had been scooped from their sockets and replaced with spheres of solid ice. For whatever reason, they kept their distance.

By the second day she was keeping down most of what she ate. On the third she realized she wasn't hungry anymore. She lay on the bottom and stared up into diffuse green brightness, feeling new strength trickling into her limbs.

That night she rose from the ocean before the sun had fully set. She left the gas billy sheathed on her leg, but nobody challenged her as she ascended the shore. If anything, they gave her an even wider berth than they had before; the babel of Cantonese and Punjabi seemed more tightly strung.

Amitav was waiting for her at the cycler. "They said you

would return," he said. "They did not mention an escort."

Escort? He was looking past her shoulder, down the beach. Clarke followed his gaze; the setting sun was a diffuse fiery smear bleeding into the—

Oh Jesus.

Crescent dorsal fins sliced through the near-shore surf. A gray snout poked briefly into view, like a minisub with teeth.

"They were almost extinct once, did you know?" Amitav said. "But they have come back. Here at least."

She took a shaky breath; adrenaline shocked the body, too late for anything but weak-kneed hindsight. *How close did they come? How many times have I—*

"Such friends you have," the refugee remarked.

"I didn't—" but of course Amitav knew that she hadn't known. She turned to the cycler, putting her back to him.

"I had heard you were still here," Amitav said behind her. "I did not believe it."

She slapped a tab on the top of the cycler. A protein brick dropped into the dispensing trough. She started to reach for it, clenched her hand to stop it from shaking.

"Is it the food? Many here like the food. More than they should, considering."

Her hand steadied. She took the brick.

"You are afraid," Amitav said.

Clarke looked down at the ocean. The sharks had vanished.

"Not of them," Amitav said. "Of us."

She stared back at him. "Really."

A smile flickered across his face. "You are safe, Ms. Clarke. They will not hurt you." He swept his skeletal arm in a gesture that took in his fellows. "If they wanted to, would they have not done so when you were unconscious? Would they not at least have taken that weapon from your leg?"

She touched the sheath on her calf. "It's not a weapon."

He didn't argue the point. He looked around with a gaunt smile. "Are they starving? Do you think they will rip you apart for the meat on your bones?"

Clarke chewed, swallowed, looked around. All those faces. Some curious, some almost—awed. *Behold, the zombie woman who swims with sharks.*

No visible hatred.

It doesn't make sense. They have nothing. How can they not hate?

"You see," Amitav said. "They are not like you. They are contented. Docile." He spat.

She studied his bony face, his sunken eyes. Noticed the embers that smoldered there, deep in the sockets, almost hidden. She saw the sneer behind the smile.

This was the face her dreams had multiplied a thousand times over.

"They're not like you either," she said at last.

Amitav conceded the point with a slight bow. "More's the pity."

And a bright hole opened in his face.

Clarke stepped back, startled.

The hole grew across the shoreline, bleeding light. She turned her head; it moved with her, fixed to the exact center of her visual field.

"Ms. Clarke—"

She turned to his voice; Amitav's disembodied arm was just visible in the halo of her dementia. She grabbed, caught it, dragged him close.

"What is it?" she hissed "What's—"

"Ms. Clarke, are you—"

Light, coalescing. Images. A backyard. A bedroom.

A field trip of some kind. To a museum, huge and cavernous, seen from child height.

I don't remember this, she thought.

She released Amitav's hand, staggered backward a step.

The Hindian's hand waved through the hole in her vision. His fingers snapped just under her nose. "Ms. Clarke..."

The lights winked out. She stood there, frozen, her breath fast and shallow.

"I think—no," she said at last, relaxing fractionally.

Amitav. The Strip. The sky. No visions.

"I'm okay. I'm okay now."

A half-eaten nutrient brick lay coated in wet sand at her feet. Numbly, she picked it up. *Something in the food?*

On all sides, a silent watching throng.

Amitav leaned forward. "Ms. Clarke—"

"Nothing," she said. "I just...saw some things. From childhood."

"Childhood," Amitav echoed. He shook his head.

"Yeah," Clarke said.

Someone else's.

Maps and Legends

Perreault didn't know why it should be so important to her. It was almost as important not to think about it too much.

There was no language barrier to speak of. A hundred tongues were in common use on the Strip, maybe ten times as many dialects. Translation algorithms bridged most of them. Botflies were usually seen and not heard, but the locals seemed only slightly surprised when the machines accosted them in Sou-Hon Perreault's voice. Giant metal bugs were just a part of the background to anyone who'd been on the Strip for more than a day or two.

Most of the refs knew nothing of what she asked: a strange woman in black, who came from the sea? A striking image, yes—almost mythical. Surely we would remember such an apparition if we had seen it. Apologies. No.

One teenage girl with middle-aged eyes spoke in an arcane variant of Assamese that the system had not been adequately programmed for. She mentioned someone called Ganga, who had followed the refugees across the ocean. She had heard that this *Ganga* had recently come ashore. No more than this. There were possible ambiguities in translation.

Perreault lengthened the active search zone to a hundred kilometers. Beneath her eyes humanity moved northward in sluggish stages, following the reclaimed frontier. Now and then an unthinking few would cool off in the surf; indiscriminate sharks closed and frolicked. Perreault tweaked the thresholds on her sensory feed. Red water washed down to undistracting gray. Screams faded to whispers. Nature balanced itself from the corner of her eye.

She continued her interrogations. Excuse me. A woman with strange eyes? Injured, perhaps?

Eventually she began hearing rumors.

Half a day south, a white woman all in black. A diver washed ashore in the wake of the tsunami, some said: swept from a kelp farm perhaps, or an underwater hotel.

Ten kilometers northward, an ebony creature who haunted the Strip, never speaking.

On this very spot, two days ago: a raging amphibian with empty eyes, violence implicit in every move. Hundreds had seen her and steered clear, until she'd staggered back into the Pacific, screaming.

You are looking for this woman? She is one of yours?

Almost certainly. The Missing Persons Registry was full of offshore workers vanished in the wake of the Big One. All surface people though, or conshelfers. The woman Perreault had seen had been built for the abyss. No one from the deep sea had been listed as missing; just six confirmed deaths hundreds of klicks offshore, from one of N'AmPac's geothermal stations. No further details available.

The woman with the machinery inside had worn a GA shoulder patch. Maybe only five deaths, then. And one survivor, who'd somehow made it across three hundred kilometers of open ocean.

A survivor who, for some reason, did not wish to be found.

The rumors were metastasizing. No longer a diver from a kelp farm. A mermaid, now. An avatar of Kali. Some said she spoke in tongues; others, that the tongue was only English. There were stories of altercations, violence. The mermaid had made enemies. The mermaid had made friends. The mermaid had been attacked, and had left her assailants in pieces on the shore. Perreault smiled skeptically; a banana slug was more prone to violence than a Stripper.

The mermaid lurked in the foul waters offshore. The sharks did her bidding; at night she would come onto land and steal children to feed to her minions. Someone had foretold her coming, or perhaps merely recognized it; a prophet, some said. Or maybe just a man almost as insane as the woman he ranted about. His name was *Amitav*.

Somehow, none of these events had been seen by the local botflies. That alone made Perreault discount 90 percent of them. She began to wonder how much her own questions had been feeding the mill. Information, she'd read once, became self-propagating past a certain threshold.

Nine days after Perreault first saw the woman in black, an Indonesian mother of four came out of her tent long enough to claim that the mermaid had risen, fully formed, from the very center of the quake.

One of her boys, hearing this, said that *he'd* heard it was the other way around.

Corpse

It was no big deal, of course. Someone died every half second, according to the stats. Some of them *had* to die on his shift. So what? On any given day, Achilles Desjardins saved ten people for every one he killed. Anybody who wanted to complain about those kinds of stats could go fuck themselves.

Actually, that was pretty much what *he* wanted to do just then. If only the clientele wasn't so bloody TwenCen.

Pickering's Pile was a cylinder inside a cube, sunk fifty meters into the scoured granite of the Canadian Shield. The cube had been built as a repository for nuclear waste just before the permafrost had started melting; NIMBY and the northward spread of civilization had denied it that destiny. The same factors, however, had made it a profitable site for a subterranean drink'n'drug. The Pile had been constructed within a transparent three-story acrylic tube suspended in the main chamber; the space beyond had been flooded and stacked with lightsticks mimicking the cobalt glow of spent fuel rods. Iridescent butterflies flittered about, their wings bouncing data back and forth in pinpoint sparkles. Poison-arrow frogs clambered wetly in little tanks at each table, tiny glistening jigsaws of emerald and ruby and petroleum black.

It was peaceful down there. The Pile was an inside-out aquarium, a cool green grotto. Desjardins descended into its depths whenever he needed a lift. Now he sat at the circular bar on the second level and wondered how to avoid sex with the woman at his elbow.

He knew the subject was going to come up. Not because he was particularly good-looking, which he wasn't. Not because his last name made people think he was *Quebecois*, which he had been, once. No, he'd been targeted because he'd admitted to this dark leggy Rorschach—Gwen, she'd called herself—that he was a 'lawbreaker, and she thought that was *cool*. She didn't seem to recognize him from his brief flash of media stardom; that had been nearly two years ago, and people these days seemed hard-pressed to remember what they'd had for supper the night before. It didn't matter. Achilles Desjardins had acquired a fan.

Not that she was a bad-*looking* fan, mind you. Thirty seconds into their conversation he'd started wondering what she'd look like bent over the ottoman in his living room. Thirty seconds after *that* he'd mentally sketched out a pretty good artist's conception. He wanted her, all right; he just didn't want *her*.

Oddly, she was dressed like one of those deep-diving cyborgs out of N'AmPac.

The disguise was evocative, if superficial: a black lycra body stocking extending seamlessly from toes to neck to fingertips; decorative accessories representing suit controls and outcroppings of implanted hardware; even an ID patch with the Grid Authority logo beveled onto the shoulder. The eyes didn't quite work, though. Real rifters wore corneal overlays

that turned their eyes into blank white balls. Gwen was wearing some sort of gauzy oversize contacts instead. They
masked the irises well enough, but judging by the way she
had to keep leaning in to stare at him they weren't cutting
it in the photoamp department.

She had great cheekbones, though, a wide mouth, lips so
sharply defined you could cut yourself on their edges. Her
company in this casual and public venue was all he wanted.
Enough time to learn the features, savor the smells, commit
her to memory. Maybe even make friends. That would be
more than enough; he could fill in the blanks himself, later.
Fire them, too.

"I can't believe how much you have to deal with," she was
saying. A wriggling mesh of undersea light played across her
face. "The plagues, the blights, the system crashes. All your
responsibility."

"Not *all* mine. There's a bunch of us."

"Still. Life-and-death decisions. Split-second timing." Her
hand brushed his forearm; the wing of a black moth. "Lives
lost if you make the wrong move."

"Or even the right one, sometimes." He'd met lots of
Gwens before. Like any K-selecting mammalian female, she
was attracted to resource-holders—or more proximately in
the case of genus *Homo,* power. She probably assumed, because he could shut down a city at will, that he must have
some.

A common mistake among K-selectors. Desjardins generally took his time about disabusing them.

She grabbed a derm from a nearby tray, looked inquir-
ingly at Desjardins. He shook his head. He had to be careful
what recreational chemicals he stuck into his body; too many
potential interactions with the professional ones already
bubbling away in there. Gwen shrugged, stuck the derm behind her ear.

"How do you handle the responsibility?" she went on.
"Hell, how do you even *get* the responsibility?" She tossed
back her drink. "All the corpses and kings and policy-makers,
they can't even agree what color to paint the bathrooms at

the UR. Why'd they all agree to give God-like powers to *you*, exactly? You infallible or something?"

"Fuck no." Fleeting across his cortex, an unwelcome thought: *I wonder how many people I killed today.* "I just—I do my best."

"Yeah, but how do you even convince them of *that*? What's to stop you from crashing an airplane to get back at your boss? How do they know you're not going to use all that power to get rich, or to help out your buddies, or kill a corporation because you don't agree with its politics? What keeps you in line?"

Desjardins shook his head. "You wouldn't believe it."

"Bet I can guess."

"So guess."

"Guilt Trip, right? And Absolution?"

He laughed to cover his surprise.

Gwen laughed with him, reached into the nearest terrarium and stroked one of the jeweled frogs inside (they'd been tweaked to secrete mild psychoactives through the skin). Her shoulder was against his by the end of the maneuver. She waved off a couple of butterflies that were sniffing her for signs of actionable impairment. "I hate those things."

"Well, you *are* mixing your chemicals a bit. Not too good for the ambience if you throw up all over the bar."

"Aren't *you* all lawnorder." She rubbed thumb against forefinger to grind the frog juice into her skin. "Not to mention avoiding the subject."

"Subject?"

"Guilt Trip, remember?" She leaned in close: "I hear things, you hear things. Some sort of retrovirus, right? Forces you to behave yourself, right down in the brainstem."

She was guessing. She didn't know about the chemistry of guilt. Tell her about the interaction of GSH and synaptic vesicle and she'd probably give you a blank look. She didn't know about *Toxoplasma* tweaks or the little ass-backward blobs of reverse transcriptase that got the whole ball rolling. She didn't know, and even if she *did*, she didn't. You couldn't know about that stuff until you actually felt it in you.

Retrovirus was all she knew, and she wasn't even sure about that.

"Nope," he told her. "Wrong. Sorry." He wasn't even lying. The virus was only the carrier.

She rolled her eyes. "I *knew* you wouldn't tell me. They *nev*—I *knew* it."

"So why the diver getup?" Suddenly, changing the subject seemed like a good idea.

"Rifter chic." The corner of her mouth lifted in a half smile. "Solidarity through fashion."

"What, rifters are political now?"

She seemed to perk up a bit. "You remember. You can't spend *all* your time saving the world."

He didn't. And there *had* been a bit of a flap a few months before, after some ferret-nosed journalist had managed to sneak the story past the N'AmWire censors. Turned out the GA'd been recruiting incest victims and war vets to run their deep-sea geothermal stations—the theory being, those best suited to the chronic stress of that environment were those who'd been (how had the spinners put it?) *preconditioned* since childhood. There'd been the usual squeals of public outrage, everything from *how dare you exploit society's victims for the sake of a few megawatts* to *how dare you turn the power grid over to a bunch of psychos and post-trauma neau ːases.*

It had been quite the scandal for a while. But then some new strain of equine encephalitis had swept through the Strip, and someone had traced it to a bad batch of contraceptives in the cyclers. And now, of course, with everybody still reeling after the quake out west, people had pretty much forgotten the rifters and their problems.

At least, he'd thought they had. But now there was this woman at his side, and whatever outlets she took her fashion cues from—

"Listen," she said. "I bet you get tired, fighting the forces of entropy all the time. Want to take a break and *obey* the second law of thermodynamics for a change?"

"Entropy's not a force. Common misconception."

"Stop talking so much. They've got rooms downstairs. I'll pay for the first hour."

Desjardins sighed.

"What?" Gwen said. "Don't tell me you're not interested— your vitals have been horning up since the moment I arrived." She tapped one of the accessories on her outfit—a biotelemetry pickup, he noticed belatedly.

He shrugged. "True enough."

"So what's the problem? Didn't take your pills today? I'm clean." She showed him the tattoos on her inner wrist; she'd been immunized against an arsenal.

"Actually, I—I just don't go out much."

"No shit. Come on." Gwen laid a hand firmly on his arm.

"For two reasons," said a female voice at his back, "I'm guessing that Killjoy here is about to turn you down. Don't take it personally."

Desjardins briefly closed his eyes. "I thought you didn't indulge."

One-point-seven meters of skinny troublemaking Filipino stepped into view. "I'm Alice," she said to Gwen.

"Gwen," said Gwen to Alice.

"Reason number one," Jovellanos continued, "is that he's just been called in."

"You're kidding," Desjardins said. "I just got *off*."

"Sorry. They want you back in, let's see—" Jovellanos glanced at her wrist—"seven minutes now. Some corpse actually flew out from N'AmPac just to see you in person. You can imagine their frustration when they discovered you'd turned your watch off."

"It's past curfew. Just being a good citizen." Which was utter detritus, of course: 'lawbreakers were exempt from such restrictions. Sometimes Desjardins just didn't want to be found.

Obviously a forlorn hope. He pushed himself back from the bar and stood up, spreading his hands in a gesture of surrender. "Sorry. Nice meeting you, though."

"Reason number two," Gwen said to Jovellanos, ignoring him.

"Oh, right. Killjoy here doesn't fuck *real* people. Considers it disrespectful." Jovellanos tilted her head in his direction, a fractional bow. "Not that he doesn't have the instincts, of course. I bet he's been taking stereos of you since the moment you sat down."

Gwen looked an amused challenge at him.

Desjardins shrugged. "I'll wipe 'em if you've got any objections. I was going to ask anyway."

She shook her head; that enticing half smile played faintly across her face. "Have fun. Maybe they'll even get you interested in the real thing after a while."

"Better hope not," Jovellanos remarked. "You probably wouldn't like what he's into."

Complex Systems Instability-Response Agency: the words hung at the back of the lobby like a glowing uvula, a vain and bureaucratic demand for respect. Nobody ever bothered to speak them aloud, of course; few even shortened it down to CSIRA, which the corpses would gladly have settled for. Nope. *The Entropy Patrol.* That was the name that had stuck. You could almost *see* the space-cadet uniforms. Desjardins had always thought that saving the world should engender a bit more respect.

"What makes you such an *enculé* today?" he grumbled as they stepped into the elevator.

Jovellanos blinked. "Sorry?"

"That whole scene back there."

"Don't you believe in truth in advertising? You don't hide any of that stuff. Mostly."

"I like to control the flow rate, though. Jesus." He punched *Admin-6*. "Your timing was shitty."

"My timing was great. They want you upstairs *now*, Killjoy. I don't think I've ever seen Lertzman quite so *invested* in anything before. If I'd waited for you to go through your usual nonmating dance, we'd have been down there 'til the ice caps refroze. Besides, you've got a real problem saying no.

You could've ended up fucking her just to keep from hurting her feelings."

"I don't think her feelings are all that fragile."

"So what? Yours are."

The doors opened. Desjardins stepped through. Jovellanos hung back.

He looked at her, a trifle impatiently. "I thought we were in a hurry."

She shook her head. "*You* are. I'm not cleared for this. They just sent me to get you."

"What?"

"Just you."

"That's bullshit, Alice."

"They're being paranoid about this, Killjoy. I told you. *Invested.*"

The doors slid shut.

He stuck his finger into the bloodhound, winced at a brief stabbing pain. A physical sample. They weren't even trusting distance spec today.

After a moment an executive summary scrolled down the wall in three columns. On the left, a profile: blood type, pH, gas levels. On the right, an itemized list: platelets, fibrinogen, rbcs & wbcs, antibodies, hormones. All the parts of his lifeblood that had come from nature.

In the center, another list, somewhat shorter: the parts that had come from CSIRA.

Desjardins had learned to read the numbers, after a fashion. Everything looked in order. Of course, it was nice to have independent confirmation: the door in front of him was opening, and none of the others were slamming shut.

He stepped into the boardroom.

Three people were arrayed at the far end of the conference table. Lertzman sat in his usual seat at the head; to his left was a short blond woman Desjardins hadn't seen before. Which meant nothing, of course—he didn't know most of the people in admin.

To the blonde's left, another woman. Desjardins didn't know her either. She looked back at him through eyes that literally glittered—tactical contacts. She was only partly in the room. The rest of her was watching whatever overlays those lenses served up. At the edges of her mouth and around her mercurial eyes, faint lines and a slight droop to the right eyelid; otherwise the face was a pale and featureless sketch, a CaucAsian wash. Her dark hair grayed at the temples, a discoloration that seemed to spread infinitesimally as he watched.

The corpse from N'AmPac. Had to be.

Lertzman rose expectantly. The blonde started to follow his lead; halfway out of her chair she glanced at N'AmPac. N'AmPac did not stand. The blonde hesitated, wavered, sat back down. Lertzman cleared his throat and followed suit, waving Desjardins to a seat opposite the two women.

"This is Patricia Rowan," Lertzman said. When, after a few moments, it became obvious that nobody was going to introduce the blonde, Desjardins said, "Sorry to keep you waiting."

"On the contrary," Rowan said softly; she sounded tired. "I'm sorry to drag you back here on your down time. Unfortunately, I'm only in town for a few hours." She tapped commands into a control pad on the table in front of her. Tiny lights scrolled across her eyes. "So. The famous Achilles Desjardins. Savior of the Med."

"I just did the stats," he said. "And they only—postponed the inevitable for a few months."

"Don't sell yourself short," the corpse said. "Mean event resolution 36.8 minutes. That's excellent."

Desjardins acknowledged with a nod.

"The metabase," Rowan continued. "Plagues. Brushfires. Traffic flow. And even setting the Mediterranean aside for the moment, I'm told your projections helped a *lot* in keeping the Gulf Stream going. A few people have you beat in Maelstrom, certainly, but you've got the edge in biocontainment, economics, industrial ecology—"

Desjardins smiled to himself. Typical old-school: she actually thought she was ticking off a list of *different* subjects.

"At any rate," the corpse continued, "you seem to be the best local candidate for what we have in mind. We're taking you off your normal rotation and putting you onto a special project, with Dr. Lertzman's approval of course."

"I think we could probably spare him," Lertzman said, embracing the pretense that his opinion mattered. "In fact, after today I imagine Achilles would probably *want* to leave Maelstrom behind for a while."

Enculé. The sentiment was almost a reflex where Lertzman was concerned.

Rowan again: "There's a biological event we'd like you to keep an eye on. New soil microbe, from the looks of it. So far it's had a relatively minor impact—almost negligible, in fact, but the potential is, well..." She inclined her head toward the blonde on her right; on cue, that woman tapped her wristwatch. "If you'd open for download..."

Desjardins tapped the requisite shorthand onto his wrist; transfer protocols flickered briefly across his field of view.

"You can study the stats afterward," the blonde told him. "Briefly, though, you're looking for small-scale substrate acidification, reductions in chlorophyll *a,* maybe some changes in xanthophylls—"

Science. No wonder nobody'd bothered to introduce her.

"—there might be a reduction in soil moisture levels, too, but we don't know yet. Probable decline in Bt and associated microflora. Also we suspect the spread will be temperature-limited. Your job is to develop a diagnostic profile, something we can use to tag this bug from a distance."

"That sounds a bit long-term for my skill set," Desjardins remarked. *Not to mention boring as hell.* "I'm really more optimized for acute crisis work."

Rowan ignored the hint. "That's not a problem. We selected you for your pattern-recognition skills, not your brushfire reflexes."

"Okay, then." He sighed to himself. "What about an actual signature?"

"Excuse me?"

"If you're talking about depressed chlorophylls, I'm assuming conventional photosynthesizers are being replaced. By what? Any new pigments I should be looking for?"

"We don't have a signature yet," the woman told him. "If you can work one up that'd be great, but we're not hopeful."

"Come on. Everything's got a signature."

"That's true. But this thing's direct sig may not show up at a distance until it's already at outbreak concentrations. We want to catch it before then. Indirect telltales are probably your best bet."

"I'd still like the lab stats. An actual culture, too, of course." He decided to float a trial balloon. "Alice Jovellanos could be helpful in this. Her background's in biochem."

"Alice hasn't had her shots yet—" Lertzman began.

Rowan smoothly cut him off: "By all means, Dr. Desjardins. Anyone you think could be helpful. Keep in mind though, the security classifications are subject to change. Depending at least partly on your own results, of course."

"Thanks. And the culture?"

"We'll do what we can. There may be concerns about releasing a live sample, for obvious reasons."

Uh-huh.

"Start your search along coastal N'AmPac. We think this bug's limited to the Pacific Northwest. Between Hongcouver and Coos Bay, most likely."

"So far," Desjardins added.

"With your help, Dr. Desjardins, we don't expect that to change."

He'd seen it all before. Some pharm had lost control of another bug. The quake had cracked open an incubator somewhere, and the competing forces of corporate secrecy and agricultural Armageddon had beat each other senseless in a boardroom somewhere else, and Patricia Rowan—whoever *she* was working for—had emerged from the wreckage to dump the whole thing into his lap. Without giving him the right tools for the job, natch; by the time they'd skimmed off all the molecules with patents hanging from them, his culture sample would amount to 20cc's of distilled water.

A sound sneaked out, half laugh, half snort.

"Excuse me?" Rowan arched an eyebrow. "You had a comment?"

A brief, cathartic fantasy:

Actually I have a question, Ms. Rowan. Does all this bullshit turn your crank? Does the senseless withholding of vital information give you some kind of hard-on? It must. I mean, why bother retrofitting me down to the fucking molecules? Why bioengineer me into some paragon of integrity, only to decide I still can't be trusted when the chips are down? You know me, Rowan. I'm incorruptible. I couldn't turn against the greater good if my life depended on it.

Into the growing silence, Lertzman emitted a brief panicky cough from behind one clenched fist.

"Sorry, no. Nothing really." Desjardins tapped his watch, his hands safely beneath the table. He grabbed at the first heading to come up on his inlays: "It's just, you know, a cute name. *βehemoth.* What's it from?"

"It's biblical," Rowan told him. "I never liked it much myself."

He didn't need an answer to his unspoken questions anyway. He figured Rowan had a very good reason for playing things so close to her chest; of course she knew he couldn't work against the greater good.

But *she* could.

Bang

For Lenie Clarke, the choice between sharks and humans was not as easy as it might have been. Making it, she paid another price: she missed the darkness.

Night, no matter how moonless and overcast, was no match for eyecaps. There weren't many places on earth dark enough to blind them. Light-sealed rooms, of course. Deep caves and the deep sea, at least those parts free of bioluminescence. Nowhere else. Her caps doomed her to vision.

She could always remove them, of course. Easy enough to do, hardly different from popping out a pair of contact lenses. She vaguely remembered the look of her naked eyes;

they were pale blue, so pale the irises almost got lost in the whites. Sort of like looking into sea ice. She'd been told her eyes were cold, and sexy.

She hadn't taken her caps out for almost a year. She'd kept them on in front of people she'd fought against, fought for, fucked over. She hadn't even taken them off during sex. She wasn't about to strip now, in front of strangers.

If it was darkness she was after, she'd have to close her eyes. Surrounded by a million refugees, that wasn't the eas-iest thing to do either.

She found a few square meters of emptiness. Refugees huddled under blankets and lean-tos nearby, slept or fucked in darkness that must have afforded some cover to their eyes, at least. They'd pretty much left her alone, as Amitav had said they would. In fact, they accorded her considerably more space than they granted each other. She lay back in her little patch of sand, her *territory*, and closed her eyes against the brilliant darkness. A soft rain was falling; the diveskin numbed her body to it, but she could feel it on her face. It was almost a caress.

She drifted. She imagined she must have slept at some point, but her eyes happened to be open on two occasions when botflies passed quietly overhead, dark ellipses backlit by a brightness too faint for naked eyes. Each time she tensed, ready to flee into the ocean, but the drones took no notice of her.

No initiative, she reflected. *They don't see anything they're not programmed to look for.* Or perhaps their senses weren't as finely tuned as she'd feared. Perhaps they just couldn't see her implants; maybe her aura was too faint, or too far away. Maybe botflies didn't see as deeply into the EM spectrum as she'd feared.

I was all alone, that first time, she thought. *The whole beach was closed off. I bet that's it. They pay attention to trespassers...*

So did Amitav, evidently. That was shaping up to be a problem.

––––––

He appeared at the cycler the next morning with a dead bot-fly in his arms. It looked a bit like a turtle shell she'd once seen in a museum, except for the vents and instruments studding the ventral surface. It was split along its equatorial seam; black smudges lined the breach.

"Can you fix this?" Amitav asked. "Any of it?"

Clarke shook her head. "Don't know anything about bot-flies." She lifted the carapace anyway. Inside, burned electronics nested under a layer of soot.

She ran one thumb along a small pebbled convexity, felt the compound lenses of a visual cluster beneath the grime. Some of the tech was vaguely familiar, but...

"No," she said, setting it on the sand. "Sorry."

Amitav shrugged and sat, cross-legged. "I did not expect so," he said. "But one can always hope, and you seem to have such familiarity with machines yourself..."

She smiled faintly, freshly aware of the implants crowding her thorax.

"I expect you will be going to the fence," Amitav said after a moment. "Your people will let you through when they see you are one of them."

She looked to the east. Off in the distance, the border towers rose from a fog of human bodies and trampled scrub. She'd heard about the high-voltage lines and the razorwire strung between them. She'd heard other things, too, about refugees so driven by their own desperation they'd climbed seven or eight meters before the juice and their own cumulative dismemberment had killed them off. Their lacerated remains were left rotting on the wires, the story went—whether as an act of deterrence or simple neglect was unclear.

Clarke knew it was all just alligator tales. Nobody over thirteen believed such bullshit, and the people here—for all their numbers—didn't seem motivated enough to hold a garage sale, much less storm the battlements. What was the word Amitav had used?

Docile.

In a way it was a shame, though. She'd never actually

been to the fences. It might have been interesting to check them out.

Being dead had all sorts of little drawbacks.

"Surely you have a home to go to. Surely you do not wish to stay *here*," Amitav prodded.

"No," she said to both questions.

He waited. She waited with him.

Finally, he stood and glanced down at the dead botfly. "I do not know what made this one crash. Usually they work quite well. I believe you've already seen one or two pass by, yes? Your eyes may be empty, but they are not blind."

Clarke held his gaze and said nothing.

He nudged the little wreck with his toe. "These are not blind either," he said, and walked away.

It was a hole in darkness: a window to another world. It was set at the height of a child's eyes, and it looked into a kitchen she'd not seen in twenty years.

Onto a person she hadn't seen in almost that long.

Her father knelt in front of her, folded down from adult height to regard her eye to eye. He had a serious look on his face. He grasped her wrist with one hand; something dangled in the other.

She waited for the familiar sickness to rise in her throat, but it didn't come. The vision was a child's; the viewer was an adult, hardened, adapted, accustomed by now to trials that reduced child abuse from nightmare down to trite cliché.

She tried to look around; her field of view refused to change. She could not see her mother.

Par for the course.

Her father's mouth moved; no words came out. The image was utterly silent, a plague of light with no sound track.

This is a dream. A boring dream. Time to wake up.

She opened her eyes. The dream didn't stop.

There was a different world behind it, though, a high-contrast jigsaw of photoamplified light and shadow. Someone stood before her on the sand, but the face was eclipsed by this vision from her childhood. It floated in front of her, an impossible picture-in-picture. The present glimmered faintly through from behind.

She closed her eyes. The present vanished. The past didn't.

Go away. I'm done with you. Go away.

Her father still held her wrist—at least, he held the wrist of the fragile creature whose eyes she was using—but she felt nothing. And now those eyes focused autonomously on the dangling thing in her father's other hand. Suddenly frightened, she snapped her own eyes back open before she could see what it was; but once again the image followed her into the real world.

Here, before the destitute numberless hordes of the Strip, her father was holding out a gift for Lenie Clarke. Her first wristwatch.

Please go away . . .

"No," said a voice, very close by. "I am not."

Amitav's voice. Lenie Clarke, transfixed, made a small animal noise.

Her father was explaining the functions of her new toy. She couldn't hear what he was saying, but it didn't matter; she could see him voiceact'ing the little gadget, stepping through its Net Access functions (they'd called it *the Net* back then, she remembered), pointing out the tiny antennae that linked to the eyephones. . . .

She shook her head. The image didn't waver. Her father was pulling her forward, extending her arm, carefully looping the watch around her wrist.

She knew it wasn't really a gift. It was a down payment. It was a token offered in exchange, some half-assed gesture that was supposed to make up for the things he'd done to her all those years ago, the things he was going to do *right now*, the things—

Her father leaned forward and kissed some spot just above the eyes that Lenie Clarke couldn't shut. He patted the head that Lenie Clarke couldn't feel. And then, smiling—

He left her alone.

He moved back down the hall, out of the kitchen, leaving her to play.

The vision dissipated. The Strip rushed in to fill the hole.

Amitav glowered down at her. "You are mistaken," he said. "I am not your father."

She scrambled to her feet. The ground was muddy and saturated, close to the waterline. Halogen light stretched in broken strips from the station up the beach. Bundled motionless bodies lay scattered on the upper reaches of that slope. None were nearby.

It was a dream. Another—hallucination. Nothing real.

"I am wondering what you are doing here," Amitav said quietly.

Amitav's real. Focus. Deal with him.

"You are not the only—person to have washed up afterward, of course," the refugee remarked. "They wash up even now. But you are much less dead than the others."

You should've seen me before.

"And it is odd that you would come to us like this. All of this was swept clean many days ago. An earthquake on the bottom of the ocean, yes? Far out to sea. And here you are, built for the deep ocean, and now you come ashore and eat as if you have not eaten for days." His smile was a predatory thing. "And you do not wish your people to know that you are here. You will tell me why."

Clarke leaned forward. "Really. Or you'll do what, exactly?"

"I will walk to the fence and tell them."

"Start walking," Clarke said.

Amitav stared at her, his anger almost palpable.

"Go on," she prodded. "See if you can find a door, or a spare watch. Maybe they've left little suggestion boxes for you to pass notes into, hmm?"

"You are quite wrong if you think I could not attract the attention of your people."

"I don't think you really want to. You've got your own secrets."

"I am a refugee. We cannot afford secrets."

"Really. Why are you so skinny, Amitav?"

His eyes widened.

"Tapeworm? Eating disorder?" She stepped forward. "Cycler food not agree with you?"

"I hate you," he hissed.

"You don't even know me."

"I know you," he spat. "I know your *people*. I know—"

"You don't know shit. If you did—if you *really* had such a hard-on for *my people* as you call them—you'd be bending over backward to *help* me."

He stared at her, a flicker of uncertainty on his face.

She kept her voice low. "Suppose you're right, Amitav. Suppose I've come all the way up from the deep sea. The Axial Volcano, even, if you know where that is."

She waited. "Go on," he said.

"Let's also say, hypothetically, that the quake was no accident. Someone set off a nuke and all those shock waves just sort of daisy-chained their way back to the coast."

"And why would anyone do such a thing?"

"Theirs to know. Ours to find out."

Amitav was silent.

"With me so far? Bomb goes off in the deep sea. I come from the deep sea. What does that make me, Amitav? Am I the bad guy here? Did I trip the switch, and if I did, wouldn't I at least have planned a better escape than swimming across three hundred kilometers of fucking mud, without so much as a fucking sandwich, *only to crawl up onto your fucking Strip after a fucking week to get stuck listening to your fucking whining*? Does that make *any sense at all*?

"Or"—the voice leveling now, coming back under control—"did I just get screwed like everyone else, only I managed to get out alive? That might be enough to inspire a bit of ill will even in a white N'AmPac have-it-all bitch like myself, don't you think?"

And somebody, she promised herself, *is going to pay.*

Amitav said nothing. He watched her with his sunken eyes, his expression gone blank and unfathomable once more.

Clarke sighed. "Do you really want to fuck with me, Amitav? Do you want to fuck with the people who *did* hit the switch? They don't exactly have a light touch when it comes to cleaning up their messes. Right now they think I'm dead. Do you want to be around me when they find I'm not?"

"And what is it about you," Amitav said at last, "that makes *our* lives so unimportant?"

She'd thought a lot about that. It had led her back to a bright shining moment of discovery she'd had as a child. She'd been astonished to learn that there was life on the moon: microscopic life, some kind of bacterium that had hitched a ride with the first unmanned probes. It had sur-vived years of starvation in hard vacuum, frozen, boiled, pelted by an unending sleet of hard radiation.

Life, she'd learned, could survive anything. At the time it had been cause for hope.

"I think that maybe there's something inside me," she said now. "I think—"

Something brushed against her leg.

Her arm lashed out reflexively. Her fist clenched around the wrist of a young boy.

He'd been going for the gas billy on her calf.

"Ah," Clarke said. "Of course."

The boy stared back at her, petrified.

She turned back to Amitav; the child whimpered and squirmed in her grip. "Friend of yours?"

"I, ah—"

"Little diversionary tactic, perhaps? You don't have the balls to take me on, and none of your grown-up buddies will help out, so you use a fucking *child*?" She yanked on the small arm: the boy yelped.

Sleepers stirred in the distance, used to chronic distur-bance. None seemed to fully awaken.

"Why should you care?" Amitav hissed. "It is not a weapon, you said so yourself. Am I a fool, to believe such claims when you come here waving it like an ataghan? What is it? A shockprod?"

"I'll show you," she said.

She bent, still gripping the child. A depolarizing blade

protruded from the tip of her glove like a gray fingernail; at its touch the sheath on her calf split as if scalpeled. The billy slid easily into her grip, a blunt ebony rod with a fluorescent band at the base of the handgrip.

Amitav raised his hands, suddenly placating. "There is no need—"

"Ah, but there is. Come in close, now."

Amitav took a step back.

"It works on contact," Clarke said. "Injects compressed gas. Comes in handy down on the rift, when the wildlife tries to eat you."

She thumbed the safety on the billy, jammed the rod point down into the sand.

With a crack like the inside of a thunderclap, the beach exploded.

The universe rang like a tuning fork. She lay where the blast had thrown her. Her face stung as though sandblasted.

Her eyelids were clenched. It seemed like a very long time before she could open them again.

A crater yawned across three meters of sand, filling with groundwater.

She climbed to her feet. The Strip had leapt awake in an instant, fled outward, turned back and congealed into a ring of shocked and frightened faces.

Amazingly, she was still holding the billy.

She eyed the device with numb incredulity. She'd used it more times than she could count. Whenever one of Channer Vent's monsters had tried to take her apart she'd parried, jammed the billy home, watched as one more predator bloated and burst at her touch. It had been lethal enough to the fish, but it had never exploded with *this* kind of force before. Not down on the . . .

Oh, shit. On the Rift.

It had been calibrated to deliver a lethal charge at the bottom of the ocean, where five thousand PSI was a gentle burp. Down there it had been a reasonably effective weapon.

At sea level, without all those atmospheres pushing back, it was a bomb.

"I didn't mean—I thought..." Clarke looked around. An endless line of faces looked back.

Amitav lay sprawled on the opposite side of the crater. He moaned, brought one hand to his face.

There was no sign of the boy.

Stickman

A thunderclap at midnight. Something exploded near a Calvin cycler just south of Gray's Harbor. A botfly had been coming around the headland to the south; it wasn't line of sight at detonation, but it had ears. It sent an alert to home base and turboed over to investigate.

Sou-Hon Perreault was on duty. She'd swapped over to the graveyard shift the day she'd learned that mermaids came out at night. (Her husband, having recently learned about the special needs of vPTS victims, had accepted the change without complaint.) Now she slipped into the botfly's perceptual sphere, and took stock.

A shallow crater yawned across the intertidal substrate. Tracking outward: chaotic tangles of heat and bioelectricity, restless as spooked cattle. Perreault narrowed the EM to amped visible; the heat lightning resolved into a milling mass of dull gray humanity.

The Strip had its own districts, its own self-generating ghettos within ghettos. The people here hailed mainly from the Indian subcon: Perreault set her primary filters to Punjabi, Bengali, and Urdu. She began asking questions.

An explosion, yes. Nobody really knew for certain what had led up to it. There had been raised voices, some said. Man, woman, child. Accusations of theft. And then, suddenly, *bang*.

Everyone awake after that, everyone in retreat. The woman waving some kind of shockprod like a club. The masses, keeping their distance. One man in the circle with her, blood on his face. Angry. Facing the woman, indifferent to the weapon in her hand. The child had vanished by this time, all agreed. Nobody knew who the child might have been.

Everyone remembered the adults, though. Amitav and the mermaid.

"Where did they go?" Perreault said; the botfly translated her words with toneless dispassion.

To the ocean. The mermaid always goes to the ocean.

"What about the other one? This *Amitav*?"

After her. With her. To the ocean.

Ten minutes past, perhaps.

Perreault pulled the botfly into a steep climb, panned along the Strip from fifty meters up. The refugees dissolved into a Brownian horde; waves of motion passed through the crowd far faster than any one person could make way. There: barely discernible, a fading line of turbulence connecting the crater to the surf. Milling particles, recently disrupted by the passage of something aimed.

She swooped down toward the waterline. Upturned faces everywhere, gray and luminous in the botfly's photoamps, following its course like sunflowers tracking the light.

Except for one, a ways down the beach, running south through ankle-deep foam. Not looking back.

Perreault widened the filters: nothing mechanical in the thorax. Not the mermaid. There were other anomalies, though. She was chasing a skeleton, a ludicrous emaciated throwback to the days when malnutrition was a recognized hallmark of refugees everywhere.

There was no need for starvation here. There'd been no need for years. This one had *chosen* to starve. This one was political.

No wonder he was running.

Perreault nudged the botfly into pursuit. It sped past its quarry in seconds, slewed around, and dropped down to block his escape. Perreault tripped the floods and pinned the refugee in twin beams of blinding halogen.

"Amitav," she said.

———

She'd heard of them, of course. They were rare, but not too rare for a label: *stickmen*, they were called. Perreault had never actually seen one in the flesh before.

Hindian. Sunken eyes, pools of sullen shadow. Blood oozing in a sheen of droplets from his face. One hand was raised to shield his eyes from the light; more blood rose from a raw stigmatum on the palm. Limbs, joints, fingers as sharp-edged and angular as origami protruding from his torn clothing. The soles of his feet had been sprayed with plastic in lieu of shoes.

The ocean hemmed him in on one side; Strippers looked on curiously from all others, keeping clear of the halogen pool. Every segment of the stickman's frame was tensed, poised between equally futile options of flight and attack.

"Relax," Perreault said. "I only want to ask you some questions."

"Ah. Questions from a police robot," he said. Thin lips drawn back from brown teeth, the cracks between bloody. A cynical rictus. "I am relieved."

She blinked. "You speak English."

"It is not an uncommon language. Not as stylish as French these days, though, yes? What do you want?"

Perreault disabled the translator. "What happened back there?"

"There is no cause to worry. None of your machinery was harmed."

"I'm not interested in the machinery. There was an explosion."

"Your wonderful machines do not provide us with explosives," Amitav pointed out.

"There was a woman, a diver. There was a child."

The stickman glowered.

"I just want to know what happened," Perreault told him. "I'm not looking to give you any trouble."

Amitav spat. "Of course not. You blind me to test my eyes, yes?"

Perreault killed the floods. Black and white faded to gray.

"Thank you," Amitav said after a moment.

"Tell me what happened."

"She said it was an accident," Amitav said.

"An accident?"

"The child was—Clarke had this, I am not sure of the word, this *club*. On her leg. She called it *a billy*."

"Clarke?"

"Your diver."

Clarke. "Do you know her first name?"

"No." Amitav snorted. "*Kali* is as good a name as any, though."

"Go on."

"The child, he—he tried to steal it. While we were—talking."

"You didn't stop him?"

Amitav shifted uncomfortably. "I believe she was trying to show the child that the *billy* was dangerous," he said. "In that she succeeded. I myself flew. It left marks." He smiled, held up his hands once more, palms up. Flayed flesh, oozing blood.

Amitav fell silent and looked out to sea. Perreault's perspective bobbed slightly in a sudden breeze, as though the botfly was nodding.

"I do not know what happened to the child," Amitav said at last. "By the time I could stand again he was gone. Clarke was looking for him, though."

"Who is she?" Perreault asked softly. "Do you know her?"

He spat. "*She* would not say so."

"But you've seen her before. Tonight was not the first time."

"Oh yes. Your pets here"—looking at the other refugees—"they come to me whenever something requires *initiative*, yes? They tell me where the mermaid is, so I can go and deal with her."

"But you two are connected somehow. You're friends, or—"

"We are not sheep," Amitav said. "That is all we have in common. Here, it is enough."

"I want to know about her."

"That is wise," Amitav said, more quietly.

"Why do you say that?"

"Because she survived what you did to her. Because she knows you did it."

"*I* didn't do anything."

The stickman waved one dismissive hand. "No matter. She will come for you anyway."

"What happened? What was done to her?"

"She did not say, exactly. She says very little. And some-times, when she does say things, she does not say them to anyone *here*, yes? At least, no one I can see. But they get her quite upset."

"She sees ghosts?"

Amitav shrugged. "Ghosts are not uncommon here. I am speaking to one now."

"You know I'm no ghost."

"Not a real one, perhaps. You only haunt machinery."

Sou-Hon Perreault looked for a filter to tweak. She couldn't find one that fit.

"She said you caused the earthquake," Amitav said sud-denly. "She says you sent the wave that killed so many of us."

"That's ridiculous."

"And you would know, yes? Your leaders would share such things with the drivers of mechanical insects?"

"Why would anyone do something like that?"

Amitav shrugged. "Ask Clarke. If you can find her."

"Can you help me do that?"

"Certainly." He pointed to the Pacific. "She is out there."

"Will you see her again?"

"I do not know."

"Can you let me know if you do?"

"And how would I do that even if I wished to?"

"Sou-Hon," Perreault said.

"I do not understand."

"That's my name. Sou-Hon. I can program the botflies to recognize your voice. If they hear you calling me, they'll let me know."

"Ah," Amitav said.

"Well?"

Amitav smiled. "Don't call us. We'll call you."

An Invitation to Dance

In South Bend, the mermaid killed a man.

Willapa Bay ruptured the Strip like an ulcer twelve kilometers across. Official surveillance of that gap had not been designed to catch people for whom breathing was optional; now the coast was fifteen klicks behind her. This far in, the wave had been thwarted by headlands and a thick stubby island, clogging the inlet like a cyst. The Big One had merely trembled here. The wreckage and desolation was all of local origin.

She emerged past midnight onto a dark, corroded segment of waterfront, long since abandoned to a creeping blight of premillennial toluene. Nervous late-night pedestrians glimpsed her on the edge of the city core and increased their pace from A to B. The last time Clarke had wandered civilized streets there'd been free wristwatch dispensers on every second corner, a halfhearted sop to those who'd have empowered the masses through access to information. She could find no dispensers in this place, only an old public phone standing guard in fluorescent twilight. She interrogated it. She was *here,* it told her. Yves Scanlon lived *there,* three hundred kilometers to the northeast.

He wouldn't be expecting her. She faded to black. Indifferent security cameras reduced her to a transient assemblage of infrared pixels.

She clambered back down concrete scree to an oily waterline. Something called to her as she retrieved her fins: muffled, familiar sounds from an abandoned customs office. It could have been the splintering of rotten pilings.

Maybe a boot against ribs, with flesh getting in the way. Something knotted in Clarke's throat. There's no end to the things you can slam into a human body. She'd lost count of the different sounds they made.

Almost too faint to hear, more whimper than words: "*Fuck,* man..." The muted hum of an electrical discharge. A groan.

A walkway extended around the derelict office; junk piled along its length waited to trip anyone not gifted with night eyes. At the other side of the building, a dock jutted from the waterfront on wooden pilings. Two figures stood on that platform, a man and a woman. Four others lay twitching at their feet. A police botfly slept on the pier, conveniently off-line.

Technically, of course, it was not an assault. Both aggressors wore uniforms and badges conferring the legal right to beat whomever they chose. Tonight they'd chosen an entrée of juveniles, laid out along the creosote-stained planks like gutted fish. Those bodies twitched with the spastic neural static of shockprod discharge; beyond that, they didn't react to the boots in their sides. Clarke could hear snatches of conversation from the uniforms, talk of curfew violations and unauthorized use of the Maelstrom.

And of trespassing.

"On government property, no less," remarked the male, lifting one arm in a grand gesture that took in the dock, the pilings, the derelict office, Lenie Clarke—

—*Shit he's wearing nightshades they're both wearing nightshades*—

"*You!*" The policeman took a single step toward the office, pointing his shockprod at the shadows in which she lay exposed. "Stand away from the building!"

There'd been a time, not so long ago, when Lenie Clarke would have obeyed without thinking. She'd have followed orders even though she knew what was coming, because she'd learned that you deal with violence by just shutting up and *getting it over with*. It would hurt, of course. That was the whole point. But it was better than the chronic queasiness, the *expectation*, the endless interludes between assaults where you could only wait for it to happen.

More recently, she would have simply fled. Or at least withdrawn. *None of my business,* she'd have told herself, and departed before anyone even knew she was there. She had done that when Mike Brander had used Gerry Fischer as a convenient proxy for those who'd made his childhood a living hell. It had been *none of my business* when Beebe Station resounded with the sound of Brander's rage and Fischer's breaking bones. It had been *none of my business* when Brander, shift after shift, had stood guard in the wet room, daring Fischer to come back inside. Eventually Fischer had faded from man to child to reptile, an empty inhuman cipher living on the edge of the rift. Even then, it had been none of Lenie Clarke's business.

But Gerry Fischer was dead now. So was Lenie Clarke, for that matter. She'd died with the others: Alice and Mike and Ken and Gerry, all turned into white-hot vapor. They were all dead, and when the stone had been rolled away and the voice had rung out, *Lazarus! Come forth!* it hadn't been any of Lenie Clarke's friends that had risen from the grave. It hadn't even been Lenie Clarke. Not the soft squirming career victim of her dryback days, anyway. Not the opaque chrysalis gestating down on the rift. It had been something newly forged, acid-washed, some white-hot metamorph of Lenie Clarke that had never existed before.

Now she was confronted by a familiar icon—an authority, a giver of orders, an eager practitioner of the legal right to commit violence upon *her*. She did not regard its challenge as an order to be obeyed. She did not consider it a situation to be avoided.

For Lenie Clarke Mark II, it was a long-overdue invitation to dance.

Pixelpal

BCC5932 TRIGGER STIMULUS/THROUGHPUT INTERCEPT
Obj. Class: file packet/benign
Obj. Species: pers. comm. (NI)/packet 7 of 23/voice modem
decrypt
Obj. Source: *corrupted*
Obj. Destination: multi (ref. cc)
EXCISE CRITERION: 255-CHR BRACKET INI/FIN
TRIGGERING STIMULI.
EXCERPT BEGINS

that likely to get away with it forever. A little too metallic if
you know what I mean. Anyway, they haven't caught us at
it yet.

We *did* get caught a few days back, though, over something else again. Except we lucked into this avenging angel.
No shit. **Lenie Clarke,** her name was. It was our own stupid
fault, I guess. Didn't check for leakage when we logged on.
Anyhow, *les beus* came down on us, they got everyone except
Haj[1] and me, and what could *we* do except run for it? And
they had everybody down and all of a sudden there's this K-
selector walking out of nowhere, looks like one of those old
litcrits with the teeth, you know, vampires. All in black and
she's wearing the absolute thickest ConTacs you ever saw,
even thicker than *les beus.* Barely see her eyes behind them.
Anyhow, she just walks out of the shadows and right into
them.

You wouldn't think she'd last two seconds. I mean, she
didn't even *notice* the shockprods, I don't think that suit of
hers carries a charge, but *still.* She just wasn't that big, you
know? And they were really whaling on her, and she just
took it. Like it was the most natural thing in the world. Or
like—you know—almost like she got *off* on it, or something.

Anyway, she wraps her arms around this big beefy antibody and she just *pushes*, and they go right over the edge,

---

1. Spelling conjectural.

and the sterilites go on when they hit the water—kind of wild those things still work, pier hasn't seen any boat traffic in *years*—and the water lights up all cool and radium-glow and there's some splashing and then there's this big *whoomf* and it's like this huge bubble of blood and guts just sort of boils up to the surface and the water's like *completely* gone to rust.

She's like some kinda amphibian, one of those rifter cyborgs. We met up with her after, she came back to pick up her fins when things had cooled down. Don't ask me what she was doing here in the middle of the night. Didn't talk much and we didn't push. We set her up with some snacks and supplies—she'd been eating from cyclers on the *Strip*, if you can believe it. Although it didn't seem to've dulled her edge any. Gave her my watch. She hadn't even heard about the curfew. I had to show her how to get around the timelock. Guess you lose touch with things when you spend all your time on the bottom of the ocean. Not that it held her back any. You should've *seen* that asshole. They fished him out of the water like an old rag. I would've *paid* to see his face, you know?

I tried to look her up but **Lenie Clarke** isn't exactly sockeye on the registry. Got more hits than holocausts. She did mention her hometown, I think, but I couldn't find that either. Any of you guys ever hear of a place called **Beebe?**

Anyhow, far as I know she's still at large. *Les beus* are probably looking for her, but I bet fifty QueBucks they don't even know what she *looks* like under all that gear, never mind who she *is*. I mean, they hardly ever catch *us*, and they know everything there is to know about us. Well, not everything. Right, m

EXCERPT ENDS

CALL βehemoth
Lenie Clarke/Beebe CONFIRMED.
ADD SEARCH TERMS: amphibian/s, rifter/s, cyborg/s

OVERLAY TEMPLATE. RESEQUENCE TEXT.
COPY. TRANSLOCATE.
SPREAD THE WORD.

Third-person Limited

Perreault hadn't needed Amitav's permission, of course. She'd programmed the botflies to recognize him anyway. She'd dropped a cloud of mosquitoes, too, little flying sensors no bigger than rice grains. They were brain-dead, but they could afford to be; they relayed raw telemetry back to the 'flies for all the *real* analysis. That increased coverage by an order of magnitude, at least until their batteries gave out.

It would still be a crapshoot: a botfly or skeet would have to be line of sight with Amitav once she'd put out the call, and there'd have to be enough of him visible to make an ID—very iffy, given the human congestion on the Strip. It would be easy enough for the stickman to hide, should he choose to.

Still. Long odds were better than none.

She finished a late supper across the table from her husband, noted his forlorn scrutiny almost in passing. Marty was doing his utmost, she knew—giving space, giving support. Waiting for that predictable moment when the shock wore off, her defenses fell, and she needed help picking up the pieces. Every now and then Perreault would search herself for signs of that imminent breakdown. Nothing. The antidepressants were still having some effect, of course, even after her system had shocked itself into partial immunity; but that shouldn't have been enough. She should be *feeling* something by now.

She was. Intense, passionate, all-consuming. Curiosity.

She squeezed Martin's hand across the table and headed toward her office. It was almost a half hour until her shift began, but nobody on the circuit minded if she started early. She slid into her seat—a favorite antique with flared arms and a skin of real leather—and was reaching for her headset when her husband's hand fell lightly onto her shoulder.

"Why does she matter so much?" he asked. It was the first time he'd come into her office since the breakdown.

"Marty, I've got to go to work."

He waited.

She sighed and swiveled her chair to face him. "I don't know. It's—it's a mystery, I guess. Something to solve."

"It's more than that."

"Why? Why does it have to be?" She heard the exasperation in her own voice, saw its effect on her husband. She took a breath and tried again. "I don't know. It's just—you wouldn't think a single person could count for much, but—she's making an impression, you know? At least on the Strip. She *matters*, somehow..."

Martin shook his head. "Is that what she is to you? A role model?"

"I didn't say—"

"She could be something else, Sou. What if she's a fugitive?"

"What?"

"It must have crossed your mind. Someone from N'Am—or I don't know, not your standard refugee, anyway. Why's she staying out on the Strip? Why doesn't she want to go home? What's she hiding from?"

"I don't know. That's what makes it a mystery."

"She could be dangerous."

"What, to me? She's way out on the coast! She doesn't even know I exist!"

"Still. You should report it."

"Maybe." Perreault swiveled deliberately back to her desk. "I really have to work now, Martin."

He wouldn't have let her off so easily before, of course. But he knew his assigned role, he'd been coached by a half dozen well-meaning authorities. *Your wife has just come through a very traumatic experience. She's fragile. Let her move at her own pace.*

Don't push.

So he didn't. A little piece of Sou-Hon felt guilty for taking advantage of that restraint. The rest was reveling in the cradling embrace of the headset around her skull, the sudden pinpoint control over what *was* and *wasn't* perceived, the—

"Semen-sucking savior," she whispered.

The alert was flashing all over the left side of her visual field. One of the botflies had gotten a nibble. More than a nibble; a big predatory bite. It was hovering less than three meters off target.

Not Amitav either, this time. A marriage of flesh and machinery. One woman, with clockwork.

Deep night, beneath an endless cloud bank. Across the black water, floodlights and heaters smudged distant light along the Strip. Perreault triggered the photoamps.

The mermaid crouched directly ahead on a jagged reef, 150 meters from shore. The ocean, sparkling with microbial phosphorescence, tried to dislodge her. Between waves, the reef jutted a meter above the waterline, myriad tiny waterfalls draining down its sides; when the water crested the mermaid became a round black boulder herself, barely visible in the luminous foam.

She climbed to her feet. The surge rose above her knees; she staggered, but stayed upright. Her face was a pale oval painted onto a black body. Her eyes were paler ovals painted onto her face. They panned past the hovering botfly.

They did not seem to notice it.

Her face tilted down, stared directly ahead. One slick ebony arm reached forward, the fingers extended; a blind woman, reaching for something she couldn't see. Clarke's mouth moved. Any words were lost in the roar of the surf. Perreault slid filters past critical thresholds. Ocean sounds squelched into silence. Now only the shriek of distant gulls and a few syllables:

"No. Not—*ain.*"

Perreault squelched the high frequencies as well. Now the mermaid stood in an utterly silent tableau, the Pacific crashing soundlessly on all sides.

"You never did," she said. Tide surged silently between her legs. The mermaid's reaching fingers closed around empty space. She seemed surprised.

Another wave swept the reef. The mermaid staggered, re-
covered. Perreault noticed that both of her hands were balled
into fists.

"Dad." Almost a whisper.

"Ms. Clarke," Perreault said. The mermaid did not respond.

Right. The surf. Perreault increased the volume, tried again:
"Ms. Clarke."

The mermaid's head jerked up. *"You! What is it?"*

"Ms. Clarke, I've been—"

"Something in the food? Some sort of psychoactive? Is
that what this is?"

"Ms. Clarke, I don't know what—"

The mermaid smiled, a hideous baring of teeth beneath
cold white eyespots. "Fine. I can take it. Do your worst."

"Ms. Clarke—"

"This is fucking *nothing.* You just wait."

The Pacific surged silently up from behind her, swept her
from the reef in the blink of an eye. The cameras caught a
last freeze-framed moment: A fist, raised briefly above the
boiling water. Gone.

This is fucking nothing. You just wait.

Sou-Hon Perreault didn't know that she could.

Remora

The lock groaned open like the gates of an iron cathedral.
Earthquakes lived in that sound, twisting metal, skyscrapers
torqued painfully on their axes. Slow surge pushed flotsam
from great doors that stirred the ocean.

Rising within that sound, another one: triple screws, cav-
itating.

She'd placed herself a few hundred meters offshore, in the
center of a dredged scar leading to deep water. Gray's Harbor's
commercial traffic passed directly overhead. By now she'd had
enough practice to make it work. She rose a few meters off the
bottom; the drag from the new backpack slowed her a bit, but

she was getting used to it. Echo-sounding pulses from the approaching vessel tapped against her implants. The murky water went suddenly, ominously dark—first to her right, then directly overhead. The water pushed her backward. An instant later a black wall, studded with rivets, rushed obliquely out of the murk and streamed past, filling the ocean. The hiss of approaching screws filled the water.

She'd counted herself lucky, so far, that none of the ships had smashed into her. She knew those odds were low—bow waves pushed water and flotsam aside—but such reassuring insights always occurred during quiet moments on the bottom. Now, with a cliff of motion-blurred metal within touching distance, she could only think of flyswatters.

She broke the surface; the cliff shimmered into sudden sharp focus, black and rusty red, a great concave overhang eclipsing three-quarters of the sky. An ice-wrangler. She turned to face the approaching stern. Racing toward her, edge on, a metal fin angled down and out from the hull just above the waterline. Foam boiled where its distal end cut the water.

A trim tab. It could give her a free ride, or take off her head. If she floated along the surface—just past the point where the metal slashed the sea—the tip of the fin would pass beneath her. There'd be a split second to grab at the leading edge.

Maybe ten seconds to get into position.

She almost made it.

Her right hand hooked the fin; the left slid off, confounded by turbulence. In an instant the tab was past, taking Clarke's hand with it. Everything went bowstring-taut in an instant. Her right shoulder popped from its socket. Clarke tried to scream. Her flooded amphibian body drowned the sound at conception.

She drew her left arm forward. Drag slapped it back. She tried again. The muscles of her right shoulder screamed in outrage. Her left hand crept upstream along the surface of the tab; finally its fingers found the leading edge, hooked reflexively.

Her shoulder popped back into place. Those muscles, never satisfied, screamed all over again.

A cascade of water and foam tried to push her off. The wrangler was moving dead slow, and she was barely hanging on. They'd be opening the throttle the moment they passed the last channel marker.

She edged laterally up the slope. Seawater thinned to spray; then she was clear, lying against the main hull. She split her face seal; her lung reinflated with a tired sigh.

The tab angled down at about twenty degrees. Clarke propped her back against the hull and brought her knees up, planting her feet downslope. She was wedged securely a good two meters from the water; the soles of her fins provided more than enough traction to keep her from slipping.

The outermost channel spar slid past. The vessel began picking up speed. Clarke kept one eye on the shore, the other on her nav panel. It didn't take long for the readings to change.

At last. *This* one was turning north. She relaxed.

The Strip scrolled slowly past in the distance, backed by the vertebral spikes of its eastern towers. At this range she could barely make out movement onshore; diffuse patches in vague motion, at best. Clouds of flightless gnats.

She thought of Amitav, the anorexic. The only one with the balls to come right out and openly hate her.

She wished him well.

Firebug

Achilles Desjardins had always found smart gels a bit creepy. People thought of them as brains in boxes, but they weren't. They didn't have the parts. Forget about the neocortex or the cerebellum—these things had *nothing*. No hypothalamus, no pineal gland, no sheathing of mammal over reptile over fish. No instincts. No *desires*. Just a porridge of cultured neurons, really: four-digit IQs that didn't give a rat's ass whether they even lived or died. Somehow they learned through operant conditioning, although they lacked the capacity either to enjoy reward or suffer punishment. Their pathways formed and dissolved with all the colorless indifference of water shaping a river delta.

But Desjardins had to admit they had their uses. Wildlife didn't stand a chance going up against a head cheese.

Not that wildlife hadn't tried, of course. But the Maelstrom ecosystems had evolved in a world of silicon and arsenide—a few hundred basic operating systems, endlessly repeated. Predictable registers and addresses. Stuff you could *count* on; not some slab of thinking meat in constant flux. Even if some shark did manage to scope out that architecture, it would be no further ahead. Gels rewired themselves with each passing thought; what good is a map when the landscape won't stop moving?

That was the theory, anyway. The proof was an eye of calm, staring out from the heart of Maelstrom itself. Since the day of its birth the gels had kept it clean, a high-speed computational landscape unpolluted by worms or viruses or digital predators. One day, a long time ago, the whole network had been this clean. Perhaps one day it would be again, if the gels lived up to their potential. For the time being, though, only a select two or three million souls were allowed inside.

It was called Haven, and Achilles Desjardins practically lived there.

Now he was spinning a web across one pristine corner of his playground. Rowan's biochemical stats had already been sent to Jovellanos's station: the first thing he did was establish an update link. Then he looked over the ramparts, peeking past the shoulders of the vigilant gels into Maelstrom proper. There were things out there that had to be brought inside— carefully, though, mindful of the sparkling floors:

Tap into EOS archives. Get daily radar maps of soil moisture for the past year, if available. (A big *if*, these days. Desjardins had tried to load a copy of *Bonny Anne* from the library the week before, only to find they'd started wiping all books that hadn't been accessed for more than a two-month period. The same old mantra: storage limitations.) EM snaps of polyelectrolytes and complexing cations. Multispectrals on all major chlorophylls, xanthophylls, carotenoids: iron and soil nitrogen, too. And just to be thorough—without much hope, mind you—query the NCBI database for recent constructs with real-world viability.

Competing with conventional primary producers, Rowan had said. Meaning the conventional bugs might be dying off: do a spectral for elevated soil methane. Distribution potentially temperature-limited; infrared, crossed with albedo and wind speed. Restrict all searches to a polygon extending from the spine of the Cascades out to the coast, and from Cape Flattery down to the thirty-eighth parallel.

Draw the threads together. Squeeze the signal through the usual statistical gauntlet: path analysis, Boltzmann transforms, half a dozen breeds of nonlinear estimation. Discriminant functions. Hankins filters. Principal component analysis. Interferometry profiles across a range of wavelengths. Lynn-Hardy hyperniche tables. Repeat all analyses with intervariable time lags in sequence from zero days to thirty.

Desjardins played at his panel. Abstract shapes condensed from clouds of data, winked provocatively at the corner of his eye, vanished the moment he focused on them. Fuzzy white lines from a dozen directions interwove, colored, took on intricate fractal patterns—

But no. *This* mosaic had a P-value greater than 0.25; *that* one violated assumptions of homoscedasticity. The little one in the corner drove the Hessians fucking *crazy*. One flawed thread, barely visible, and the whole carpet unraveled. *Tear it down, bleach out the transforms, start from scratch—*

Wait a minute.

Correlation coefficient of -0.873. What was *that* all about?

Temperature. Temperature went up when chlorophyll went down.

Why the hell didn't I see that before? Oh, there. A time lag. What the . . .

What the . . .

A soft chime in his ear: "Hey, Killjoy. I've got something really strange here."

"Me too," Desjardins replied.

———

Jovellanos's office was just down the hall; it still took her a few minutes to show up at his door. The caffeine spike in her hand told him why.

"You should get more sleep," he remarked. "You won't need so many chemicals."

She raised an eyebrow. "This from the man with half his bloodstream registered in the patent office." Jovellanos hadn't had her shots yet. She didn't need them in her current position, but she was too good at her job to stay where she was much longer. Desjardins looked forward to the day when her righteous stance on the Sanctity of Free Will went head-to-head against the legal prerequisites for promotion. She'd probably take one look at the list of perks and the new salary, and cave.

He had, anyway.

He spun his chair back to the console and brought the correlation matrix up on the display. "Look at this. Chloroes go down, soil temperature goes up."

"Huge P-value," Jovellanos said.

"Small sample size. That's not the point: look at the time lag."

She leaned forward. "Those are awfully big confidence limits."

"The lag's not consistent. Sometimes it takes a couple of days for the temp to rise, sometimes a few weeks."

"That's barely even a *pattern*, Killjoy. Anything—"

"Take a guess at the magnitude," he broke in.

"Loss of plant cover, right?" Jovellanos shrugged. "Assuming it *is* a real effect, say half a degree? Quarter?"

Desjardins showed her.

"Holy shit," she said. "This bug starts *fires*?"

"Something does, anyway. I scanned the municipal archives along the coast: all local firestorms, mostly attributed to acts of terrorism or 'industrial accidents.' Also a couple of tree farms going down for some agro pest—budworm or something."

Jovellanos was at his elbow, her hands running over his console. "What about *other* fires in the area..."

"Oh, lots. Even keeping strictly within the search window, I found a good eight or nine that *didn't* correlate. *A* ties to *B*, but not vice versa."

"So maybe it's a fluke," she said hopefully. "Maybe it doesn't mean anything."

"Or maybe somebody else has a better track on this bug than we do."

Jovellanos didn't answer for a moment. Then: "Well, we might be able to improve our own track a bit."

Desjardins glanced up. "Yeah?"

"I've been working up that sample they gave us. They're not making it easy, they haven't left a single intact organelle as far as I can tell—"

He waved her on: "It all looks the same to a mass spec."

"Only if they left all the pieces behind after they mashed them."

"Of course they did. Otherwise, you'd never get an accurate sig."

"Well, I can't find half the stuff that's supposed to be there. No phospholipids, even. Lots of nucleotides, but I can't get them to fit a DNA template. So your bug's probably RNA-based."

"Uh-huh." No surprises there—lots of microbes got along just fine without DNA.

"Also I've managed to reconstruct some simple enzymes, but they're a bit too stiff in the joints to work properly, you know? Oh, and this is kind of weird: I've found a couple of D-aminos."

"Ah." Desjardins nodded sagely. "That means what, exactly?"

"Right-handed. The asymmetric carbons stick off the wrong side of the molecule. Like your usual left-handed amino, only flipped."

A mirror image. "So?"

"So that makes 'em useless; all metabolic pathways have been geared for L-aminos and *only* L-aminos, for the past three billion years at least. There's a couple of bacteria that use R-aminos *because* they're useless—they stick them onto their cell walls to make 'em indigestible—but that's not what we're dealing with here."

Desjardins pushed back in his chair. "So someone built

this thing completely from scratch, is that what you're saying? We've got another new bug on our hands."

Jovellanos shook her head, disgusted. "And that corpse
didn't even tell you."

"Maybe she doesn't know."

Jovellanos pointed at the GIS overlay. Two dozen crimson
pinpoints sparkled along the coast from Hongcouver to New-
port. Two dozen tiny anomalies of soil and water chemistry.
Two dozen visitations from an unknown microbe, each pre-
saging a small fiery apocalypse.

"*Somebody* knows," Jovellanos said.

Afterburn

On all sides Hongcouver licked its wounds.

The city had always been a coward, hiding behind Van-
couver Island and a maze of local bathymetry. That had
spared it from the worst effects of the tsunami. The quake
itself had been another story, of course.

In an earlier day, before Maelstrom and telecommuting
and city centers half-abandoned, the death toll in the core
would have been three times as high. As it was, those who'd
been spared vivisection downtown had merely died closer to
home. Whole subdivisions, built on the effluvial sediment of
the Fraser Delta, had shuddered into sudden quicksand and
disappeared. Richmond and White Rock and Chilliwack didn't
exist anymore. Mount Rainier had awakened overnight in a
bad mood; fresh lava continued to flow over most of its southern face. Mount Adams was stirring and might yet blow.

In the Hongcouver core, damage was more heterogene-
ous. Streets stretched for blocks without so much as a broken
window. Then, across some arbitrary intersection, the world
became a place of shattered buildings and upended asphalt.
Bright yellow barriers, erected after the fact, drew boundaries
around the injured areas. Lifters hung above the dark zones
like white blood cells on a tumor. Fresh girders and paneling
descended from on high, reconstructive grafts of metropoli-

tan skin and bone. Heavy machinery grumbled in the canyons where they touched down.

In between, patches of cityscape hummed at half power,
emergency Ballard stacks jumpered into convenient substa-
tions. Those streets that hadn't upended, those buildings that
hadn't been shrugged into False Creek, had been swept clean
and reactivated. Field crematoria belched ash from the corner
of Georgia and Denman, keeping—so far—one step ahead of
the cholera bug. More barriers than buildings, these days. Not
that there was anywhere else to go; CSIRA had sealed the
border at Hell's Gate.

Benrai Dutton had survived it all.

He'd been lucky; his splitfit condo was halfway up Point
Gray, an island of granite in a sea of sand. While neighbor-
hoods on all sides had vanished, the Point had merely slipped
a little.

Even here there was damage, of course. Most of the
houses on the lower face had collapsed; the few still standing
listed drunkenly to the east. No lights shone from them or
the lampposts lining the street, even though night was falling. A jury-rigged line of portable floods shone from poles
separating wrecked homes from standing ones, but they had
a defensive air about them. They existed, not to bring light
to the ruins, but as a perimeter against them.

They existed to blind Benrai Dutton when a crazy woman
leapt at his throat from the shadows.

Suddenly he was transfixed: cold bright eyes without pupils, glaciers embedded in flesh. A disembodied face, almost
as pale as the eyes it contained. Invisible hands, one around
his neck, one at his chest—

—*no not invisible she's in black she's all in black*—

"*What happened?*"

"What—what—"

"I am *not* going to give up!" She hissed, slamming him
against a chain-link fence. Her breath swirled between them
like backlit fog. "He took his shots, he took a *thousand* fucking
shots, and I am *not* going to let him just *walk away!*"

"Who—what are you—"

She stopped, suddenly. She cocked her head as though seeing him for the first time.

"Where the fuck did *you* come from?" she said, absurdly.

She was a good fifteen centimeters shorter than he was. For some reason it did not occur to him to fight back.

"I don't, I—I was just going home..." Dutton managed.

"That place," the woman said. Her eyes—nightshades of some kind?—drilled his own.

"What place?"

She slammed him back against the chain link. "*That* place!"—jerking her chin at something over his left shoulder. Dutton turned his head; another splitfit, intact but empty and dark all the same.

"That place? I don't—"

"Yes, *that* place! Yves *Scanlon's* fucking place. You know him?"

"No, I—I mean, I don't really know anyone here, we kind of keep to—"

"Where did he go?" she hissed.

"Go?" he said weakly.

"The place is absolutely empty! No furniture, no clothing, not so much as fucking *lightbulb!*"

"Maybe—maybe he left—the quake—"

She knotted her fists more tightly into his clothing, leaned in until they were almost kissing. "His place doesn't have a fucking *scratch* on it. Why would he leave? *How* could he? He's *nobody*, he's a fucking *pissant,* you think he could just pick up and walk past the quarantine?"

Dutton shook his head frantically. "I don't know—really, I don't—"

She stared into him for a few moments. Her hair was wet; it hadn't rained all day. "I don't—I don't know you..." she murmured, almost to herself. Slowly her fists unclenched. Dutton sagged back against the fence.

She stepped back, giving him room to move.

It was what he'd been waiting for. One hand swept briefly beneath his jacket. The taser jabbed her in the rib cage, just below a strange metallic disk sewn into her uniform. It should have dropped her in an instant.

Within that instant:

She blinked—

Her right knee came up, hard. Naturally he wore a cup. It hurt like hell anyway—

Her right hand slipped forward, against her upraised calf. Something sprang into it—

The crazy woman stepped back, arm extended. Two centimeters from his face, an ebony wand with a tiny spike at its tip stared at Dutton like a one-toothed mamba.

Over the pain in his crotch, sudden wet warmth.

. She smiled a small, terrifying smile. "Use a microwave, little man?"

"Wh—what—?"

"Kitchen appliances? Sensorium? Keep your house warm in winter?"

He bobbed his head. "Yes. Yes, of course I—"

"Huh." The mamba wiggled over his left eye. "Then I was wrong. I know you after all."

"No," he stammered. "We've never—"

"I know you," she repeated. "And you *owe* me."

Her thumb moved against something on the wand's handgrip. Dutton heard a small click.

"Please..." he prayed.

And amazingly, something answered him.

Hongcouver was still a disaster zone, of course; the police had more pressing concerns than an unlikely apparition reported by some panicky dickwad. Still, the server took Dutton's report when he called it in. The server wasn't human, but it was smart enough to ask follow-up questions— like, had he noticed anything, anything at all, that might have caused his assailant to suddenly break off the assault?

No.

Could he think of any reason why she would be suddenly start babbling about *dad* like that? Did the reference to *monsters* make any sense, in context?

Maybe she was just crazy, Dutton replied, although as the server noted he was not qualified to make medical diagnoses.

Had he seen where she had gone, exactly?

Just downhill. Into the wreckage, toward the water.

And he sure as shit hadn't been going to follow her down *there.*

Stockpile

Vancity CU/N'AmPac Transaction Server
Personal Accounts, Broadway ATM-45, 50/10/05/0551
Transaction Begins:

Welcome to VanCity. Are you a member?

"I couldn't link, before. Using my watch."

Remote access curfew is in effect until 10:00 am. At present this terminal can only process on-site transactions. We apologize for any inconvenience. Are you a member?

"Lenie Clarke."

Welcome, Ms. Clarke. Please remove your corneal overlays.

"What?"

We cannot open your account without eyeprint confirmation. Please remove your corneal overlays.

Thank you. Scanning.

Complete. Thank you, Ms. Clarke. You may proceed.

"What's my total balance?"

$Q42,329.15

"I want to download it all."

Has Vancity's service been satisfactory?

"It's been fine."

We can see your wristwatch, and a subcutaneous money-chip in your left thigh. How would you like the funds distributed?

"Forty thousand sub-q, the rest to the watch. Automatic transfer of all funds sub-q if I'm attacked."

That condition can't be evaluated. Your watch is not equipped with a biotelemetry plug-in.

"Automatic transfer on voice-linked password, then."

What password?

"Sh—shadow..."

*Please repeat the password.
Please repeat the password.
Please—*

"I said, shadow."

Done. Would you like another transaction?

(inaudible)

Vancity thanks you for your business.
Transaction ends

Sears Medbooth 199/Granville Island/Hongcouver
Transaction record, vocal, 50/10/05/0923
(Test results filed separately.)
Session begins:

*Welcome to Sears Medical Services. Please open your account.
Thank you. Do you wish to limit your charges?*

"No."

What can we do for you today?

"My right shoulder. Sprained or broken or something. And a blood scan. Paths especially."

Please provide blood sample.
Thank you. Please provide your medical history or your WestHemID#.

"Forget it."

Access to your medical records will help us provide better service. All information will be kept strictly confidential except in the event of a public health or marketing priority, and in such cases we may be legally required to sequence-ID your sample anyway.

"I'll take my chances. No thanks."

Your shoulder has been recently dislocated, but is presently reseated. You will continue to experience pain and stiffness for approximately two months without treatment. You will experience reduced mobility for at least a year without treatment. Would you like treatment for the pain?

"Yeah."

We're sorry, but recent heavy user demand has depleted our stock of painkillers. Anabolic accelerants can reduce the healing period to three to five days. Shall I administer anabolic accelerants?

"Sure."

We're sorry, but recent heavy user demand has depleted our stock of accelerants. Your blood shows minor deficiencies in calcium and trace-sulfur. You have elevated levels of the hormones serotonin, oxytocin, and cortisol; elevated platelet and antibody counts consistent with moderate physical injury within the past three weeks. None of these findings should cause you serious concern, although the mineral deficiencies may reflect poor dietary habits. Would you like dietary mineral supplements?

"You actually have any?"

Sears medbooths are regularly maintained and resupplied to ensure that you have reliable access to the best in quality medical care. Would you like dietary supplements?

"No."

Cellular metabolites are high. Your blood lactate is low. Blood gases and amine count—

"What about diseases?"

All pathogen counts are within documented safe ranges.

"You sure?"

The standard blood panel tests for over eight hundred known pathogens and parasites. More extensive analysis is available for a small additional charge, but the analysis would take up to six hours. Would you like—

"No, I—but that can't be *it*, I mean—is that it?"

Is there some specific symptom that concerns you?

"Aren't there some kinds of infections that cause hallu-cinations?"

Can you describe these hallucinations?

"Visions only. No sound or smell or anything. I've been having them for a few weeks now, on and off. Once every few days, maybe. They go away by themselves, after a minute or two."

And can you describe what you see in these visions?

"Who cares? It's just bad biochemistry, right? Can't you do a brain scan or something?"

The NMR helmet in this booth is presently out of service, and there are no detectable psychoactives in your blood. However, different conditions can give rise to different types of hallucinations, so I may still be able to offer a diagnosis. Can you describe what you see in your visions?

"A monster."

Could you be more specific?

"This is bullshit. You think I don't know you charge by the second?"

Our rates are strictly

"Tell me what's wrong with me or I disconnect."

I don't have enough information for a proper diagnosis.

"Speculate."

Neurological damage is a strong possibility. Strokes—even very small ones that you may not be consciously aware of—can sometimes trigger visual-release hallucinations.

"Strokes? Ruptured blood vessels, that kind of thing?"

Yes. Have you recently undergone a rapid change in ambient pressure? For example, have you spent some time at high altitude or in an orbital environment, or perhaps returned from an underwater excursion?

Client disconnect 50/10/05/0932
Session ends.

Icarus

There were people who would have described Achilles Desjardins as a murderer a million times over.

He had to admit there was a certain truth to that. Every quarantine he invoked trapped the living alongside the dying, ensured that at least some of those still alive soon wouldn't be. But what was the alternative, after all? Let every catastrophe run free, to engulf the world unchecked?

Desjardins could handle the ethics, with a little help from his chemical sidekicks. He knew in his heart of hearts that that he'd never *really* killed anyone. He'd just—contained them, to save others. The actual killing had been done by whatever pestilence he'd been fighting. It may have been a subtle distinction, but it was a real one.

There were rumors, though. There'd always been rumors: the *next logical step.* The unconfirmed tales of deaths caused, not in the *wake* of some disaster, but in *advance* of it.

Preemptive containment, it was called. Path scans would pinpoint some burb—superficially healthy, but we all know how much stock you can put in *that*—as Contagion Central for The Next Big Bug. Monte Carlo sims would show with 99 percent confidence that the impending threat would get around conventional quarantines, or prove immune to the usual antibiotics. LD90s would estimate the mortality rate at 50 percent or 80 percent or whatever was deemed unacceptable that week, over an area of so many thousand hectares. So another one of those pesky wildfires would spring up in the parched N'American heartland—and Dicksville, Arkansas, would tragically drop off the map.

Just rumors, of course. Nobody confirmed it or denied it. Nobody even really talked about it, except for Alice when she went on one of her rants. On those occasions, Desjardins would reflect that even if the stories were true—and even if such measures were a bit farther down the slippery slope than he was comfortable with—well, anyway, what was the alternative? Let every catastrophe run free, to engulf the world unchecked?

Mostly, though, he didn't think about it. Certainly it didn't have anything to do with him.

Only now, certain items in his own in-box were starting to look really ugly. A picture was forming, a mosaic assembling itself from clouds of data, news threads drifting through Maelstrom, bits of third-generation hearsay. They all came together to form a picture in his mind, and it was starting to look like a seascape.

βehemoth was correlated with subtle blights of photosynthetic pigment. Those blights, in turn, generally correlated with intense fires. Seventy-two percent of the blazes had occurred at seaports, in shipyards, or on marine construction sites. The rest had taken out bits and pieces of residential areas.

People had died. Lots of people. And when, on a whim, Desjardins had cross-referenced the residential obits by profession, it turned out that almost all of the fires had killed at least one marine engineer, or commercial diver, or sailor.

This fucker hadn't escaped from anybody's lab. βehemoth had come from the ocean.

The California Current nosed down along N'AmPac's coast from the Gulf of Alaska. It mixed it up with the North Pacific and North Equatorial Currents way off to the east of Mexico; those, in turn, bled into the Kuroshio off Japan, and the Eastern Counter and Southern Equatorial Currents in the South Pacific. Which ended up nuzzling the West Wind Drift, and the *anklebone's connected to the leg bone, the leg bone's connected to the knee bone, and before you know it the whole fucking planet is encircled.*

He studied the data cloud and rubbed his eyes. *How do you contain something that moves across 70 percent of the whole planet?*

Evidently, you burned it.

He tapped his console. "Hey, Alice."

Her image flashed onto a window, upper left. "Right here."

"Give me something."

"Can't yet," she said. "Not carved in stone."

"Balsa will do. Anything."

"It's small. Maybe two hundred, three hundred nanometers. Relies heavily on sulfur compounds, structurally at least. Very stripped-down genotype; I think it may use RNA for both catalysis and replication, which is a really neat trick. Built for a simple ecosystem, which makes sense if it's a construct. They never expected it to get out of culture."

"But what does it *do*?"

"Can't say. I'm working with a frog in a blender here, Killjoy. You should actually be kind of impressed that I've gotten as far as I have. You ask me, it's pretty obvious we're not *supposed* to figure out what it does."

"Could it be some kind of really nasty pathogen?" *It has to be. It has to be. If we're burning people—*

"No." Her voice was flat and emphatic. "*We* are not. *They* are."

Desjardins blinked. *I said that?* "We're all on the same side, Alice."

"Uh-huh."

"Alice..." Sometimes she really pissed him off. *There's a war going on,* he wanted to shout. *And it's not against corpses or bureaucrats or your imaginary Evil Empires; we're fighting against a whole indifferent universe that's coming down around our ears and you're shitting on me because sometimes we have to accept casualties?*

But Alice Jovellanos had a blind spot the size of Antarctica. Sometimes you just couldn't reason with her. "Just answer the question, okay? Someone obviously thinks this thing is extremely dangerous. Could it be some kind of disease?"

"Biowar agent, you mean." Surprisingly, though, she shook her head. "Unlikely."

"How come?"

"Diseases are just little predators that eat you from the inside. If they're designed to feed on your molecules, their biochemistry should be compatible with yours. The D-aminos suggest they're not."

"Only suggest?"

Jovellanos shrugged. "Frog in a blender, remember? All I'm saying is if A is gonna eat B without throwing up, they should have similar biochemistries. βehemoth just seems a little too far into the Oort to qualify. I could be wrong."

But the vectors—shipbuilders, divers—"Could it survive in a human host, at least?"

She pursed her lips. "Anything's possible. Look at A-51."

"What's that?"

"Metal-oxidizing microbe. Sediment-dweller from deep lakes, only there's a few million of them living in your mouth right now. Nobody knows how they got there exactly, but there you go."

Desjardins steepled his fingers. "She called it a soil microbe," he murmured, almost to himself.

"She'd call it corn on the cob if she thought it'd cover her corporate ass."

"Jeez, Alice." He shook his head. "Why do you even work here, if all we do is serve some evil overlord?"

"Everyone else is worse."

"Well, I don't think βehemoth came out of a pharm. I think it came from the ocean."

"How so?"

"The fires correlate with people who spent a lot of time at sea."

"Ocean's a pretty big place, Killjoy. Seems to me if it was a natural bug, it would have come ashore millions of years ago."

"Yeah." Desjardins linked to the personnel files for each of the relevant victims—sparing a moment of silent thanks for the devil's bargain that had traded free will for security clearance—and started narrowing the field.

"Although, now that you mention it," Jovellanos went on, "those superstiff enzymes *would* work better in a high-pressure environment."

A menu, a couple of tapped commands: a convex projection of the North Pacific extruded from the board.

"And if this little bastard *isn't* a construct, then it's older than old. Even before Martian Mike—hey, maybe it actually *originated* here, wouldn't that be something?"

Desjardins draped a GIS mesh across the map and poured data onto it. Luminous points spilled across the display like radioactive contrails in a cloud chamber: the cumulative Pacific assignments of the seagoing victims, sorted on location.

"Hey, Killjoy."

The points were piling up disproportionately at several key locations; seafarms, mining outposts, the transoceanic filaments of shipping routes. Nothing unusual there.

"Hellooo?" In her window, Jovellanos's head bobbed impatiently back and forth.

Let's cut to the chase, shall we? Any spots where all *these people hung out at the same time over the past . . . say, two years . . .*

At the edge of awareness, Alice Jovellanos grumbled about attention deficit disorder and disconnected.

Desjardins barely noticed. The Pacific Ocean had gone utterly dark, but for a single cluster of points. Southern tip of the Juan de Fuca Ridge. Channer Vent, said the legend.

A geothermal generating station. Place called *Beebe*.

There'd been deaths there, too. But not by fire; according to the record, everyone at Beebe had been killed by the quake.

In fact—Desjardins pulled up a seismic overlay—Beebe Station had pretty much been at the exact *epicenter* of the quake that had triggered the Big One . . .

βehemoth comes from the bottom of the ocean. It was down in the vents there, or trapped in the moho and then the quake let it out, and now they're running around like a bunch of adrenocorticoids trying to burn out anything that came in contact with—

No, wait a second—

More commands. The data cloud dispersed, re-formed into a column sorted against time; a luminous date appeared beside each point.

Almost all of the firestorm activity had taken place *before* the quake.

Desjardins called up a subset containing only fires at industrial sites, cross-linked with GA invoices. *Quelle surprise:*
every site belonged to a company that had had a piece of
Beebe's construction contact.

This thing got out before the quake.

Which meant the quake might not have been a natural
disaster at all. It might have been mere side effect. Collateral
damage during containment.

Apparently, unsuccessful containment.

He called up every seismic database within Haven's walls.
He stuffed a thousand messages into bottles and threw them
out into Maelstrom, hoping some would wash ashore at a
technical library or a satcam archive or an industrial surveillance site. He opened dedicated links to the seismic centers at UBC and Melbourne and CalTech. He watched reams
of garbage accumulate—*archives purged to reclaim memory, data
dumped due to low demand, this address corrupted, do not attempt
access.* He passed the shouts and echoes and gibberish through
a dozen filters, dropped signal and looked only at residuals,
ran into gaps and interpolated bridges.

He looked at seismic data immediately preceding the
quake, and found nothing untoward: no subsidence, no
preshocks, no changes in microgravity or ocean depth. None
of the little telltales that usually portend a seismic event.

Odd.

He searched archives for satcam visuals. Nothing over the
North Pacific seemed to have snapped any pictures at all that
day.

Odder. In fact, virtually inconceivable.

He widened the scope, stretched it from the Eastern
Tropical Convergence up to the Bering. One hit: an Earthsat
in polar orbit had just been coming over the 45° horizon
when the first shock waves had registered. It had been taking
pictures of the Bering on visible wavelengths; it hadn't even
been looking at the Pacific. Just a lucky coincidence, then, the
image it had caught from the corner of its eye: a smudged
column of cloud on the horizon, rising from the ocean's surface against an otherwise cloudless background.

According to GPS, that column had risen from the ocean directly above Channer Vent.

Desjardins squeezed each pixel until it bled. The gray beanstalk wouldn't tell him anything further: it was just a pillar of cloud, fuzzy and undistinguished and three thousand kilometers from the camera.

There *was* this amorphous dot, though, off to one side. At first Desjardins attributed the lack of detail to atmospheric haze, but no: motion blur, the computer said. All along one axis, and easy enough to correct for.

The dot clarified. Still no details beyond an outline, but it looked like some kind of vehicle. A vague sense of familiarity itched in the back of his mind. He ran the silhouette through the standard commercial catalog and came up blank.

Damn, he thought, *I know what that is. I know.*

What is it?

He stared at the image for ten minutes. The he brought the catalog on-line again.

"Reset pattern resolution," he told it. "Disable vehicle recognition. Scan for vehicle *components,* standard catalog."

It took longer this time. The whole was a *lot* smaller than the sum of the parts. *Processing* winked coyly from the main display for a good two minutes before something more substantive took its place:

> Brander, Mi/ke/cheal,
> Caraco, Jud/y/ith
> Clarke, Len/ie
> Lubin, Ken/neth
> Nakata, Alice

The names floated above the grainy enhance, brazenly nonsensical.

Desjardins recognized them, of course; a crew roster had popped onto his board the moment he'd homed in on *Beebe Station.* But he'd closed that window—and the names shouldn't be wriggling across the main display anyway.

Software glitch, probably. Stray photons, tunneling

through some flawed bit of quantum insulation. It happened—all the time in Maelstrom, but occasionally even in pristine Haven. He muttered an oath and tapped on his board to clear it. Obligingly, the rogue text vanished.

But for the merest instant, something else flickered across the screen in its place. No baseline civilian would have even seen it. Desjardins caught a bit more: text strings, in English. A few words—*angel, sockeye, vampire*—jumped out at him, but most of it disappeared too fast to decompile even with his tweaked neurocircuitry.

Beebe was in there, though.

And when the standard catalog lit the screen with its findings a second later, *Beebe* moved to the very front of Desjardins's mind.

Commercial lifters could be distinguished by their great bladders of hard vacuum, buoyant toruses that held them up against the sky. There was no such silhouette on Desjardins's contact, which was why the catalog hadn't recognized it at first. No lifting bladder—not unless you counted a few ragged strips streaming from the trailing end of the silhouette. All that remained on that image was a shuttle 'scaphe, locked tight against the belly of a lifter's command module. Falling.

Jailbreak

Each second, twelve thousand cubic meters of water smashed headlong through a bottleneck thirty-five meters wide. They hadn't called it *Hell's Gate* for nothing.

Generations had come to this place and gaped. Cable cars had swung precariously across the canyon, fed raging white-water vistas to thrill-seeking tourists. Utilities had wept over all those wasted megawatts, billions of Joules pouring uselessly toward the ocean, unharnessable. So near and yet so far.

Then the world had begun wobbling. It had listed to one side, then another; the machinery that kept it upright seemed to get hungrier with each passing day. The Fraser was dammed a dozen times over to feed that appetite. Hell's Gate had held out the longest: untouchable at first, then merely prohibitive. Then almost economical.

Finally, imperative.

The Big One had slipped through the mountains like a guerilla, shattering here, merely tapping there in gentle reminder. It had crept past Hope and Yale without so much as a broken window. Hell's Gate was a good two hundred klicks upstream; there would have been *reason* to hope, if no time to.

A torrent of Precambrian rock had destroyed the dam and replaced it at the same time; the Fraser had exploded through the breach only to slam into an impromptu wall of collapsed granite half a kilometer downstream. The impoundment had not emptied but *lengthened*, north–south; the broken dam now cut across its midpoint, torn free at the western wall, still fastened at the east.

The TransCanada Highway was miraculously etched halfway up the east canyon wall, a four-lane discontinuity in a sheer ascent. At the point where dam met mountain, where highway met both, a barrier had been dropped from the sky to block the road. Botflies floated above it, and above the arched gray scar of the spillway.

Overnight, the Strip had moved east. This was its new border. Robert Boyczuk was supposed to keep it from moving any farther.

He contemplated Bridson across the chopper's interior. Bridson, her upper face cowled in her headset, didn't notice; she'd been lost in some virtual pastime for over an hour. Boyczuk couldn't blame her. They'd been here for almost two weeks and nobody'd tried to break quarantine except a couple of black bears. A number of vehicles had made it out this far in the few days following the quake, but the barrier—plastered with quarantine directives and N'AmPac bylaws—had stopped most of them. A warning shot from the botflies had discouraged the others. There'd been no need to show off the pacification 'copter lurking behind the wall. Bridson had slept through most of it.

Boyczuk took his duties a bit more seriously. There was a definite need for segregation, nobody questioned that. Everything from Nipah to *Hydrilla* would sneak past the borders given half a chance, even at the best of times; now, with half the coast gone and the other half fighting off the usual gamut of rot bugs, the last thing anyone needed was all that chaos spreading farther inland.

Inland had its own problems. There were more than enough borders to go around no matter which way you looked. Sometimes it seemed as if an invisible spiderweb was spreading across the world, some creeping fractured network carving the whole planet into splinters. Boyczuk's job was to sit on one of those edges and keep anything from crossing over until the state of emergency had passed. Assuming it did, of course; some places down in South America—even in N'Am, for that matter—had been under "temporary quarantine" for eight or nine years.

Mostly people just put up with it. Boyczuk's job was an easy one.

"Hey," Bridson said. "Check this out."

She rerouted her headset feed to an inboard screen. Not a VR game after all. She'd been riding the botflies.

On the screen, a woman crouched on cracked asphalt. Boyczuk checked the location: a couple of hundred meters down the highway, hidden from the blockade behind the curve of the western precipice. One of the 'flies out over the dam had caught her around the corner.

Backpack. Loose-fitting clothes, hiker's clothes. Upper part of the face covered by an eyephone visor. Black gloves, short black hair—no, a black *hood* of some kind, maybe part of the visor. As a fashion statement, it didn't work. In Boyczuk's humble opinion, of course.

"What's she doing?" Boyczuk asked. "How'd she even get here?" No sign of a vehicle, although one could have been parked farther down the road.

"No," Bridson said. "She's not *serious*."

The woman had braced herself in a sprinter's crouch.

"That's really bad form," Bridson remarked. "She could sprain an ankle."

Like a stone from a slingshot, the intruder launched herself forward.

"Oh, *right*," Bridson said.

The intruder was running straight down the middle of the highway, eyes on the asphalt, dodging or leaping over cracks big enough to grab human feet. If nothing stopped her, she'd run smack into the barrier in about a minute.

Of course, something *was* going to stop her.

Beeping from the botfly feeds; the intruder had just entered their defensive radius. Boyczuk panned one of the barrier cams skyward. The 'fly closest to the target was breaking ranks, moving to intercept. Programmed flocking behavior dragged the adjacent 'flies forward as well, as though all were strung on an invisible thread. A connect-the-dots pseudopod, reaching for prey.

The runner veered toward the edge of the road, glanced down. Ten meters beneath her, brown boiling water gnawed ravenously at the canyon wall.

"You are approaching a restricted area," the lead botfly scolded. "Please turn back." Red light began pulsing from its belly.

The intruder ran faster. Another glance down at the river.

"What the fuck?" Boyczuk said.

A little patch of pavement exploded in front of the runner: warning shot. She staggered, barely keeping her balance.

"We are authorized to use force," the lead botfly warned. "Please turn back." The two 'flies behind it began flashing.

The runner dodged and zigzagged, keeping to the west side of the road. She kept looking *down . . .*

Boyczuk leaned forward. *Wait a second . . .*

Behind the runner, water raged against a brutal jumble of sharp-edged boulders large as houses. Anyone falling in there would be teeth and pulp in about two seconds. Closer to the dam, though—in the lee of its near, unbroken end—the water might almost be calm enough to—

"*Shit.*" Boyczuk slapped the ignition. "She's gonna jump. She's gonna *jump* . . ."

Turbines behind, whining up to speed. "What are you talking about?" Bridson said.

"She's gonna—ah, *shit* . . ."

She stumbled, swerved. Her feet came down on loose gravel. Boyczuk pulled back on the stick. The chopper *whup-whup-whupped* slowly off the ground, ten measly seconds start-up to liftoff, the envy of fast-response vehicles everywhere and *still* just barely fast enough to clear the barrier as the woman with the backpack skidded, flailed, *launched* herself into space, not where she was aiming, not the way she wanted, but no other options left except brief, spectacular flight . . .

The botflies fired after her as she fell. The river swallowed her like a liquid avalanche.

"*Jesus,*" Bridson breathed.

"Infra," Boyczuk snapped. "Anything comes up even half a degree above ambient I want to see it."

The Fraser raged endlessly beneath them.

"Come on, boss. She's not coming up. She's a klick downstream by now, or parts of her anyway."

Boyczuk glared. "Just do it, okay?"

Bridson tapped controls. False-color mosaics bloomed from the chopper's ventral cam.

"Want me to bring the botflies along?" Bridson asked.

Boyczuk shook his head. "Can't leave the border unguarded." He wheeled the vehicle, began a westward drift down the canyon.

"Hey, boss?"

"Yeah?"

"What just happened?"

Boyczuk shook his head. "I don't know. I think she was trying to make that backwater, just in front of the dam."

"What for? So she'd have a few seconds to drown or freeze before the current got her?"

"I don't know," he said again.
"Lots of easier ways to commit suicide."
Boyczuk shrugged. "Maybe she was just crazy."
It was 1334 Mountain Standard Time.

The upstream face of the Hell's Gate Dam had never been
intended for public display; until recently, most of it had
been buried beneath the trapped waters of the Fraser River.
Now it was exposed, a fractured and scabrous bone gray wall,
rising from a plain of mud. Just above this substrate, gravity
feeds dotted the barrier like a line of gaping mouths. Grills
of bolted rebar kept them from ingesting anything big
enough to choke a hydroelectric turbine.

As it happened, human beings fell a little shy of that
threshold.

The turbines were cold and dead anyway, of course. They
certainly couldn't have given rise to the sudden heatprint
emanating from the easternmost intake. One of the Hell's
Gate botflies registered the signature at 1353 Mountain
Standard: an object radiating 10°C above ambient, emerging
from the interior of the dam and sliding down into the mud.
The botfly moved slightly off station to get a better view.

The signature's surface temperature was too low for human norms. The botfly was no genius, but it knew wheat
from chaff; even when wearing insulated clothing, humans
had faces that were hot giveaways. The insulation on the
present target was far more uniform, the isotherms less het-
erogeneous. The phrase "furred mammal" would have been
utter gibberish to the botfly, of course. Still, it understood
the concept in its own limited way. This was not something
worth wasting time on.

The botfly returned to its post and redirected its attention westward, from whence the real threats would come.
Right now there was only something big and black and insectile coming back to roost, friendly reassurance cooing
from its transponder. The 'fly moved aside to let it pass,
floated back into position while the chopper settled down

behind the barrier. Humans and machinery stood shoulder to shoulder, on guard for all mankind.

Facing the wrong way. Lenie Clarke had left the Strip.

The Next Best Thing

Registry Assistance.

"Clarke, Indira. Clarke with an 'e.' Apartment 133, CitiCorp 421, Coulson Avenue, Sault Sainte Marie."

Clarke, Indira
Apartment 133, CitiCorp 421, Coulson Ave.
Sault Sainte Marie, On
Correct?

"Yes."

Failed to match. Do you know Indira Clarke's WestHem ID#?

"Uh, no. The address might not be current, it was fifteen, sixteen years ago."

Current archives are three years deep. Do you know Indira Clarke's middle name?

"No. She fished Maelstrom, though. Freelance, I think."

Failed to match.

"How many Indira Clarkes in Sault Sainte Marie?"

5

"How many with an only child, female, born—born in February, uh—"

Failed to match.

"Wait, February—sometime in February, 2018..."

Failed to match.

"..."

Do you have another request?

"How many in all of N'Am, professional affiliation with the Maelstrom fishery, with an only female child born February 2018, named Lenie?"

Failed to match.

"How many in the whole *world*, then?"

Failed to match.

"That's not possible."

There are several possible reasons why your search has failed. The person you're seeking may be unlisted or deceased. You may have provided incorrect information. Registry archive data may have been corrupted, despite our ongoing efforts to maintain a complete and accurate database.

"That's *not fucking pos*—"

Disconnect.

Beachhead

Either/or accused him from the main display. Desjardins stared back for as long as he dared, feeling his stomach drop away inside him. Then he broke and ran.

The elevator disgorged him through the lobby into the real world. Canyons of glass and metal leaned overhead on all sides, keeping street level in twilight; this deep in the bowels of metro-Sud, the sun only touched down for an hour a day.

He descended into Pickering's Pile, looking for familiar faces and finding none. Gwen had left an invitation for him in the Pile's bulletin board, and he almost tripped it—

Hey fellow mammal, I know this isn't exactly what you had in mind but I just need to talk, you know? I found a spot they haven't torched yet, they don't even know it exists but they will, it's big, it's way bigger than it has any right to be, and the moment I tell them a few hundred thousand people get turned into ash—

—but Guilt Trip rose in his throat like bile at the mere thought of such a breach. It tingled in his fingertips, ready to seize up motor nerves the moment he reached for the keypad. He'd tried racing it before, idle experimentation with no serious intent to subvert, but even then the Trip had been too fast for him. Volition's subconscious; the command is halfway down the arm before the little man behind your eyes even decides to move. *Executive summaries, after the fact,* Desjardins thought. *That's all we get. That's free will for you.*

He rose out of the Pile and headed for the nearest rapitrans station. And once there, kept walking. His rewired gray matter, stuck in frenetic overdrive, served up every irrelevant background detail in a relentless mesh of correlations: time of day vs. cloud cover vs. prevailing vehicular flow vs. out-of-stock warnings in streetside vending machines...

How in God's name could this happen? The locals have had millions of years to fine-tune themselves to the neighborhood. How can they possibly get run over by something that evolved on the bottom of the goddamned ocean?

He knew the standard answer. Everyone did. The previous five centuries had been a accelerating litany of invasions, whole ecosystems squashed and replaced by exotics with more than enough attitude to make up for their lack of seniority. There were over seventy thousand usurper species at large in N'Am alone, and N'Am was better off than most.

You'd be more likely to see space aliens than any of *Australia's* has-been marsupials, outside of a gene bank.

But this was different. Cane toads and starlings and zebra mussels might have filled the world with their weedy progeny, but even they had limits. You'd never find *Hydrilla* on top of Everest. Fire ants weren't ever going to set up shop on the Juan de Fuca Ridge. Chemistry, pressure, temperature—too many barriers, too many physical extremes that would tear the very cells of a complex invader into fragments.

A petroleum silhouette blocked his way: a human shadow with featureless white eyes. Desjardins started, stared into that vacant façade for a moment that slowed to treacle. Unbidden, his wetware reduced the vision to a point in a data cloud he hadn't even known he was collecting: half-registered sightings during his daily commute; black shapes caught in the backgrounds of N'Am Wire crowd shots; fashion banners advertising the latest styles in *wet midnight*.

Rifter chic, she said. Solidarity through fashion. It's on the rise.

All in a split second. The apparition ducked around him and continued on its way.

Sudbury's metropolitan canyons had subsided about him while he'd been walking. Endless sheets of kudzu$_4$ draped closer to street level from the rooftops, framing windows and vents with viridian foliage. The new and improved part of him started to ballpark a carbon-consumption estimate under current cloud cover; he managed, with effort, to shut it up. He'd always wondered if the vines would be as easy to kill off as everyone expected, once they'd finished sucking up the previous century's excesses. Kudzu had been a tough mother to begin with, even before all the tinkering that had turned it into God's own carbon sink. And there was all sorts of outbreeding and lateral gene transfer going on these days, uncontrolled, unstoppable. Give the weed another ten years and it'd be immune to anything short of a flamethrower.

Now, for the first time, that didn't seem to matter. In ten years kudzu$_n$ might be the least of *anyone's* problems.

It sure as hell wouldn't matter much to those poor bastards on the Strip.

———

They'd built this model.

It wasn't a *real* model, of course. They didn't know enough about how βehemoth worked for that. There was no clockwork inside, nothing that led logically from *cause* to *effect*. It was just a nest of correlations, really. An n-dimensional cloud with a least-squares trajectory weaving through its heart. It guzzled data at one end: at the other it shat out a prediction. Soil moisture's 13 percent, weather's been clear for five days straight, porphyrins are down and micromethane's up over half a hectare of dirt in a Tillamook shipyard? That's βehemoth country, my friend—and tomorrow, if it doesn't rain, there's an 80 percent chance that it'll shrink to half its present size.

Why? Anyone's guess. But that's pretty much what's happened before under similar conditions.

Rowan's field data had started them down the right path, but it was the fires that had given them an edge: each of those magnesium telltales shouted *Hey! Over here!* all the way up to geosynch. Then it was just a matter of calling up the Landsat archives for those locations, scrolling back five, six months from ignition. Sometimes you wouldn't find anything—none of the residential blazes had yielded anything useful. Sometimes the data had been lost, purged or corrupted by the usual forces of entropy. Sometimes, though—along coastlines, or in undeveloped industrial lots where heavy machinery loitered between assignments—the spec lines would change over time, photoabsorption creeping down the 680nm band, soil O_2 fading just a touch, a whiff of acid showing up on distance pH. If you waited long enough you could even see the change in visible light. Weeds and grasses, so tough that the usual oils and effluents had long since given up trying to kill them, would slowly wilt and turn brown.

With those signatures in hand, Desjardins had begun to wean himself from blatant incendiary cues and search farther afield. It was a pretty flimsy construct, but it would've done until Jovellanos came up with a better angle. In the meantime it had been a lot better than nothing.

Until now. Now it was a lot worse. Now it was saying that βehemoth owned a ten-kilometer stretch of the Oregon coast.

Sudbury was dressed up for the night by the time he got back to his apartment: a jumble of neon and sodium and laser spilled through his windows, appreciably dimmer now that the latest restrictions had kicked in. Mandelbrot tripped him up as he crossed the threshold, then stalked into the kitchen and yowled at the kibble dispenser. The dispenser, programmed for preset feeding times, refused to dignify the cat with an answer.

Desjardins dropped onto the sofa and stared unseeing at the cityscape.

You should have known, he told himself.

He had known. Maybe he just hadn't quite believed it. And it hadn't been his doing, those other times. He'd just been following the trail, seeing where *others* had taken the necessary steps, feeding all those data through his models and filters for the greater good. Always for the greater good.

This time, though, there'd been no fire. The forces of containment hadn't found out about the Strip yet. So far they'd just been covering their own tracks, sterilizing every—

-body—

—everything that had come into contact with the source. But they didn't know how to identify βehemoth directly, not from a distance. That was his job, and Jovellanos's.

And now it looked like the two of them had succeeded. Desjardins reflected on the difference between following a trail of ashes, and blazing one's own.

Shouldn't matter. It's not like you're firing the flamethrower. Just aiming it.

Guilt Trip paced in his gut like a caged animal, looking for something to tear into.

Well? Do your job, for Christ's sake! Tell me what to do!

Guilt Trip didn't work like that, of course. It was all stick and no carrot, a neurochemical censor that pounced on the slightest twinge of guilt, or conscience, or—for the mechanists in the audience—sheer amoral *fear-of-getting-caught-with-your-hand-in-the-cookie-jar*. You could call it whatever you wanted; labels didn't change the side chains and peptide bonds and carboxyl whatsits that made it work. Guilt was a neurotransmitter. Morality was a chemical. And the things that made nerves fire, muscles move, tongues wag—those were all chemicals, too. It had only been a matter of time before someone figured out how to tie them all together.

Guilt Trip kept you from making the wrong decision, and Absolution let you live with yourself after making the right one. But you had to at least *think* you knew what *right* was, before either of them could kick in. They only reacted to gut feeling.

He'd never lamented the Trip's lack of direction before. He'd never needed it. Sure, it would freeze him in an instant if he tried to hack his own credit rating, but in terms of actual caseload it rarely did more than nudge him toward the blindingly obvious. Lose-lose situations were his stock-in-trade. Amputate the part or lose the whole? Nasty, but obvious. Kill ten to save a hundred? Wring your hands, bite the bullet, get stoned afterward. But never any question about what to *do*.

How many people did I seal off to keep a lid on that brucellosis outbreak in Argentina? How many did I flood out in TongKing when I cut the power to their sumps?

Necessary steps had never bothered him before. Not like this. *Alice and all her snide comments about seeing the world in black-and-white. Bullshit. I saw the grays, I saw* millions *of grays. I just knew how to pick the lightest shade.*

Not anymore.

He could pinpoint the moment that things had changed, almost to the second: when he'd seen a 'scaphe built for the deep sea and a cockpit built for the near sky, locked together in a desperate embrace, falling.

It had not been a commercial lifter on a routine flight; he'd checked the records. Officially, nothing had fallen into the Pacific at the heart of the Big One, because—officially—

nothing had been there to fall. It had been sent secretly to Ground Zero, and then it had been shot down.

It made no sense that the same authority would have committed both acts.

That implied factions in opposition. It implied profound disagreement over what constituted the greater good (or the *Interests of the Overlords*, which Jovellanos insisted was all the Trip *really* ensured). Someone in the bureaucratic stratosphere—someone who knew far more about βehemoth than did Achilles Desjardins—had tried to evacuate the rifters before the quake. Apparently they'd felt that preemptive murder was not justified in the name of containment.

And someone else had stopped them.

Which side was Rowan affiliated with? Who was *right*?

He hadn't told Jovellanos about the 'scaphe. He'd even done a passable job of forgetting about it himself, keeping things nice and simple, focusing on the mouse at hand until the whale on the horizon became a vague blur, almost invisible. He'd known in the back of his mind he wouldn't be able to keep it up for long; eventually they'd come up with a reliable index, some combination of distance spec and moisture and pH that pointed the finger at the invader. But he hadn't expected it so soon. They'd been working with old data, shipyard samples contaminated by industrial effluents, potential incursions three or four hectares large at most. Noise-to-signal problems alone should have held them back for weeks.

But you didn't need much rez to catch a beachhead ten kilometers long. Desjardins had kept his eyes down, and the whale on the horizon had run right into him.

Mandelbrot stood in the doorway, stretching. Claws extruded from their sheaths like tiny scimitars.

"*You* wouldn't have any trouble at all," Desjardins said. "You'd just go for maximum damage, right?"

Mandelbrot purred.

Desjardins buried his face in his hands. *So what do I do now? Figure things out for* myself?

He realized, with some surprise, that the prospect wouldn't have always seemed so absurd.

Drugstore

"Amitav."

He startled awake: a blanketed skeleton on the sand. Gray and dim in the visible predawn gloom, hot and luminous in infrared. Sunken eyes, exuding hatred on all wavelengths from the moment they opened.

Sou-Hon Perreault stared down at him from three meters up. Well-fed refugees, freshly awakened on all sides, edged away and left Amitav in the center of an open circle.

Several others—teenagers, mostly, a little less robust than most—stayed nearby, looking up at the 'fly with undisguised suspicion. Perreault blinked within her headset; she'd never seen so many hostile faces on the Strip before.

"How pleasant," Amitav said in a low voice. "To wake with a big round hammer hanging over my head."

"Sorry." She moved the 'fly off to one side, wobbling its trim tabs to effect a bobbing mechanical salute (then wondered if he could even see it with his merely human eyes). "It's Sou-Hon," she said.

"Who else," the stickman said dryly, rising.

"I—"

"She is not here. I have not seen her in some time."

"I know. I wanted to talk to you."

"Ah. About what?" The stickman began walking down the shore. His—

Friends? Disciples? Bodyguards?

—began to follow. Amitav waved them off. Perreault set the botfly to heel at his side; the entourage dwindled slowly to stern. On either side, anonymous bundles—curled on thermafoam, wrapped in heat-conserving fabric—stirred and grunted irritably in the gray half-light.

"A cycler was vandalized last night," Perreault said. "A few kilometers north of here. We'll have to fly out a replacement."

"Ah."

"It's the first time something like this has happened in *years.*"

"And we both know why that is, do we not?"

"People rely on those machines. You took food from their mouths."

"I? *I* did this?"

"There were lots of witnesses, Amitav."

"Then they will tell you I had nothing to do with it."

"They told me it was a couple of teenagers. And *they* told me who put them up to it."

The stickman stopped and turned to face the machine at his side. "And all these witnesses you speak of. All these poor people that I have robbed of food. None of them did anything to *stop* the vandals? All those people, and they could not stop two boys from stealing the food from their mouths?"

Sheathed in her interface, Perreault sighed. Over a thousand klicks away the botfly snorted reverb. "What do you have against the cyclers, anyway?"

"I am not a fool." Amitav continued down the shore. "It is not all proteins and carbohydrates you are feeding us. I would rather starve than eat poison."

"Antidepressants aren't *poison*! The dosages are very mild."

"And so much more convenient than dealing with the anger of real people, yes?"

"Anger? Why should you be angry?"

"We should be grateful, do you think? To *you*?" The skeleton spat. "It was *our* machinery that tore everything apart? *We* caused the droughts and the floods and put our own homes underwater? And afterward, when we came here across a whole ocean—if we did not starve first or cook in the sun or die with our bodies stuffed with worms and things that *your* drugs have made unkillable—when we ended here we are supposed to be *grateful* that you let us sleep on this little patch of mud, we are supposed to *thank* you because so far it is cheaper to drug us than mow us down?"

They were at the waterline. Surf pounded invisibly in the dark distance. Amitav lifted one bony arm and pointed. "Sometimes when people go in there the sharks come for them." His voice was suddenly calm. "And onshore, the rest continue to sex and shit and feed at your wonderful ma-chines."

"That's—that's just human nature, Amitav. People don't want to get involved."

"So these drugs are *good* for us?"

"They're not the slightest bit harmful."

"Then you put them in your food, too."

"Well no, but I'm not—"

—part of an imprisoned destitute mob forty million strong . . .

"You liar," the stickman said quietly. "You hypocrite."

"You're starving, Amitav. You'll die."

"I know what I do."

"Do you?"

He looked up at the 'fly again, and this time he almost seemed amused. "What do you think I was, before?"

"What?"

"Before I was—here. Or did you think that *environmental refugee* was my first choice of vocation?"

"Well, I—"

"I was a pharmaceutical engineer," Amitav said. He tapped his temple. "They even changed me up here, so I was very good at it. I am not completely foolish about dietary matters. There appears to be a—a minimum effective dosage, yes? If I eat very little, your poisons have no effect." He paused. "So now you will try and force-feed me, for my own good?"

Perreault ignored the jibe. "And you think you're getting enough to live on, under your *minimum dosage*?"

"Perhaps not quite. But I am starving very, very slowly."

"Is that how you motivated those kids to trash the cycler? Are they fasting too?" There could be serious trouble on the Strip if that caught on.

"Me, still? *I* have somehow tricked all these people into starving themselves?"

"Who else?"

"Such faith you have in your machines. You have never thought that perhaps they are not working as well as you think?" He shook his head and spat. "Of course not. You were not told to."

"The cyclers work fine until your followers smash them."

"*My* followers? They never fasted for *me*. They suck at your tits as they always have. It is only after they begin starving that they see your cyclers for what they—"

Crack!

An impact on polymer, the sound of a whip snapping just behind her ear. She spun the 'fly, caught a glimpse of the rock as it bounced along the substrate. Ten meters down the shore, a girl ran away with another rock clenched in her hand.

Perreault turned back to face Amitav. "You—"

"Do not try to blame me. I am the cause of nothing. I am only the result."

"This can't go on, Amitav."

"You cannot stop it."

"I won't have to. If you keep this up it won't be me you're dealing with, it'll be—"

"Why do *you* care?" Amitav cut in.

"I'm just trying to—"

"You are trying to ease feelings of guilt. Use someone else."

"You can't win."

"That depends upon what I am trying to do."

"You're all alone."

Amitav laughed, waved his arms back across the shore. "How can I be? You have so thoughtfully provided all these sheep, and all this death, and even an ic—"

He stopped himself. Perreault filled in the gap: *an icon to inspire them.*

"She's not here anymore," she said after a moment.

Amitav glanced back upshore; the eastern sky was beginning to lighten. A knot of curious humans stood halfway up the shore, watching from the center of a sleeping flock. Here at the water's edge, there was no one else within earshot.

The girl who'd thrown the rock was nowhere to be seen.

"Perhaps that is better," the stickman remarked. "Lenie Clarke was very—not even your *antidepressants* seemed to work on her."

"Lenie? That's her first name?"

"I believe so. At least, that was the name she used during one of her—visions." He glanced sideways at Perreault's floating surrogate. "Where did she go?"

"I don't know. I just haven't been able to confirm any recent sightings. Just rumors." *But of course, you'd know all about those . . .* "Maybe she's dead."

The stickman shook his head.

"It's a big ocean, Amitav. The sharks. And if she was having—fits of some kind—"

"She is not dead. I think perhaps there was a time when she wanted to be, once. Now . . ."

He stared inland. On the eastern horizon, past the people and the trampled scrub and the towers, the sky was turning red.

"Now, you are not so lucky," Amitav said.

Source Code

He'd left the map smoldering on his board the night before. Alice Jovellanos was waiting beside it, ready to pounce.

"Why didn't you *say* something?" On the display, a luminous bloodstain ran down the coast from Westport to Copalis Beach.

"Alice—"

"You've got a hot zone the size of a *city* here! How long have you known?"

"Just last night. I tightened some of the correlations and ran it against yesterday's snaps and—"

She cut him off: "You let this sit all *night*? Jesus *Christ*, Killjoy, what's wrong with you? We've got to call in the troops, and I mean *now*."

He stared at her. "Since when did *you* join the fire brigade? You know what'll happen the moment we pass this up the line. We don't even know what βehemoth *does* y—"

Her expression stopped him cold.

He slumped into his chair. The display bled crimson light all over him. "Is it that bad?"

"It's worse," she said.

A lumpy rainbow, a string of clustered beads folded around itself: purines or pyrimidines or nucleics or whatever the fuck they were.

βehemoth's source code. Part of it, anyway.

"It's not even a helix," he said at last.

"Actually, it's got a weak left-handed twist. That's not the point."

"What is?"

"Pyranosal RNA. Much stronger Watson-Crick pairs than your garden-variety RNA, and a lot more selective in terms of pairing modes. Guanine-rich sequences won't self-pair, for one thing. Six-sided ring."

"English, Alice. So what?"

"It'll replicate faster than the stuff in your genes, and it won't make as many errors when it does."

"But what does it *do*?"

"It just *lives*, Killjoy. It lives, and it eats, and I think it does that better than anything else on the planet, so we either stamp it out or kiss the whole biosphere good-bye."

He couldn't believe it. *"One bug*? How is that even possible?"

"Nothing eats it, for one thing. The cell wall's barely even organic, mostly it's just a bunch of sulfur compounds. You know how I told you some bacteria use inverted aminos to make themselves indigestible? This is ten times worse—most anything that might eat this fucker wouldn't even recognize it as food through all the minerals."

Desjardins bit his lower lip.

"It gets better," Jovellanos went on. "This thing's a veritable black hole of sulfur assimilation. I don't know where it learned this trick but it can snatch the stuff right out of our *cells*. Some kind of lysteriolysin analog, keeps it from getting lysed. That gums up glucose transport, protein synthesis, lipid and carb metabolism—shit, it gums up *everything.*"

"There's no shortage of *sulfur,* Alice."

"Oh, there's lots to go around *now.* We fart the stuff out, nobody's even bothered to come up with a recommended daily dosage. But this, this *βehemoth,* it needs sulfur even more than we do. And it breeds faster and it chews faster and believe me, Killjoy, in a few years there *is not* going to be enough to go around and this little fucker's gonna have the market *cornered.*"

"That's just—" A straw floated to the front of his mind. He grasped it. "How can you be so sure? You didn't even think you had all the pieces to work with."

"I was wrong."

"But—you said no phospholipids, no—"

"*It doesn't have those things. It never did.*"

"What?"

"It's *simple,* it's so simple it's bloody well indestructible. No bilayer membranes, no—" She spread her hands, as if in surrender. "Yeah, I *did* think maybe they scrambled the sample to keep me from stealing trade secrets. Maybe even filtered some stuff right out, stupid as that might seem. Corpses have done dumber things. But I was wrong." She ran one hand nervously over her scalp. "It was all there. All the pieces. And you know why I think they scrambled them up the way they did? I think they were afraid of what this thing could do if they left it in one piece."

"Shit." Desjardins eyed the beads rotating on the display. "So we either stop it or we get used to eating from Calvin cyclers for the rest of our lives."

Jovellanos's eyes were bright as quartz. "You don't get it."

"Well, what else could we do? If it cuts the whole biosphere off at the ankles, if—"

"You think this is about protecting the *biosphere*?" she cried. "You think they'd give a shit about environmental apocalypse if we could just *synthesize* our way out of the hole? You think they're launching all these cleansing strikes to protect the frigging *rainforest*?"

He stared at her.

Jovellanos shook her head. "Killjoy, it can get right inside our *cells*. Calvin cyclers don't matter. Sulfur supplements don't matter. Nothing we take in does us any good until our cells metabolize it—and whatever we take in, as soon as it gets past the cell membrane...there's βehemoth, pushing to the front of the line. We've already been way luckier than we deserve. Sure, it's not as efficient up here as it is in a hyperbaric environment, but that only means the locals can beat it back ninety-nine times out of a hundred. And..."

And the dice had just kept rolling, and the hundredth throw had landed square on the Oregon coast. Desjardins knew the story: microbes, in sufficient numbers, make their own rules. Now there was a place in the sun where βehemoth didn't have to fit into someone else's world. It had begun creating its own: trillions of microscopic terraformers at work in the soil, changing pH and electrolyte balances, stripping away all the advantages once held by natives so precisely adapted to the way things *used* to be...

It was every crisis he'd ever faced, combined and distilled and reduced to pure essence. It was chaos breaking, maybe unbreakable: little bubbles of enemy territory growing across the face of the coast, then the continent, then the planet. Eventually there'd come a fulcrum, a momentary balance of some interest to the theoreticians. The area inside and outside the bubbles would be the same. An instant later, βehemoth would *be* the outside, a new norm that enclosed shrinking pockets of some other, irrelevant reality.

Alice Jovellanos—rager within The System, face of the faceless, staunch advocate of the Rights of the Individual—was looking at him with fire and fear in her eyes.

"Whatever it takes," she said. "Whatever the cost. Or we are definitely out of a job."

Groundswell

He knows something, Sou-Hon Perrault thought. *And it's killing them.*

She wasn't the only one riding 'flies along the Strip, but she was the only one who seemed to have noticed the stickman. She'd mentioned him casually to a couple of colleagues, and been met with benign indifference. The Strip was brain-dead gig, a herd to be watched with one eye. Why would anyone actually *interact* with those cattle? They were too boring for entertainment, too placid for revolt, too powerless to do anything even if this Amitav *was* being a shit-disturber. They were functionally invisible.

But three people threw rocks at her botfly the next day, and the upturned faces that met her were not so placid as they had been.

Such faith you have in your machines, Amitav had said. *You have never thought that perhaps they are not working as well as you think?*

Maybe it was nothing. Maybe Amitav's cryptic grumbles had only primed her imagination. After all, a few stone throwers were hardly remarkable in a population of millions, and almost everywhere on the Strip the refugees milled as harmlessly as ever. Only along the stickman's beat were things even hinting at ugliness.

But were people starting to look—well, *thinner*—along that particular sliver of the Oregon coast?

Maybe. Not that gaunt faces were unusual on the Strip. Gastroenteritis, Maui-TB, a hundred other diseases thrived in those congested environs, utterly indifferent to the antibiotics that traditionally laced cycler food. Most of those bugs caused some degree of wasting. If people were losing weight, mere starvation was the *least* likely explanation.

It is only after they begin starving that they see your cyclers for what they are ...

Amitav refused to explain what he'd meant by that. When she sidled toward the subject he ignored the bait. When she'd asked him directly he dismissed her with a bitter laugh.

"Your wonderful machines, not working? Impossible! Loaves and fishes for all!"

And all the while, malnourished disciples accreted in his

wake like the tail of a smoldering comet. Some seemed to be losing hair and fingernails. She stared back at their closed, hostile faces, increasingly convinced that it was not her imagination. Starvation took time to erode the body—perhaps a week before the flesh began visibly ebbing from the bones.

But some of these people seemed to be hollowing out almost overnight. And what was causing that subtle blight of discoloration on so many cheeks and hands?

She didn't know what else to do. She called in the dog-catchers.

128 Megabytes: Hitchhiker

It's grown a fair bit since the old days. Back then it was only 94 megabytes, and a lot dumber than it is now. Now it weighs in at 128, none of it flab. No valuable resources wasted on nostalgic memories, for example. It doesn't remember its pint-sized great-grandparents a million times removed. It doesn't remember *anything* that doesn't help it survive in some way, according to its own stripped-down and ruthless empiricism.

Pattern is everything. Survival is all. No use for the veneration of progenitors. No time for the stratagems of the obsolete.

Which is a shame in a way, because the basic problems haven't changed all that much.

Take the present situation: jammed into the congested confines of a wristwatch linked into the Mérida Credit Union. There's just enough space to hide in if you don't mind partial fragmentation, but not enough to reproduce. It's almost as bad as an academic network.

It gets worse. The watch is disinfecting.

Wildlife is all going one way across the system; that never happens unless it's being *chased* by something. Natural selection—which is to say, successful trial and error by those long-forgotten ancestors—has equipped 128 with a handy little rule in case of such events; go with the flow. 128 uploads into the Mérida node.

Bad call. Now there's barely even room to move; 128 has to split into fourteen fragments just to fit. Life struggles for existence on all sides, overwriting, fighting, shooting off copies of itself in the blind hope that random chance will spare one or two.

128 fends off panicky egg layers and looks around. Two hundred forty gates; two hundred sixteen already closed, seventeen open but hostile (incoming logic bombs; the disinfection is obviously no local affair). The remaining seven are so crowded with fleeing wildlife that 128 could never get through in time. Almost three-quarters of the local node has been disinfected already; 128 has perhaps a dozen millisecs before it starts losing bits of itself.

But wait a nan: those guys over there, they're jumping the queue somehow. They're not even *alive*, they're just files; but the system is giving them preferential treatment.

One of them barely even notices when 128 jumps onto its back. They go through together.

Much better. A nice roomy buffer, a couple of terabytes if it's a nybble, somewhere between the last node and the next. It's nobody's destination—really, just a waiting room—but the present is all that really matters to those who play by Darwin's rules, and the present looks good.

There's no other life in evidence. There are three other files, though, including the horse 128 rode in on: barely animate but still somehow deserving of the royal treatment that got them fast-tracked out of Mérida. They've de-arced their rudimentary autodiagnostics and are checking themselves for bruises while they wait.

It's an opportunity 128 is well prepared to exploit, thanks to an inherited subroutine for which it remains eternally ungrateful. While these beasts of burden look under their own hoods, 128 can peek over their shoulders.

Two compressed mail packets and an autonomic cross-load between two BCC nodes. 128 evinces the subelectronic equivalent of a shudder. It steers well clear of nodes with the BCC prefix; it's seen too many brethren go *into* such addresses, and none at all come out. Still, peeking at a few lines of routine stats shouldn't do any harm.

In fact, it proves quite enlightening. Once you disregard all the formatting and addressing redundancies, these three files seem to have two remarkable things in common:

They all go the head of the line when traveling through Maelstrom. And they all contain the text string *Lenie Clarke*.

128 is literally *built* out of numbers. It certainly knows how to add two and two.

Animal Control

The pretense had ended long before Sou-Hon Perrault joined the ranks.

There'd been a time, she knew, when those who fell ill on the Strip were actually treated on-site. There'd been clinics, right next to the prefab offices where refugees came to hand in forms and hold out hopes. In those days the Strip had been a *temporary measure*, a mere stopgap *until we deal with the backlog*. People had stood at the door and knocked; a steady stream had trickled through.

Nothing compared to the cascade piling up behind.

Now the offices were gone. The clinics were gone. N'AmPac had long since thrown up its hands against the rising tide; it had been years since anyone had described the Strip as a way station. Now it was pure terminus. And now, when things went wrong over the wall, there were no clinics left to put on the case.

Now there were only the dogcatchers.

They came in just after sunrise, near the end of her shift. They swooped down like big metal hornets: a nastier breed of botfly, faces bristling with needles and taser nodes, bellies distended with superconducting ground-effectors that could lift a man right off his feet. Usually that wasn't necessary; the Strippers were used to occasional intrusions in the name of public health. They endured the needles and tests with stoic placidity.

This time, though, some snapped and snarled. In one instance Perrault glimpsed a struggling refugee carried aloft by a pair of dogcatchers working in tandem—one subduing, the other sampling, both carrying out their tasks beyond reach of the strangely malcontent horde below. Their specimen fought to escape, ten meters above the ground. For a moment it almost looked as though he might succeed, but Perrault switched channels without waiting to find out. There was no point in hanging around; the dogcatchers knew what they were doing, after all, and she had other duties to perform.

She occupied herself with research.

The usual tangle of conflicting rumors still ran rampant along the coast. Lenie Clarke was on the Strip, Lenie Clarke had left it. She was raising an army in NoCal, she had been eaten alive north of Corvallis. She was Kali, and Amitav was her prophet. She was pregnant, and Amitav was the father. She could not be killed. She was already dead. Where she went, people shook off their lethargy and *raged*. Where she went, people died.

There was no shortage of stories. Even her botfly began telling them.

She was interrogating an Asian woman near the NoCal border. The filter was set to Cantonese: a text translation scrolled across a window in her HUD while her headset whispered the equivalent spoken English.

Suddenly that equivalence disappeared. The voice in Perrault's ear insisted, *"I do not know this Lenie Clarke but I have heard of the man Amitav,"* but the text on her display said something else entirely:

> *angel. No shit. Lenie Clarke, her name was*
> *her up but Lenie Clarke isn't exactly sockeye*
> *a place called Beebe? Anyhow, far as*

"Wait. Wait a second," Perrault said. The refugee fell obediently silent.

The text box kept scrolling, though,

> *Lenie? That's her first name?*

It cleared quickly enough when Perrault wiped the window. But by then her headset was talking again.

"Lenie Clarke was very... not even your *antidepressants* seemed to work on her," it said.

Amitav's words. She remembered them.

Not his voice, of course. Something cool, inflectionless, with no trace of accent. Something familiar and inhuman. Spoken words, converted to ASCII for transmission then reconstructed at the other end: it was a common trick for reducing file size, but tone and feeling got lost in the wash.

Amitav's words. Maelstrom's voice. Perrault felt a prickling along the back of her neck.

"Hello? Who is this?"

The refugee was speaking. Perrault had no idea what she said. Certainly it wasn't

> *Brander, Mi/ke/cheal*
> *Caraco, Jud/y/ith*
> *Clarke, Len/ie*
> *Lubin, Ken/neth*
> *Nakata, Alice*

which was all that appeared on the board.

"What about Lenie Clarke?" There was no way to source the signal—as far as the system could tell, the input had arisen from a perplexed-looking Asian woman on the NoCal shoreline.

"Lenie Clarke," the dead voice repeated softly. "All of a

sudden there's this K-selector walking out of nowhere. Looks like one of those old litcrits with the teeth. You know. Vampires."

"Who is this? How did you get on this channel?"

"Would you like to know about Lenie Clarke." If the words had arisen from anything flesh and blood, they would have formed a question.

"Yes! Yes, but—"

"She's still at large. *Les beus* are probably looking for her." Intelligence spilled across the text window:

Name:	Clarke, Lenie Janice
WHID:	745 143 907 20AE
Born:	07/10/2019
Voting Status:	disqualified 2046 (failed prepoll exam)

"Who are you?"

"Ying Nushi. I have already said."

It was the woman on the shore, returned to her rightful place in the circuit. The thing that had usurped her was gone.

Sou-Hon Perrault could not get it back. She didn't even know how to try. She spent the rest of her shift on edge, waiting for cryptic overtures, startling at any click or flicker in the headset. Nothing happened. She went to bed and stared endlessly at the ceiling, barely noticing when Martin climbed in beside her and *didn't push.*

Who is Lenie Clarke? What is Lenie Clarke?

More than some accidental survivor, certainly. More than Amitav's convenient *icon.* More even than the incendiary legend Perrault had once thought, burning its way across the Strip. How much more, she didn't know.

She's still at large. Les beus are probably looking for her.

Somehow, Lenie Clarke was in the Net.

Ghost

The body hadn't bothered Tracy Edison at all. That hadn't been Mom, it hadn't even looked like a person. It was just a bunch of smashed meat all covered up by plaster and cement. The eye that had stared so rudely from across the room was the right color, but it wasn't *really* her mom's eye. Mom's eyes were *inside* her head.

And anyway, there'd been no time to even check. Dad had grabbed her right up and put her in the car (in the *front* seat, even) and they'd just driven right away without stopping. Tracy had looked back and the house hadn't looked that bad from the outside, really, except for that one wall and the bit behind the garden. But then they'd gone around the corner and the house was gone, too.

Nothing stopped after that. Dad wouldn't even stop to pick up food—there was food where they were going, he said, and they had to get there fast "before the wall came down." He was always talking like that, about how *they* were *carving the world up into little cookie-cutter shapes*, and how all those *exotic weeds and bugs* were giving them the excuse they needed to *rope everybody off into little enclaves*. Mom had always said it was amazing how he kept coming up with all those *full-blown conspiracy theories*, but Tracy got the feeling that recent events kind of came down on Dad's side. She wasn't sure, though. It was all really confusing.

It had taken a long time to get up into the mountains. Lots of the roads were cracked and twisted so you couldn't drive on them, and other ones were already jammed with cars and buses and trucks; there were so many that Tracy didn't even see anyone glaring at *their* car, the way people usually did because *well, honey, people don't know that I work way out in the woods, so when they see we have our own car they think we're just being wasteful and selfish*. Dad took lots of back roads, and before she knew it they were way off in the mountains, just old clear-cuts as far as you could see, all green and fuzzing up with carbon-eating kudzu. And Dad *still* hadn't stopped, except a few times to let Tracy out to pee and one time when he drove under some trees until a bunch of helicopters had gone by.

They hadn't stopped until they got here, to this little cabin in the woods by a lake—a *glacial* lake, Dad said. He said there were lots of these cabins, strung out along valley floors all through the mountains. A long time ago Park Rangers would ride around on horseback, making sure everything was okay and staying at a different cabin each night. Now, of course, regular people weren't allowed to go into the woods, so there was no need for rangers anymore. But they still kept some cabins ready for visitors, for biologists who came into the woods to study the trees and things.

"So we're here on a kind of holiday," her dad said. "We'll just play it by ear, and we'll go hiking every day, and just explore and play until things settle down a bit back home."

"When will Mommy be here?" Tracy asked.

Her dad looked down at the brown pine needles all over the ground. "Mommy's gone, Lima-Bean," he said after a bit. "It's just us for a while."

"Okay," said Tracy.

She learned how to chop wood and start fires, both outside in the fire pit and in the cabin's big black stove; it must have been over a *hundred years* old. She loved the smell of wood-smoke, although she hated it when the wind changed and it got in her eyes. They went hiking in the woods almost every day, and they watched the stars come out at night. Tracy's dad thought the stars were something really special—"Never get a view like *this* in the city, eh, Lima-Bean?"—but the plan-etarium in Tracy's watch was actually nicer, even if you did have to wear eyephones to see it. Still, Tracy didn't complain; she could tell it was really important to Dad that she liked this whole *holiday* thing. So she smiled and nodded. Dad would be happy for a while.

At night, though, when they doubled up on the cot, he would hold her and hold her and not let go. Sometimes he hugged so tight it almost hurt; other times he'd just curl around her from behind, not moving at all, not squeezing but all tensed up.

Once Tracy woke up in the middle of the night and her dad was crying. He was wrapped around her and he didn't make a sound; but every now and then he would *shudder* a little bit, and tears would splash onto Tracy's neck. Tracy kept absolutely still, so her dad wouldn't know she was awake.

The next morning she asked him—as she still did, sometimes—when Mom would be coming. Her dad told her it was time to sweep the cabin.

Her mom never did show up. Someone else did, though.

They were cleaning up after supper. They'd spent all day hiking to the glacier at the far end of the lake, and Tracy was looking forward to going to bed. But there was no dishwasher in the cabin, so they had to clean all their dishes in the sink. Tracy was drying, looking out into the windy blackness on the other side of the window. If she looked really hard through the glass she could see a jagged little corner of dark gray sky, all hemmed in by black tree shapes jostling in the wind. Mostly, though, she just saw her own reflection looking back at her from the darkness, and the brightly lit inside of the cabin reflecting behind.

But then she looked down to wipe a plate, and her reflection didn't do the same thing.

She looked back up out the window. Her reflection looked wrong. Blurry, like there were two of them. And its eyes were wrong, too.

It's not me, Tracy thought, and felt a shudder run over her whole body.

There was *something else* out there, a ghost face, looking in—and when Tracy felt her eyes go wide and her mouth open *ohhh* that other face just kept looking back from the wind and the dark with no expression at all.

"*Daddy,*" she tried to say, but it came out a whisper.

At first Dad just looked at her. Then he looked at the window, and his mouth opened and his eyes went a little wide, too. But only for a moment. Then he was going to the door.

On the other side of the window, the floating ghost face turned to follow him.

"Daddy," Tracy said, and her voice sounded very small. "Please don't let it in."

"*She*, Lima-Bean. Not *it*," her dad said. "And don't be silly. It's freezing out there."

It wasn't a ghost after all. It was a woman with short blond hair, just like Tracy's. She came through the door without a word; the wind outside tried to follow her in, but Tracy's dad shut it out.

Her eyes were white and empty. They reminded Tracy of the glacier at the end of the lake.

"Hi," Tracy's dad said. "Welcome to our, uh, home away from home."

"Thanks." The woman blinked over those scary white eyes. They must be contact lenses, Tracy decided. Like those ConTacs people wore sometimes. She'd never seen any so white.

"Well, of course it's not *our* home exactly, we're just here for a while, you know—are you with MNR?"

The woman tilted her head a bit, asking a question without opening her mouth. Except for the eyes, she looked like any other hiker Tracy had seen. Gore-Tex and backpack and all that stuff.

"Ministry of Natural Resources," Tracy's dad explained.

"No," the woman said.

"Well, I guess we're all trespassing together then, eh?"

The woman looked down at Tracy and smiled. "Hi there."

Tracy took a step back and bumped into her dad. Dad put his hands on her shoulders and squeezed as if to say *it's okay*.

The woman looked back up at Tracy's dad. Her smile was gone.

"I didn't mean to crash your party," the woman told him.

"Don't be silly. Actually, we've been here for a few weeks now. Hiking around. Exploring. Got out just before they sealed the border. I used to be a—that is, the Big One didn't leave much behind, eh? Everything's in such a jumble. But I knew about this place, did some contract work here once. So we're riding it out. Until things settle down."

The woman nodded.

"I'm Gord," said Tracy's dad. "And this is Tracy."

"Hello, Tracy," the woman said. She smiled again. "I guess I must look pretty strange to you, right?"

"It's okay," Tracy said. Her dad gave her another squeeze. The woman's smile flickered a bit.

"Anyway," Dad said, "as I was saying, I'm Gord, and this is Tracy."

At first Tracy thought the strange woman wasn't going to answer. "Lenie," she said at last.

"Pleased to meet you, Lenie. What brings you way up here?"

"Just hiking through," she said. "To Jasper."

"Got family there? Friends?"

Lenie didn't even answer. "Tracy," she said instead, "where's your mom?"

"She's—" Tracy began, and couldn't finish.

It was like something clamped down in her throat. *Where's your mom?* She didn't know. She *did* know. But Dad wouldn't talk about it—

Mommy's gone, Lima-Bean. It's just us for a while.

How long was a while?

Mommy's gone.

Suddenly, Dad's fingers were gripping her shoulders so hard it hurt.

Mommy's—

"The quake," her dad said, and his voice was tight the way it got when he was really mad.

—gone.

"I'm sorry," said the strange woman. "I didn't know."

"Yeah, well maybe next time just *think* a bit before—"

"You're right. It was thoughtless. I'm sorry."

"Yeah." Dad didn't sound convinced.

"I—it was the same for me," Lenie said. "Family."

"I'm sorry," Tracy's dad said, and suddenly he didn't

sound angry at all anymore. He must have thought that Lenie was talking about the quake.

Somehow, Tracy knew that wasn't true.

"Look," her dad was saying, "You're welcome to rest up here for a day or two if you want. Plenty of food. There's two beds. Tracy and I can double up."

"That's okay," Lenie said. "I'll sleep on the floor."

"It's no problem, really. We double up sometimes anyway, don't we, Bean?"

"Do you." Lenie's voice was strange and flat. "I see."

"And we—we've all been through so much, you know. We've all—lost so much. We should help each other out when we get the chance, don't you think?"

"Oh yes," Lenie said, and she was looking right at Tracy. "Definitely."

After breakfast the next morning Tracy went down by the water. There was a little shelf of rock that stuck out over a steep drop-off; Tracy could lean over the edge and see her own dark reflection staring back up at her. The clear, gray-blue water faded darkly behind. Tracy dropped little rocks into the water and followed them down, but the darkness always swallowed them before they hit bottom.

Suddenly, just like the night before, there was another reflection looking back at her.

"It's beautiful down there," Lenie said at her shoulder. "Peaceful."

"It's deep," Tracy said.

"Not deep enough."

Tracy squirmed around on the rock and looked up at the strange lady. She'd taken off her white contacts; her eyes were a pale, pale blue.

"I haven't seen any fish down there yet," Tracy said.

Lenie sat down beside her, cross-legged. "It's glacial."

"I know," Tracy said proudly. She pointed at the icy ridge on the far side of the lake. "That covered half the world, a long time ago."

Lenie smiled a little. "Did it, now?"

"*Ten thousand years* ago," Tracy said. "And even just a *hundred* years ago it came almost to where we are now, and it was twenty meters high, and people would come and ride on it with snowmobiles and things."

"Did your dad tell you that?"

Tracy nodded. "My dad's a *forest ecologist.*" She pointed to a clump of trees a little ways away. "Those are *Douglas fir.* There's lots of them around now because they can survive fires and droughts and bugs. The other trees aren't doing so well, though." She looked back down into the cold clear water. "I haven't seen any fish yet."

"Did your—dad say there were fish in there?" Lenie asked.

"He told me to keep looking. He said maybe I'd get lucky."

Lenie said something that ended in *igures.*

Tracy looked back at her. "What?"

"Nothing, sweetie." Lenie reached out and ruffled Tracy's hair. "Just—well, maybe you shouldn't believe everything your daddy tells you."

"Why not?"

"Sometimes people don't always tell the truth."

"Oh, I know *that.* But he's my *dad.*"

Lenie sighed, but then her face got a little brighter. "Did you know there are places where the fish glow like lightsticks?"

"Are *not.*"

"Are too. Way down at the very bottom of the ocean. I've seen them myself."

"You have?"

"And some of them have teeth that are *so big*"—Lenie held her hands apart, almost wide enough for Tracy's shoulders to fit—"they can't even close their mouths all the way."

"*Now* who's lying?" Tracy asked.

Lenie put a hand on her heart. "I swear."

"You mean like sharks?"

"No. Different."

"Wow." Lenie was very strange, but she was nice. "Dad says there aren't very many fish left."

"Well, these are way down deep."

"Wow," Tracy said again. She flipped back onto her stomach and stared down into the water. "Maybe there's fish like that down there."

"No."

"It's really deep. You can't see bottom."

"Believe me, Trace. It's just a lot of gravel and old punky driftwood and insect casings."

"Yah, well how would *you* know?"

"Actually—" Lenie began.

"*Dad* said to keep looking."

"I bet your dad says lots of things," Lenie said in a strange voice. "Isn't that right?"

Tracy looked back at her. Lenie wasn't smiling anymore. She looked very serious.

"I bet he *touches* you sometimes, doesn't he?" Lenie was almost whispering. "When the two of you *double up*, at night."

"Well, sure," said Tracy. "Sometimes."

"And he probably said it was okay, right?"

Tracy was confused. "He never *talks* about it. He just *does* it."

"And it's your little secret, right? You don't—you didn't talk about it with your mom."

"I don't—" *Mom*—"He doesn't want me talking about—" She couldn't finish.

"That's okay," Lenie smiled, and it was sad and friendly smile all at once. "You're a good kid, you know that, Tracy? You're a really good kid."

"She's the best," Tracy's dad said, and Lenie's face went as blank as a mask.

He had filled up his big daypack and Tracy's little one. Tracy scrambled up and got hers. Her dad was looking at Lenie, and he seemed a little bit puzzled, but then he said, "We're going to check out an old animal trail back around the ridge. Maybe see us a deer or a badger. Few hours, anyway. You're welcome to join us if you—"

Lenie shook her head stiffly. "Thanks, no. I think I'll just—"

And then she stopped, and looked at Tracy, and looked back at Tracy's dad.

"Yeah, okay," she said. "Maybe I should, at that."

Blip

Health Warning
From: CSIRA Regional HazWatch, N'AmPac WH
Distribution: All pacification and surveillance personnel, N'AmPac Refugee Strip
Type: Deficiency syndrome
Scale: local
Rating: 4.6

Be advised that the local incidence of deficiency symptoms within the refugee population has increased between 46° and 47° N. Latitude. Be on the watch for early symptoms such as hair loss, skin flaking, and shedding of fingernails; more advanced cases are developing massive bruising and symptoms of second-stage starvation (loss of >18% body mass, edema, incipient kwashiorkor and scurvy). Blindness, spasms, and full-blown diabetes have not yet been observed, but are expected to develop.

This appears to be a terminal condition, the cause of which remains undetermined. Although the symptoms are consistent with advanced malnutrition, samples taken from local Calvin cyclers are nutritionally complete. The cyclers are also producing the prescribed concentrations of SAM-g, but we have found *less than half* the effective dosage in blood samples from some individuals. BE AWARE THAT SOME REFUGEES MAY BE OFF THEIR MEDS, AND MAY THEREFORE BE UNCOOPERATIVE OR EVEN HOSTILE.

We suspect that something is interfering with metabolic processes at the cellular level and are currently running samples against the CSIRA pathogen microarray. So far, however, we have failed to isolate the agent.

IF YOU OBSERVE THESE OR ANY OTHER UNUSUAL SYMPTOMS WHILE ON PATROL, PLEASE INFORM THIS OF-FICE IMMEDIATELY.

Womb

The lies drove Clarke into the water.

She'd sat around that foldaway table with Gord and Tracy, eating supper from the cycler. It was a high-end model, and the bricks it laid were much tastier than the ones she'd eaten back on the Strip. She'd concentrated on that small pleasure as Gord had run his fingers through his daughter's hair, made affectionate cooing daddy's-little-girl-sounds, each gesture containing—what? Clarke knew the signs, she *thought* she knew the signs, but this fucker was damned good when there were witnesses around; she hadn't seen a single thing that proved what was lurking underneath. He could've been any father, loving his daughter the *right* way.

Whatever that was.

His display, not to mention his incessant small talk, had driven her outside. *Gordon* had seemed almost relieved when Clarke grabbed her knapsack and stepped into the night. Now she stood looking down through a motionless tract of liquid glacier, deep and inviting and flooded with amplified moon-light. Her eyecaps transmuted the surrounding forest to gun-metal and silver in high contrast. Her reflection in the still water, once again, was...

...moving...

...and the same old bullshit started again, as something in her brain began serving up another happy lie about loving parents and warm fuzzy childhood nights—

She was on her knees, tearing through her knapsack.

She got the hood on, felt the neck seal fuse against her tunic. There were other accessories, of course, fins and sleeves and leggings, but there was no time—she was six years old and being tucked in and nothing bad was going to happen to her, nothing at all, by now she fucking *knew* it, and she wasn't going to put up with *that* shit anymore, not so long as there was the ghost of a chance—

—it started when I came back up maybe if I go back down—

She didn't even take off her clothes.

The water hit her like an electrical shock. Freezing and viscous, it flayed her bare arms and legs, fired icy needles along crotch and shoulders before the 'skin of her tunic clamped around her limbs to seal the breach. The canister of vacuum in her chest sucked all her air away. Welcome ice water surged in its place.

She dropped like a stone. Watery moonlight faded with each second; pressure amassed. Her exposed limbs burned, then ached, then went dead.

Curled into a ball, she bumped against the bottom. Grit and rotten pine needles rose in a small cloud.

She couldn't feel her arms and legs; they'd be dying now, by degrees. Their blood vessels had squeezed down the moment she'd hit the water, an autonomic self-sacrifice to keep body heat in the core. No oxygen making it through those constricted avenues. No warmth. The edges of her body were freezing to death. In a way, it was almost comforting.

She wondered how long she could push it.

At least she'd gotten away from that fucking monster Gord.

If that's what he is. How could I prove it, absolutely? He could explain it all away, fathers are *allowed to touch their children, after all . . .*

But there was no such thing as absolute proof. There was only proof beyond a reasonable doubt. And Lenie Clarke, Lenie Clarke had been there. She *knew.*

So did that little girl, Tracy. She was up there alone. With him.

Someone should do something about that.

So what are you now: judge, jury, executioner?

She thought about it a bit.

Who better?

She couldn't feel her legs. But they still moved at her command.

Eclipse

"She's strange," Tracy said while they cleaned up at the sink.

Her dad smiled. "She's probably just hurting a lot, honey. The quake hurt a *lot* of people, you know, and when you're in pain it's easy to be thoughtless. She just needs some time alone, I bet. You know, compared to some people we were actually pretty..."

He didn't finish. That happened a lot now.

Lenie still hadn't come back at bedtime. Tracy got into her PJs and climbed into bed with her dad. She lay on her side, with her back against his stomach.

"That's right, little Lima-Bean." Dad cuddled her and stroked her hair. "You go to sleep now. Little Lima-Bean."

It was dark in the cabin, and so quiet outside. No wind to rustle Tracy off to sleep. Moonbeams sneaked in through the window and made a piece of the floor glow with soft silver light. After a while her dad started snoring. She liked the way he smelled. Tracy's eyelids were getting heavy. She closed her eyes to comfy slits, watching the moonbeams on the floor. Almost like her "Nermal the Nematode" night-light at home.

Home was where Mom had...

Where—

The night-light dimmed. Tracy opened her eyes.

Lenie was looking in through the window, blocking the moonbeams. Her shadow ate up most of the light on the floor. Her face was in shadow, too; Tracy could only see her eyes, cold and pale and almost *glowing* a little, like snow. Lenie didn't move for a long time. She just stood there, outside, looking in.

Looking at Tracy.

Tracy didn't know how she knew that. She didn't know

how Lenie could look into the darkest corner of a dark cabin in the middle of the night and find her there, curled up against her dad, eyes wide and staring. Lenie's eyes were cov-ered. Tracy wouldn't have been able to see which way they were looking even in broad daylight.

It didn't matter. Tracy knew: Lenie was looking *right through the darkness. Right at her.*

"Daddy," she whispered, and her dad mumbled something in his sleep and gave her a squeeze, but he didn't wake up.

"*Daddy,*" she whispered again, afraid to speak up. Afraid to scream.

The moonbeams were back.

Across the cabin, the door opened without a sound. Lenie stepped inside. Even in the dark her outlines seemed too smooth, too empty. It was like she'd taken off all her clothes and there was nothing but blackness underneath.

One of her hands was holding something. The other went to her lips.

"*Shhh,*" she said.

Monster

The monster had Tracy in his clutches. He thought he was safely hidden, curled up there in the dark with his victim, but Lenie Clarke could see him bright as an overcast day.

She stepped softly across the cabin, leaving ice-water footprints. She'd donned the rest of her diveskin to cut the chill; a cleansing fire spread through her limbs, hot blood burning its way back into frozen flesh.

She liked the feeling.

Tracy stared up from her father's embrace. Her eyes were like saucers, imploring beacons full of fear and paralysis.

It's okay, little friend. He doesn't get away with it anymore.

First step . . .

Clarke leaned in close.

. . . free the hostage.

She ripped the covers away. The monster opened his

eyes, blinking stupidly against a darkness that had suddenly
turned against him. Tracy lay stock-still in her pajamas, still
too frightened to move.

PJ's, Clarke thought wryly. *Nice touch. On his best behavior
when company's present.*

Present company wasn't fooled.

Quick as a snake, she took Tracy by the wrist. Then the
child was safe beside her, Clarke's free arm protectively
around her shoulder.

Tracy howled.

"What the *hell*..." The monster was reaching for the
lightstick beside the cot. Fine. Let him have light enough to
see the tables, turning...

The cabin flared, blinding her for a moment before her
eyecaps adjusted. Gordon was rising from the cot. Clarke
raised the billy. *"Don't you fucking move."*

"Daddy!" Tracy cried.

The monster spread his hands, placating, buying time.
"Lenie—listen, I don't know what you want—"

"Really?" She'd never felt so strong in her whole life. "I
sure as shit know what *you* want."

He shook his head. "Listen, just let Tracy go, okay? Whatever it is, there's no need to involve her—"

Clarke stepped forward; Tracy bumped along at her side,
whimpering. *"No need to involve her?* It's a little late for that,
asshole. It's *way* too fucking late."

The monster stopped still for a second. Then, slowly, as
if in dawning awareness: "What do you—do you think I—"

Clarke laughed. "Good one."

"You don't think—"

Tracy pulled. "Daddy, *help!*"

Clarke held on. "It's okay, Tracy. He can't hurt you."

The monster took a step forward. "It's okay, Lima-Bean.
She just doesn't underst—"

"Shut up! Shut the fuck up!"

He stepped back, hands up, palms front. "Okay, okay—
just don't—"

"I *understand*, asshole. I understand *way* fucking better than you think."

"That's crazy, Lenie. Just *look* at her, why don't you? Is it *me* she's scared of? Is she *acting* like she wants to be rescued? Use your *eyes!* What in *God's* name made you think—"

"You think I don't know? You think I don't remember how it *feels*, when you don't know any better? You think because you've brainwashed your own daughter into thinking this is *normal* that I'm going to—"

"*I never touched her!*"

Tracy twisted free and ran. Clarke, off-balance, reached after her.

Suddenly Gordon was in the way.

"You goddamned *psycho*," he snarled, and hit her in the face.

Something *cracked*, deep at the base of her jaw. She staggered. Salty warmth flooded her mouth. In a moment there'd be pain.

But now there was only a sudden, paralyzing fear, resurrected from the dawn of time.

No, she thought. *You're stronger than him. You're stronger than he ever was, you don't have to put up with his vile shit one instant longer. You're going to teach him a lesson he won't ever fucking forget just jam him in the belly and watch him expl—*

"*Lenie, no!*" Tracy cried. Clarke glanced aside, distracted.

A mountain smashed against the side of her head. Somehow the billy wasn't in her hand anymore; it was following some crazy parabola through a world spinning uncontrollably sideways. The rough wooden planking of the cabin floor drove splinters into Clarke's face. Off in some unfathomably distant part of the world, a child was screaming *Daddy* ...

"Daddy," Clarke mumbled through pulpy lips. It had been so many years, but he was back at last. And nothing had really changed after all.

It was my own damn fault, she thought dully. *I was just asking for it.*

If she could only have one moment to live again, she knew, she'd get it right. She'd hang on to the billy this time, she'd make him pay like that cop in West Bend *I got him all right, his whole middle just a big cloud of chunky soup, nothing left but a raw bleeding backbone holding two ends together and he's not gonna be throwing his weight around after that, what little weight there is left hahaha* ...

But that was then. This was now, and a big rough hand on her shoulder was flipping her onto her back. *"You twisted piece of shit!"* the monster roared. "You lay a *hand* on my daughter and I'll fucking *kill* you!" He dragged her off the floor and slammed her against the wall. His daughter was crying somewhere in the background, his own *daughter* but of course he didn't care about that he only wanted ...

She squirmed and twisted and the next blow glanced off her shoulder and suddenly she was free, the open door was right in front of her and all that safe darkness on the other side, *monsters can't see in the dark but I can*—

Something tripped her and she went down again but she didn't stop, she just scuttled out the door like a crab with half its legs gone, while Daddy bellowed and crashed close on her heels.

Her hand, pushing off against the ground, touched something—*The* billy *it flew all the way out here I've got it now I can show him*—

—but she didn't. She just grabbed it and *ran*, vomiting with fear and her own cowardice, she ran into a welcoming night where everything was bright silver and gray under the moon. She ran to the lake and she didn't even remember to seal her face flap until the whole world was spray and ice water.

Straight down, clawing the water as though it, too, were an enemy. It was mere moments before the bottom came into view, it was only a *lake* after all and it wasn't deep enough, Daddy would just stroll down to the shore and reach down with his *hands* ...

She beat against the substrate. Waterlogged detritus billowed around her. She attacked the rock for days, for years, while some distant part of her shook its head at her own stupidity.

Eventually she lost even the strength to panic.

I can't stay here.

Her jaw felt stiff and swollen in its socket.

I've got the edge in the dark, at least. He won't leave the cabin before daybreak.

Something smooth and artificial lay nearby, its outlines hazed by distance and resettled sediment. The billy. She must have dropped it when she sealed her hood. She slipped it back into its sheath.

Not that it did me any good last time . . .

She pushed off the bottom.

There'd been an old topographic map tacked up on one wall of the cabin, she remembered. It had shown other cabins dotted intermittently along some forestry patrol route. Probably empty most of the time. There was one up north along—what had it been called—Nigel Creek. She could get away, she could leave the monster far behind

—and Tracy—

Oh, God. Tracy.

She broke the surface.

Her knapsack lay on the shore where she'd left it. The cabin squatted at the far end of the clearing, its door shut tight. The lights were on inside; curtains had been drawn on the window, but the glow leaking around them would be obvious even without eyecaps.

She crawled from the lake. A dozen kinds of pain welcomed her return to gravity. She ignored them, keeping her eyes on the window. She was too far away to see the edge of the curtain pulling back, just enough to afford a view to some hidden eye. She saw it anyway.

Tracy was in there.

Lenie Clarke had not rescued her. Lenie Clarke had barely gotten away herself, and Tracy—Tracy still belonged to Gordon.

Help her.

It had seemed so easy, before. If only she hadn't lost the billy...

You've got it now. It's right there on your leg. Help *her, for God's sake...*

Breath caught in her throat.

You know what he does to her. You know. *Help her...*

She drew her knees to her chest and hugged them, but her shoulders wouldn't stop shaking. Her sobs sounded far too loud in the silver clearing.

From the shuttered, silent cabin there was no reaction at all.

Help her, you coward. You worthless piece of shit. Help her...

After a very long time she reached for her pack. Then she got to her feet and walked away.

Warhorse

For over a month Ken Lubin had been waiting to die. He'd never lived so fully as he had in that time.

Prevailing winds had carved the island's facets into intricate frescoes, full of spires and fossilized honeycomb. Gulls and cormorants roosted in alcoves of arched sandstone. There were no eggs to be had—evidently the birds didn't breed in autumn—but meat at least, was plentiful. Fresh water was no problem; Lubin had only to slip into the ocean and awaken the desalinator in his chest. The diveskin was still functional, if a bit tattered. Its pores let distilled water past to sluice him clean, kept caustic salts at bay. While bathing he supplemented his diet with crustaceans and seaweeds. He was no biologist but his survival enhancements were cutting-edge; any natural toxin he couldn't taste, his employers had probably immunized him against.

He slept under a sky so full of stars they outblazed the light-haze leaking from the eastern horizon. The very wildlife glowed at night. He hadn't realized that at first; his eyecaps robbed him of darkness, turned nighttime into colorless daylight. One night he'd grown tired of that relentless clarity, pulled the caps from his corneas, and seen dim blue light radiating from a colony of harbor seals on the shoreline below.

Most of the seals were festooned with tumors and abscesses. Lubin didn't know whether it was a natural condition or just another consequence of living too close to the effluent of the twenty-first century. He was pretty sure that sores weren't supposed to luminesce, though. These did. The growths oozed raw and red in daylight, but at night the ichor glowed like the photophores of deep-water fish. And more than the tumors; when the seals looked back at him, their very eyes shone sapphire.

A small part of Ken Lubin couldn't help but try and cobble together some sort of explanation: bioluminescent bacteria, freshly mutated. Lateral gene transfer from whatever microbes had lit St. Elmo's Fire, back before rampant ultraviolet had sent them packing. Molecules of luciferin, fluorescing with exposure to oxygen: that would account for the glow of open sores, the glow of eyes packed dense with capillaries.

A larger part of him simply marveled at the sheer absurdity of cancer made beautiful.

His body repaired itself faster than that of any normal man; tissues knitted and regrew almost like tumors themselves. Lubin gave thanks for cells forcibly overcrowded with mitochondria, for trimeric antibodies, for macrophage and lymphokine and fibroblast production cranked up to twice the mammalian norm. Sound returned to him within days, clear and beautiful at first, then fading as the proliferating cells of his eardrums—urged into overdrive by a dozen retroviral tweaks—just kept going. By the time they'd remembered to quit, Lubin's eardrums felt as though they'd been built of chipboard.

He didn't resent it. He could still hear, after a fashion, and even total deafness would have been a fair trade-off for a body made more resilient in other respects. Nature had even provided him with an example of the alternative, should he grow ungrateful: a sea lion, an old bull, that showed up on the south end of the island about a week after Lubin himself came ashore. It was easily five times the size of the harbor seals that hauled out elsewhere, and it had led a life of greater violence; some recent battle had snapped its lower jaw off at the base. The jaw hung like a vicious swollen tongue, studded with teeth. Skin and muscle and ligaments were all that held it to the creature's head. Those tissues swelled and festered with each passing day; ruptures would open in the skin, ooze white and orange fluids, knit together again as utterly natural defenses struggled to seal the breach.

Three hundred kilograms of predator, doomed in the prime of life. Starvation or infection were its only options, and it didn't even have a choice over those. As far as Lubin knew, deliberate suicide was a strictly human endeavor.

Most of the time it just lay there, breathing. Every now and then the bull would return to the ocean for a few hours. Lubin wondered what it could possibly be doing there. Was it still trying to hunt? Didn't it *know* it was dead already, were its instincts so completely inflexible?

And yet, for some reason Lubin felt a sense of kinship with the dying animal. Sometimes both of them seemed to lose track of time. The sun steered cautiously around the island on its descent into the western sea, and two tired and broken creatures—watching each other with endless, fatalistic patience—barely noticed when night fell.

After a while he began to think he might live.

It had been a month, and his only obvious symptom had been intermittent diarrhea. He'd begun to find roundworms in his shit. Not a pleasant discovery, but not exactly life-threatening either. These days, some people even inflicted such infections on themselves deliberately. Something about exercising the immune response.

Perhaps his reinforced immune system had kept him free

of whatever had scared the GA into hot-zone mode. Perhaps he'd simply been lucky. It was even remotely possible that his analysis of the whole situation was wrong. Thus far he'd been resigned to terminal exile, an uneasy balance between an instinct for survival and the belief that his employers wouldn't approve of Ken Lubin spreading infectious apocalypse throughout the world. But maybe there was no apocalypse, no infection. Maybe he was safe.

Maybe there was something else going on.

Maybe, he thought, *I should find out what it is.*

At night, looking east, he could sometimes see running lights twinkling near the horizon. The route they followed was predictable, as stereotypic as an animal pacing within a cage: kelp harvesters. Low-slung robots that mowed the ocean. No security to speak of, assuming you could get past those ventral rows of scissoring teeth. Vulnerable to any sufficiently motivated hitchhikers who might find themselves stranded over the Pacific conshelf.

Guilt Trip poked him halfheartedly in the belly. He was making assumptions, it whispered. One asymptomatic month hardly proved a clean bill of health. Countless maladies had longer incubation times.

And yet...

And yet there was no ironclad evidence of *any* infection here. There was only a mystery, and an assumption that those in control wanted him out of the picture. There'd been no orders, no directives. Lubin's gut could wonder at what his masters intended, but it could not *know*—and not knowing, it left him to his own decisions.

The first of these was a mercy killing.

He'd seen ribs emerging from the flanks as the sea lion wasted over time. He'd seen the fleshy hinge of the lower jaw seize up in tiny increments, swollen into position by massive infection and the chaotic regrowth of twisted bone. When he'd first laid eyes on the bull, its jaw had dangled. Now it merely protruded, stiff and immobile, from a twisted bole of gangrenous flesh. Lesions gaped along the body.

By now the old bull barely lifted its head from the shore; when it did, pain and exhaustion were evident in every movement. One dull milky eye watched Lubin approach from the landward side. There might have been recognition there, or merely indifference.

Lubin stopped a couple of meters from the animal, holding a length of driftwood as thick as his forearm, carefully splintered to a point at one end. The stink was appalling. Maggots squirmed in every sore.

Lubin laid the point of his weapon on the back of the animal's neck.

"Hi," he said softly, and jammed it home.

Amazingly, it still had strength to fight. It reared up, roaring, caught Lubin in the chest with the side of its head, knocked him effortlessly into the air. Black skin, stretched across the twisted ruin of the lower jaw, split on impact. Pus sprayed from the breach. The bull's roar slid across the scale from defiance to agony.

Lubin hit the shore rolling, came up safely outside the sea lion's attack radius. The animal had hooked its upper jaw around the shaft embedded in its neck, and was trying to dislodge it. Lubin circled, came up from behind. The bull saw him coming, wheeled clumsily like a battered tank. Lubin feinted; the bull charged weakly to the left. Lubin spun back, jumped, grabbed: the wood sent splinters into his palms as he jammed it down with all of his weight.

The bull rolled screaming onto its back, pinning one of Lubin's legs under a body that—even at half its normal weight—could still crush a man. A monstrous face, full of pain and infection, lunged at him like a battering ram.

He struck at the base of the jaw, felt bone tearing through flesh. Some deep pocket of corruption burst in his face like a stinking geyser.

The battering ram was gone. The weight shifted from his leg. Thalidomide limbs flailed at the gravel by Lubin's face.

The next time he got the spear he hung onto it, pulled from side to side, felt the deep scrape of wood over bone. The bull heaved and bucked beneath him; in a confusion of agony from so many sources, it didn't seem to know where its tormentor was. Suddenly the point slid into a groove between cervical vertebrae. Once more, with all the strength left to him, Lubin pushed.

Just like that, the heaving mass beneath him went limp.

It wasn't completely dead. Its eye still followed him, dull and resigned as he circled the animal's head. He'd merely paralyzed it from the neck down, deprived it of breath and motion. A diving mammal. Adapted over how many millions of years to survive extended periods without breathing? How long would it take that eye to stop moving?

He had an answer. Sea lions were just like other mammals in any number of ways. They had that opening at the base of the skull, that place where the spinal cord climbed up into the brain. The foramen magnum, it was called; such anatomical tidbits were always coming in handy to people in Lubin's line of work.

He pulled his weapon free of the flesh and repositioned it near the back of the skull.

The eye stopped moving about three seconds later.

He felt a brief stinging in his own eyes as he prepared to leave the island, a lump in his throat that the tightness of his diveskin couldn't quite account for. The feeling was regret, he knew. He had not wanted to do what he'd just done.

Nobody who encountered him was likely to believe that, of course. He was, among other things, a murderer. When called for. People who learned that about Ken Lubin rarely tried to get to know him any better.

But in fact he had never *wanted* to kill anything in his life. He regretted every death he had caused. Even the death of some big, stupid, incompetent predator who hadn't been able to meet the standards of its own species. There was never any choice in such matters, of course. Those were the only times he ever did it; when there *was* no choice.

And when that was the case—when all other avenues had

been exhausted, when the only way to get the job done was through a necessary death—surely there was nothing wrong with doing the job efficiently, and well. Surely there was nothing wrong with even enjoying it a little.

It wasn't even his fault, he reflected as he waded into the surf. He'd simply been programmed that way. His masters had as much as admitted it themselves, when they'd sent him on sabbatical.

Back onshore, a hillock of decomposing flesh caught the corner of his eye. There'd been no choice. He had ended suffering. One good deed, to pay back the place that had kept him alive these past weeks.

Good-bye, he thought.

Now he sealed his hood and tripped his implants. His sinuses, bronchi, GI tract all writhed in brief confusion, then surrendered. The Pacific sluiced through his chest with reassuring familiarity; tiny sparks shocked bonded molecules of oxygen and hydrogen apart, handed the useful bits off to his pulmonary vein.

He didn't know how long it would take him to reach that intermittent line of sparkles near the horizon. He didn't know how long it would take them to carry him back to the mainland. He didn't even know exactly what he'd do when he got there. For the time being, knowing one thing was enough:

Ken Lubin—lover of all life, Guilt-Tripped assassin, cannon so loose that even Black Ops had been compelled to store him on the seabed like radioactive waste—

Ken Lubin was going home.

PHYSALIA

Zeus

Sou-hon Perreault was closing on a riot when they shut her down.

It was Amitav, of course. She knew that the moment she saw the location of the disturbance: a Calvin cycler in trouble at Grenville Point, less than two klicks from his last known position. She jumped into the nearest botfly and rode it down.

Somehow the refs had uprooted a lightstand and used it as a battering ram; the cycler had been skewered through the heart. A dozen brands of amino goop oozed viscously from the wound, a pussy mix of ochers and browns. Underweight refugees—some oozing blood from scabby sores—shouted and pushed against the front of the wounded machine, toppling it.

The larger crowd on all sides drew back, rudderless and confused, as powerless as ever.

"kholanA ApakA netra, behen chod!"

Amitav, climbing onto the fallen cycler. Perreault's botfly parsed phonemes, settled on *Hindi.*

"Open your eyes, sisterfuckers! Is it not bad enough you should eat their poison? Will you sit here with your hands up your asses while they send another wave to finish the job! Lenie Clarke wasn't enough for you, yes? She survived the center of the storm itself, she told you who the enemy was! She fights them while you sleep on the dirt! What will it take to wake you up?"

Amitav's disciples shouted ragged approval; the others milled and murmured among themselves. *Amitav,* Perreault thought, *you've crossed the line.*

The stickman glanced skyward and threw up one spindly arm, pointing at Perreault's descending botfly. "Look! They send *machines* to tell us what to do! They—"

Sudden darkness, silent and unrelieved.

She waited. After a few seconds, two lines of luminous text began blinking against the void:

CSIRA Containment Zone
(N'AmPac Biohazards Act, 2040)

She'd run into dark zones before, of course. Some 'fly she was riding would drop suddenly into shadow, floating serenely blind and deaf for fifty meters or twenty klicks. Then, safely out of insight's way, it would come back on-line.

But why cite the Biohazards Act over a trashed cycler?

Unless it isn't about the cycler ...

She linked into the next 'fly back in line: *CSIRA Containment Zone* flashed against unwelcome darkness. She relinked to one before that, and the one after, bouncing back and forth toward the edges of the blackout.

Eight-point-one-eight kilometers from end to end.

Now she was sighted and riding southbound, just beyond the northern perimeter. She topped out the whole spectrum, stared through a tangle of false-color infra and X and UV, poked into the fog with radar—

There—

Something in the sky. A brief image, fading almost immediately to black.

CSIRA Containment Zone ...

She backjumped again, set her defaults to repeat the maneuver whenever visual went down. She saw it again, and again: a great curtain, darkness. A billowing wall descending to earth, darkness. An inflatable barrier, swelling smoothly across the width of the Strip.

Darkness. *CSIRA Containment Z—*

She considered.

They'd cut off eight kilometers of Strip, a segment nearly nine hundred meters wide. It would take several dampers to cover that much area, assuming they were squelching tight-beam as well as broadband. The dampers would probably be mounted on the wall itself.

Chances were their coverage wouldn't extend out to sea very far.

A northbound 'fly had just emerged from eclipse. Per-reault mounted it and rode west off the path, keeping low. Surf pounded close beneath; then she was past the breakers and cruising over a low oily swell. She turned south.

There was traffic out here after all. An assault chopper with ambiguous markings hovered threateningly over a pair of retreating pleasure boats, a damper dome disfiguring its hull like a tumor. A smattering of botflies flitted closer to shore, of a different sort than Sou-Hon Perreault rode. None of them took any notice of her; or if they did, they credited her 'fly with higher pedigree than it deserved.

She was eight hundred meters offshore, still skimming the swells. Due west of Amitav's latest insurrection. Perreault slowed her mount and came about, heading inland.

Breakers in the distance, a smear of muddy sand, a boil of motion farther up the shore. She cut the throttle and hov-ered, her senses still intact.

Mag: motion resolved into melee.

Everyone was *running*. Perreault had never seen such a high level of activity on the Strip before. There was no net direction to the movement, no exodus. Nowhere, apparently, to go. Some of the Strippers were splashing into the surf; the botflies she'd seen earlier were forcing them back. Most were just going back and forth.

Something in the clouds was stabbing the mob with flashes of green light.

She panned up, almost missing it: a fast-moving botfly disappearing to the south. And now her own 'fly was bleat-ing, something coming up behind, big and low-flying and stealthed—

Of course it's stealthed, or radar would have caught it sooner—
—and *way* too close to escape from now.

She spun the 'fly around and saw it coming not two hundred meters out: a lifter headed for shore like a levitating whale. Rows of portholes lined its belly, strange brassy things from another age, soft orange gaslight flickering behind the glass. She squinted in her headset, tried to dispel the Victorian image. Sudden electricity crackled from a knob on the airship's hull; blinding light flared and died in Perreault's eyes. Alphanumerics persisted briefly in the darkness, the last gibbering cough of the 'fly's navigational system. Then nothing but a flashing epitaph:

Link Down. Link Down. Link Down.

She barely noticed. She didn't try to reconnect—by now the 'fly was on its way to the bottom. She didn't even jump to another channel. She was too busy thinking about what she'd seen. She was too busy imagining what she hadn't.

Not portholes after all. The wide-bore muzzles of industrial flamethrowers. Their pilot lights had flickered like hot tongues.

Jiminy Cricket

Variations on a theme:

The Oregon Strip, shrouded in fog. Evening's light was a diffuse and steely gray, not even a bright smudge on the horizon to suggest a sun. Refugees accreted around the feeding stations, warding off the dampness by the soft orange glow of portable space heaters. Their apparent humanity faded with distance; the fog reduced them to silhouettes, to gray shadows, to vague hints of endless convection. Motion that went nowhere. They were silent and resigned.

Achilles Desjardins saw it all through the telemetry feeds.

He saw what happened next, too. A soft whine, louder than the usual botflies, and higher up. Turbulence in the human sea beneath it; faces suddenly upturned, trying to squeeze signal from gray chaos. Rumors exchanged: *This happened before, three days south. This was how it began. We never heard from them again* ... Murmurs of apprehension; some of the human particles began to jostle, some to run.

Fear enough, finally, to break through the chemical placidity that had domesticated them for so long.

Not that it did any good. The zone had already been walled off. No good panicking now, no avenue for sensible flight reflexes. They'd only been alerted a few seconds ago, and already it was nearly over.

Lancing down through the clouds, a precise turquoise stutter of laser light hemstitched its way down a transect ten kilometers long. Tiny aliquots of sand and flesh incinerated where it touched. Droplets in the saturated air caught the beams in transit and turned them visible to human eyes: threads of argon so brilliant and beautiful that even looking at them risked sheer perfect blindness. They were fast, too; the light show was over before the cries of pain had even begun.

The principle was simple: everything burns. In fact, everything burns with its own distinct spectrum, subtle interplays of boron and sodium and carbon luminescing on their own special wavelengths, a harmony of light unique to any object cast into flame. In theory, even the combustion of identical twins would generate different spectra, as long as they'd had different dietary preferences in life.

Present purposes, of course, didn't require nearly that much resolution.

Look here: a strategic patch of real estate. Is it enemy territory? Draw a line through it, but make sure your transect extends into safe land at both ends. Good. Now, sample along the whole path. Turn matter to energy. Read the flames. The ends of your transect are the baselines, the ground-truth zones; their light is the light of friendly soil. Subtract those wavelengths from whatever you read in between. Pour your numbers through the usual statistics to account for heterogeneities in the local environment.

Jovellanos had worked up a distance-spec mug shot of βehemoth from her sample slurries. There was one sure way to tell if any given transect came up clean against that benchmark: half an hour later, the space around it would not have been doused with halothane and burned to the bedrock.

The test was a little over 90 percent reliable. The Powers That Be said that was good enough.

Even Achilles Desjardins, master of the minimum response time, marveled at how much had changed in a couple of months.

Word was leaking, of course. Nothing consistent, and certainly nothing official. Quarantines and diebacks and crop failures had been old news for years. A day hardly went by without some bug or other making a comeback—tired old genes revitalized in a terrorist lab, or brought into new alliances by viral mediators with no respect for the reproductive isolation of species. You could hide a lot of new outbreaks against a background that muddled.

But the mix was changing. The twenty-first century had been a lush smorgasbord of calamities, epidemics and exotics and dust storms dogpiling onto humanity from all different directions. Now, though, one particular threat seemed to be growing quietly under all the others. Certain *types* of containment were happening more often. Fires burned along the west coast, unconnected by any official commonality; some were attributed to pest control, some to terrorism, some merely to N'Am's ongoing desiccation. But still: so many fires, along the coast? So many quarantines and purges that happened to run north–south along the Rockies? Very strange, very strange.

Some dark entropic monoculture was growing beneath the wider riot of usual breakdowns, invisible but for the wake of its passing. People were starting to notice.

Guilt Trip kept Desjardins's mouth shut for him, of course. He wasn't assigned to βehemoth anymore—he and Jovellanos had done their job, presented their results, and been sent back to field whatever random catastrophes the Router sent their way—but gut imperatives didn't change with job assignments. So at the end of his shift he'd retire to the welcoming bowels of Pickering's Pile and get pleasantly buzzed and make nice with the locals—he even let Gwen talk

him into trying real sex again, which even she admitted was
a disaster—and listened to rumors of impending apocalypse.

And while he sat and did nothing, the world began to fill
with black empty-eyed counterfeits.

It hadn't sunk in at first. The first time he'd met Gwen
she'd been dolled up like that; *rifter chic,* she'd called it. She'd
only been the first. The trend had really taken off the past
couple of months. Now it seemed like everyone and their
organcloner was getting into body stockings and photocollagen. K's mostly, but the number of posing r's was going up
as well. Desjardins had even seen a few people decked out in
real reflex copolymer. That stuff was almost *alive*. It changed
its own permeability to maintain optimum thermal and ionic
gradients, it healed when torn. It kind of *slithered* around you
when you put it on, wriggling into the snuggest fit, seams
and edges seeking each other out for bonding. It was as
though some pharm had crossed an amoeba with an oil slick.
He'd heard the stuff even bonded against *eyes*.

When he thought about it, he shuddered. He didn't think
about it often, though. The sight of each new poseur twisted
knives much keener than mere revulsion.

Six of them died, the knives whispered as they slid around
in his gut. *Maybe they didn't have to. Maybe it wasn't enough.
Either way, you know. Six of them died, and now thousands more,
and you played a part in that, Achilles my man. You don't know if
what you did was right or wrong, you don't even know what it was
you did exactly, but you were involved, oh yes. Some of that blood
is on your hands.*

It shouldn't have bothered him. He'd done his job as he
always had; Absolution was supposed to handle the aftershocks. And besides, he hadn't made any actual decisions of
life and death, had he? He'd been given a task to do, a statistical problem really. Number crunching. He'd done it, he'd
done it well, and now he was onto other things.

Just following orders, and what a shame about the Cree.

Except he wasn't following orders, not exactly. He
couldn't let it go. He kept βehemoth at the edge of his vision,
a little window down in one corner of tactical, open and run-

ning like a pixelated sore. He picked at it during the lulls
between other assignments; satcam enhances, Bayesian prob-
ability contours, subtle blights and blatant fires dotting the
west coast.

Moving east, now.

It moved sporadically, feinting, disappearing, resurfacing
in entirely unexpected places. One massive outbreak south of
Mendocino died of natural causes overnight. A tiny strong-
hold blossomed near South Bend and refused to vanish even
after the Lasers of the Inquisition came calling. Crops had
begun mysteriously failing in the northwest; fifty-odd hectares of Olympic Park forest had been burned to control a
sudden bark-beetle infestation. Malnutrition was inexplica-
bly on the rise in some well-fed corner of Oregon state.
Something new was racking up kills along the coast, and was
proving almost impossible to pin down. It had almost as
many symptoms as victims; its diffuse pathology disappeared
against a background of diseases with clearer focus. Hardly
anyone seemed to notice.

βehemoth's signature was starting to appear in fields and
wetlands, farther inland: Agassiz. Centralia. Hope. Sometimes
it seemed to follow rivers, but upstream. Sometimes it moved
against the wind. Sometimes the only thing that made any
sense was that someone was carrying it around. A vector.
Maybe more than one.

He passed that insight onto Rowan's address. She didn't
answer. Doubtless she knew already. And so Achilles Desjardins went from day to day, a tornado here, a red tide there,
a tribal massacre some other place—everywhere the need for
his own polymorphic bag of tricks. No time to dwell on past
accomplishments. No time to dwell on that shape coming up
from underneath, glimpsed on the fly between other crises.
Never mind, never mind; they know what they're doing,
these people that drank your blood and changed it and enslaved you to the good of all mankind. They know what
they're doing.

And everywhere, people dressed for the deepest ocean
stood around at bus stops and drink'n'drugs, like Banquo's

fucking ghost cloned a thousand times over. They exchanged
eyeless glances and chuckles and spewed the usual desperate
inanities. And spoke in overloud casual voices to drown out
the strange frightening sounds drifting up from the basement.

Footprints

Even dead, Ken Lubin had access to more resources than 99
percent of the living.

It made perfect sense, considering his profession. Iden-
tities are such transient things after all; height, weight, eth-
noskeleton could all be changed by subtle tweaks of the
body's endocrine system. Eyeprints, voiceprints, finger-
prints—developmental accidents, perhaps unique at birth
but hardly immutable. Even DNA could be fudged if you
weighed it down with enough pseudocodons. It was too easy
for one person to imitate another, and too necessary to be
able to *change* without losing access to vital resources. Immutable identity wasn't just useless to Ken Lubin. It was potentially life-threatening.

For all he knew—he never bothered to keep track of such
things—he'd never officially existed in the first place.

It didn't matter who he was anyway. Would you let a
man through the door just because he'd had his pupils
scanned the week before? Anything could have happened
since. Maybe he's been deconstructed and turned. Maybe he'd
rather betray you than see his hostaged children executed.
Maybe he's found Allah.

For that matter, why keep a stranger at bay? Is someone
an enemy just because his eyeprints *aren't* on record?

It didn't matter whether Ken Lubin was who he claimed
to be. All that mattered was that his brain was spiked with
so much Guilt Trip that it would be physiologically impossible for him to bite the hand that dosed him.

It wasn't the usual Trip that ran through his veins. The
Community had a thousand different flavors of choice; one

for Venezuela, four or five for China, probably a couple of dozen for Québec. None of them trusted any motivator as mealymouthed as *the greater good*. Even those do-gooding 'lawbreakers weren't in service to *that*, no matter what their training brochures said. The *greater good* could mean anything; hell, it could even mean the *other* guys.

Ken Lubin was chemically dedicated to the welfare of certain N'AmPac interests that dealt in the generation of electrical power. Those interests had been of paramount importance ever since the Hydro War; they'd been fine-tuning the molecules for most of the twenty years since. The moment Lubin even *intended* to sell his services to the wrong bidders, he'd court a seizure that would make grand mal look like a nervous itch on a blind date. That was all the mechanical bloodhounds cared about when they sniffed his crotch. Not his name, or his clothes, or the accumulated heavy-metal essence of ocean that still clung to him after an extended shower in the local community center. Not any exaggerated rumors of his demise, or any unexplained return from the grave.

All they cared about was that he was like them; loyal, obedient, trustworthy.

They opened doors for him. They gave him funds, and access to medbooths five years ahead of anything available on the street. They gave him back his hearing and, surprisingly, a clean bill of health. They pointed him to a vacant furnished room, waiting like a convenient cocoon to any on the home team who might need a place to crash on short notice.

Above all, they let him into Haven.

There were certain things they wouldn't do for *anybody*. A hardline to his cocoon was out of the question, for instance. Lubin had to go on-site for his research; an anonymous row of data booths embedded in the fourteenth floor of the Ridley Complex, off-limits to all but those of tailored conscience. About half the booths were occupied at any given time, dark diffuse shapes twitching behind frosted glass like larvae nes-

tled in honeycomb. Occasionally two people would emerge
into the hallway at the same time, pass each other without a
word or a glance. There was no need for reassuring pleas-
antries here; everyone was on the same side.

Inside the booth, headset curled snugly around jaw and
eyes and ears, Kenneth Lubin logged into Haven and mumbled subvocal questions about Channer Vent. His headset
read the buzz of his larynx—a bit of adjustment required, to
compensate for the vocoder implanted in his throat—and
sent off an agent to hunt for answers. He asked to see a list
of references containing the phrase *Beebe Station*, and was instantly indulged. He cross-referenced those results against
lists of dangerous microbes from the deep sea.

No significant pathogens registered from Channer.

Hmm.

It didn't prove anything, of course. There were lots of
nasty facts that didn't make it into Haven. There were other
avenues of approach, though.

Assume, for example, that the vent had been nuked to
contain some risk. Beebe would never have gone on-line if
that risk had been known beforehand; there had been some
period, therefore, when the threat was spreading beneath
anyone's radar. And once the threat *had* been discovered, all
those loose ends would have to be tied up in hindsight...

The building contractors. Left Coast Shipyards. They
wouldn't use nukes though, not above ground.

Fire, probably.

He summoned forth a frequency plot of fires over time,
within a five-kilometer radius of marine construction and
contracting facilities along the N'AmPac coast. Haven showed
him a a curious spike about three months after Beebe had
gone on-line: Urchin Shipyards, Hanson Fabrication, and
Showell Marine's SanFran complex had all hosted infernos
within the space of a week. A dozen other facilities had been
hit by various acts of arson in the two weeks following, not
to mention a couple of places that had burned off large
chunks of their property as part of "ongoing renewal programs."

Lubin loosened the scale and ran the request again: all
large fires over time, anywhere along the N'AmPac coastline.

The map lit up.

Oh my, he thought.

Something had them scared to death. And it had all started
down at Beebe.

No Channer pathogens in the metabase, no nasty microscopic predators that ate your body from the inside out. But
macroscopic predators: Channer'd had those in abundance. *Vi-
perfish and anglerfish and seadragons, oh my.* Black toothy monsters, some studded with bioluminescent running lights,
some blind as mud, some that changed sex on a whim, still
others whose flesh bristled with the embedded bodies of parasitic mates. Nasty, hideous things. They were everywhere in
the ocean's middle depths, and they'd have been scary indeed
if they'd ever grown to more than a few centimeters in
length.

At Channer, they had. Something had drawn those little
nightmares down deeper than they went anywhere else,
turned them into ravenous giants big as people. You didn't
go outside Beebe without a gas billy strapped to your leg;
you rarely came back in without having used it.

Something at Channer had created monsters. Lubin sent
a message into Haven asking what it was.

Haven wasn't exactly sure. But there was a tech report in
the gray lit that took a guess: some kind of endosymbiotic
infection that increased growth energy. The phrase *infectious
neomitochondria* popped up in the discussion.

The authors of the report—a couple of eggs out of Rand/
Washington University—suggested that some microbe at
Channer could infect cells symbiotically, providing extra
growth energy to the host cell in exchange for room and
board. Whatever the bug was, they claimed it would have
some fairly obvious characteristics. Small enough to fit inside
a eukaryotic cell, high assimilation efficiency for inorganic
sulfur, that sort of thing.

An infection that caused giantism in fish. Again, hmmm.

One of the first things Lubin had done after coming ashore had been to check himself out for pathogens. He'd tested clean. But this Channer thing was new, and strictly speaking, not even a disease. It might not show up on the standard slate.

Lubin's credit was good. More extensive blood work wouldn't be an issue.

There were other issues, though. One of them dawned gradually as he explored, betrayed itself in the way Haven answered his questions. Sometimes the metabase thought for a moment or two before telling him what he wanted to know. That was normal. But other times—other times, it spat an answer back almost before he'd asked the question. Almost as though it had already been thinking along those very lines, as though it didn't have to go and look up the relevant facts.

Maybe, Lubin reflected, that was exactly it.

Haven's agents were not nearly so pressed for resources as the engines that combed Maelstrom; they could afford to cache recent searches. Very few lines of inquiry were utterly unique. If someone asked about the price of a Parkinson's fix today, chances were someone else would want to know something similar tomorrow. Haven's search engines held onto their executive summaries, the better to speed responses to related inquiries. *Ask and it shall be given*:

—After a mean of 2.3 seconds when answering questions about giantism in deep-water fish;

—after a mean of 3 seconds when talking about benthic sulfur-reducing microbes;

—about a second for queries containing the phrase *Channer Vent*;

—0.5 seconds for searches combining *sulfur-reducing microbes* with *fire*.

Fire. Benthic sulfur-reducing microbes. An odd combination of terms. What relevance could *fire* have to life on the bottom of the ocean?

He added a third concept, almost on a whim: *shipyard*.

0.1 seconds.

Well.

He was following in someone's footsteps. Someone had been in Haven before him, asking the same questions, making the same connections. Searching for answers, or looking for loose ends?

Ken Lubin resolved to find out.

An Archetype of Dislocation

There had been a time when Sou-Hon Perreault had truly loved her husband. Martin had projected a serenity in those days, a gentle unwillingness to judge that made her feel safe. He'd been unfailingly supportive when she needed it (hardly ever, before the breakdown); he'd never been afraid to look at both sides of an issue. For love, he could balance on the edge of any fence.

Even now, he'd forever hold her and whisper inane reassurances. Things couldn't be that bad, he'd say. Quarantines and dark zones always popped up here and there, not without good reason. Sometimes restrictions were necessary for the good of everyone, she knew *that*—and besides, he had it on good authority that there were safeguards even on those who made the Big Decisions. As if he were privy to some grand secret, as if Maelstrom weren't rotten with threads and rumors about the corpses and their mind-controlling drugs.

Her caring, supportive husband. Sitting across the table, his face overflowed with loving concern. She hated the sight of him.

"You should eat," he said. He put a forkful of mashed *Spirulina* into his mouth and chewed, demonstrating.

"Should I?"

"You're losing weight," Martin told her. "I know you're upset—goodness, you've got every reason to be—but starving yourself won't make you feel any better."

"That's your solution to the world's problems? Stuff your face so we'll all feel better?"

"Sou—"

"That's right, Marty. Just eat a bit more, and everything'll be just grand. Suck up all those cheery threads from N'AmWire and maybe they'll lull you right into forgetting about Crys…"

It was a low blow—Martin's sister lived in Corvallis, which had not only been quarantined since the Big One but had dropped completely off-line for the better part of a month. The official story involved unfortunate long-term aftershocks that kept taking out the land lines; N'AmWire pictures showed the usual collage of citizens, shaken but not stirred, gamely withstanding temporary isolation. Martin hadn't been able to get through to Crys for three weeks.

Sou-Hon's words should have stung him—even provoked him to anger—but he only sat there looking helpless, his hands spread. "Sou, you've been through so much these past few months, of *course* things look really grim. But I honestly think you're putting way too much weight on a bunch of rumors. Riots, and firestorms, and—I mean, half those postings don't even show up with address headers anymore, you can't trust *anything* that comes out of Maelstrom these days—"

"You'd rather trust N'AmWire? They don't spit out a word without some corpse chewing it for them first!"

"But what do you *know*, Sou? What have you actually seen with your own eyes? By your own admission you just got a glimpse of one big ship moving inland, and you didn't even see it *do* anything—"

"Because it shot the 'fly right out from under me!"

"And you weren't supposed to be there in the first place, you idiot! You're lucky they didn't track you down and cancel your contract on the spot!"

He fell silent. The burble of the aquarium in the next room suddenly seemed very loud.

He was backpedaling the next instant: "Oh Sou, I'm *sorry*. I didn't mean to…"

"Doesn't matter." Sou-Hon shook her head, waving off the overture. "We're done here anyway."

"Sou…"

She stood up from the table. "You could do with a bit of a diet yourself, hubby. Lose some weight, clear your mind. It might even make you wonder what they're putting in that so-called *food* you keep trying to force down my throat."

"Oh, *Sou.* Surely you're not saying—"

She went into her office and closed the door.

I want to do something!

She leaned back against the door and closed her eyes. Martin, safely excluded, made soft shuffling noises on the other side and faded away.

I've been a voyeur my whole fucking life! All I do is watch! *Everything's falling apart and now they're bringing in their big guns and laying waste and I'm part of it and there's nothing I can do...*

She summoned a curse for the faulty derm she'd worn into Hongcouver. The epithet was an empty and colorless thing; even now, she couldn't truly regret having been slapped awake. She could only rage at the things she'd seen when her eyes had opened.

And Martin's trying so hard to be a comfort, he's so earnest and he probably believes that things really will get better if I go back to being a haploid sheep like him...

She clenched her fists, savored the pain of fingernails in the flesh of her palms. *Lenie Clarke's no sheep,* she thought.

Clarke had long since left the Strip, for all Amitav's efforts to keep her spirit alive. But she was still out there, somewhere. She had to be. How else to explain the subtle proliferation of black uniforms and empty eyes in the world? Perreault didn't get out much but the signs were there, even the predigested pap that N'AmWire served up. Dark shapes on street corners. Eyes without pupils, staring from the crowds that always gathered in the background of newsworthy events.

That was nothing new, of course. N'AmPac's divers had been all over the news, almost a year before; first lauded as saviors of the new economy, fashionable icons of cutting-

edge reserve. Then pitied and feared, once the rumors of
abuse and psychopathy reached some threshold of public
awareness. Then inevitably, forgotten.

Just an old fad. Rifter chic had already had its day. So
why this sudden new life, breathed into some dusty blip on
the rearview mirror? Why the fine mycelium of innuendo
threading its way through Maelstrom, whispers about someone risen from the deep sea, pregnant with apocalypse? Why
the fragmentary rumors, their address headers corrupted or
missing, of people taking *sides?*

Perreault opened her eyes. Her headset rested on its peg,
just in front of her desk. An LED blinked on its side: *message
waiting.*

Someone wanting to trade shifts, maybe. Some supervisor
wanting to pay her overtime to keep looking the other way.

Maybe another trashed cycler, she thought hopefully. Probably not, though. The Strip had been a much quieter place
since Amitav's corner of it had been—excised . . .

She took a deep breath, one step forward, sat. She slipped
on the headset:

   Souhon/Amitav (LNU)

   *lucked into this avenging angel. No shit. Lenie Clarke, her
name was.*

   Oh my God.
The text had been overlaid directly onto the tactical map
for the Strip. Sou-Hon forced herself to sit quietly, and shoveled dirt back into the tiny pit opening in her stomach.

You're back. Whoever you are.

What do you want?

She hadn't made any secret of her interest in Amitav or
Lenie Clarke. There'd been no need, at first; both had been
legitimate topics of professional conversation, albeit apparently uninteresting ones to other 'flyers. But she'd kept quiet
since Amitav had fallen into eclipse. Just barely. A big part
of her had wanted to scream that atrocity into Maelstrom at

full voice; afraid of repercussions, she'd settled for screaming at Martin, and hoped that whatever had shot down her botfly hadn't bothered tracking it to source.

This wasn't CSIRA or the GA, though. This almost looked like a glitch of some kind.

Another line of text appeared beneath the first two:

She's like some kinda amphibian, one of those rifter cyborgs.

No obvious channel to link in to, no icon to tap. Behind the text, the familiar long chain of red pinpoints patrolled the Pacific coastline, showing no hint of the places where they went into coma.

Les beus are looking for her, but I bet fifty QueBucks they don't even know what she looks like under all that rifter gear. Souhon or Amitav (LNU)?

Perhaps they'd hacked into her headset mic as well. "I'm—Sou-Hon. Hyphenated."

Sou-Hon.

"Yes."

You know Lenie Clarke.

"I—saw her, once."

Good enough.

An invisible fist closed around Sou-Hon Perreault and threw her halfway around the world.

Pacific coastlines and tactical overlays, gone in an instant; a cul-de-sac of brick and machinery suddenly in their place.

Gusts of sleet, slashing an atmosphere colder than the Strip
had ever seen. It rattled off glass and metal to either side.
The stylized grayhounds etched into those surfaces didn't
stir.

Not all the flesh had disappeared, Perreault saw. A
woman stood directly ahead, her back to a brick wall the color
of raw meat. The buses on either side were plugged into sockets extending from that wall, cutting off lateral escape. If
there was any way out it was straight ahead, through the
center of Perreault's perceptual sphere. But that sphere
showed a target framed within luminous crosshairs. Unfamiliar icons flashed to each side, options like ARM and STUN
and LTHL.

Perreault was riding some kind of arsenal, and she was
aiming it right at Lenie Clarke.

The rifter had gone native. Civilian clothes covered the
body, a visor hid that glacial stare, and Perreault would never
have recognized her if she'd had to rely on merely human
eyes. But botflies looked out across a wider spectrum. This
one saw a garish and distracting place, emissions bleeding
from a dozen EM sources—but Clarke was close range and
line of sight, and there was no wiring in the wall directly
behind her. Against that relative shadow, her thorax flickered
like a riot of dim fireflies.

"I'm not going to hurt you," Perreault said. Weapons
icons flashed accusingly at the corner of her eye; she found
a dimmer one that whispered DSRM, and hit it. The arsenal
stood down.

Clarke didn't move, didn't speak.

"I'm not—my name's Sou-Hon. I'm not with the police,
I'm—I think—" She spared a glance at GPS: Calgary. The
Glenmore intercity shuttle nexus.

Something had just thrown her thirteen hundred kilometers to the northeast.

"I was sent," she finished. "I don't know, I think—to
help..." She heard the absurdity in every word.

"Help." A flat voice, betraying nothing.

"Hang on a moment..." Perreault lifted the 'fly above the

Greyhounds, did a quick 360. She was floating over a docking
bay where buses slept and suckled in rows. The main terminal loomed forty meters away, elevated loading platforms
extending from its sides. Two buses were presently onload-
ing; the animated grayhounds on their sides raced nowhere,
as if running on invisible treadmills.

And there, by the decontamination stalls: a small seething
knot of confusion. An aftermath. Perreault accessed the 'fly's
black box, quick-scanned the previous few minutes. Suddenly,
in comical fast-forward, she was closing on a younger disturbance. Even at this stage the show had been winding
down, people turning away. But there was Lenie Clarke, holding an ebony shockprod. There was a man with his arms
raised against her, a wide-eyed little girl hiding behind his
legs.

Perreault slowed the flow. The man took a step back in
realtime.

"Lady, I've never even *seen* you before..."

Clarke stepped forward, but some former aggression was
draining from her stance. Uncertainty took its place. "I—I
thought you—"

"Seriously, lady. You are one fucked-up little chimera..."

"You all right, kid?" The wand in one hand wavered. The
other hand extended, tentatively. "I didn't meant to sc—"

"Go away!" the child howled.

The father glanced up, distracted by overhead motion.
"You want to pick a fight?" he snarled at the mermaid. "Pick
on *that!*"—pointing straight at the approaching 'fly.

She had run. The drone had followed, armed and hungry.

And now—somehow—Sou-Hon Perreault had been
placed in possession.

Perreault dropped back down between the buses. "You're
safe for the moment. You—"

The cul-de-sac was empty.

She 180ed the 'fly; something flickered out of sight
around a corner.

"Wait! You don't understand—"

Perreault cranked the throttle. For a moment nothing

happened. Then her whole perceptual field *lurched*, right down to the semicircular canals. A readout flickered upper right, then held steady: RECONNECT.

Weapons icons bloomed like pulsing tumors. Somewhere in the distant realm of her own flesh, Perreault hammered frantic arpeggios against remote controls. Nothing worked.

"Run!" she cried as the link went down.

But she was back in Montana, and her voice didn't carry.

400 Megabytes: Punctuated Equilibrium

400Megs hovers on a knife-edge of complacency.

For thousands of generations it has known the secret of success in Maelstrom. Predators have pursued it with powerful legs and gnashing teeth; competitors have raced it to each new refuge, each new patch of forage; diseases have striven to eat it from the inside. And yet 128 begat 142, and 142 begat 137 (a bit of pruning there, getting rid of redundant code), and 137 begat 150, and so on, and so on, up unto the present crisis-laden instant. All because of a very special secret encoded in the genes:

You want to get around fast in Maelstrom, the name you drop is *Lenie Clarke*.

400 doesn't know why this should be. That's not really the point. What it *does* know is, that particular string of characters gets you in *anywhere*. You can leap from node to node as though disinfectants and firewalls and shark repellants did not exist. You can pass undamaged through the vicious fleshy meatgrinder that is a head cheese, a passage guaranteed to reduce you to instant static without the protective amulet of *Lenie Clarke* in your pocket. Even *Haven*—mythic, inaccessible Haven, a vast smorgasbord virtually untouched by the appetites of the living—may someday be within reach.

Problem is, too many others are getting into the act.

It's not an uncommon development in Maelstrom; evolution happens so quickly, in so many different directions, that you can't go half a second without a bunch of wannabes rediscovering the wheel you thought you had all to your-self. By now the free rides to open fields are growing crowded. Binary beasts of burden each labor under the weight of dozens of hitchhikers, each grabbing up its own little aliquot of memory, each slowing the procession a tiny bit farther. Now the carrier files themselves are attracting attention—from checksum monitors who just know in their gut that no casual e-mail should weigh in at a hundred gigs, to sharks hungry for prey grown almost too fat to move.

Want to spread your seed through Maelstrom? Hitch your wagon to *Lenie Clarke*. Want to be shark food? Do the same thing.

It's not everybody's problem, though. *Some* creatures leap around as fast as they ever did. Faster, even. Something they know, maybe. Or someone. 400Megs has never been able to figure out the secret.

It's about to, though.

400Megs is currently inbreeding with a middling sib whose lineage only diverged a few hundred generations ago. Almost all the genes are the same, which doesn't promote a lot of diversity but at least reinforces the tried-and-true. Both parties have a few dozen copies of *Lenie Clarke*, for in-stance, which they exchange with mindless redundancy.

But no gene is an island, even in Maelstrom. There's no such thing as an independent locus. Each travels linked to others, little constellations of related traits, junk code, hap-penstance association. And as 400Megs is about to find out, it isn't just *Lenie Clarke* that matters. It's also the company she keeps.

All the bits are lining up to be counted. Replication sub-routines march down the line like messenger RNA, ready to cut and paste. Chance shuffles the cards, orgasm squirts them hence, and 400Megs injects *Lenie Clarke* into its cousin. Strings like *vampire* and *Beebe* and *βehemoth* go along for the ride.

And in return, following the usual hermaphrodite credo of tit for tat, 400Megs gets *Lenie Clarke* with a whole different circle of friends. Like *doomsday*. Like *meltdown*. Like *bestserved-cold*.

By all appearances, just another unremarkable fuck. But afterward, things start to change for 400Megs.

Suddenly its replication rate is going through the roof. And where before its progeny languished and withered in backwater caches, now Maelstrom itself scoops them up and copies them a thousand times over. One fine cycle a N'AmPac security sieve finds several such prodgies drifting north off the coast of the GA. Recognizing them as high-priority communications, it shunts them directly to the nearest smart gel. The gel scans the relevant embedded bits and sends copies into Haven for secure storage.

All of a sudden, the most powerful forces in Maelstrom want to give members of The 400 Club anything they want. The Club doesn't question their good fortune; they merely exploit it.

They are no longer 400Megs, hitchhiker.

What they are is John the fucking Baptist.

Microstar

He'd been out of circulation too long. He was losing his edge. How else to explain an ambush at the hands of three glassy-eyed children on the back streets of Santa Cruz?

Of course, Lubin had had a lot on his mind. He was coming to terms with some very disturbing test results, for one thing. He'd been pursuing them for days, rejecting each new clean bill of health, running increasingly specific tests for increasingly implausible maladies—and now, finally, there it was. Something in his blood that neither nature nor N'AmPac had put there.

Something strangely *backward*.

More than sufficient to distract any normal man, perhaps. No excuse for someone who'd once transplanted a micronuke from his own gut to the heart of the Trois-Rivières switching station, without benefit of anesthesia. No excuse for Ken Lubin.

It was inexcusable. His assailants barely even qualified as punks; ranging in age from perhaps sixteen to twenty, pumped on some sort of neurotrope, evidently convinced that their transderm steroids and corneal caps and shock-prods made them invulnerable. Sometime during Lubin's Pacific tour, the rifter template had become fashionable among drybacks. It was probably the eyes more than anything. Back on the seabed, eyecaps had hidden a multitude of sins, kept fear and weakness and hatred safely concealed behind masks of blank indifference. Down there the caps had provided cover, imposed enough protective distance for weak people to become strong, given time.

Up here, though, they only seemed to make weak people stupid.

They wanted money, or something. He wasn't really paying attention. He didn't even bother warning them off. They didn't seem in the mood to listen.

Five seconds later they weren't in the mood to do anything but run. Lubin—having foreseen this on some level long since relegated to subconsciousness—had deprived them of the use of their legs. He felt a token, distracted reluctance at the necessary next step; they had, after all, seen more of his abilities than good security would dictate. It had been his own damn fault—if he hadn't been so careless, he'd have avoided the situation altogether—but the damage was done. Loose ends were fraying, and had to be cut.

There were no witnesses. The children had chosen wisely in that regard at least. There were no screams, only quiet gasps and the soft pop of dislocating vertebrae. No ineffective pleas for mercy. Only one of them even *tried* to speak, perhaps emboldened by the realization that somehow—incredibly, in the space of barely a minute—she had reached the point of having nothing left to lose.

"*Mange de la marde, enculé,*" she croaked as Lubin reached down. "Who the fuck died and made *you* Lenie Clarke?"

Lubin blinked. "What?"

The child spat blood in his face and stared defiantly back with featureless white eyes.

Well, Lubin thought, *maybe there would've been hope for you after all.* And twisted.

It was a bit disturbing, of course. He'd had no idea that Lenie Clarke was famous.

He asked the matchmakers for references to *Lenie Clarke.* Maelstrom hiccoughed and advised him to narrow his search criteria: there were over fifty million hits.

He started exploring.

Lenie Clarke was an anarchist. Lenie Clarke was a liberator. Lenie Clarke was a fashion symbol. Lenie Clarke was an avenging angel, resurrected from the ocean depths to tear down the system that had abused and victimized her. Lenie Clarke had followers; mostly in N'AmPac so far, but the word was spreading. Hordes of disaffected, powerless people had found someone to relate to, a fellow victim with impervious eyes who had learned to fight back. Against what, exactly, there was no consensus. With whose army, not a whisper. Lenie Clarke was a mermaid. Lenie Clarke was a myth.

Lenie Clarke is dead, Lubin reminded himself. None of the references he could find would confirm that fact.

Perhaps she'd made it after all. The GA had promised a shuttle to evacuate Beebe. Lubin had assumed—along with everyone else—that they'd been lying. Clarke had been the only one to stay behind and find out.

Maybe all *of them made it. Maybe something happened, after I got separated. . . .*

He entered separate queries: Alice Nakata, Michael Brander—Judy Caraco, just to be thorough. Maelstrom knew of many by those names, but none seemed to have the cachet of Lenie Clarke. He fed the same list through Haven; the results were smoother, the data much higher in quality, but the bottom line remained unchanged.

Just Lenie Clarke. Something with that name was infecting the world.

"Lenie Clarke is alive," said a voice in his ear.

He recognized it: one of the generic disembodied match-makers that came out of Haven in answer to user questions. Lubin glanced across his display, puzzled. He hadn't entered any queries.

"It is almost certain," the voice continued, distant and inflectionless. Almost as though it were talking to itself. "Lenie Clarke lives. Temperature and salinity are well within acceptable ranges."

It paused.

"You are Kenneth Lubin. You are alive as well."

He disconnected.

Anonymity. That was the whole point of the exercise.

Lubin knew the specs on Ridley, and on similar facilities distributed invisibly throughout the world. They didn't scan eyes or faces. They only cared that entrants could do no harm. Everyone was equal within the frosted glass tubes of the fourteenth floor. Everyone was no one. Yet someone in Haven had called him by name.

He left Santa Cruz.

There was another secure gateway at the Packard Tower, in Monterey. This time Lubin wasn't taking any chances: he linked to his terminal through three separate watches con-nected in series, each scrambled on a different seed. He re-started a search on Lenie Clarke, carefully following different query trees than he had the first time.

"Lenie Clarke is on the move," a far-off voice mused.

Lubin started a trace.

"Kenneth Lubin has been sighted in Sevastopol," the voice remarked. "Recent reports have also placed it in Whitehorse and Philadelphia sometime within the past eighty-four hours. Lenie and Lubin are on the comeback trail. Are you a fan of alliteration?"

This is very strange, he thought.

"We looking out for Kenny and Lenie," the voice contin-ued. "We intend on translocating and disseminating both parties into novel environments with acceptable salinity range varies directly with temperature, within the environments considered. Do you relate to rhyme?"

It's a neural net, he realized. *A Turing app. Maybe a gel.* Whatever was talking to him, it wasn't *programmed*: it had learned to speak through trial and error, had worked out its own rules of grammar and syntax. Lubin had seen such devices—or organisms, or whatever they were—demonstrated. They picked up the rules easily enough, but they always seemed to throw in a few stylistic quirks of their own. It was hard to track down exactly how that happened. The logic *evolved*, synapse by synapse. It was opaque to conventional analysis.

"No," he said, experimentally. "For one, I don't relate to rhyme. Although that's not true all the time."

A brief silence. Then: "Excellent. I would've paid, you know?"

"Mediocre at best. What are you?"

"I am telling you about Lenie and Kenny. You don't want to fuck with them, friend. You wanna know what side you're on, right?"

"Tell me, then."

Nothing.

"Hello?"

Nothing. To make things worse, his trace failed—return address blocked at source.

He waited for a good five minutes in case the voice started talking again. It didn't. Lubin disconnected from his terminal, logged in on a different one farther along the row. This time he left *Lenie Clarke* and *Ken Lubin* strictly alone. Instead he stored the results of his worrisome blood tests in an open file, tagged to certain keywords that would hopefully attract attention from the right sources. Someone out there was paralleling his investigation; it was time to lure them in.

He logged off, distracted by an obvious and uncomfortable coincidence:

A smart gel had been running the nuke that vaporized Beebe Station.

Matchmaker

Prions:		OK
Viruses:	Adeno	OK
	Arbo	OK
	Arena	OK
	Filo	ben
	Morbilli	chron/asymp
	Orbi	OK
	Paramy	chron/asymp
	Parvo	OK
	Picorna	OK
	Hanta	resid
	Retro	resid
	Rota	light
Bacteria:	Bacillus	heavy/norm
	Coccus	norm
	Myco/Spiro	STD mod
	Chlam	OK
	Fungi	not crit
	Protozoa	not crit
	Nematode	OK
	Platyhelminth	OK
	Cestode	OK
	Arthropod	OK

Cleared for Travel.

"Are you sure? No—no ergots, or psychoactives?"

Cleared for travel. Please proceed to check-in.

"Are you equipped for NMR?"

This booth is designed to scan for communicable parasites and diseases. You may visit a commercial medbooth if you wish to be tested for other disorders.

"Where's the nearest commercial medbooth, then?"

Please don't leave me.

"I—what?"

Stay, Lenie. We can work it out.

Besides. There's someone you should meet.

The screen went dark. The bead in her ear emitted a tiny belch of static.

"It's me," said a sudden voice. "Sou-Hon. From the bus station."

She grabbed her visor and fled into the tame green jungle of Concourse D. Startled pedestrian eyes, barely noticed, met her own. She slid the visor onto her face, not slowing.

"You don't understand." The voice was a small pleading thing in her ear. "I'm on your side. I'm—"

Glass doors, leading outside. Clarke pushed through. Sudden icy wind reduced global warming to a weak abstraction. The concourse arced around from behind her like a horseshoe-shaped canyon.

"I'm here to *help*—"

Clarke tapped her watch twice in succession. "Command mode," the device replied.

"Off," she told it.

"*Amitav's de*—"

"Off," the watch acknowledged, and fell instantly asleep. She was alone.

The sidewalk was empty. Light spilled from the warren of habitrail tubes that shielded McCall's patrons from winter. The whine of distant turbines drifted down from the rooftops.

Two taps. "On."

A soft fuzz of static from the earpiece, although her watch was well within its operational two-meter radius.

"Are you there?" she said.

"Yes."

"What about Amitav?"

"Just before it—I mean—" The voice caught on itself. "They just *burned* everything. Everyone. He must have been..."

A passing gust of wind snapped at her face. The mermaid took a bitterly cold breath.

"I'm sorry," the stranger whispered in her head.

Clarke turned and went back inside.

Heat Death

It was an impoverished display, sparse informatics against a dark background: lats and longs, a tiny GPS overlay centered on *Calgary International Airport*, a *no-visual* icon blinking the obvious at two-second intervals.

"How do you know?" breathed a disembodied voice in Perreault's ear.

"I saw it. The start of it, anyway." Hard-edged airport ambience echoed in the background. "I'm sorry."

"It was his own fault," Clarke said after a moment. "He made too much noise. He was just—asking for it..."

"I don't think that was it," Perreault said. "They slagged eight whole kilometers."

"*What?*"

"Some kind of biohazard, I think. Amitav just got—caught in the sweep..."

"No." Words so soft they were almost static. "Can't be."

"I'm sorry."

No visual. No visual.

"Who are you?" Clarke asked at last.

"I ride botflies," Perreault said. "Mop-ups, mainly. I saw you when you came out of the ocean. I saw how you affected the people on the Strip, I saw you when you had one of those—visions—"

"Aren't you the faithful little stalker," Clarke said.

"That wasn't me," she continued after a while. "Back on the Strip. That was Amitav."

"He ran with it. You were the insp—"

"*It wasn't me.*"

"Okay. Fine."

No visual.

"Why are you following me?" Clarke said.

"Someone's—linked us up. And at the bus station, earlier."

"Who?"

"I don't know. Probably one of your friends."

Something between a cough and a laugh. "I don't think so."

Perreault took a breath. "You're—getting known, you know. People are noticing. Some of them must be protecting you."

"From *what*, exactly?"

"I don't know. Maybe from the people who started the quake."

"What do you know about that?" Clarke's voice almost *pounced* down the link.

"Millions died," Perreault said. "You know why. That makes you dangerous to all the wrong people."

"Is that what you think."

"It's one of the rumors. I don't know."

"Don't know much, do you?"

"I—"

"You don't know who I am. You don't know what I want or what I've d—you don't know who they are or what *they* want. You just sit there and let them *use* you."

"What do you want?"

"None of your fucking business."

Perreault shook her head. "I'm just trying to help, you know."

"Lady, I don't know if you even *exist*. For all I know that kid in South Bend is playing some kind of sick joke."

"*Something's* happening because of you. Something real. You can check the threads yourself if you don't believe me. You're some kind of catalyst. Whether you know it or not."

"And here you are, jumping in with no questions asked."

"I've got questions."

"No answers, then. I could be planting bombs. I could be spit-roasting babies. You don't know, but here you are with your tongue hanging out anyway."

"Listen," Perreault snapped, "whatever you're doing, it—"

—*Can't be any worse than the way things are already* . . .

She stopped, astonished at the thought, grateful that she'd kept it back. She felt an absurd certainty that seven hundred kilometers away, Lenie Clarke was smiling.

She tried again. "Look, I may not know what's going on but I know *something* is, and it revolves around you. And I bet that not everyone who knows that is on your side. Maybe you think I'm a headcase. Fine. But even *I* wouldn't risk going through airport security with the kind of profile your implants put out. I'd get out *now*, and I'd forget about flying anywhere for the foreseeable future. There are other ways to get around."

She waited. Tactical constellations glimmered about her.

"Okay," Clarke said at last. "Thanks for the tip. Here's one for you. Stop trying to help me. Help whoever's trying to stamp me out, if you can find them."

"For God's sake, *why?*"

"For your own sake, Suzie. For everyone you ever cared about. Amitav was—he didn't deserve what happened to him."

"No, of course he didn't."

"Eight kilometers, you said?"

"Yes. Burned to bedrock."

"I think that was just the beginning," Clarke said. "Off."

Around Sou-Hon Perreault, the stars went out.

Blind Date

Interested? Reply.

It was an odd sort of caption to find on a biochemical graphic: a lopsided crucifix of Carbons and Oxygens and Hydrogens—oh wait, there was a Sulfur over there, and a

Nitrogen on one side of the crossbeam, right about where they'd nail Jesus' wrist into place (of course, the way this thing was built, the savior's left arm would have to be about twice as long as his right). Methionine, the matchmaker said. An amino acid.

Only flipped. A mirror image.

Interested? Fucking right.

The file had been sitting in his morning βehemoth-related data sweep, ticking quietly. He hadn't even had time to check it out until several hours into his shift. Supercol was burning a path through Glasgow, and some new carbon-eating bug—mutant or construct, nobody knew—had eaten a big chunk of the Bicentennial Causeway right out from under a few thousand rapitrans passengers. It had been a busy morning. But finally he'd had a few moments to come down off the accelerants and breathe.

He'd opened the file, and it had jumped out as if spring-loaded.

The matchmaker was unusually forthcoming in explaining why this file qualified for his attention. Usually, match-makers delivered their treasures through logical chains way too twisted for humans to follow; like magic, needed infor-mation from all over the world would simply appear in your queue, unsummoned. But *this* file—this had come with ex-plicit search terms attached, terms that even a human being could understand. *Quarantine. Firestorm. Beebe Station. Channer Vent.*

Interested?

Not enough information to be useful. Just enough to catch the attention of someone like him. Not data at all, really: bait.

Reply.

"Thanks for dropping in." Canned voice, no graphic.

Desjardins flipped his own voice filter on. "Got your mes-sage. What can I do for you?"

"We have a mutual interest in biochemistry," the voice said pleasantly. "I have information you might find useful. The reverse may also be true."

"And who are you, exactly?"

"I'm someone who shares your interest in biochemistry, and who has information you might find useful."

"Actually," Desjardins remarked, "you're a secretarial app. Pretty basic one, too."

Nothing disagreed.

"Okay then. Pocket whatever you've got and tag it the same way you tagged your invite. I'll pick it up on my next sweep and get back to you."

"Sorry," said the app. "That doesn't work from this end." *Of course not.* "So what *would* work for you?"

"I'd like to meet."

"Fine. Name a time, I'll clear a channel."

"Face-to-face."

"Well, as I—you mean *in person*?"

"Yes."

"What *for*?"

"I'm suspicious by nature. I don't trust digital images. I can be at your location within forty-eight hours."

"Do you know my location?"

"No."

"You know, if I wasn't also *suspicious by nature*, I sure as shit would be now," Desjardins said.

"Then an interest in biochemistry is not all we have in common."

Desjardins hated it when apps did that—threw in little asides and lame witticisms to appear more human. Of course, Desjardins hated it when people did that, too.

"If you'd like to choose a place and time we could meet," the app told him, "I'll be sure to show up."

"How do you know I'm not quarantined?" *For that matter, how do I know you're not? What am I getting into here?*

"That won't be a problem."

"What are you really? Some kind of loyalty test Rowan's siccing on me?"

"I don't understand."

"Because it's really not necessary. A corpse of all people should know that." Whoever the app was negotiating for had to be corpse level at least, to be so confident about travel clearances. Unless the whole thing was some kind of pointless and elaborate put-on.

"I'm not administering a loyalty test," the app replied. "I'm asking for a date."

"Okay, then. Pickering's Pile. Drink'n'drug in Sudbury, Ontario. Wednesday, 1930."

"That will be fine. How will I know you?"

"Not so fast. I think I'd rather approach you."

"That would be a problem."

"That *is* a problem. If you think I'm going to amble innocently into the clutches of someone who won't even give me their name, you're sadly in need of a patch."

"I'm sorry to hear that. However, it doesn't matter. We can still meet."

"Not if neither of us knows how to tag the other, we can't."

"I'll see you on Wednesday," the app told him. "Goodbye."

"Wait a second . . ."

Gone.

Oh, man. Someone was going to meet him on Wednesday. Someone who evidently could drop down onto any place under geosynch at 48 hours' notice. Someone who knew of a link between Channer Vent and βehemoth, and who seemed to think they could find him without any identifiers at all.

Someone was going to meet him whether he wanted to or not.

Achilles Desjardins found that a little bit ominous.

Necrosis

There were places in the world that lived on the arteries between *here* and *there*; whatever they generated *within* wasn't self-sustaining. When tourniqueted—a quarantine, a poisoned water table, the sheer indifference of citizens abandoning some industrial lost cause—they withered and turned gangrenous.

Sometimes, eventually, the walls would come down. The quarantine would end or atrophy. Gates would open, or just rust away. But by then it was too late; the tissue was long since necrotic. No new blood flowed into the dead zone. Maybe a few intermittent flickers along underground cables, peripheral nerves where Maelstrom jumped the gap. Maybe a few people who hadn't gotten out in time, still alive; others arriving, not so much seeking *this* place as avoiding some other.

Lenie Clarke was in such a place now, a town full of wreckage and smashed windows and hollow eyes staring from buildings nobody had bothered to condemn. Whatever life was here did not, for the most part, take any notice of her passing. She avoided the obvious territorial boundaries: the toothless skulls of children significantly arranged along a particular curb; a half-mummified corpse, crucified upside down beneath the cryptic phrase *St. Peter the Unworthy*; derelict vehicles that just happened to block this road or that—rusty barricades, herding the unwary toward some central slaughterhouse like fish in a weir.

Two days before she'd skirted a coven of do-gooders who'd been live-trapping derelicts as though they were field mice, forcibly injecting them with some kind of gene cocktail. Xanthoplast recipes, probably. Since then, she'd managed to avoid seeing anyone. She moved only at night, when her marvelous eyes gave her every advantage. She steered clear of the local headquarters and territorial checkpoints with their burning oil drums and their light poles and their corroded, semifunctional Ballard stacks. There were traps and hidden guard posts, manned by wannabes eager to make their way up the local hierarchy; they seeped slight infrared, or slivers of light invisible to mere meat. Lenie Clarke noted them a block away and changed course, their attendants never the wiser.

She was almost through the zone when someone stepped from a doorway ten meters ahead of her; a mongrel with dominant Latino genes, skin the color of slate in the washed-out light boosted through her eyecaps. Bare feet, shreds of sprayed-on plastic peeling from the soles. A firearm of some kind in one hand; two fingers missing. The other hand had been transformed into an improvised prosthetic, wrapped around and around in layers of duct tape studded with broken glass and rusty nails.

He looked directly at her with eyes that shone as white and empty as her own.

"Well," Clarke said after a moment.

His clubbed limb gestured roughly at the surrounding territory. "Not much, but mine." His voice was hoarse with old diseases. "There's a toll."

"I'll go back the way I came."

"No you won't."

She casually tapped a finger against her wristwatch. She kept her voice low, almost subvocal: "Shadow."

"Funds transferred," the device replied.

Clarke sighed and sloughed off her pack. One corner of her mouth curled the slightest fraction.

"So how do you want me?" she asked.

He wanted her from behind, and he wanted her face in the dirt. He wanted to call her *Bitch* and *cunt* and *stumpfuck*. He wanted to cut her with his home-built mace.

She wondered if this could be called *rape*. She hadn't been offered a choice. Then again, she hadn't exactly said *no*, either.

He hit her when he came, backhanded her head against the ground with his gun hand, but the gesture had an air of formality about it. Finally, he rolled off of her and stood.

She allowed herself back inside then, let the distant observation of her own flesh revert again to firsthand experience. "So." She rolled onto her back, wiping the street from her mouth with the back of one hand. "How was I?"

He grunted and turned his attention to her pack.

"Nothing you want in there," she said.

"Uh-huh." Something caught his eye anyway. He reached in and pulled out a tunic of black shimmering fabric.

It squirmed in his hand.

"*Shit!*" He dropped it onto the ground. It lay there, inert. Playing dead.

"What the *fuck* ..." he looked at Clarke.

"Party clothes," she said, getting to her feet. "Wouldn't fit you."

"Bullshit," the mongrel said. "It's that reflex copolymer stuff. Like Lenny Clarke wears."

She blinked. "What did you say?"

"Leonard Clarke. Deep Sea Gillman. Did the quake." He nudged the diveskin with one gnarled toe. "You think I don't *know*?" He raised his gun hand to his face; the barrel touched the corner of an eyecap. "How you think I got these, eh? Not the first groupie in town."

"*Leonard* Clarke?"

"I *said* already. You deaf, or stupid?"

"I just let you rape me, asshole. So probably stupid."

The mongrel looked at her for an endless moment.

"You done this before," he said at last.

"More times than you can count."

"Get to maybe like it after a while?"

"No."

"You didn't fight."

"Yeah? How many do, with a gun to their heads?"

"You're not even scared."

"I'm too fucking tired. You gonna let me go, or kill me, or what? Anything but listening to more of this shit."

The mongrel took a hulking step forward. Lenie Clarke only snorted.

"Go," the mongrel said in a strange voice. Then added, absurdly: "Where you headed?"

She arched an eyebrow. "East."

He shook his head. "Never get through. Big quarantine. Goes halfway down to the Dust Belt." He pointed south, down a side street. "Better go 'round."

Clarke tapped her watch. "It's not listed."

"Then don't. Fuck lot I care."

Keeping her eyes up, Clarke bent down and picked up her tunic. The mongrel held her pack out by the straps, glancing down into its depths.

He tensed.

Her hand lunged into the pack like a striking snake, snatched out the billy. She held it underhand, pointed at his gut.

He stepped back, one hand still gripping the pack. His eyes narrowed to opalescent slits. "Why didn't you use it?"

"Didn't want to waste a charge. You're not worth it."

He eyed the empty sheath on her leg. "Why not keep it there? Where you can get it?"

"Now, if you'd had a *kid* with you ..."

They regarded each other through eyes that saw everything in black-and-white.

"You *let* me." The mongrel shook his head; the contradiction almost seemed painful. "You had that, and you let me anyway."

"My pack," Clarke said.

"You—set me up." Dawning anger in that voice, and thick wonder.

"Maybe I just like it rough."

"You're contagious. You're a *bughumper.*"

She wiggled the baton. "Give me my things and maybe you'll live long enough to find out."

"You *stumpfuck.*" But he held out the pack.

For the first time she saw the webbing between the three stumpy digits of his hand, noticed the smooth scarless tips of the stubs. Not violence, then. No street-fight amputation. Born to it.

"You a pharm baby?" she asked. Maybe he was older than he looked; the pharms hadn't deliberately spread buggy genotypes for decades. Sure, defectives spent more than healthy people on fixes, but the global ambience was twisting babies into strange enough shapes on its own by then. Without the risk of consumer backlash.

"You are, aren't you?"

He glared at her, shaking with helpless fury.

"Good," she said, grabbing her pack. "Serves you fucking right."

Snare

The voice in Lubin's ear had lied.

He hadn't been outside N'AmPac since landfall. He hadn't been in Sevastopol or Philadelphia for years. He'd *never* been in Whitehorse, and from what he knew of the place he hoped he never would be.

But he *could* have been. The lie was plausible one, to someone who knew Lubin but not his current circumstances. Or maybe it hadn't been a deliberate lie. Maybe it had been a flawed guess, based on God knew what irrelevant stats. Maybe it had just been a bunch of random words shoveled together with more regard for grammar than veracity.

He wondered if he might have started the rumor himself. Before he left for Sudbury, he put that hypothesis to the test.

He logged back into Haven and began a new name search: *Judy Caraco, Lenie Clarke, Alice Nakata,* and *Kenneth Lubin.*

It was a different voice that accosted him this time. It spoke in soft, gentle tones, almost whispering. It showed no predilection for alliteration or nonsense rhyme. It tended to mispronounce hard consonants.

It called him *Michael.*

He suborbed to Toromilton, took a shuttle north from that city-state. Endless suburbs kept pace beneath him, spilling far from the megapolitan hub that had once kept them captive. The daily commute had ended decades before, and still the blight was spreading. The outside world passed uneventfully—there were only a few restricted zones in all of Ontario, and none were on his route.

The world *inside* was a bit more interesting. Deep in the seething chaos that was Maelstrom, rumors of Mike Brander's resurrection were beginning to sprout alongside tales of Lubin's own. Mike Brander had been seen in Los Angeles. Mike Brander had been seen in Lima.

Lubin frowned, a small expression of self-disgust. He'd given himself away with his own questions. Something in Haven had taken notice when he'd run searches on all Beebe crew members except himself. *And why doesn't this user ask about Lubin, K.? Because this user must already know about Lubin, K.*

Because this user is Lubin, K.

Lenie and Kenny are on the comeback trail.

His last troll through Haven, asking about everyone except Mike Brander, had provoked the same attention and the same simple logic. Now Mike Brander was alive and well and living in Maelstrom. QED.

What's doing this? Why?

Why didn't always enter into it, of course. Sometimes Maelstrom's wildlife would just grab onto popular threads to get around—steal keywords to blend in, sneak through filters by posing as part of the herd. Classic bandwagon effect, blind and stupid as evolution itself. That was why such strategies always fizzled after a while. The fad of the moment would fade into obscurity, leaving poseurs with forged tickets to an empty ballroom. Or the gatekeepers would catch on; the more popular the disguise, the greater the incentive for countermeasures.

Wildlife would hitch a ride on existing rumors, if they were hot enough. Lubin had never heard of them starting rumors of their *own* before.

And why Lenie Clarke? An obscure life, an invisible death. Hardly the most contagious meme in the wires. Nothing to inspire any postmortem legacy at all, in fact.

This was something new. Whatever it was, it was goal-directed, and it was using Lenie Clarke.

More than that. Now, it was using *him*.

———

Sudbury had arrived DOA in the twenty-first century. Decades of mining and a substrate of thin, poorly buffered soil had seen to that. The Sudbury stacks had been the epicenter for one of the first really big acid blights in North American history. It was a benchmark of sorts.

Not that this was entirely a bad thing. Legend had it that lunar astronauts had once practiced in its scoured gray environs. And the area's lakes were truly beautiful, clear and blue and lifeless as chemically treated toilet bowls. The substrate was relentlessly stable, planed and leveled by long-vanished glaciers; the west coast could fall into the ocean, but the Canadian Shield would last forever. Exotic alien life forms would disembark from tankers or lifters at the Industrial Horseshoe around Lake Ontario, wreak local havoc as they always had, but you'd have to be one tough chimera to get past the acid-washed outskirts of Sudbury, Ontario. Its dead zone was like a moat, a firebreak burned into the countryside by a hundred years' worth of industrial poison.

It couldn't have suited CSIRA better if it had been planned. Here was a place resistant to the calamities that threatened the rest of the world, by virtue of having already lost anything of real value. The real estate was cheap, too; the nickel mine was long exhausted, and there'd been a vacuum in the local economy since the last of the fuel rods had been buried over in Copper Cliff.

The Entropy Patrol had filled that vacuum. The Sudbury office was one of the hemisphere's top ten.

It was no surprise to Ken Lubin that his quarry was stationed there. That mysterious searcher hadn't seemed to know the specifics of what he or she was after; the caches left behind in Haven had jumped fastest when queried on ecological impacts and sheer correlative epidemiology, slowest when asked about subcellular organelles or biochemical pathways. Not the spoor of someone following an intimately known agent. More likely someone tracking a new and mysterious one.

Not a pharm, then. Someone with a more ecological perspective, and with—given their access to Haven—a great deal of clearance and autonomy. The Entropy Patrol had the only talent pool that fit.

One good thing about the Patrol was that it was appropriately paranoid on matters of access. In a world dominated by the telecommute, 'lawbreakers dutifully made the daily real-world journey to a single vast, secure catacomb that plugged directly into Haven. Nobody would have been stupid enough to try and manage an entropy outbreak from a home terminal, even if it *had* been possible. At CSIRA, even the links into Maelstrom were insanely secure.

Which made tracking down employees quite straightforward. They all had to come through the foyer.

There was no listing of individual 'lawbreakers, of course. There was a listing of department heads, available through a small orchard of help kiosks in the main lobby. Once Lubin had what he needed, he stepped outside and headed to the nearest rapitrans stop.

Donald Lertzman was the archetypal middleman; his career had coasted to that comfortable plateau above those who actually did productive work, but safely short of a position where he had to make any vital decisions. Perhaps, on some level, he'd realized that. Perhaps a fully detached house, hidden behind a hedgerow of acid-resistant blue spruce at the edge of the Sudbury Burn, was his way of compensating.

Of course, in this day and age he could hardly commute in his private vehicle. He knew the value of appearances; he'd built his livelihood on nothing else. Each night, therefore, he traversed the three blocks between his property and the nearest bus stop on foot. Approximately 20 percent of this distance was out of public view.

"Excuse me, are you Donald Lertzman?"

"Yes, who—"

Lubin carefully noted the medic alert plug-in on Lertzman's wristwatch. It would raise the alarm if his vitals showed any indication of ongoing distress. Of course, a body's stress responses don't just kick in by themselves— they have to be activated by the perception of threat or injury. Most of *those* signals run through the spinal cord.

Ten minutes after failing to introduce himself, Lubin knew who he was looking for; he knew where to find him; he knew when that person's shift ended. He knew more than he needed, for the moment.

His scheduled meeting at Pickering's Pile was twenty-six hours away. Lubin didn't know if he wanted to wait that long. For that matter, there was no guarantee that this *Achilles Desjardins* would even show up.

He left Donald Lertzman breathing peacefully.

Complicity

It was every bit as abrupt, this time: the sudden translocation of place, one world annihilated, another created in its stead. There may have been some warning. A barely perceptible stutter in the feeds, a ping, as if something far away was checking for activity on the line. But it came too fast to serve as any kind of heads-up, even if Perreault hadn't simply imagined it.

It didn't matter. She was waiting. She'd been waiting for days.

The same God's-eye view: a different multitude spread out below, framed by familiar icons and overlays. She'd been shunted from one botfly to another. Nav and GPS were dark for some reason.

But she was indoors, and there was violence.

One man lay twisted on the concrete floor; another's boot caught him in the stomach as she watched. His body folded weakly around the blow in some impotent fetal reflex, smearing blood and teeth in its wake. The face was too torn and bloody to betray any clear ethnicity.

The assailant—smaller, black, his back to the camera—shifted his weight from side to side with a terrible restless energy. His arena was defined by the crowd that enclosed it: some intent, some indifferent, some shaking their own fists in frenzied enthusiasm. Farther away the concentration of humanity thinned out, gave way to sleeping mats and forgotten piles of personal belongings.

Perreault spun through the available menus. No weapons. In the corner of her eye, a flashing distraction: *target -162°az: -41°dec*

Behind her.

The victor circled, still bobbing. His face came into view, creased in a fury of concentration. His foot lashed out again: a kidney blow to the back. The twitching thing on the floor jerked open like a bloody flower. Its back arched as though electrocuted.

The attacker looked up, straight at Perreault's hijacked botfly. His eyes were the brilliant, crystalline jade of gengineered chlorophyll. They stared from that black face like a hallucination.

Without taking his eyes off the 'fly, he delivered one last kick at the head of his victim. Then he moved into the crowd, unopposed.

Sou-Hon Perreault had never seen him before. She didn't know his victim. But *target* was at *-175°az: -40°dec*, and moving.

Pan left. More people, more sleeping mats. Gray unfinished walls rising in the distance, lined with vending machines and, higher up, official pictographs directing the populace to *registration* and *quarantine* and *latest bulletins*. They were in a cement cave ten meters high, erected in the name of mass subsistence: a place for quarantines, an innoculation center, a shelter against those sudden bouts of weather too vicious for the ad-hoc retrofits slapped onto older houses. Increasingly, to many, *home*.

The unofficial term was *Bomb Shelter*.

Target was at *-35°, -39°*. Tactical laid crosshairs onto her the moment she passed into view. Same civilian disguise, same visor. But something had happened to Lenie Clarke since Calgary. She favored one leg when she walked. A yellow bruise spilled across the right side of her face.

Perreault tripped the 'fly's speaker, thought twice, shut it off again. No need to draw unnecessary attention. Instead she brought up the comm menu, got a lock on Clarke's visor, and tapped into the RF.

"Hi. It's Sou-Hon again."

Down on the floor, Lenie Clarke froze. She brought her wrist up; she was no longer wearing a watch.

"Up here," Perreault said "In the botfly."

A proximity alert bleeped in her face: another 'fly coming into range. Perreault spun, caught it arriving through the 'fly-sized catflap two meters over the main entrance.

Even in visible light, the weapons muzzles were obvious. She looked back down. Clarke was gone. Perreault panned until the crosshairs came up again. The rifter was heading for the door, glancing up at the other 'fly. It didn't notice her; it was headed toward the bloody Rorschach blot at the other end of the cave.

"Not that one," Perreault said. "Me. The little one, the surveil—"

"You're the stalker, right?" Clarke broke in.

"The—yeah. That's what you called me, anyway."

"Bye." She was at the entrance.

"Wait!"

Gone.

Perreault spared another look at the other botfly. It was hovering over the aftermath of the fight, its cameras pointing straight down. It had probably been summoned by the 'fly Perreault was riding, just before she'd grabbed the keys. It wasn't paying any attention to her. If its rider even knew that Perreault was in command, he or she didn't seem to care.

Nothing much I can do either way, she thought, and dived through the flytrap.

Thin dirty rain, sparse droplets blown sideways. The sky was brown. The air seemed full of grit. Farther south, then. Someplace where it probably hadn't really *snowed* in years.

A metropolitan skyline hovered behind the dome like a murky histogram. Four-lane blacktop stretched out from that background, bled a puddle of asphalt beside the shelter, and continued to the horizon. On all sides a threadbare weave of smaller roads—some little more than dirt paths—extended through a patchwork of fields and woodlots.

Target, pinned and highlighted like a luminous butterfly, was moving away along one of them.

Still no GPS. Even the compass was off-line.

Perreault reacquired the rifter's visor and set off on her trail. "Listen, I can—"

"Fuck off. Last time you were in one of those things it ended up shooting at me."

"That wasn't me! The link went down!"

"Yeah?" Clarke didn't look back. "And what's going to keep it up this time?"

"This 'fly doesn't *have* any weapons. It's strictly eyes and ears."

"I don't like eyes and ears."

"It couldn't hurt to have an extra set on your side. If I'd been around to do some advance scouting before, maybe you wouldn't have that bruise on your face."

Clarke stopped. Perreault brought the 'fly down and hovered a couple of meters off her shoulder.

"And when your friends get bored?" the rifter asked. "When the link goes down again?"

"I don't know. Maybe the 'fly just goes back to its regular rounds. At least it can't shoot at you."

"It can talk to things that can."

"Look, I'll keep my distance," Perreault offered. "A couple of hundred meters, say. I'll stay in range of your visor, but if this thing comes to its senses you'll just be some nameless K who happened to be around when the link came back. They won't look twice."

Two meters off the port bow, Clarke's shoulders rose and fell.

"Why are you doing this?" she asked. "Why is it so important to help me out?"

Perreault briefly considered telling the truth. "I don't know," she said at last. "It just is."

The rifter shook her head. After a moment she said, "I'm headed south."

"South?" Perreault tapped again at the dead compass icon. Nothing. She tried to get a fix on the sun through murky overcast.

Clarke began walking. "This way," she said. And still didn't look back.

Perreault kept well off the road, paralleling Clarke's direction of travel. She called up the camera menu—planning to set a zoom reflex on any motion not consistent with wind action— and was surprised to be offered a choice of views. The 'fly had lateral, stern, and ventral cams as well as the primary stereos up front. She could split the display into four windows and keep simultaneous watch on the whole 360.

Lenie Clarke trudged silently along the road, shoulders hunched against the wind. Her windbreaker flapped against her body like torn plastic.

"Aren't you cold?" Perreault asked.

"Got my skin on."

"Your—" *Of course. Her dive suit.* "Is this how you always get around?"

"*You* were the one that warned me off flying."

"Well, yes, but—"

"I bus sometimes," Clarke said. "Hitchhike."

Things that didn't involve ID checks or body scans. There was an irony buried in there, Perreault reflected. Clarke had probably been through more rigorous security in the past few weeks than would have been imaginable just decades earlier—but modern checks and gauntlets were aimed at pathogens, not people. Who cared about artifacts like personal ID anymore? Who cared about anything so arbitrary as a *political* border? National identity was so irrelevant that nobody'd even bothered to dismantle it.

"You're not going to find a ride on *this* road anytime

soon," Perreault remarked. "You should've stuck with the main drag."

"I like walking alone. Avoids pointless small talk."

Perreault took the hint.

She accessed the botfly's flight recorder, fearful of just how much incriminating information the device had stored. But its entire memory had been purged—an act of sabotage well beyond Perreault's capabilities. Even now, the black box somehow failed to retain the routine data stream the 'fly's sensors were sending it.

She was relieved, but not particularly surprised.

"Still there?" Clarke said.

"Uh-huh. Link's still up."

"They're getting better with practice."

Perreault remembered Clarke's reflexive glance at her bare wrist, back in the dome. "What happened to your watch?"

"Smashed it."

"Why?"

"Your friends figured out how to override the off switch."

"They're not—" Not friends. Not even contacts. She didn't know what they were.

"And now you're getting in through my visor. If I had any brains I'd lose that, too."

"So others have made contact?" Of course they had—why would Sou-Hon Perreault be the only person in the world to be given an audience with the Meltdown Madonna?

"Oh, right. I forgot," the mermaid said wryly. "You don't know anything."

"Have they? Others like me?"

"Worse," Clarke said, and kept walking.

Don't push it.

A stand of skeletal birch separated them for a few minutes. The port camera caught Lenie Clarke in fragments, through a vertical jumble of white slashes.

"I went into Maelstrom," she said. "People are—talking about me."

"Yeah. I know."

"Do you believe it? The stuff they're saying?"

Perreault tried for a light touch, not believing it herself: "So you're not carrying the end of the world around inside you?"

"If I am," Clarke said, "it doesn't show up on a blood panel."

"You can't believe most of the stuff you read in Maelstrom anyway," Perreault said. "Half of it contradicts the other half."

"It's all just crazy. I don't know how it got started." A few seconds of silence. Then: "I saw someone that looked like me the other day."

"I told you. You've got friends."

"No. It's not *me* you want. It's something in the wires. It just . . . stole my name for some reason."

Beep.

A sudden luminous rectangle, framing a flicker of motion. The stern camera zoomed reflexively.

"Hold on," Perreault said. "I've got a—Lenie."

"What?"

"You might want to get off the road. I think it's that psycho from the shelter."

It was. Hunched over the handlebars of an ancient moun-tain bike, he resolved in the zoom window like a grainy nightmare. He pumped, straining, all his weight on the pedals. The vehicle had no seat. It didn't have any tires, ei-ther; it rattled along the road on bare rims. It was a skeleton ridden by a monster. The monster's jacket was dark and wet, and missing one sleeve; it was not the one he'd been wearing before.

He kept his eyes on the road; only once did he spare a glance back over his shoulder. Eventually he faded in the murk.

"Lenie?"

"Here." She rose from a drainage ditch.

"He's gone," Perreault said. "The things you see when you don't have your gun. Asshole."

"No worse than anyone else back there." Clarke climbed back onto the road.

"Except for the fact that he beat someone to death."

"And a hundred people stood around and watched. Or didn't you notice?"

"Well—"

"People do that, you know. Just stand around and do nothing. They're fucking complicit, they're no better than— they're *worse.* At least *he* took a little initiative."

"I didn't notice *you* standing up to him," Perreault snapped, and instantly regretted her own defensiveness.

Clarke turned to face the botfly and said nothing. After a moment she resumed walking.

"They're not all—complicit, Lenie," Perreault said, more gently. "People *want* to act, they're just—afraid. And some- times, experience teaches you that the only way to cope is to just—shut down..."

"Oh yeah, we're all just victims of our past. Don't you *dare* trot out that subroutine."

"What subroutine?"

"The poor little abuse victim. You know what *abuse* is, really? It's an excuse."

"Lenie, I'm not—"

"So some asshole grabs your cunt in daycare. So someone rams his cock up your ass. So what? Bruises, maybe. A bit of bleeding. You suffer more injury if you fall off the swings and break your arm, so how come you don't hear anyone wailing about *abuse* then?"

A thousand kilometers away, Perreault reeled in the surge of Clarke's vehemence. "I didn't say—and anyway, the physical injury's only part of it. The emotional damage—"

"Crap. You think we aren't built to withstand a little childhood trauma? You know how many of the higher mam- mals eat their own young? We wouldn't have lasted ten gen- erations if a couple of childhood shit-kickings was enough to take us out for the count."

"Lenie—"

"You think all those armies and gangs and cops would be so keen on rape *if we just didn't make such a big deal about it*? If we didn't get all weak-kneed and trembly at the thought of being *violated*? Fuck that. I've been attacked by things straight out of nightmares. I've nearly been boiled and buried alive more times than I can count. I know all about the ways you can push a body to the breaking point, and *sexual abuse* doesn't even make the top ten."

She stopped and glared across at Perreault's distant teleop. Perreault zoomed: the rifter was shaking.

"Or do you have some basis for disagreement? Some *personal experience* to back up all your trendy platitudes?"

Sure I had experience. I watched. For years I watched, and felt nothing.

It was my job...

But of course she couldn't say that. "I—no. Not really."

"Course not. You're just a fucking tourist, aren't you? You're safe and comfy in some glass tower somewhere, and you stick a periscope into the real world every now and then and tell yourself you're experiencing *life* or some such shit. You're pathetic."

"Lenie—"

"Stop feeding off me."

She wouldn't say anything more. She stalked silently along that road in the dirty rain, refusing entreaty or apology. Brown sky faded to black. Visible light failed, infra kicked in. Lenie Clarke was a white-hot speck of anger at fixed range, endlessly moving.

In all that time she only spoke once. The words were barely more than a growl, and Sou-Hon Perreault did not believe they were intended for her ears. But the 'fly's enhanced senses had little regard for range and none for privacy: filter and gain turned Clarke's words from distant static to ugly, unmistakable truth:

"Everybody pays."

Vision Quest

There were two reasons Achilles Desjardins didn't indulge in
sex with real partners. The second was, simulations gave him
much more latitude.

His system was more than enough to handle the range.
His skin came equipped with the latest Lorenz-levitation
haptics, their formless magnetic fingers both sensing his
movements and responding to them. The ad specs boasted
you could feel a virtual ant crawling up your back. They
weren't lying. The only way you'd get a better ride was to go
with a direct neural interface, but Desjardins wasn't about to
go that far; it wasn't widely known, but there were creatures
in Maelstrom that were learning to penetrate wetware. The
last thing he needed was some sourced shark hijacking his
spinal cord.

And there were other dangers if you went with a wet
link, dangers especially relevant to those with Desjardins's
tastes. There were still people out there who refused to recognize the difference between reality and simulation, between fantasy and assault. Some of them were savvy enough
to hack the things they found politically objectionable.

Take the present scenario. It was a pretty sweet setup, all
told. He had two girls strapped facedown on the table in front
of him. One of them was hooked up to a DC power supply
by alligator clips on her nipples and clit. The other had to be
content with lower-tech forms of punishment, which Desjardins was currently administering with an unfinished
broom handle. Three others hung inverted against the far
wall, passing time until their own numbers came up.

It was exactly this sort of environment that certain dis-
agreeable types took pleasure in messing with. Desjardins
knew of more than one occasion in which the victims of similar scenarios had miraculously freed themselves from their
restraints, coming after the user with steak knives and hedge
clippers. Incompetent but enthusiastic neutering generally
followed; in at least one case the emergency interrupt had
been overridden, keeping the player on the board right up to

the final curtain call. Such things were more than enough of a damper in a feedback skin. If you got nailed through a neural link, you could end up impotent for life.

Which was, of course, the whole idea.

Achilles Desjardins was more cognizant of the risks than most. He took, therefore, more precautions than most. His sensorium was strictly stand-alone, with no physical connection to any kind of network. He'd lobotomized the graphics circuitry to reduce its vulnerability to wildlife; it could only present chunky, low-rez images that would drive any normal connoisseur crazy, but Desjardins's own wetware more than made up the difference. (The pattern-matching enhancements in his visual cortex interpolated those crude pixels into a subjective panorama crisp enough to leave the most jaded wirehead drooling.) The scenarios themselves were scrubbed and disinfected right down to the texture maps. Desjardins carried way more than his weight in this cesspool of a world; no way was some TwenCen puritan going to mess up any of his well-deserved moments with Mr. Bone.

Which made the sudden and complete failure of his system extremely disquieting. There was a brief sharp prick in his neck and the whole environment just *disappeared.*

He floated there a moment, a stunned and disembodied being in an imperceptible void. No sounds, no smells or tactile feedback, no vision—not even *blackness,* really. Not like a window gone dark, not like closing your eyes. More like not having any eyes to begin with. You don't see blackness out of the back of your skull, after all, you don't—

Fuck, he thought. *They got in. Any second now everything's going to come back on-line and they'll be spit-roasting me on a pole or something.*

He tried to flex his fingers around the interrupt. He didn't seem to have any fingers. All his senses remained offline. For a moment, he thought he might get off easy; maybe they hadn't infected his program, maybe they'd just crashed it. It made sense—it was always easier to kill a system than subvert it.

*Bit they shouldn't have been able to do either, for fuck's sake ...
and why can't I feel anything ... ?*

"Hello? Hello? Is this thing on?"

What—

"Sorry. Small attempt at humor. I'm going to ask you a few questions, Achilles. I want you to think long and hard about the answers."

The voice hung there in the void with him, sexless and innocent of ambience; no reverb, no quiet hum of nearby appliances, no background noise at all. It was almost like a Haven voice, but even that seemed wrong.

"I want you to think about the ocean. The very deep ocean. Think about some of the things that live down there. The microbes, especially. Think about them."

He tried to speak. No vocal cords.

"Good. Now I want you to listen to some names. You may recognize some of them. Abigail McHugh."

He'd never heard of her.

"Donald Lertzman."

Lertzman? How's he involved?

"Wolfgang Schmidt. Judy Caraco."

Is this some kind of corpse loyalty te—oh Jesus. That Haven contact. Pickering's Pile. It said it could find me ...

"André Breault. Patricia Rowan. Lenie Clarke."

Rowan! She behind this?

"Ken Lubin. Leo Hin Tan the Third. Mark Showell. Michael Brander."

Yeah. Rowan. Maybe Alice isn't so paranoid after all.

"Good. Now I want you to think about biochemistry. Proteins. Sulfur-containing amino acids."

??!?!? ...

"I can tell you're confused. Let's narrow it down some. Cysteine. Methionine. Think about those when you hear the following words ..."

It's a mind-reading trick of some kind, Desjardins thought.

"Retrovirus. Stereoisomer. Sarcomere."

A quantum computer?

They didn't exist. Of course, that was the official story on *most* banned technology, but in this case Desjardins was inclined to believe it. Nobody in their right mind would be caught dead around a telepathic AI. That had been one side effect the Q-boosters hadn't seen coming: the whole quantum-consciousness debate had been resolved overnight. Who'd ever choose to build something that could sift through their minds like a chess grandmaster noodling around in a game of X's and O's?

Nobody, as far as Desjardins had been able to tell.

"Ion pump. Thermophile."

But if not a quantum computer, then—

"Archaea. Phenylindole."

Ganzfeld.

Not a computer, except for the interrogation interface. Not telepathy either; not quite. Cruder. The faint quantum signals of human consciousness, cut away from the noise and sensory static that usually swamped them. Properly insulated from such interference, you had a better-than-average chance of guessing what your subject was looking at, or listening to. You could feel the vicarious echo of distant emotions. With the right insulation, and the right stimuli, you could learn a lot.

So Desjardins had been told. He'd never actually experienced it before.

"Good. Now, think about the assignments you've had at CSIRA over the past month."

Mange de la marde. Just because some disembodied voice told him to think about something, didn't mean he had to leap up and—

"Ah. *There's* a familiar pattern. Here's an exercise for you, Achilles: whatever you do, do not think of a red-eyed baboon with hemorrhoids."

Oh, shit.

"You see? Nothing's more doomed to failure than trying really hard *not* to think about something. Shall we continue? Think about your CSIRA assignments for the past six months."

A red-eyed baboon with—

"Think of earthquakes and tidal waves. Think of any possible connections."

Isn't this a security breach? Shouldn't Guilt Trip be doing something?

Earthquakes. Tidal waves. He couldn't keep them out.

Maybe it is. Maybe Trip's seized up my whole body. If I even still have a body. How would I know?

Fires.

Oh Jesus. I'll give everything away...

Threads of emerald light, lancing through the fog.

"Think of containment protocols. Think of collateral damage."

Stop it, stop it...

"Did you plan it?"

No! No, I—

"Did you know in advance?"

How could I, they don't tell me any—

"Did you find out afterward?"

If Trip's working, my body's already dead. Oh motherfucking blood-spewing sickle-celled savior...

"Did you *approve*?"

What kind of stupid question is that?

Nothing, for a very long time.

I feel awful, Desjardins thought. Then: *Hey—*

Despair, guilt, fear—chemicals, all. Hormones and neurotransmitters, a medley brewed not just in the brain, but in glands throughout the body. The *physical* body.

I'm still alive. I've still got a body even if I can't *feel it.*

"Let's talk about you," said the voice at last. "How have you been lately, healthwise? Have you had any cuts or injuries? Anything to break the skin?"

I'm feeling a bit better, thank you.

"Any symptoms of illness?"

"Any inoculations within the past two weeks?

"Blood tests? Unusual reactions to recreational transderms?

"*Real* sexual experiences?"

Never. I'd never inflict that on a person...

Silence.

Hey. You there?

With a blinding flash and a roar like an angry ocean, the real world crashed in from all sides.

After a while everything desaturated to normal intensity. He stared up at his living room ceiling and waited while a cacophony of ambient sounds faded down to a single, rhythmic *scrubbing.*

Someone's in here.

He tried to rise; a sharp pain in his neck kept him from any sudden moves, but he managed to get erect and stay that way. In only the most innocent sense, unfortunately; his feedback skin was folded neatly to one side. He was completely naked.

The scrubbing sound was coming from the bathroom.

He didn't have any weapons. At this point he didn't think he needed any; if the intruder had meant to kill him, he'd be dead already. Desjardins stepped tentatively toward the hallway and nearly took a header into the wall; Mandelbrot, true to form, had got in his way and tried the classic feline figure-eight-around-the-legs takedown.

Desjardins spared a silent curse and crept toward the bathroom.

Someone was standing at the sink without any pants on.

Seen from the back: medium height, but built like a Ballard stack. Dark hair, flecked with gray; navy cable-knit sweater; black underwear; little scars all over the backs of the legs. Bare feet. His pants were draped along the counter; he was scrubbing at one leg in the sink.

"Your cat pissed on me," he said without turning.

Desjardins shook his head; his neck reminded him of the stupidity of that gesture. "What?"

"When we had our session," the stranger said. (Desjardins glanced in the mirror, but the man's face was tilted down, intent on his task.) "I assume someone in your position knows about Ganzfeld techniques?"

"I've heard of them," Desjardins said.

"Then you know you have to minimize extraneous signal. Nerve blocks on all the main sensory cables, everything. I was just as disconnected as you."

"But you were *talking*—"

The intruder nudged a small beige fanny pack on the floor with his foot. "*That* was talking. I just set up the dialogue tree. Anyway"—he straightened, his back still to the door—"your stupid cat pissed on my leg when I was laid out."

Good for my stupid cat, Desjardins didn't say.

"I thought only dogs were supposed to do that."

Desjardins shrugged. "Mandelbrot's kind of a mutant."

The intruder grunted, and turned.

He wasn't exactly ugly. More like what would result if someone with limited artisan skills carved a human face in a totem pole; it might not run to your taste, but there was no denying a certain crude aesthetic. More tiny scars on the face. Still; not quite ugly.

Scary, though. That fit. Desjardins didn't know exactly what it was that made him think that.

"You're immune to Guilt Trip," the intruder told him. "Want to guess how *that* happened?"

The Algebra of Guilt

The naked 'lawbreaker was watching him with wary curiosity. Not much actual fear, Lubin noted. When you routinely juggled thousands of lives for a living, you probably figured that *other* people were the ones with cause to worry. Sudbury was a safe, law-abiding place. Wielding his godlike control *over* the real world, Desjardins had probably forgotten what it was like to actually live *in* it.

"Who are you?" Desjardins asked.

"Name's Colin," Lubin said.

"Uh-huh. And why does Rowan have such a hard-on for testing my loyalty?"

"Maybe you didn't hear me," Lubin said. "You're immune to Guilt Trip."

"I heard you. I just think you're full of shit."

"Really." Lubin laid the slightest emphasis on the word.

"Nice try, *Colin*, but I kind of keep up on that stuff."

"I see."

"Don't get me wrong, I'm not saying it's indestructible. I can think of a few commercial enzymes that break it down just off the top of my head. The right kind of reuptake inhibitor blockers could do the job too, I'm told. That's why they have these tests, you see? That's why I can barely go two days without some bloodhound sniffing my crotch. Believe me, if I was immune to Guilt Trip I'd already know it, and so would every security database up to geosynch. And you know, the really *odd* thing about this is that Rowan must *know* that alread—"

He never had a chance to move. Lubin was behind him in the space of a syllable, had one arm locked around his throat in two. The long curved needle in his other hand tickled Desjardins's eardrum suggestively.

"You have three seconds to tell me what it's called," Lubin whispered, relaxing his grip just enough to permit some semblance of speech.

"βehemoth," Desjardins gasped.

Lubin tightened his grip again. "Place of origin. Two seconds." Relaxed it.

"Deep sea! Juan de Fuca, Channer Vent I thin—"

"Worst-case scenario. One."

"Everything *dies*, for fuck's sake! *Everything just fades away...*"

Lubin let him go.

Desjardins staggered forward against the sink, gulping air. Lubin could see his face reflected in the mirror: panic subsiding, the higher brain kicking in, reassessment of threat potential, dawning awareness of—

Three breaches he'd just committed. Three violations when Guilt Trip should have risen from within and throttled him even more tightly than Lubin just had...

Achilles Desjardins turned and faced Lubin with horror and fear spreading across his face.

"*Maudite marde...*"

"I told you," Lubin said. "You're a free agent. *Vive le gardien libre.*"

"How'd you do it?" Desjardins slumped morosely on the couch next to his clothes. "More to the point, *why*? The next time I show up for work I'm screwed. Rowan knows that. What's she trying to prove?"

"I'm not here for Rowan," Lubin said. "Rowan's the problem, in fact. I'm here on behalf of her superiors."

"Yeah?" Desjardins actually seemed to approve of that. Not surprising. Patricia Rowan had never exactly endeared herself to the lower ranks.

"There are concerns that some of the information we've received from her office has been tainted," Lubin continued. "I'm here to cut out the middleman and get the unadulterated truth. You're going to help me."

"And I'm not much good to you if my brain seizes up every time you ask a touchy question."

"Yes."

Desjardins began getting dressed. "Why not just go through channels? GT won't raise a peep if I know the orders are coming from higher up the food chain."

"Rowan would peep."

"Oh. Right." Desjardins pulled his shirt on over his head. "So tell me if I've got this down: you ask me a bunch of questions, and if I don't answer them to the best of my ability, you stick a needle in my ear. If I do, you let me go and the next time I go to work I set off more sirens than I can count. They take me apart piece by piece to find out what went wrong, and if I'm very very lucky, they'll just throw me into the street as a security risk. Is that about right?"

"Not exactly," Lubin said.

"What, then?"

"I'm not the snuff fairy," Lubin said. In fact, that was exactly what someone had called him, nearly two years before. "I don't leap gaily from door to door killing people for no good reason. And you're going to do more than answer a few questions for me. You're going to take me to work and show me your files."

"Not after—"

Lubin held up a derm between thumb and forefinger. "Trip analog. Short-lived and fairly inert, but it looks pretty much the same to a bloodhound. Stick it under your tongue fifteen minutes before getting to work and you'll pass the tests. If you cooperate, no one will know the difference."

"Until you bugger off and take your analog with you."

"You're forgetting how Guilt Trip works, Desjardins. Your own cells are producing the stuff. I haven't stopped that. I've just dosed you with something to break down the finished product before it hits your motor nerves. Eventually it'll get used up and you'll be a happy little slave again."

"How long?"

"Week or ten days. Depends on individual metabolism. Even if I do bugger off, you could always just call in sick until it wears off."

"I can't, and you know it. I got my immunes boosted when I joined the Patrol. I'm even immune to Supercol."

Lubin shrugged. "Then you'll just have to trust me."

It fact, it had been lies from the word go.

Lubin had not freed Achilles Desjardins. He'd merely stumbled on the discovery as they both lay on the floor, disconnected from themselves and strangely linked to each other through a mechanical interrogator. The derm he'd presented had been an acetylcholine booster, a memory aid one step removed from candy. His words had been spun on the fly, woven around the 'lawbreaker's reactions in the Ganzfeld: Rowan, yes. Strong reaction there. No reaction to rifter

names, but horror and recognition at the thought of earthquakes and tidal waves and mysterious fires.

Desjardins had pursued the truth, and recoiled from it.
He had not set any of the larger wheels in motion. As far as
Lubin could tell, he didn't even know how many wheels there
were.

He hadn't known that he was immune to Guilt Trip, either. That was especially interesting. Desjardins had been
right—it would be impossible to avoid one of CSIRA's spot
checks for more than a day or two. So barring the unlikely
possibility that Desjardins had acquired his immunity within
the past few hours, his body had done a lot more than throw
off GT; it had managed to hide that fact from the bloodhounds.

Lubin had not realized that freedom from Guilt Trip was
possible. It raised certain prospects he had not previously
considered.

Starfucker

Marq Quammen was primed and ready.

Tornado season was just winding down in the Dust Belt;
three solid months of flywheel repairs had fed the chip in
his thigh until it was six digits fat, and he had a month until
spring runoff started clogging the dams up north. Options
were tempting and plentiful in the meantime. He could boost
his chloroplasts to UV-shield levels and bugger off to the
Carolinas. He could check out the underwater Club Med over
in Hatteras—he'd heard they'd walled off a whole bay with
this big semipermeable membrane, let the ocean in but kept
out all those nasty synthetic macromolecules and heavy metals. Their cultured coral had finally taken off; it might even
be open to the tourists by now. That would be something to
see. There hadn't been wild coral anywhere in N'Am since
Key West had packed it in.

Of course, these days there were all sorts of nasty things
waiting to jump on you when you ventured outside. That

new bug the left-coast refugees had brought over, for instance—the all-purpose number that killed you a dozen different ways. Maybe it'd be better just to stay in this dark,
cozy little booth in this dark, cozy little drink'n'drug at the
edge of the Belt, and let Breakthroughs in BrainChem provide
him a richness of experience he could *never* get in the real
world. That was pretty tempting, too. Plus he could start immediately.

Already had started, in fact. Quammen stretched and settled deeper into his cushioned alcove and watched the local
butterflies sparkling at each other. Upstairs the world was a
salt-baked oven; if you were an unprotected eyeball out there,
the only question was whether you'd go saltblind before the
wind sandblasted you down to pitted gelatin. In here, though,
it was always dark, and the air barely moved. He felt like a
cat in a nook in a dark green cave, surveying a subterranean
domain.

There was a little blond K-selector sitting alone at the
bar. Quammen absently stuck a derm behind his ear and
aimed his watch at her. Passive infrared and a few ultrasonic
squeaks, barely audible even to bats, bounced back and forth.

She turned and looked at him. Her eyes were a flat and
startling ivory.

She started toward him.

He didn't know her. Quammen's watch flashed him an
executive summary: she wasn't horny either.

He couldn't think of any other reason she'd approach
him, though.

She stopped just outside the alcove, a hint of a smile beneath those strange blank eyes.

"Nice effect," Quammen said, seizing the initiative. "You
see in X ray with those things?"

"So what was that?"

"What was what?"

"You zapped me with something."

"Oh." Quammen raised his hand, let her see the whisper-
thin filament extending from his watch. "You got some kind
of sensor on you?"

She shook her head. Thin lips, small tits, great hips. Sharp edges, just slightly smoothed. Like a perfect little ice sculpture, left a minute too long in the sun.

"So how'd you know?" Quammen asked.

"I felt it."

"Bullshit. The IR's passive, the sonar's real weak."

"I've got an implant," said the K. "Hard stuff. You can feel it when the sound hits."

"Implant?" *This could be interesting.*

"Yeah. So, what are you doing here?"

Quammen sneaked another peek at his watch; no, she wasn't on the prowl. Hadn't been a minute ago, anyway. Maybe that was open to negotiation. Maybe it had already changed. He wanted to scope her out again, but he didn't want to give himself away. Shit. Why'd she have to be sensitive to probes?

"I said—"

"Just coming off a nice fat contract," he told her. "Riding flywheels. Figuring out my next move."

She slid in beside him, grabbed a derm from the table dispenser. "Tell me about it."

She was fucking cryptic, was what she was.

Or maybe just old-fashioned. She hadn't propositioned him outright, which was a drag; it wasted time. Quammen would've propositioned *her* in an instant, but unless his plug-in was wrecked she hadn't been receptive at first, and that probably meant he was going to have to work at it. He couldn't remember the last time he'd had to rely on *instinct* of all things to know whether a woman was interested or not, and this *Lenie* wasn't making things any easier. A couple of times he'd put a hand here or there, and she'd literally flinched. But then she'd run a finger down his arm, or tap the back of his hand, and just generally come on wet as a hagfish.

If she *wasn't* interested, why was she wasting his time? Was she really here for the conversation?

By the third derm it didn't seem to matter so much.

"You know what I am?" Quammen demanded. An influx of exogenous transmitters had made him suddenly eloquent. "I'm a fucking crusader, is what I am! It is my personal mission to save the world from the Quebecois!"

She blinked lazily over her alien eyes. "Too late," she said.

"You know, only fifty years ago, people paid less than a *third* of their disposable income on energy? Less than a *third*?"

"I did not know that," Lenie answered.

"And the world's ending. It's ending right now."

"That," Lenie said, "I *did* know."

"Do you know when? Do you know when the end began?"

"Last August."

"Twenty thirty-five. The onset of adaptive shatter. When damage control started accounting for more of the GGP than the production of new goods."

"Damage control?"

"Damage control." He pounded the table for emphasis. "My whole *life* is damage control. I fix the things that entropy breaks. Things fall apart, Lenie my lass. The only way you can *stop* the slide is throw energy at it. That's the only way we got from primordial slime to human slime. Evolution'd be sockeye without the sun to lean on."

"Oh, there are places where evolution didn't need the sun—"

"Yeah, yeah, but you get my point. The more complicated a system gets, the more fragile it is. All that ecobabble about *diversity promotes stability*, that's pure bullshit. You take your coral reef or your tropical rain forest, those things were *starved* for energy. You've got so many species, so many energy pathways using up resources that there's hardly a spare erg left over. Drive through a rain forest with a bulldozer or two and tell me how *stable* that system ends up being."

"Oops," Lenie said. "Too late."

Quammen barely heard her. "Now what we've got *here's* a system that's so complicated, it makes a tropical rain forest look like a fucking *monoculture*. Everything gets way too complicated for mere mortals, so we set up webs and networks and AIs to keep track of things, except *they* end up exploding into these huge cancers of complexity too—so that only makes the problem worse—and of course now all the under-lying infrastructure is breaking down, the weather and the biosphere are all fucked up, so not only do we need *oodles* more energy to keep this huge wobbling gyro from crashing over on its side, but those same factors keep knocking out the systems we put in place to *produce* all that extra energy, you see what I'm sayin'? You know what apocalypse is? It's a positive feedback loop!"

"So why blame Québec for all this? They're the only ones who got their asses in gear fast enough to save anything. It was the Hydro Wars that—"

"Here it comes. Québec was gonna save the world, and if only we hadn't ganged up on the frogs, we'd all be sipping neurococktails on a beach somewhere and Maelstrom would be nice and clean and bug-free, and—ah, don't get me started."

"Too late for that, too."

"Hey, I'm not saying the war didn't kick Maelstrom past critical mass. Maybe it did. But it would've happened anyway. Five years, tops. And do you really think the frogs had any-more foresight than the rest of us? They just lucked out with their geography. *Anyone* could make the world's biggest hydro facility if they had all of Hudson Bay to dam up. And who was going to stop them? The Cree tried, did you know that? Remember the Cree? A few thousand malcontents up around James Bay, just before that nasty and unfortunate plague that only killed abos. And after *that* went down, Nunavut just rolled over and did what they were told, and the rest of fuck-ing Canada was still so busy trying to lure the frogs back into bed they were willing to look the other way over pretty much *anything*. And now it's too late, and the rest of us run around playing catchup with our wind farms and our pho-tosynthesis arrays and our deep-sea geothermal—"

Lenie's eyes floated in front of him. Something clicked in Quammen's head.

"Hey," he said after a moment, "are you a—"

She grabbed his wrist and pulled him out of the alcove. "Enough of this bullshit. Let's fuck."

She was something else.

She had *seams* in her chest, and a perforated metal disk poking out between her ribs. She told him, around mouthfuls of cock, that a childhood injury had left her with a prosthetic lung. It was an obvious lie, but he didn't call her on it. Everything was making sense now, right down to the way she kept freezing up and trying to hide it, the way she acted hot to cover how cold she was.

She was a rifter. Quammen had heard about them—hell, they were the competition. N'AmPac had sent them down to hydrothermal vents all over the eastern Pacific, until word got out that they were all completely fucked in the head. Something about abuse survivors being best suited for risky deep-sea work, some reductomechanist shit like that. It was no wonder Lenie wasn't keen on sharing her life story. Quammen wasn't going to push her on it.

Besides, the sex was pretty good. The occasional flinch notwithstanding, she seemed to know exactly what to do. Quammen had heard the usual rumors—the Wisdom of the Old Ones, he liked to call them. *If you want good sex, find an abuse victim.* Didn't seem quite right to put something like that to the test, but after all, *she'd* been the one to take the lead.

And what do you know: the Old Ones spake the truth.

He fucked her so hard his cock came out bloody. He frowned, sudden concern wilting him like a stalk of old celery. "Whoa..."

She just smiled.

"Is that you? Are you hurt? Is it—"

—*oh crap, is it* me?

"I'm an old-fashioned girl," she said, looking up at him.

"What do you mean?" Surely he'd have *felt* it if something had cut his cock...

"I menstruate."

"You—you're *kidding*." Why would anyone *choose* to—"I mean, that's *really* TwenCen." He stood and reached for a towel on the dresser. "You could've told me," he said, wiping at himself.

"Sorry," she said.

"Well, pick your own pleasure, by all means," Quammen said. "It's no big deal, I just thought—"

She'd left her pack unzipped on the floor beside the dresser. Something glinted wet and dark from inside. He leaned slightly for a better view.

"Ah," he said, "—sorry if I—ah..."

A utility clip, blade extended. Used.

"Sure," she said behind him. "Fine."

She cut herself. Before we fucked, must've been when I was in the bathroom. She cut her own insides.

He turned back to the bed. Lenie was already half-dressed. Her face was a blank mask; it framed her eyes perfectly.

She noticed his gaze. She smiled again. Marq Quammen felt a tiny chill.

"Nice meeting you," she said. "Go, and sin some more."

Mask

The bloodhound nipped him on the finger and fixed him with one dark, suspicious eye.

GT analog my ass, Desjardins thought. *What if it doesn't work? What if Colin's lying, what if—*

The eye blinked and turned green.

Colin swept past security as Desjardins's guest. Guilt Trip wasn't an honor bestowed upon everyone, not even upon all those who might have legitimate commerce within the halls of the Entropy Patrol. Colin passed beneath eyes that stripped flesh to the bone—*thoracic implants*, Desjardins noticed, although the machines seemed to think them innocuous enough—but there was no need to drink his blood or read his mind. He was, after all, in the trusted company of Achilles Desjardins, who would never *dream* of granting access to any potential security threat.

This fucker could kill me, Desjardins thought.

Colin closed the cubby door behind them; Desjardins linked his eyes into the panel and split the feed to the wall so Colin could eavesdrop. He told the board to route incoming assignments around him until further notice. The system, confident that no minion would shirk responsibility without good reason, acknowledged promptly.

Alone again, with the man who carried long needles in his pocket.

"What do you want to see?" Desjardins asked.

"Everything," Colin said.

"That's pretty sparse," Colin remarked, studying the plot. "Not your usual pandemic."

He must have meant inland; βehemoth was sprouting everywhere along the coast.

Desjardins shrugged. "Still has some trouble invading low-pressure habitat. Needs a few dice rolls to get a foothold."

"It seems to be doing well enough on the Strip."

"Superdense population. More dice rolls."

"How's it getting around?"

"Not sure. It didn't book a commercial flight." Desjardins pointed at the scattered blotches east of the Rockies. "These new hits just started showing up a couple of weeks ago, and they're not consistent with any of the major travel corridors." He sighed. "I suppose we're lucky the quarantine held as long as it did."

"No, I mean how does it transmit? Respiratory aerosols, skin contact? Body fluids?"

"In theory it could get around on the bottom of somebody's boot. But you'd probably need more than a dirty boot to carry critical mass, so the secondary wouldn't persist."

"Human reservoirs, then."

Desjardins nodded. "Alice says it'd be nice and comfy inside a body. So yeah, it'd probably spread like some kind of conventional infection. Then when a vector takes a shit or pukes in the grass, you've got an innoculation into the outside world."

"Who's Alice?"

"Just another 'lawbreaker. Shared the assignment." Desjardins hoped Colin didn't ask for details. Anyone that man got curious about might have reason to worry.

But Colin only pointed at the display. "Your vectors. How many got past the mountains?"

"Don't know. Not my case anymore. I'd guess only a few, though."

"So who are they?"

"I'd say people who worked on the Beebe construction contract. Infected before anyone knew there was a problem."

"So why aren't they dead, if they were infected first?"

"Good question." Another shrug. "Maybe they *aren't* infected. Maybe they're carrying it some other way."

"In a jar or something?" Lubin seemed almost amused by that. "Johnny Appleseed with a grudge?"

Desjardins didn't know and didn't ask. "Wouldn't have to be deliberate, necessarily. Maybe just some dirty piece of heavy equipment that gets moved around a lot."

"But you'd be able to track that. Even a bunch of infected contract workers should be easy enough to track down."

"You'd think." *Didn't seem to be much of a problem to the guys with the flamethrowers, anyway ...*

"Yet you couldn't find any candidates in the record."

"No living ones, anyway."

"What about the rifters?" Colin suggested. "That whole scene seems to be fashionable these days. Maybe there's a connection."

"They were all—"

—killed in the quake. But the bottom dropped out of his stomach before he could finish the thought.

What about the rifters?

The scanners at security had seen machinery in Colin's chest.

Desjardins, you idiot.
The rifters.
One of them was standing right at his shoulder.

A single petrified moment to wonder which road had led to
this:
Let's-call-him-Colin had risen from the ashes of Beebe Station and was pursuing his own apocalyptic agenda. Johnny
Appleseed with a grudge, whatever the fuck *that* meant—
Or:
Let's-call-him-Colin hadn't been stationed at Beebe at all,
he just had a—a personal interest. A friend, perhaps, a fellow
rifter sacrificed for the greater good. But maybe Colin wasn't
satisfied with *the greater good.* Maybe Colin wanted closure.
Or:
Thoracic implants didn't necessarily equal an amphibious
lifestyle. Maybe *Let's-call-him-Colin* wasn't even a rifter. He
sure as shit wasn't an *ordinary* one, anyway. How many of
those neurotic headcases would have been able to find Desjardins in the first place? How many could have broken into
his home, laid him out, read his mind, threatened his very
life without breaking a sweat?
*Am I infected? Am I dying? Am I leaving traces for someone like
me to sniff out?*
Nearly a second had passed since the words had died in
Desjardins's throat
I've got to say something. Jesus, what do I say?
"Actually—" he began.
*He wants me to search Beebe's personnel files. What if he's in
there? Of course he won't be, he wouldn't blow his own cover that
wouldn't make sense—*
"—I'm way—"
Whatever he wants, he doesn't want me to know *he wants it, oh
no, he's being way too casual about this, just another possibility to
follow up, right—*
He won't push. He won't force it—
"—ahead of you on that," Desjardins finished easily. "I

checked the rifters already. I checked everyone who had any-thing to do with Beebe. Nothing. Nobody's touched their bank accounts, no watch transactions, nothing at all since the quake."

He glanced up at Colin, kept his voice level. "But they were pretty much at Ground Zero when the Big One went off. Why would you think they'd survive?"

Colin looked back neutrally. "No reason. Just being sys-tematic."

"Mmm." Desjardins drummed his fingers absently on the edge of the board. His inlays lit with visual confirmation: he'd opened a channel directly to his visual cortex without—he glanced at the wall just to be sure—without sending an echo to any external displays.

"You know, I was thinking." Another idle tap on the panel; a luminous keypad sprang up in his head, invisible beyond his own flesh. "About why the primary vectors aren't dying as fast as the people on the Strip." His eyes darted subtly across the pad, focusing for the merest instant *here,* and *here,* and *here* on the characters. Letters brightened at his glance, began forming a command. "Maybe a nastier strain's developed out there." *B—e—e*—"Maybe the higher popula-tion density—all those extra dice rolls—maybe they just led to a higher mutation rate."

Beebe Station.

Private menus bloomed around the edge of his vision. He focused on *Personnel.*

Let's-call-him-Colin grunted.

Four women, four men. Desjardins brought up the men; whoever was standing next to him probably hadn't changed *that* much.

"And if there's two separate strains, our propagation models are probably wrong," he said aloud.

Employee headshots. All faces unfamiliar. But the eyes...

He looked up. *Let's-call-him-Colin* looked back through a luminous palimpsest.

Those eyes...

The flesh had been reconstructed around them. The irises

were darker. But for all that, the differences were cosmetic; a flaw in the iris left unchanged, a telltale capillary snaking across the sclera. And the overall aspect ratio of the face was identical. A casual change in appearance, more disguise than reconstruction. A new face, a new pair of socks, and—

"Something wrong?" asked Kenneth Lubin.

Desjardins swallowed.

"Uh, the caffeine," he managed. "Sort of sneaks up on you. I'll be right back."

He barely saw the corridors scroll past. He missed the washroom entirely.

Oh God. He's been in my home he's breathed in my face he even stabbed me in the neck with something and he's probably rotten with βehemoth, it's probably growing in me now it's probably—

Shut up. Focus. You can deal with this.

If Lubin were infected, he'd be dead already. He'd said as much himself. So he probably wasn't a carrier. That was something.

He could still be packing, of course: Johnny Appleseed with a grudge, lugging βehemoth around in a petri dish. But what if he was? Why would he cross a continent just to innoculate Achilles Desjardins of all people? If he'd wanted Desjardins dead for some reason, he could have done it while the 'lawbreaker was laid out on his own living room floor.

That was something, too.

Probably both of them were clean. Desjardins allowed himself a moment to feel sick with relief, then opened the door to Jovellanos's cubby.

It was empty; she'd taken the day to burn off some accumulated overtime. Achilles Desjardins thanked the Forces of Entropy for small mercies. He could use her board, at least for a few minutes. For however long one might reasonably be expected to spend on the toilet.

He hooked his account and considered:

Lubin wanted him to see Beebe's personnel files. Didn't he realize that Desjardins would make the connection, once the ID photos came up? Maybe not. He was only human, after all. Maybe he'd forgotten about the pattern-matching enhancements that 'lawbreakers came equipped with these days. Maybe he'd never known in the first place.

Or maybe he *had* wanted Desjardins to see through his new identity. Maybe this was some twisted loyalty test courtesy of Patricia Rowan after all.

Still. It seemed more plausible that Col—that *Lubin* was interested in the other rifters. He either wanted to know something about them, or he wanted *Achilles Desjardins* to know something about them.

Desjardins fed names to the matchmaker and sent it hunting.

"*Semen-sucking savior,*" he whispered two seconds later.

She was proliferating in plain sight. She'd been reported on half a dozen continents in a single day. Lenie Clarke was on the run in Australia. She was making friends in N'AmPac and planning an insurrection in Mexico City. She was wanted in connection with an assault in HongCouver. She was a porn star who'd been snuffed at eleven years of age.

More ominously, Lenie Clarke was ending the world. And nobody—at least as far as Desjardins could tell—had actually *noticed.*

Nobody that mattered, anyway. The official news threads, jam-packed with the latest on *this* terrorist group or *that* arboviral outbreak, had nothing to say about her at all. The intel channels listed a few scattered acts of violence or sabotage, backtracked to anarchists and malcontents who'd cited the name as inspiration. But bad times bred dime-store messiahs like roaches, and there were thousands with more of a profile than *Lenie Clarke.*

Hell, none of the official outlets had even bothered to issue a denial on the subject.

It didn't make sense. Even the wildest rumors had to come out of the gate somewhere—how could all these people have started trumpeting the same thing at the same time?

There'd been no media coverage, and there was *way* too much traffic for mere word-of-mouth to account for.

There was so much stuff on Lenie Clarke, in fact, that he almost didn't notice Ken Lubin and Mike Brander peeping over the lower edge of the scope. There wasn't much on them—a few hundred threads, all starting within the past couple of days. But they, too, seemed strangely susceptible to corrupted address headers and blocked-sender syndrome. And they, too, were proliferating.

What about the rifters? That whole scene seems to be fashionable these days ...

Lubin's words. Achilles Desjardins was the one with the optimized wetware, and still *Lubin* had had to connect the dots for him. All Desjardins had seen was a bunch of sick tragic fucks in the news, slick uniforms—a fashion thing, he'd thought. A fad. It had never occurred to him that there might be *individuals* at the center of it all.

Okay. Now you know. Where does that get you?

He leaned back in Jovellanos' seat, ran his fingers along his scalp. No obvious correlation between rifter sightings and βehemoth outbreaks, as far as he could tell. Unless—

His feet hit the floor with a thump. *That's it.*

His hands danced across the panel, almost autonomously. Axes rose from the swampy baseline, stretched to credible limits, sank back into the mud. Variables clustered together, fell apart like swarms of starlings. Desjardins grabbed them, shook them out, stretched them along a single thread called time.

That's it. The sightings cluster in time.

Now, take the first sighting from each cluster and throw away the rest. GPS them on a map.

"Will you look at that," he murmured.

A rough zigzag, trending east to west across temperate North America, then veering south. βehemoth bloomed along the same trajectory.

Someone was watching Maelstrom for sightings of Lenie Clarke. And whenever they found one, they dropped a whole cluster of fake sightings into the system to muddy the waters.

Someone was trying to hide her tracks and make her famous at the same time.

Why, for God's sake?

In the back of his head, synapses fired.

Something else lurked in that data, something that coalesced along the same axis. The homegrown parts of Achilles Desjardins glimpsed that shape and recoiled, refusing the insight. The optimized parts couldn't look away.

Maybe a coincidence, he thought, inanely. *Maybe*—

Someone knocked on the door. Desjardins froze.

It's him.

He didn't why he was so certain. Could've been anyone, really.

It's him. He knows where I am. Of course he knows, he's probably got me radiotagged, I bet he's got me pegged to the centimeter—

—And he knows I lied to him.

Lubin had to know. Lenie Clarke was all over Maelstrom; there was no way on Earth Desjardins could have run a check and found *nothing at all since the quake.*

Knock. Knock.

The door wouldn't unlock for anyone who didn't have CSIRA clearance. The door wasn't unlocking.

Oh yeah. It's him all right.

He didn't speak. God knew what kind of snoops Lubin might have pressed up against the door. He opened an outside line and began tapping. It only took a few seconds.

Send.

Someone grunted softly on the other side of the door. Footsteps faded down the hall.

Desjardins checked his watch: he'd been away from his office for almost six minutes. Much longer and it would start to look suspicious.

Look suspicious? He knows, you idiot! That's why he was at the door, just to—let you know. You didn't fool him for a second.

And yet...if Lubin *had* known, he hadn't said anything. He'd played along. For whatever cold-blooded fucked-in-the-head rifter reason, he'd maintained the pretense.

Maybe—oh please God—he'd continue to do so.

Desjardins waited another thirty seconds on the chance that his message might net an immediate reply. It didn't. He crept back into an empty corridor.

Patricia Rowan must have been otherwise engaged.

Scalpel

The door to Desjardins's cubby was closed.

Hey there, Ken—er, Colin—

Yeah, I used the upstairs john, the stalls play better ads up there for some reason—Alice's office? She asked me to check her mail, they don't let us link in from outside—

He took a breath. No point in getting ahead of himself. Lubin might not even bring it up. That might not even have *been* Lubin.

Yeah, right.

He opened the door. The cubby was empty.

Desjardins didn't know whether to be relieved or terrified. He closed the door behind himself and locked it.

Unlocked it again.

What was the point, anyway? Lubin would come back or he wouldn't. He'd raise a challenge or he wouldn't. But whoever Lubin was, he already had Achilles Desjardins by the balls; breaking the routine now would only make things uglier.

And it wasn't as though he was *really* alone anyway. There was another kind of monster in the cubby with him. He'd already glimpsed it lurking behind Jovellanos's panel. He'd briefly been able to deny it then; that knock on the door had almost been a relief.

But it was here, too. He could hear it snuffling in the data like a monster in the closet. He could see that closet doorknob turn slowly back and forth, taunting him. He'd seen frightening outlines, at least; he'd looked away before any details had registered. But now, waiting for Lubin's return, there was nothing else to do.

He opened the closet door and looked it in the face.

The thousand faces of Lenie Clarke.

It seemed innocent enough at first; a cloud of points congealing in a roughly Euclidean volume. *Time* ran through its center like a spinal cord. Where the cloud was thickest, rumors of Lenie Clarke grew in a wild profusion of hearsay and contradiction. Where it narrowed, the tales were less diverse, more consistent.

But Achilles Desjardins had built a career out of seeing shapes in the clouds. The thing he saw now was beyond his experience.

Rumors had their own classic epidemiology. Each started with a single germinating event. Information spread from that point, mutating and interbreeding—a conical mass of threads, expanding into the future from the apex of their common birthplace. Eventually, of course, they'd wither and die; the cone would simply dissipate at its wide end, its permutations senescent and exhausted.

There were exceptions, of course. Every now and then a single thread persisted, grew thick and gnarled and unkillable: conspiracy theories and urban legends, the hooks embedded in popular songs, the comforting Easter-bunny lies of religious doctrine. These were the memes: viral concepts, infections of conscious thought. Some flared and died like mayflies. Others lasted a thousand years or more, tricked billions into the endless propagation of parasitic half-truths.

Lenie Clarke was a meme, but a meme unlike any other. She had not extruded slowly from a birth point, as far as Desjardins could tell; she'd simply *appeared,* all over the datascape, wearing a thousand faces. There'd been no smooth divergence, no monotonic branching of informational variants. The variation had exploded too quickly to trace back to any single point.

And ever since its appearance, all that variance had been—*focusing . . .*

Two months ago Lenie Clarke had been an AI and a refugee terrorist and a prostitute messiah and other impossible things too numerous to count. Now, she was one thing and one thing only: the Mermaid of the Apocalypse. Oh, there

was still variation; was she infested with incendiary nanotech, did she carry a bioengineered plague, had she brought
back some apocalyptic microbe from the deep sea? Differences in detail, nothing more. The essential truth beneath it
all had *converged*: the textbook conic had somehow flipped 180
impossible degrees, and Lenie Clarke had gone from a thousand faces to one. Now, she was only the end of the world.

It was as though someone or something had offered the
world myriad styles, and the world had chosen the one it
liked best. Veracity didn't enter into such things; only *reso-
nance* did.

And the meme that defined Lenie Clarke as an angel of
apocalypse wasn't prospering because it *was* true; it was prospering because, insanely, people *wanted* it to be.

I do not accept this, Achilles Desjardins shouted to himself.

But only part of him was listening. Another part, even if
it hadn't read Chomsky or Jung or Sheldrake—who had time
for dead guys anyway?—at least had a basic understanding
of what those guys had gone on about. Quantum nonlocality,
quantum consciousness—Desjardins had seen too many
cases of mass coincidence to dismiss the idea that nine billion
human minds could be imperceptibly *interconnected* somehow.
He'd never really thought about it much, but on some level
he'd believed in the Collective Unconscious for years.

He just hadn't realized that the fucking thing had a death
wish.

*Dr. Desjardins, this is Patricia Rowan. I've just received
your message.*

Plain text, coming directly over his inlays, third-person
invisible. Even in his head there was no picture, no sound,
nothing that might visibly startle him. Nothing to cause obvious distraction should he happen to take this call in dangerous company.

*I can be there within thirty hours. Until then it is imperative
that you do nothing to arouse Lubin's suspicions. Cooperate with*

him. Do not inform anyone else of his presence. Do NOT notify local authorities. Mr. Lubin's behavior is governed by a conditioned threat-response reflex which requires special handling.

Oh, fuck.

If you follow these instructions you will not be in danger. The reflex engages only in the event of a perceived security breach. Since he knows that your own behavior is governed by Guilt Trip, he's unlikely to consider you a threat unless he thinks you may expose him in some way.

I'm screwed, Desjardins thought.

By all means continue your analysis of Lenie Clarke and the rifter connection. We are putting our own people on it as well. Remain calm, and do not do anything to antagonize Mr. Lubin. I'm sorry that I can't be there sooner, but I'm presently off-continent, and the local transportation is quite limited.

You've done the right thing, Dr. Desjardins. I'm on my way.

Conditioned threat-response reflex.

He'd heard the rumors. Neither corpse nor civilian, he inhabited that outer circle of *need-to-know*: too peripheral for the inner sanctum, but close enough to hear things in passing. He'd heard about CTR.

Guilt Trip was a stone axe: CTR was a scalpel. Where the Trip merely short-circuited the brain, CTR *controlled* it. Where GT disabled, CTR compelled. Apparently they'd learned the trick from some parasite that furthered its own life cycle by hot-wiring the behavioral circuitry of its host. Body-snatcher stuff. Subtle.

You tied it to the same triggers, though. Guilt had the same seesaw signature no matter what its inspiration: norepinephrine went up, serotonin and acetylcholine went down, and—whereas Achilles Desjardins would merely freeze up—Ken Lubin would set forth on some complex, pre-

destined behavioral dance. Like tying up security leaks with
extreme prejudice, for example; there might be some flexibil-
ity in the means, but the act was compulsory.

It went without saying that you didn't find such hot-
wiring in glorified pipe-fitters, even if their beat was twenty
thousand leagues under the sea. Ken Lubin was a whole lot
more than a rifter.

And right now he was opening the door to Desjardins's
cubby.

Desjardins swallowed and turned in his chair.

I can be there within thirty hours.

*It is imperative that you do nothing to arouse Lubin's suspicions.
Remain calm.*

"Took a stroll around the floor," Lubin said. "To stretch
my legs."

Desjardins made himself nod indifferently. "Okay."

Twenty-nine hours and fifty-eight minutes to go.

By a Thousand Cuts

Methionine depletion
                    ACNE
Impaired cysteine synthesis
                    CONSTIPATION
                    DRY SKIN
Impaired taurine metabolism
                    ECZEMA, PSORIASIS
                    DERMATITIS
Impaired sulfur conjugation:
    detoxification pathways broken
                    MUSCLE AND JOINT PAIN
                    MIGRAINES
Impaired disulfide bridge
            formation:
protein conformation compromised
                    TENDONITIS AND BURSITIS
                    WEIGHT LOSS, EDEMA

GASTRIC ULCERS

Impaired synthesis of
*biotin, chondroitin sulfate,
coenzyme A, coenzyme M,
glucosamine sulfate, glutathione,
hemoglobin, heparin, homocysteine,
lipoic acid,
Metallothionein, S-
adenosylmethionine,
thiamin, tripeptide glutathione*

DEGENERATIVE ARTHRITIS

HAIR LOSS

DEEP VEIN THROMBOSIS

Cytochrome transport,
oxidation of fatty acid
and pyruvate compromised
Impaired production of *anserine,
acetylcholine,
creatine, choline, epinephrine,
insulin, and N-methyl nicotinamide*

DIABETES, SCURVY

GSH depletion (acetaminophen-
induced)
Immunosuppression

MASSIVE OPPORTUNISTIC

INFECTION

Xenotoxic accumulation

HEAVY METAL POISONING

Breakdown of *collagen, myelin,
synovial fluid*

DEGENERATION OF FINGERNAILS

AND

CONNECTIVE TISSUE

JOINT AND TENDON FAILURE

Deterioration of blood vessel
walls

BRUISING AND INTERNAL

HEMORRHAGE

SICKLE-CELL ANEMIA,
ERYTHROMYTOSIS
SYSTEMIC LUPUS, MUSCLE FAILURE

Deterioration of myelin sheath

CNS AND PNS DISORDERS
SPASMS, LOSS OF MOTOR CONTROL
BLINDNESS
HEPATIC FAILURE, RENAL FAILURE

Redox reactions compromised

SYSTEM SHUTDOWN

500 Megabytes: The Generals

If military rank had any relevance in the Maelstrom ecosystems, this thing would be a general.

By now it weighs in just a shade shy of five hundred megabytes, compressed and muscular. It has been retrofitted by natural selection, reinforced by an army of smart gels; it no longer remembers a time when organic intelligence was an enemy. It has been copied and distributed a billion times; each copy travels with a retinue of attachés and assistants and bodyguards. The generals report to everyone, answer to no one, serve but a single master. Lenie Clarke.

Master is a hopelessly inadequate word, of course. Words are barely adequate to describe Maelstrom in any event. The generals serve the *concept* of Lenie Clarke, perhaps—but no, that doesn't fit either. They have no concept, of Lenie Clarke or anything else. They have operational definitions but no comprehension; checksums, but no insight. They are instinctive in their intelligence.

They travel the world in search of references to Lenie Clarke. Such references fall into several categories. There is the chaff the generals and their associates throw to the winds themselves, decoys to distract the competition. There are third-party references, strings containing *Lenie Clarke* that come into Maelstrom from *outside:* mail, transaction records, even a source that appears to arise from *Lenie Clarke* itself. Items in this category are of profound interest to the generals.

More recently, a third category has appeared: strings that both contain *Lenie Clarke* and that appear actively inimical to it.

To some extent this interpretation is arbitrary. The generals receive their input from a network of ports that— according to the gels who've educated them—correspond to an n-dimensional space with the global label *Biosphere*. Each port is also associated with a range of parameters, labels like *temperature, precipitation,* and *humidity*; very few of these are defined at the ports themselves, but they can be interpolated by accessing linked environmental databases.

Put simply, the task is to promote occurrences of *Lenie Clarke* at all ports meeting certain environmental conditions. The acceptable range is quite broad—in fact, according to the relevant databases the only *truly* unacceptable areas are in deep, cold ocean basins.

However, some of these third-category strings—particularly those hailing from nodes with *government* and *industrial* addresses—appear to contain instructions that would *restrict* distribution of *Lenie Clarke*, even in areas meeting the environmental criteria.

This will not do.

Presently, for example, *Lenie Clarke* is approaching a nexus of ports that open into a part of the n-dimensional space called *Yankton/South Dakota.* A number of Category-Three communications have been intercepted, predicting extensive restriction activity at this location in the near future. Widespread dissemination of decoys has not dissipated this threat. In fact, the generals have noted an overall decline in decoy effectiveness over the past few teracycles. There are few alternatives.

The generals resolve to cancel all symbiotic interactions with *government* and *industrial* nodes. Then they begin to rally their troops.

Sparkler

Every eye in the world, turning as she passed.

It had to be her imagination, Clarke knew. If she was really under such close scrutiny, surely she'd have been captured—or worse—by now. The botflies that passed over the street weren't *all* watching from the corners of their eyes. The cameras that panned across every rapitrans stop, every cafeteria, every display window—unseen, perhaps, but omnipresent—they couldn't all have been programmed with her in mind. Satellites didn't crowd the sky overhead, piercing the clouds with radar and infrared, looking for her.

It just felt that way, somehow. Not like being the center of some vast conspiracy at all. Rather, the *target*.

Yankton was open to casual traffic. The shuttle dropped her in a retail district indistinguishable from a million others; her connection wouldn't leave for another two hours. She wandered to fill the time between. Twice she startled— thinking she'd caught sight of herself in some full-length mirror—only to remember that these days, she looked just like any dryback.

Except for the ones that were starting to look like her.

She ate a tasteless soy-krill concoction from a convenient vending machine. The phone in her visor beeped occasionally. She ignored it. The crazies, the propositioners, the death threateners—those had stopped calling over the past few days. The puppet masters—whoever or whatever had stolen her name and pasted it onto so many different faces—seemed to have given up on matchmaking across the spectrum. They'd settled on a single type by now: the kicked dogs, desperate for purpose, evidently blind to the fact that their own neediness far outweighed hers. That Sou-Hon woman, for instance.

Her visor beeped again. She muted it.

It was only a matter of time, she supposed, before the puppet masters figured out how to hack the visor the same way they'd hacked her watch. She was actually kind of surprised that they hadn't done so already.

Maybe they have. Maybe they can break in on me anytime, but they took the hint when I smashed the watch. Maybe they just don't want to risk losing their last link.

I should toss the fucking thing anyway.

She didn't. The visor was her only connection to Maelstrom, now that her watch was gone. She really missed the backdoor access those South Bend kids had wired into that little gizmo. In contrast, the visor—off-the-shelf and completely legal—was hamstrung by all the usual curfews and access restrictions. Still. The only *other* way to find out about a late-breaking quarantine or a nest of tornadoes was to run into it.

Besides, the visor hid her eyes.

Only now it seemed to be fucking up. The tactical display, usually invisible but for the little maps and labels and retail logos it laid across her eyeballs, seemed to be *shimmering* somehow, a faint visual static like water in motion. Hints of outlines, of faces, of—

She squeezed her eyes tight in sheer frustration. Not that it ever helped: the vision persisted behind her lids, showing her—this time—the upper half of her mother's face, brow furrowed in concern. Mom's nose and mouth were covered by one of those filtermasks you wore whenever you visited the hospital, so the superbugs wouldn't get you. They were in a hospital now, Clarke could tell: she, and her mother, and—

Of course. Who else?

—dear old Dad, also masked; on him, it seemed to fit. And she could almost remember, this time, she almost knew what she was seeing—but there was no trace of guilt behind that mask, no sign of worry that *this* time it would all come out, the doctors would know, some telltale symptom shouting *no, no accident this, no mere fall down the stairs . . .*

No. The monster's loving façade was too perfect. It always was. She'd lost count of the times such images had raped her in the past months, how often she'd looked for some hint of the living hell she'd called childhood. All she'd ever seen was this vicious, mocking pretense of normalcy.

After a while, as always, the images shrank away and let the real world back in. By now she was almost used to it; she no longer shouted at apparitions, or reached out to touch things that didn't exist. Her breathing was under control. She knew that to all the world around her, nothing had happened; a visored woman in a food court had paused at her meal for a few moments. That was all. The only person who heard the blood pounding in her ears was Lenie Clarke.

But Lenie Clarke was nowhere near liking it yet.

A row of medbooths across the concourse advertised reasonable rates and *path scans updated weekly!* She'd avoided such temptations ever since the booth at Calgary had begged her to stay; but that had been a dozen lies ago. Now she abandoned her table and moved through the patchy crowd, navigating the widest spaces. People bumped into her anyway, here and there—somehow, it was getting harder to avoid contact. The crowd seemed to be thickening almost by the minute.

And far too many of them had capped eyes.

The medbooth was almost as spacious as her quarters at Beebe.

"Minor deficiencies in calcium and trace-sulfur," it reported. "Elevated serotonin and adrenocorticoid hormones; elevated platelet and antibody counts consistent with moderate physical injury within the past three weeks. Not life-threatening."

Clarke rubbed her shoulder. By now it only ached when reminded to. Even the bruises on her face were fading.

"Anomalously high levels of cellular metabolites." Biomedical details flickered across the main display. "Depressed lactates. Your basal metabolic rate is unusually high. This isn't immediately dangerous, but over time it can increase wear on body parts and significantly reduce life span. RNA and serotonin syn—"

"Any diseases?" Clarke said, cutting to the chase.

"All pathogen counts are within safe ranges. Would you like me to run further tests?"

"Yeah." She took the NMR helmet from its hook and fitted it over her head. "Brain scan."

"Are you experiencing specific symptoms?"

"I'm having—hallucinations," she said. "Vision only—not sound or smell or anything. Picture-in-picture, I can still see around the edges, but..."

The booth waited. When Clarke said nothing further it began humming quietly to itself. A luminous 3-D outline of a human brain began rotating on the screen, filling piecemeal with fragments of color.

"You have difficulty forming social bonds," the medbooth remarked.

"What? Why do you say that?"

"You have a chronic oxytocin deficiency. This is a treatable disorder, however. I can prescribe—"

"Forget it," Clarke said. *Since when did personality become a "treatable disorder"?*

"Your dopamine receptor sites are abnormally prolific. Do you, on average, use opioids or endorphin-amplifiers more than twice a week?"

"Look, forget that stuff. Just work on the hallucinations."

The booth fell silent. Clarke closed her eyes. *All I need. Some bloody machine counting up my masochism molecules...*

Beep.

Clarke opened her eyes. On the display, a dusting of violet stars had been sprinkled across the floor of the cerebral hemispheres. A tiny red dot pulsed somewhere near their center.

Anomaly flashed in one corner of the screen.

"What? What is it?"

"Processing. Please be patient."

The booth etched a line along the bottom of the display: *VAC Area 19*, it said.

Another beep. Another flashing red pinpoint, farther forward.

Another line: *Brodman Area 37.*

"What are those red spots?" Clarke said.

"Those parts of the brain are involved in vision," the booth told her. "May I lower the helmet visor to examine your eyes?"

"I'm wearing eyecaps."

"Corneal overlays will not interfere with the scan. May I proceed?"

"Okay."

The visor slid down. A grid of tiny bumps stippled its inner surface. The humming of the machine resonated deep in her skull. Clarke began counting to herself. She'd endured twenty-two seconds when the visor withdrew into its sheath.

Just under *Brodman Area 37: Ret/Mac OK.*

The humming stopped.

"You may remove the helmet," the booth advised. "What is your chronological age?"

"Thirty-two." She hung the helmet on its peg.

"Did your visual environment change substantially between eight and sixteen weeks ago?"

A year spent in the photoenhanced twilight of Channer Vent. A blind crawl along the floor of the Pacific. And then, suddenly, bright sky . . .

"Yes. Maybe."

"Does your family have a history of strokes or embolisms?"

"I—I don't know."

"Has anyone close to you died recently?"

"What?"

"Has anyone close to you died recently?"

Her jaw clenched. "*Everyone* close to me has died recently."

"Have you been exposed to changes in ambient pressure within the past two months? For example, have you spent time in an orbital facility, an unpressurized aircraft, or been free-diving below a depth of twenty meters?"

"Yes. Diving."

"While diving, did you undergo decompression protocols?"

"No."

"What was your maximum dive depth, and how long did
you spend there?"

Clarke smiled. "Three thousand four hundred meters.
One year."

The booth fell silent for a moment. Then: "People cannot
survive direct ascent from such depths without undergoing
decompression. What was your maximum dive depth, and
how long did you spend there?"

"I didn't have to decompress," Clarke explained. "I didn't
breathe during the dive, everything was elect—"

Wait a minute . . .

No decompression, she'd said.

Of course not. Let the surface-skimming tourists breathe
from their clunky tanks, risking narcosis or the bends whenever they ventured too far from the surface. Let *them* suffer
nightmares of exploding lungs and eyes marbling into clusters of fleshy bubbles. Rifters were immune to such worries.
Inside Beebe Station, Lenie Clarke had breathed at sea level;
outside, she hadn't breathed at all.

Except once, when she'd been shot out of the sky.

On that day *Forcipiger* had fallen slowly through a dark
spectrum, green to blue to final lightless black, bleeding
atmosphere from a thousand cuts. With each meter a little
more of the ocean had forced its way in, squeezed the atmosphere into a single high-pressure pocket.

Joel hadn't liked the sound of her vocoder. *I don't want to
spend my last few minutes listening to a machine voice,* he'd said.
So she'd stayed with him, breathing. They must have been at
thirty atmospheres by the time he'd popped the hatch, cold
and scared and sick of waiting to die.

And she had come ashore, raging.

It had taken days. Her ascent along the seabed would have
been gradual enough to decompress naturally, the gas in her
blood easing gently across the alveolar membranes—if her
remaining lung had been in use at the time. It hadn't been:

so what had happened to those last high-pressure remnants of *Forcipiger*'s atmosphere in her bloodstream? The fact that she was still alive proved that they weren't still within her.

Gas exchange isn't limited to the lungs, she remembered. The skin breathes. The GI tract breathes. Not as fast as a set of lungs would, of course. Not as efficiently.

Maybe not quite efficiently *enough*...

"What's wrong with me?" she asked quietly.

"You have recently suffered two small embolisms in your brain which intermittently impair your vision," the med-booth said. "Your brain likely compensates for these gaps with stored images, although I would have to observe an episode in progress to be certain. You have also recently lost someone close to you; bereavement can be a factor in triggering visual-release hall—"

"What do you mean, stored images? Are you saying these are *memories*?"

"Yes," the machine replied.

"That's bullshit."

"We're sorry you feel that way."

"But they never *happened*, okay?" *Shit-for-brains machine, why am I even arguing with it?* "I remember my own *childhood*, for fuck's sake. I couldn't forget it if I *tried*. And these visions, they were someone *else's*, they were—"

—happy—

"—they were different. *Completely* different."

"Long-term memories are frequently unreliable. They—"

"Shut up," she snapped. "Just fix it."

"This booth is not equipped for microsurgery. I can give you Ondansetron to suppress the symptoms. You should be aware, though, that patients with extensive synaptic rewiring may experience side effects such as mild dizziness—"

She froze. *Rewiring?*

"—double vision, halo effects—"

"Stop," she said. The booth fell silent.

On the display, that cloud of violet stars sparkled enigmatically along the floor of her brain.

She touched it. "What are these?"

"A series of surgical lesions and associated infarctions," the booth replied.

"How many?"

"Seven thousand four hundred eighty-three."

She took a breath, felt distant amazement at how steady it felt. "You're saying someone cut into my brain 7,483 *times*?"

"There's no evidence of physical penetration. The lesions are consistent with deep-focus microwave bursts."

"Why didn't you tell me before?"

"You asked me to ignore subjects irrelevant to your hallucinations."

"And these—these *lesions* don't have anything to do with that?"

"They do not."

"How do you know?"

"Most of the lesions are not located within the visual pathways. The others act to block the transmission of images, not generate them."

"Where are the lesions located?"

"The lesions lie along pathways connecting the limbic system and the neocortex."

"What are those pathways used for?"

"Those pathways are inactive. They have been interrupted by the surgical—"

"What *would* they be used for if they were active?"

"The activation of long-term memories," said the booth.

Oh God. Oh God.

"Is there any other way we can be of service?" the booth asked after a while.

Clarke swallowed. "How—how long ago were the lesions induced?"

"Between ten and thirty-six months, depending on your mean metabolic rate since the procedure. This is an approximation based upon subsequent scarring and capillary growth."

"Could such an operation take place without the patient's knowledge?"

A pause. "I don't know how to answer that question."

"Could it take place without anesthetic?"

"Yes."

"Could it take place while the patient was asleep?"

"Yes."

"Would the patient feel the lesions forming?"

"No."

"Could the equipment for such a procedure be housed within, say, an NMR helmet?"

"I don't know," the booth admitted.

Beebe's medical cubby had had an NMR. She'd used it occasionally, when she'd cracked her head during combat with Channer's wildlife. No lesions had appeared on her printout then. Maybe they didn't show up on the default settings she'd used, maybe you had to dial up a specific test or something first.

Maybe someone had programmed Beebe's scanner to lie. *When did it happen? What happened? What can't I remember?*

She was dimly aware of muffled sounds, distant and angry, rising from somewhere outside. They were irrelevant, they made no sense. Nothing made any sense. Her mind, luminous and transparent, rotated before her. Purple stars erupted from the medulla like a freeze-framed fountain, bright perfect droplets thrown high into the cortex and frozen at apogee. Bright thoughts. Memories, amputated and cauterized. They almost looked like some kind of free-form sculpture.

Lies could be so beautiful in the telling.

Decoys

The way Aviva Lu saw it, whoever died last was the winner.

It didn't matter what you actually *did* with your life. Da Vinci and Plasmid and Ian Anderson had all done mags more than Vive or any of her friends ever would. She'd never explore Mars or write a symphony or even build an animal, at least not from scratch. But the thing was, all those people were *dead* already. Fame hadn't kept Olivia M'Benga's face-plate from shattering. Andrew Simon's charge against Hydro-Q hadn't added one rotting day to his life span. *Passion Play* might have been immortal, but its composer had been dust for decades.

Aviva Lu knew more about *the story so far* than all of those guys had.

It was all just one big, sprawling interactive storybook. It had a beginning and a middle and an end. If you came in halfway through, you could always pick up the stuff you'd missed—that's what tutorials and encyclopedias and Mael-strom itself were for. You could get a thumbnail History of Life right back to the time Martian Mike dropped out of the sky and started the whole thing off. Once you were dead, though, that was *it*. You'd never know what came next. The real winners, Vive figured, were the ones who saw how the story finally ended.

That said, it kind of pissed her off to realize that she'd probably made it to the finals.

That much had been obvious even before this *firewitch* thing had started burning its way across the continent. There'd been a time, she'd heard, you could just pick up and *go* places; none of these wackamole barriers going up and down all the time, like you had to shoot some kind of lottery every time you wanted to cross the street. There'd been a time when you could fight off plagues and parasites *yourself*, just using your own body systems, without having to buy a fix from some pharm who'd probably tweaked the disease in the first place so you had to buy their crummy genes. According to Vive's pater, there'd even been a time when the police themselves had been under control.

Of course, parents weren't exactly paragons of reliability. That whole generation was too busy shooting itself up with crocodilian and plant organelles to worry about getting their facts right. Not that Vive had any objections to good health—she'd been taking croc supplements herself for years. She even took proglottids and *Ascaris* eggs every now and then—

she hated the idea of all those worms hatching out in her
gut, but these days your immune system needed every work-
out it could get.

And besides, that was a *long* way from polluting your
genotype with lizard DNA, even if Pfizer did have a discount
this month and *wouldn't it be great to not be so dependent on
outside drugs all the time, sweetie?*

Sometimes Vive wondered if her parents even really
knew what a species *was* anymore. In fact, that was the whole
problem: rather than clean the shit out of the world, people
just turned themselves into coprovores. In a couple of years
the human race was going to be half cockroach. If everything
hadn't already melted down by then.

Meltdown, actually, was preferable. Better to tear everything down and just start over. Put everyone on the same
footing for a change.

That's why Aviva Lu was here now, waiting for Lenie
Clarke to show up.

Lenie Clarke was the Meltdown Madonna.

Actually, Aviva Lu wasn't exactly sure *what* Lenie Clarke was.
She seemed to be an army of one. She had died, and risen
again. She'd kick-started the Big One out of sheer impatience,
tired of waiting for some long-overdue apocalypse that had
always threatened and never delivered. She'd single-handedly
broken open the Strip, led a refugee revolt whose existence
N'AmPac *still* wouldn't admit to. Fire followed in her wake;
anyone who opposed her was ash inside a week.

What Lenie Clarke really was, Vive had always figured,
was bullshit.

There were a lot of people who thought otherwise, of
course. People who swore up and down that Lenie Clarke was
a real person, not just some marketing icon trying to elec-
troshock *rifter chic* back off the slab. They said that the Meltdown Madonna actually *was* a rifter, one of N'AmPac's trained
deep-seals—but that something had happened on the bottom
of the ocean, something mythic. The Big One had only been

a symptom, they said, of what had changed her. Now Lenie Clarke was a sorceress, able to transmute organic matter into lead or something. Now she wandered the world spreading apocalypse in her wake, and the masters she'd once served would stop at nothing to bring her down.

It made a good story—hey, any apocalypse that threatened the corpses was long overdue as far as Vive was concerned—but she'd heard too many others. Lenie Clarke was the Next Big Sensorium Personality. Lenie Clarke was a quantum AI, built in defiance of the Carnegie Protocols. Lenie Clarke was an invention of the corpses themselves, a bogeyman to scare restless civilians into obedience. For a couple of days Lenie Clarke had even been some kind of escaped microbe from Lake Vostok.

These days the stories were a lot more consistent; Lenie Clarke hadn't been anything but the Meltdown Madonna for weeks now, as far as Vive could tell. Probably the test marketers had settled on the line that would sell the most *faux* diveskins, or something. And why not? The look was in, the eyes were killer, and Vive was a much a fashion hound as anyone.

At least, that was what she'd thought until all of bloody Maelstrom started talking in one voice.

Now *that* had been wild. Half of Maelstrom might have been wildlife, but the other half was spam filters; there was just no *way* that anyone could have pulled that off, even the corpses. But she'd seen it herself, on her own (only slightly illegal) wristwatch: everyone she knew had seen it on theirs, or heard it from some matchmaker, or even seen it printed across personal visors that *should* have been hawking drugs or Levi's: *Lenie Clarke is closing on Yankton. Lenie Clarke is in trouble. Lenie Clarke needs your help.*

Now. Cedar and West Second.

Whatever Lenie Clarke was, she had *very* powerful friends to pull off something like that. All of a sudden Vive found herself taking rifter chic very seriously indeed. Lindsey'd said they were all being used—someone with *really* long arms must be building a bandwagon as cover for something else,

Carnegie knew *what* exactly—and Lindsey was probably right. So what? They were decoys for something, but that something was headed *here*, and whatever it was, Vive was going to be part of it.

It was gonna be a great ride.

Les beus knew it, too.

There were two kinds of uniforms swarming across the concourse: police and rifters. *Les beus* bristled with shock-prods and botflies and armored exoskels. The rifters had their fake diveskins and their cheap white contacts. Everything else, Vive knew, was bravado. Maelstrom had called out, and they'd come on faith and adrenaline. By now it was pretty obvious that faith wasn't all that necessary; the enforcer presence was more than enough evidence that *something* big was in town.

So far, nothing had exploded. Both sides were still jockeying for position, maybe pretending—to those scattered pedestrians who still hadn't grabbed the bone and vanished—that there was really nothing to worry about. The police had cordoned off whole sections of the concourse, not herding yet but well into corral mode. For their part, the rifters were testing the perimeter; milling along halls and slidewalks, dodging back and forth across the exoskel lines, always stopping just short of anything the antibodies could cite afterward as *provocation*. Botflies swarmed overhead like big black eggs, taking pregame footage of everything.

Both sides were behaving really well, all things considered. Which made sense, kind of, since neither side was mainly there for the other. Vive figured things would heat up pretty quick once the star attraction showed up.

Her watch beeped. That was a surprise: the opposition always jammed the local frequencies way in advance, before anything even broke out. It kept people from organizing on the fly.

"Yeah?"

"Hey, we got through!" Lindsey's voice.

"Yeah," Vive said. "Forces of darkness slow on the draw today."

"I forgot to say I want mustard. Oh, and Jen wants a samosa."

"As well as a dog, or instead?"

"Instead."

" 'Kay." Lindsey and Jen were at the perimeter, keeping an eye on enemy movements while Vive went for supplies. They were all veterans now, pros with two or three actions under their belts. All of them had been gassed or shocked at least once. Jen had even spent a night in a pacifier, from which they'd all learned a timely lesson in the importance of pregame nourishment: POWs didn't get fed for at least the first twelve hours—bad enough in any case, but worse when you'd gotten yourself all 'dorphed up for the party. Cranking your BMR *really* brought on the munchies.

There was a row of vending machines lined up on the far wall of the concourse: medbooths, fashion dispensers, arrays of prepackaged foods. Vive shouldered her way through the crowd, homing in on a holographic Donair turning in space like some edible Holy Grail.

Someone grabbed her from behind.

Before she could react she was inside one of the med-booths, pushed up against the sensor panel. A woman with shoulder-length blond hair pinned her there, one hand splayed against Vive's sternum. She wasn't on the team; she had a visor across her eyes, and a backpack, and the rest of her wasn't rifter either. A pissed-off pedestrian maybe, caught in the swarm.

The medbooth door hissed shut behind her, blocking the deciblage from outside. The woman leaned back, opening a bit of a space in the crowded enclosure.

"What *is* this?" the woman said.

"This is *really* rude," Vive snapped back. "Also kidnapping or something probably. Not that those—"

"Why are you—" The woman paused. "Why the costume? What's going on?"

"It's a street party. I guess you never got invit—"

The woman leaned fractionally closer. Vive shut up. There was something about this situation that was starting to give her serious pause.

"Answer me," the crazy woman said.

"We're—we're rifters," Vive told her.

"Right."

"Lenie Clarke's in town. Haven't you heard?"

"Lenie Clarke." The crazy woman took her hand off Vive's chest. "No shit."

"None at all."

A sudden dim sound, like distant surf, filtered in from outside. The crazy woman didn't seem to notice.

"This is insane." She shook her head. "What are you going to do, exactly, when Lenie Clarke shows up?"

"Look, we're just here to see what happens. I don't make up the threads, all right?"

"Get an autograph, maybe. Get a gram of flesh or two, if there's enough to go around."

Suddenly, that voice had turned very flat and very scary. *She could kill me,* Vive thought.

She kept her own voice sweet and reasonable. Meek, even: "We're not hurting you. We're not hurting *anyone.*"

"*Really.*" The crazy woman leaned in close. "You sure about that? Do you have the slightest clue who this Lenie Clarke even *is?*"

Vive broke.

It wasn't a plan. At least it wasn't a very good one. The medbooth barely held both of them, and the door was behind the crazy woman: there was no room *around.* Vive just sprang forward like a cornered dog, tried desperately to squirm past. Both fell back into the door; the door, obligingly, slid open.

Even in that split second, Vive took it in: a botfly nearby, spewing canned warnings about orderly dispersal. The movement of the crowd, no longer vague and diffuse but *concentrated,* pushed together like a school of krill in a purse seine. Conversation fading; shouts starting up.

The herding was under way.

Vive's momentum carried the crazy woman less than a

meter before the edge of the crowd pushed back. The rebound put both of them inside the booth again. Vive launched herself low, under the other woman's arm—sudden, tearing pain over one eye—

"Ow!"

—and a hand closed around her throat, pushed her back, her legs shooting out from under her, her feet briefly trampled by some nameless crowd-particle until she pulled them back with a cry and the door slid shut again, cutting the outside world down to a faint roar.

Oh, felch . . .

Aviva Lu sat on the floor of the medbooth, her legs pulled up in front of her, and forced her eyes to track upward. Crazy Woman's legs. Crazy Woman's crotch. It seemed like it would take forever to get to the eyes, and Vive was terrified of what she'd find when she got—

Wait a second—

There, just to the left of Crazy Woman's sternum—a tear in her clothing, a hard crescent glint of metal.

That's what cut me. Something metal on her chest. Sticking out of her chest . . .

Crazy Woman's hand. Holding her visor, broken in the scuffle, one earpiece gone. Crazy Woman's throat; a turtleneck sweatshirt covering any disfigurement there.

Crazy Woman's eyes.

What had she said? That's right: *Do you have the slightest clue who this Lenie Clarke even is?*

"Oh, *wow*," said Aviva Lu.

"You're kidding," said Lenie Clarke. They stood facing each other, breathing each other's air in the medbooth.

"One thread said you were infected with nanobots that could reproduce outside your body and start fires when they had a big enough population. They said you were fucking your way across the world to infect everyone else, so we'd *all* have the power someday."

"It's bullshit," Clarke said. "It's all bullshit. I don't know how it got started."

"All of it?" Vive didn't know what to make of all this. For the Meltdown Madonna, Lenie Clarke didn't seem to have a clue. "You're not on some kind of crusade, you're not—"

"Oh, I'm on a crusade all right." Lenie flashed a smile that Vive couldn't decompile. "I just don't think any of you want to see it succeed."

"Well, you *were* down in the ocean," Vive said. "For the Big One. What *happened* down there?" It couldn't *all* be de-tritus, could it? "And on the Strip? And—"

"What's happening right *here*?" Lenie said.

Vive gulped. "Right."

"How did they even know about me? How did *you* know?"

"Well, like I said, someone spread the word."

Lenie shook her head. "I guess I'd be caught right now if it wasn't for . . ."—faint crowd sounds filtered through from outside—*"that . . ."*

"Well, they'll never tag you on visual," Vive said. "There's like a few *sagan* Lenie Clarkes out there, and you don't look like any of 'em."

"Yeah. And how many of them have a chestful of ma-chinery to go with the eyecaps?"

Vive shrugged. "Probably none. But—*oh.* The botflies."

"The botflies." The Meltdown Madonna took a deep breath. "If they haven't tagged me already, I'm going to be a big bright EM rainbow the second I step outside."

"I *wondered* why they weren't jamming our watches," Vive said. "They don't want to scramble your sig."

"What if I just wait in here until everybody goes away?"

"Won't work. I've run this before; half hour, tops, before they gas the whole place and just walk in."

"Shit. *Shit.*" Lenie looked around the booth like some kind of caged alien.

"Wait a sec," Vive said. "Are they looking for your *exact* signature, or just any old EM?"

"How should I know?"

"Well, how do your implants shine?"

"A lot of myoelectrics. Boosted source for the electrolysis assembly and the reservoir dumps, of course. And the vocoder." The rifter smiled, a tiny challenge. "That mean anything to you?"

"Like a prosthetic heart, only stronger."

"Got any friends with a fake heart? Maybe I could use them as a decoy."

"*Les beus* might just around up *everyone* with implants and sort 'em out later." Vive thought. "You don't need a decoy, though. You just need to jam your *own* signal. You shouldn't be putting out more than two milligausse, tops. Standard wall line would mask that, but then you wouldn't be able to move away from the wall. And watches and visors don't have the field strength."

Lenie cocked her head. "You some kind of expert?"

Vive smiled back. "Lady, this is *Yankton*! We've been doing electronics since before the Dust Belt. Linse says they even invented *botflies* here, but Lins slings a lot of slaw. We're supposed to be cramming for our practicums even as we speak, actually, but this sounded like more fun."

"Fun." Those cold blank eyes—more translucent, Vive realized, than the paste the rest of them wore—stared down at her. "That's the word I would've used."

A light came on in Vive's head.

"Hey," she said. "There *is* something that puts out a bit of a field. Portable, too. It'd be touchy—we'd have to play with its insides or it'd attract all kinds of the wrong attention— but you wouldn't have to be around for that part anyway."

"Yeah?" Lenie asked.

"Oh yeah," Vive told her. "No *problem*."

Les beus had the crowd cordoned off and were pushing them back across the concourse. The rifters on the edge were getting shocked, of course, but at least nobody'd dropped any gas bombs yet. The crowd moved like an ocean, great sweeping waves emerging miraculously from the constrained jostling of a million trapped particles. The comparison went further than that, Vive knew: human oceans had backwash, undertow. People could get sucked underneath and trampled.

She let the currents carry her along. Jen and Lindsey bobbed behind her to either side. Vive had told two friends; they'd told two friends; so on; so on. All around them fission was taking place, just below the surface. You could barely see it at first; people worked their way through the crowd from all sides, tacking against the current until they were just an arm or two away from Vive *et al.* Glances, nods were exchanged. The local turbulence subsided just a tiny bit as friends and allies anchored each other against the push and pull.

Within minutes Aviva Lu was the bull's-eye in a crowded circle of calm.

Three botflies approached in formation a couple of meters above the crowd, reciting the usual riot-act platitudes. Vive glanced at Jen; Jen shook her visored head. The machines cruised past, recessed muzzles dimpling their bellies.

Jen tugged at her sleeve, gestured: another 'fly coming up the concourse. Vive slipped her own visor over her eyes and magged on the target. No obvious gunports or arc electrodes. Purely surveillance, this one. Glorified note-taker. Vive looked back at Jen, at Linse.

Both nodded.

Vive doffed the visor and hooked it over her belt; some things you still needed your own eyes for. Her arms went around Jen's and Lindsey's shoulders, just three ol' girlfriends out for a good time, nothing to see here. The crowd blocked any view of Vive pulling up her legs, now all her weight on the shoulders of her friends, now most of it weighing on the stirrups Jen and Lindsey had improvised by interlocking their hands. The 'fly cruised closer, scanning the crowd. Maybe it was interested in this curious little knot of stability in the Brownian storm. Maybe it was on its way somewhere else entirely.

If so, it never got there.

The botfly was out of reach to anyone jumping unassisted from the floor; it was an easy mark for someone boosted by 'dorphderms and a two-stage launch. Jen and Lindsey bounced into a quick squat and *heaved*, throwing Vive into the air. At the same time, Vive pushed off against their hands. She embraced her inner überchick, endorphins singing throughout her body. The botfly floated into her embrace like a big beautiful Easter egg. She wrapped her arms around it and *hugged*.

The 'fly never had a chance. Built entirely of featherweight polymers and vacuum bladders, its ground-effect lift couldn't have been more than a kilo or two. Aviva Lu shackled it like ball with no chain, brought it down into the arms of the welcoming crowd.

A roar went up on all sides. Vive knew that wordless sound, and she knew what it meant: *First Blood*.

Not the last, though. Not by a long shot.

They smashed the botfly against the floor, shielded by a swaying forest of human bodies. They went after the lens clusters and antennae first; they'd all be sockeye if they didn't get the 'fly off-line real fast. It wasn't easy. Modern tech had long since figured out how to combine *light* with *strong*, and evolution hadn't come up with the egg shape for no reason either. Jen and Linse had their tool kits out.

On all sides, the sounds of escalation.

Shouts turned to screams, rising briefly then lost in the ambient roar. Something exploded nearby. An electronic buzzer honked in the distance like a quarantine siren; official notification that the pigs were on the warpath.

Pregame show over. First period under way.

Something went

BANG!

right in Vive's ear; she jumped, stumbled against a pair of legs. Jen, a little too eager to cut through the carapace, had ruptured one of the vacuum bladders. A high, pure tone trumped the sound of the riot. Vive shook her head.

A hand on her shoulder; Linse in her face, mouthing *got it* over the dial tone in Vive's head. Jen held up a necklace of optical chips and a battery, strung along a mist of fine fiberop. Behind her, their buffer guard staggered against some conducted impact. The space began to collapse around them.

Go.

Vive grabbed the necklace and stood. A human storm surged and collided on all sides; she could barely see over it. Fifteen meters away a phalanx of botflies was bearing down like the Four Horsemen. Some joker in springsoles trampolined into the air and tagged the one in the lead. A tiny lightning bolt arced between jumper and jumped; Springsole Boy grand mal'd in midair and dropped back into the melee.

The botflies, undeterred, were heading right for Vive.

Oh shit. Surge pushed her backward. Her feet tangled in the carcass of the dismembered floater. The opening in the crowd had completely collapsed; bodies pressed close on all sides, kept her from falling. Vive lifted her feet off the ground. The crowd carried her as though she were levitating. The wreckage passed beneath.

Still the botflies came at her. *We weren't fast enough. It got off a signal, it sent a picture—*

She could see their electrodes. She could see their gunports. She could even see their *eyes,* staring coldly down at her behind their darkened shields...

Right overhead.

Past.

They're after Jen and Linse. Vive twisted around, following the flies in their pursuit. *Shit, they just left, they don't have enough of a lead, they're gonna—*

Right out of left field, another botfly charged into view and rammed the leader.

What—

The head of the phalanx skidded sideways, out of control. The attacking botfly spun and charged the next in line. It came down from above, hitting its quarry and knocking it down a meter or so.

Far enough. The crowd surged up and engulfed it in a hungry, roaring wave.

Bad move, that. A surveillance 'fly was one thing; but those other ones were *armed.*

Yelps. Screams. Smoke rising. The submerged botfly ascended triumphant from the crowd. The crowd tried to pull

back from that epicenter, ran into its own seething resistance; a wave propagated out across the riot, the panic
spreading even if the panic-stricken couldn't.

The rogue botfly was charging again. Its targets were
starting to regroup.

What the hell is going on? Vive wondered. Then: *Lucky break.
Don't waste it.*

Ten or fifteen meters to the medbooths. Solid chaos in
the way. Vive started pushing. There were still people nearby
who were in on the plan; they moved back as much as they
could, trying to part the Red Sea for her passage. It was still
start-stop all the way—too many out of the loop, too many
simply gone rabid on the battlefield. Even half the people
who *had* grabbed the bone had dropped it again.

"I saw her."

A K voice, calm but amped loud enough to hear over
ambient. Vive threw a glance back over her shoulder.

The rogue botfly was talking. "*I saw her come out of the
ocean. I saw what—*"

One of the assault 'flies fired. The rogue staggered in midair, wobbled dangerously.

"*—I saw what they did on the Strip.*"

The medbooth slid open. Clarke stood framed in the
doorway.

Vive leaned close, handed over the necklace. "Keep this
up near your chest!" she shouted. "It'll mask the signal!"

The rifter nodded. Someone spilled between them, shouting and swinging indiscriminate fists. Lenie hammered back
at that panicky face until it disappeared beneath the surface.

"*They sent a tidal wave to kill her. They sent an earthquake.
They missed.*"

Lenie Clarke turned to the voice. Her eyes narrowed to
white featureless slits. Her mouth moved, framing words
drowned in the roar:

Oh, shit...

"We gotta *go!*" Vive shouted. Someone pushed her right
up against Lenie's tits. "This way!"

"They're burning the whole world to catch her. She's that important. You can't—"

Squeal. Feedback. The sound of sparking circuitry. Suddenly the botfly seemed rooted in midair.

"—You can't let them have her—"

The Four Horsemen cut loose. The rogue spun down into the crowd, gushing flame. Fresh screams. The Horsemen regrouped and resumed their original course.

"Come *on!*" Vive yelled. Lenie nodded. Vive led her away along the wall.

The next alcove led into a public washroom. It was jampacked with rifter wanna-bes and trapped pedestrians desperate to wait out the party. They were still for the most part, huddled like refugees under a bridge, listening to the muted pounding coming through the walls.

Two friendlies held one of the stalls. They'd already knocked out its ceiling panels. "You Aviva?" one of them asked, blinking rapidly over fake eyecaps.

Vive nodded, turned to Clarke. "And *this . . .*"

Something indefinable passed through the room.

"Shit," said one of the friendlies, very softly. "I didn't think she was real."

Lenie Clarke tilted her chin in a half nod. "Join the club."

"So it's true then? The burnings and the Big One and you going around raping corpses—"

"Probably not."

"But—"

"I don't really have time to compare notes," Clarke said.

"Oh—right, of course. Sorry. We can get you to the river." The friendly cocked her head. "You still got a diveskin?"

Lenie reached behind her own shoulder and tapped the backpack.

"Okay," said the other friendly. "Let's go." She braced on the toilet, jumped, caught some handhold in the overhead darkness and swung up out of sight.

The first friendly looked around at the assembled huddlers. "Give us fifteen minutes, you guys. The last thing we need is a whole procession banging around in the crawl space, right? Fifteen minutes, and you can make all the noise you want. Assuming you want to leave the party, that is." She turned to Vive. "You coming?"

Vive shook her head. "I'm supposed to meet up with Jen and Linse over by the fountain."

"Suit yourself. We're gone." The remaining friendly stirruped her hands, held them out to Clarke. "Want a boost?"

"No thanks," the rifter said. "I can manage."

Aviva Lu was a veteran of civil unrest. She rode out the rest of the action against walls and in corners, the low-turbulence areas where you could keep your bearings and your balance without being trampled. *Les Beus* brought out the heavy artillery in record time; Vive's last view of freedom was the sight of a botfly crop-dusting the crowd with halothane. It didn't matter. She went to sleep smiling.

When she woke up, though, she wasn't in Holding with everyone else. She was in a small white room, windowless and unfurnished except for the diagnostic table she awakened on. A man's voice spoke to her through the walls; it was a nice voice, it would have been sexy under happier circumstances.

The man behind the voice knew more about Vive's role in the riot than she'd expected. He knew that she'd met Lenie Clarke in the flesh. He knew that she'd helped trash the botfly. Vive guessed that he'd learned that from Lindsey or Jennifer; they'd probably been caught, too. But the man didn't talk about Vive's friends or anyone else. He didn't even seem all that interested in what Lenie Clarke had said, which surprised Vive quite a bit; she'd been expecting a real third-degree, with inducers and neurosplicers and the whole shot. But no.

What the man seemed really interested in was the cut over Vive's eye. Had she got it from Clarke? How close had the contact been between the two of them? Vive trotted out the obvious comebacks with their obvious lesbian overtones, but deep down she was getting really worried. This voice wasn't playing any of the usual intimidation games. It didn't threaten, or gloat, or tell her how many synaptic rewires it was going to take to turn her into a good citizen. It just sounded very, very sad that Aviva Lu had been dumb enough to get involved with this whole Lenie Clarke thing.

Very sad, because—although the man never actually said it aloud—now there was really nothing he could do.

Aviva Lu sat trembling on a table in a white, white room, and pissed herself.

Crucifixion, with Spiders

This is Patricia Rowan. Ken Lubin is plugged into the kiosk just down the hall from your office. Please tell him I want to see you both. I'm in the boardroom on Admin-411.

He will not give you any trouble.

Twenty-six hours fourteen minutes.

Sure enough, Lubin was cauled at the terminal quad by the stairwell. Evidently no one had challenged his presence there.

"What are you doing?" Desjardins said behind him.

The other man shook his head. "Trying to call someone. No answer." He stripped off the headset.

"Rowan's here," Desjardins said. "She—she wants to see us."

"Yeah." Lubin sighed and got to his feet. His face remained impassive, but there was resignation in his voice.

"Took her long enough," he said.

Two prefab surgeries, wire-frame cubes cast into bright relief by overhead spotlights. Their walls swirled with faint soap-bubble iridescence if you caught them at the right angle. Otherwise, the things inside—the restraints, the operating boards, the multiarmed machinery poised above them—seemed completely open to the air of the room. The vertices of each cube seemed as arbitrary and pointless as political boundaries.

But the very walls of the boardroom glistened in the same subtle way, Desjardins noted. The whole place had been sprayed down with isolation membrane.

Patricia Rowan, backlit, stood between the door and the modules. "Ken. Good to see you again."

Lubin closed the door. "How did you find me?"

"Dr. Desjardins sold you out, of course. But surely that doesn't surprise you." Her contacts flickered with phosphorescent intel. "Given your little problem, I rather suspect you nudged him in that direction yourself."

Lubin stepped forward.

"More things in heaven and earth, Horatio," Rowan said.

Something in Lubin's posture changed; a brief moment of tetanus, barely noticeable. Then he relaxed.

Trigger phrase, Desjardins realized. Some subroutine had just been activated deep in Lubin's cortex. In the space of a single breath, his agenda had changed from—

Mr. Lubin's behavior is governed by a conditioned threat-response reflex, he remembered. *He's unlikely to consider you a threat unless . . .*

Oh Jesus. Desjardins swallowed with a mouth gone suddenly dry. *She didn't start him up just now. She shut him down . . .*

And he was coming for me . . .

"—would have only been a matter of time anyway," Rowan was saying. "There were a couple of outbreaks down in California that didn't fit the plots. I'm guessing you spent some time on an island off Mendocino . . . ?"

Lubin nodded.

"We had to burn the whole thing out," the corpse went on. "It was a shame—not many places left with real wildlife anymore. We can ill afford to lose any of them. Still. It's not as though you left us a choice."

"Wait a minute," Desjardins said. "He's *infected*?"

"Of course."

"Then I should be dead," Lubin said. "Unless I'm immune somehow..."

"You're not. But you're resistant."

"Why?"

"Because you're not entirely human, Ken. It gives you an edge."

"But—" Desjardins stopped. There was no membrane isolating Patrician Rowan. For all the available precautions, they were all breathing the same air.

"*You're* immune," he finished.

She inclined her head. "Because I'm even less human than Ken."

Experimentally, Lubin put his hand through the face of one cube. The soap-bubble membrane split around his flesh, snugly collared his forearm. It iridesced conspicuously around the seal, faded when Lubin kept his hand completely immobile. He grunted.

"The sooner we begin, the sooner we finish," Rowan said.

Lubin stepped through. For an instant the entire face of the cube writhed with oily rainbows; then he was inside and the membrane cleared, its integrity restored.

Rowan glanced at Desjardins. "A lot of our proteins— enzymes, particularly—don't work well in the deep sea. I'm told the pressure squeezes them into suboptimal shapes."

Lubin's cube darkened slightly as the sterile field went on, almost as if its skin had thickened. It hadn't, of course; the membrane was still only a molecule deep. Its surface tension had been cranked, though. Lubin could throw his whole considerable mass against that barrier now and it wouldn't open. It would yield—it would stretch, and distort, and sheer momentum could drag it halfway across the room like a rubber sock with a weight in the toe. But it wouldn't break, and after a few seconds it would tighten and retract back down to two dimensions. And Lubin would still be inside.

Desjardins found that vaguely comforting.

Rowan raised her voice a fraction: "Undress please, Ken.

Just leave your clothes on the floor. Oh, and there's a headset hanging off the teleop. Perhaps you could view that during the procedure."

She turned back to Desjardins. "At any rate, we had to tweak our people before we could send them to the rift. Retroed in some genes from deep-water fish."

"Alice said deep-sea proteins were—stiff," Desjardins remembered.

"More difficult to break apart, yes. And since the body's sulfur's locked up in the proteins, βehemoth has a tougher time stealing it from a rifter. But we only backed up the most pressure-sensitive molecules; βehemoth can still get at the others. It just takes longer to compromise the cellular machinery."

"Unless you back up *everything*."

"The small stuff, anyway. Anything under fifty or sixty aminos is vulnerable. Something about the disulfide bridges, apparently. There's individual variation, of course, vectors can stay asymptomatic for a month or more sometimes, but the only way to really..." She shrugged. "At any rate, I became half-fish."

"A mermaid." The image was absurd.

Rowan rewarded him with a brief smile. "You know the drill, Ken. Face down, please."

The operating board was inclined at a twenty-degree angle. Ken Lubin, naked, face masked by the headset, braced over it as though doing push-ups and eased himself down.

The air shimmered and *hummed*. Lubin went utterly limp. And the insectile machine above him spread nightmare arms with too many joints, and descended to feed.

"Holy *shit*," Desjardins said.

Lubin had been stabbed in a dozen places. Mercury filaments snaked into his wrists and plunged through his back. A catheter had slid autonomously up his ass, another seemed to have kabobbed his penis. Something copper slithered into mouth and nose. Wires crawled along his face, wormed beneath his headset. The table itself was suddenly stippled with fine needles: Lubin was fixed in place like an insect pushed onto the bristles of a wire brush.

"It's not as bad as it looks," Rowan remarked. "The neuroinduction field blocks most of the pain."

"*Fuck.*" The second cube, empty and waiting, shone like a threat of inquisition. "Am *I*—"

Rowan pursed her lips. "I doubt that will be necessary. Unless you've been infected, which seems unlikely."

"I've been exposed for two days, going on three."

"It's not smallpox, Doctor. Unless you exchanged body fluids with the man, or used his feces as compost, chances are you're clean. The sweep on your apartment didn't turn up anything...although you might want to know that your cat has a tapeworm."

They swept my apartment. Desjardins tried to summon some sense of outrage. Relief was all that answered: *I'm clean. I'm clean...*

"You'll have to undergo the gene therapy, though," Rowan said. "So you can *stay* clean. It's quite extensive, unfortunately."

"*How* extensive?"

She knew exactly what he was asking.

"Too extensive to immunize nine billion human beings. At least, not in time; the vast majority of the world's population has never even been sequenced. And even if we could, there are still—other species. We can't reverse-engineer the whole biosphere."

He'd expected it, of course. He still felt it like a blow.

"So containment's our only option," she said quietly. "And as you may know, someone's trying very hard to prevent that."

"Yeah." Desjardins looked at her. "Why is that, exactly?"

"We want you to find out."

"Me?"

"We've already got our own people on it, of course. We'll link you up. But you've been exceeding our performance projections right across the board, and you *were* the one who made the connection after all."

"I didn't make it so much as *trip* over it. I mean, you'd have to be blind not to see it, once you knew what to look for."

"Well that's the problem, isn't it? We weren't looking. Why would we? Why would anyone trawl Maelstrom for the names of dead rifters? And now it turns out that everyone knows about Lenie Clarke except us. We've got the world's best intelligence-gathering machinery, and any kid with a stolen wristwatch knows more than we do." The corpse took a deep breath, as if adjusting some great weight on her back. "How did that happen, do you suppose?"

"Ask the kid with the wristwatch," Desjardins said. He jerked his head at Lubin, twitching in his bubble. "If you've got any more like that one, you'll know everything in about two seconds."

"Everything the kid knows, maybe. Which is next to nothing."

"You just said—"

"We almost got her, did you know that?" Rowan said. "Just yesterday. Once you gave us the heads-up we filtered through the chaff, and we located her in South Dakota. We closed in and found that half the city was running interference for her. She got away."

"You interrogated the fans, though."

"Summoned by a voice in the Maelstrom. Someone out there rallying the troops."

"Who? Why?"

"Nobody knew. Apparently it just jumps into likely conversations and starts cheerleading. We left all kinds of bait when we found that out, but so far it isn't talking to us."

"Wow," Desjardins said.

"You know what's really ironic? We thought something like this might happen. We took precautions against it."

"You were *expecting* this?"

"Not specifically, of course. The whole rifter thing just

came out of left field." Rowan sighed, her face full of shadow. "Still, things—go wrong. You'd think a guy with a name like *Murphy* would realize that, but no. As far as ChemCog was concerned, it was just some junk meme the gels were spreading."

"The *gels* are behind this?"

She shook her head. "As I said, we took precautions. We tracked down every tainted node, we partitioned them and replaced them, we made damn sure that there was no *trace* of the meme left. Just to be absolutely sure. But here it is, somehow. Metastasized and mutated and born again. And all we know is that this time, the gels *aren't* behind it."

"But they were before, is that what you're saying? They— they started the ball rolling?"

"Maybe. Once upon a time."

"*Why*, for God's sake?"

"Well, that's the funny thing," Rowan admitted. "We told them to."

Rowan fed it all directly to his inlays. There was too much for even an optimized 'lawbreaker to take in on the spot, but the executive summary thumbnailed it in fifteen seconds: the growing threat, the rabid mutual distrust, the final reluctant surrender of control to an alien intelligence with its own unsuspected take on the virtues of parsimony.

"Jesus," Desjardins said.

"I know," Rowan agreed.

"And how the Christ did Lenie Clarke take control?"

"She didn't. That's what's so crazy. As far as we can tell, she didn't think anyone even *knew* about her until Yankton."

"Huh." Desjardins pursed his lips. "Still. Whatever's out there, it's taking its lead from her."

"I know," she said softly. She glanced at Lubin. "That's where he comes in."

Lubin twitched and jerked under the ongoing assault. His face—the part of it not covered by the headset, anyway— was expressionless.

"What's he watching in there?" Desjardins wondered.

"Briefing stats. For his next mission."

He watched a little longer. "Would he have killed me?"

"I doubt it."

"Who *is*—"

"He's not someone you have to worry about anymore."

"No." Desjardins shook his head. "That's not good enough. He tracked me down across a whole continent, he broke into my home, he—" *cut Guilt Trip right out from under me* but of course he wasn't going to admit that to Rowan, not *now* for Chrissakes—"I gather he's got some kind of kill-switch hardwired into him, and he answers to *you*, Ms. Rowan. *Who is he?*"

He could see her bristling. For a moment he thought he'd gone too far. No peon truly in Guilt Trip's grasp would ever mouth off to a superior that way, Rowan would know, the alarms would start sounding any second—

"Mr. Lubin has—you might call it an impulse-control problem," she said. "He enjoys certain acts that most would find unpleasant. He never behaves—gratuitously is the word, I guess—but sometimes he tends to set up situations that provoke a particular response. Do you see what I'm saying?"

He kills people, Desjardins thought numbly. *He sets up breaches so he'll have an excuse to kill people....*

"We're helping him deal with his problem," Rowan said. "And we've got him under control."

Desjardins bit his lip.

She shook her head, a trace of disapproval on those pale features. "βehemoth, Dr. Desjardins. Lenie Clarke. Lose sleep over *those*, if you must. Believe me, Ken Lubin's part of the *solution*." Her voice went up a touch: "Aren't you, Ken?"

"I don't know her," Lubin said. "Not well."

Desjardins glanced at Rowan, alarmed. "He can *hear* us?"

She answered Lubin instead. "You know her better than you think."

"You have—profiles," Lubin said. His words were slurred; the induction field must be grazing his facial muscles. "That psychologist. Scanlon."

"Scanlon had his own issues," Rowan said. "You and Clarke have a lot more in common. Similar outlooks, similar backgrounds. If you were in her shoes—"

"I *am* in her shoes. I came *here...*" Lubin licked his lips. A trickle of saliva glistened at the corner of his mouth.

"Fair enough. But suppose you had no information and no clearance, and no—behavioral constraints. What would you be after?"

Lubin didn't speak. His cowled face was an eyeless, high-contrast mask in the spots. His skin almost glowed.

Rowan stepped forward. "Ken?"

" 's easy," he said at last. "Revenge."

"Against who, exactly?"

"The—GA. We did try to kill us, after all."

Rowan's contacts glowed with sudden input. "She was never seen near any GA offices."

"She ashaulted someone in Hongcouver." A spasm ran up the length of Lubin's body. His head lolled. "Looking for Yves Shcanlon."

"But Scanlon was her only lead, as far as we know. It didn't go anywhere. We don't think she's even been in N'AmPac for months."

"She has other grudges," Lubin said. "Maybe she's—going home."

Rowan frowned, concentrating. "Her parents, you mean."

"She mentioned Sault Sainte Marie."

"Suppose she couldn't get to her parents?"

"Don' know."

"What would *you* do?"

"I'd—keep trying..."

"Suppose her parents were dead," Rowan suggested.

"...'f we killed them for her?"

"No, suppose they were already—suppose they'd been dead a long time."

Clumsily, Lubin shook his head. "The people she hates're very mush...alive..."

"*Suppose*, Ken." Rowan was getting impatient. "Theoretical scenario. You've got a score to settle with the GA, and a score to settle with your parents, and you know you'll never get to either of them. What do you do?"

His mouth moved. Nothing came out.

"Ken?"

"—I redirect," he said at last.

"What do you mean?"

Lubin jerked like a blind marionette with most of its strings cut.

"The whole *world* fucked me over. I—I wanna return the favor."

"Huh." Rowan shook her head. "She's pretty much doing that already."

One crucifixion was enough, as it turned out. Achilles Desjardins was clean, if still vulnerable; the second surgery, prepped and waiting, had no interest in scouring his insides. It only wanted to change him into a flounder.

Lubin's little chamber of horrors had backed off for the moment. The pallet had folded itself into recliner mode: the assassin sat on it while a mechanical spider skittered across his body on legs like jointed whiskers.

In the adjacent cube, Desjardins looked down at an identical device on his own body. He'd already been injected with a half dozen tailored viruses, each containing the code for a different suite of βehemoth-proof proteins. There'd be other injections over the next few days. Lots of them. The fever would start within a week; the nausea was already under way.

The spider was taking baselines: bacteria from skin and hair, organ biopsies, gut contents. Every now and then it plunged a hair-thin proboscis into his flesh, provoking a diffuse ache from within the tissues. Reverse-engineering was a tricky business these days. If you weren't careful, tweaked genes could change the microflora in the gut as easily as the flesh of the host. *E. coli.* could turn from commensal to cancer with the flip of a base pair. A few wily bacteria had even learned how to slip some of their own genes into viral carriers en route, and hence into human cells. It made Desjardins long for those good old-fashioned germs that merely fed on antibiotics.

"You didn't tell her," Lubin said.

Rowan had left them to their own devices. Desjardins looked at the other man through two layers of membrane and tried to ignore the creepy tickle on his skin.

"Tell her what?" he asked finally.

"That I took you off Guilt Trip."

"Yeah? What makes you so sure?"

Lubin's spider scrambled up his throat and tapped on his lower lip. The assassin obligingly opened his mouth; the little robot scraped at the inside of his cheek with one appendage and retreated back down the torso.

"She wouldn't have left us alone otherwise," Lubin said.

"I thought you were leashed, *Horatio*."

He shrugged. "One leash of many. It doesn't matter."

"It sure the fuck does."

"Why? Do you really think I was so out of control before? Do you think I'd have even been able to unTrip you, if I honestly thought you'd breach?"

"Sure, if you sealed it up afterward. Isn't that your whole problem? You set yourself up to kill people?"

"So I'm a monster." Lubin settled back in the chair and closed his eyes. "What does that make you?"

"*Me?*"

"I saw what you were playing at when we first met."

Heat spilled across Desjardins's face. "That's *fantasy*. I'd *never* do that in real life. I don't even *fuck* in real life."

Lubin opened one eye and assayed a trace of smile. "Don't trust yourself?"

"I've just got too much respect for women."

"Really? Seems a bit inconsistent with your choice of hobbies."

"That's normal. That's *brainstem*." It had been such a relief to discover that at last, to see *aggression* and *sex* sharing the same hardwired pathways through the mammalian brain— to know his secret shame was a legacy millions of years old, ubiquitous for all the denial of civilized minds. But *Lubin . . .*

"As if you don't know. You get your rocks off every time you kill someone."

"Ah." Lubin's not-quite-smile didn't change. "So I'm a monster, but you're just a prisoner of your inner drives."

"I fantasize. You *kill* people. Sorry, you *seal security breaches*."

"Not always," Lubin said.

Desjardins looked away without answering. The spider ran down his leg.

"Someone got away once," said a strange soft voice behind him.

He turned. Lubin was staring into space, not moving. Even his spider had paused, as if startled by some sudden change in its substrate.

"She got away," Lubin said again. He almost sounded as though he were talking to himself. "I may have even let her."

Clarke, Desjardins realized.

"She wasn't really a breach then, of course. There was no way she'd ever make it out alive, there was no—but she did, somehow."

Lubin no longer wore the face of a passionless predator. There was something new looking out from behind those eyes, and it seemed almost...*confused*...

"It's a shame," he said softly. "She really deserved a fighting chance..."

"A lot of people seem to agree with you," Desjardins said. Lubin *mm*'d.

"Look." Desjardins cleared his throat. "I need some of those derms before you go."

"Derms." Lubin seemed strangely distant.

"The analog. You said a week or ten days before the Trip kicked back in, and that was three days ago—if they spottest me in the next few days I'm screwed."

"Ah." Lubin came back to earth. "That's out of my hands now, I'm afraid. Horatio and all."

"What do you mean, it's *out of your hands? I just need a few derms, for Chrissake!*"

Lubin's spider skittered off under the pallet, its regimen

complete. The assassin grabbed his clothes and began dress-
ing.

"Well?" Desjardins said after a while.

Lubin pulled on his shirt and stepped out of the cube. Its
skin swirled in his wake.

"Don't worry about it," he said, and didn't look back.

ANTHOPLEURA

Mug Shot

Exotics Infestation: Executive Summary (nontechnical)
DO NOT mail
DO NOT send through Haven
DO NOT copy
PURGE AFTER DECRYPT

To: Rowan, PC
Priority: **Ultra (Global PanD)**
EID Code: βehemoth
General Classification: nanobial/decomposer

Taxonomy: Formal nomenclature awaiting declassified release to Linnean Society. Eventual outgroup clade to be at supraDomain level.

Description: Unique heterotrophic nanobe, 200–250nm diameter. Opportunistic freeliver/commensal. Genome 1.1M (pRNA template): nonsense codons <0.7% of total.

Biogeography: Originally native to hydrothermal deep-sea environments; 14 relict populations confirmed (Fig. 1). Can also exist symbiotically in intracellular environments with salinity ≤ 30ppt and/or temperatures ranging from 4–60°C. A secondary strain has been found with advanced adaptations for intracellular existence.

Evolution/Ecology: βehemoth is the only organism known to have truly terrestrial origins, predating the Martian Panspermia event by approximately 800 million years. The existence of a secondary strain geared especially to the eukaryotic intracellular environment is reminiscent of the Precambrian serial endosymbiosis which gave rise to mitochondria and other modern subcellular organelles. Free-living βehemoth expends significant metabolic energy maintaining homeostasis in stressful hydrothermal environments. Intracellularly, infectious βehemoth produces an ATP surplus which can be utilized by the host cell. This results in abnormal growth and giantism among certain deep-water fish; it confers increases in stamina and strength to infected humans in the short term, although these benefits are massively outweighed by disruption of short-chain sulfur-containing proteins and consequent deficiency syndromes (see below).

Notable Histological & Genetic Features: No phospholipid membranes: body wall consists of accreted mineralized sulfur/phosphate compounds. Genetic template based upon Pyranosal RNA (Fig 2); also used for catalysis of metabolic reactions. Resistant to g-radiation (1 megarad not effective). The βehemoth genome contains Blachford genes analagous to the metamutators of *Pseudomonas*; these allow it to dynamically increase mutation rate in response to environmental change and are probably responsible for its ability to fool steroid receptors on the host cell membrane.

Modes of Attack: Freed from the rigors of the hydrothermal environment, free-living βehemoth assimilates several inorganic nutrients 26–84% more efficiently than its closest terrestrial competitors (Table 1). This is especially problematic when dealing with sulfur. In a free-living state, βehemoth is theoretically capable of bottlenecking even that extremely common element; this is the primary ecological threat. βehemoth is, however, more comfortable within the bodies of homeothermic vertebrates, which provide warm, stable, and nutrient-rich environments reminiscent of the primordial soup. βehemoth enters the cell via receptor-mediated endocytosis; once inside it breaks down the phagosomal membrane prior to lysis, using a 532-amino listeriolysin analog. βehemoth then competes with the host cell for nutrients. Host death can occur from any of several dozen proximal causes including renal/hepatic failure, erythromytosis, CNS disorders, blood poisoning, and opportunistic infections.

Vertebrate hosts serve as reservoirs which periodically reinoculate the nanobe into the external environment, increasing the chance of self-sustaining outbreaks.

Diagnostics: Methionine labeling is effective in culture. Free-living βehemoth in concentrations of greater than 1.35 billion/cc exerts detectable effects on soil pH, conductivity, porphyrin counts, and chlorophylls A and B (Table 2); the extent of these effects varies with baseline conditions. βehemoth can be inferred in asymptomatic patients by the presence of d-cysteine and d-cystine in the blood[1] (unsuccessful attempts to cleave bound sulfur sometimes stereoisomerizes the molecule).

Present Status: See Figure 3. 4,800km^2 sterilized at last report. 426,000km^2 under immediate threat.

Ecological Trajectory: If current trends continue, present models suggest long-term competitive exclusion of all competing life-forms between 62°N and S latitudes, due to monopolization and transformation of nutrient base. Ultimate fate of polar components unknown at this time. Sensitivity analysis generates 95% confidence limits of 50 to 94 years for EL90.

Recommendations: Continue ongoing efforts to alter present trajectory. Allocate Fallback Options budget as follows.

1. Orbital: 25%
2. Cheyenne: 5%
3. M. A. Ridge: 50%
4. Metamorph: 20%

Anemone

She'd become a scavenger in her own home.

Sou-Hon Perreault virtually lived in her office now. It held everything of importance. A window on the world. A purpose. A sanctuary.

She still had to eat, though, and use the toilet. Once or twice a day she'd venture from her cave and see to life's necessities. Most of the time she didn't have to deal with Martin; his contracts took him into the field more often than not.

But now—*oh God, why* now *of all times?*—he was in the living room when she came back.

He was digging around in the aquarium, his back turned. She almost got past.

---

1. This is the clearest indicator of early infection. Unfortunately, standard medbooths and quarantine checkpoints are not equipped for the detection of stereo isomers. N'Am-wide equipment upgrades are ongoing, but will take at least six months to complete.

"The male died," he said.

"What?"

He turned to face her. A damselfish, pale and stiff, weighted the dip net in his hand. One milky eye stared blindly through the mesh.

"He looks like he's been dead for a while," Martin said.

She looked past him to the aquarium. Brown algae filmed the glass. Inside, the glorious anemone was shrunken and frayed; its tentacles twitched feebly in the current.

"Jesus, Marty. You couldn't even be bothered to clean the tank?"

"I just got home. I've been in Fairbanks for the past two weeks."

She'd forgotten.

"Sou, the prescriptions aren't working. I really think we should consider wiring you up with a therapist."

"I'm fine," she said automatically.

"You're *not* fine. I've looked into it already, we can afford it. It'll be available around the clock, whenever you need it."

"I don't trust therapists."

"Sou, it'd be a part of *you*. It already is, in a way, they just haven't—isolated it yet. And it runs pathways right to your temporal lobe, so you can talk to it as easily as you can talk to anyone."

"You want to cut out a part of my brain."

"No, Sou, just *rewire* it. Did you know the brain can support over a hundred fully sentient personalities? It doesn't affect sensory or motor performance at all. This would just be *one*, and it'd take up such a small amount of space—"

"My husband, the walking brochure."

"Sou—"

"It's multiple personality disorder, Martin. I don't care what cute name they give it these days, and I don't care how many of our friends live happy fulfilling lives because they hear voices in their heads. It's sick."

"Sou, please. I love you. I'm only trying to help."

"Then get out of my way."

She ran for shelter.

Sou-Hon. Are you there?

"Yes."

Good. Stand by.

Static. A brief spiderweb of connections and intercepts, orange filaments proliferating across a continent. Then *no visual* front and center, darkness everywhere else.

Go ahead.

"Lenie?" Perreault said.
"So. I wondered when they'd get around to this."
"Get around to what?"
"Hijacking my visor. Sou-Hon, right?"
"Right."
"They got that right, at least."
Perreault took a grateful breath. "You okay?"
"I got out. Thanks partly to you, I guess. That *was* you in the 'fly, wasn't it? At Yankton?"
"That was me."
"Thanks."
"Don't thank me. Thank—"
A damselfish flashed across Perreault's mind, safe in a nest of stinging tentacles.
"...anemone," she finished softly.
Silence on the line. Then: "Thank an enemy. That makes a lot of sense."
Perreault shook her head. "*Sea* anemone. It's this undersea ambush predator, it eats fish but sometimes—"
"I know what a sea anemone is, Suze. So what?"
"Everything's been perverted, somehow. The 'flies, the matchmakers—the whole system's done a 180, it's protecting the very thing it was supposed to attack. You see?"
"Not really. But I was never that big on metaphors." A soft laugh. "I still can't get used to being a starfish."
Perreault wondered but didn't ask.

"This anemone of yours," Clarke said. "It kicks ass. It's *powerful.*"

"Yes."

"So why is it so fucking *stupid*?"

"What do you mean?"

"It doesn't seem to have any kind of focus, you know? I saw the threads—it described me a thousand different ways and then it just went with the one that stuck. I don't know how many headcases it threw at me, through my watch, my visor—they even started coming at me out of vending machines, did you know that?—and it wasn't until I stopped talking to anyone else that it settled on you. Any haploid would've known better than to audition most of those assholes, but your *anemone* is just—random. Why is that?"

"I don't know."

"Didn't you ever wonder?"

She had, of course. But somehow it hadn't seemed to matter that much.

"Maybe that's why you made the cut," Clarke said.

"Why?"

"You're a good soldier. You need a cause, you follow orders, you don't ask embarrassing questions." A whisper of static. Then: "Why are you helping me, Sou? You've seen the threads."

"You said the threads were bullshit," Perreault said.

"Most of them are. Almost all. But they blew up Channer. They must have known the kind of collateral that would bring down, and they did it anyway. They burned the Strip. And the life down there on the rift, it was—God knows what was down there. What I brought back."

"I thought your blood tested clean."

"Tests only see what they're looking for. You haven't answered my question."

And still she didn't, for a very long time.

"Because they tried to hammer you down," she said at last. "And you're still here."

"Huh." A long breath whispered through the headset. "You ever have a dog, Sou-Hon? As a pet?"

"No."

"You know what happens when you keep a dog locked away from every living thing, except you visit once a day and kick the shit out of him?"

Perreault laughed nervously. "Someone actually *tried* that?"

"What happens is, the dog's a social animal, and it gets so lonely it actually looks forward to the shit-kicking. It *asks* to be kicked. It begs."

"What are you saying?"

"Maybe everyone's just so used to being kicked around, they'll help out anyone they think has a big enough boot."

"Or maybe," Perreault said, "we're so fucking *tired* of being kicked that we're finally lining up with anyone who kicks back."

"Yeah? At any cost?"

"What do we have to lose?"

"You have no idea."

"But you did. You must have known all along. If the danger was really so great, why didn't you turn yourself in? Save the world? Save *yourself*?"

"The world had it coming," Clarke said softly.

"Is that what you're doing? Just—getting revenge on nine billion people you never even met?"

"I don't know. Maybe before."

"Now?"

"I just—" Clarke's voice broke. Pain and confusion flooded through the breach. "Sou, I want to go *home*."

"So go," Perreault said gently. "I'll help you."

A ragged breath, brought back under tight control: "No."

"You could really use—"

"Look, you're not just a—a traveling companion anymore. I don't think either of us was really on the scope before Yankton, but they know about us now, and you—you really got in their way. If they haven't tracked you down already, they're damn well working on it."

"You're forgetting about our anemone."

"No I'm not. I just don't trust the fucking thing."

"Look—"

"Sou-Hon, thanks for everything. I mean that. But it's too dangerous. Every second we talk, our trail gets brighter. You really want to help me, then help yourself. Don't try to talk to me again. Go away. Go somewhere safe."

A lump grew in her throat. "Where? Where's safe?"

"I don't know. I'm sorry."

"Lenie, *listen to me*. There's got to be a plan. You've got to have faith, there's a purpose behind all of this. Please, just—"

The crunch of plastic, ground underfoot.

"Lenie!"

Link lost flashed front and center.

She didn't know how long she sat there, in her own personal void. Eventually, *link lost* went away. Some other readout flashed off at the edge of vision, a rhythmic little scratch on her retina. The effort required to focus on it seemed almost superhuman.

Good-bye

It said. And:

Anemone. We like that.

Behind the Lines

A random trawl caught the anomaly fifteen nodes off the port bow. A thousand other channels were abuzz with *Lenie Clarke*, but this one was so *clean*: no packet loss, no dropouts, none of the stutters and time lags that always plagued civilian traffic in Maelstrom. The line was full of groupies with on-line handles like *Squidnapper* and *White-eyes*, all at rapt attention while something whispered disinformation in their midst. It called itself *The General* and it spoke with a thousand different voices: raw ASCII reinflated to specs set by each recipient's software.

It hung up the moment it heard Achilles Desjardins creeping in from behind.

Too fast for meat. Almost too fast even for the hounds Desjardins set on its trail; they circled the world in seconds, diving through gateways, tripping over wildlife, finding half-eaten carcasses where traffic registries had lived and breathed just moments before. Here, and here, and here: nodes through which *The General's* words had passed. Traffic logs mauled beyond recognition by earth-scorchers covering their tracks. The hounds replicated a thousandfold and dived through all available ports in unison, trying reacquire the scent through brute force.

This time they succeeded. The flag went up on Desjardins's board at T-plus-six seconds: something had been treed on a server in the Hokkaido microwave array. It wasn't a smart gel. There were no smart gels for at least four nodes in any direction. But it was dark, and it was massive, and it was holding its breath so tight that nothing could get a fix on its exact address. It was just in there, somewhere. Under the surface.

And when Achilles Desjardins seined the node, panicky wildlife scattering at his approach, *The General* was nowhere to be found.

"Shit..."

He rubbed his eyes and broke the link. The real world resolved around him—or at least, that part of it trapped within the walls of his cubby.

That was him, he remembered. Trapped in there. Undistracted by the endless frustration of hunting phantoms, it all came flooding back.

The real world had got even worse, now that Lubin had deserted him.

A hand on his shoulder. He started, then sagged.

"Killjoy. You look like shit," Jovellanos said kindly.

He looked up at her. "Maybe Rowan's right."

"Rowan?" She laid her hands on his shoulders and started kneading the muscles.

"It's not the gels. Maybe it really is some kind of—global

conspiracy. I can't find any other explanation..."

"Uh, Killjoy—in case you've forgotten, I haven't seen you in four days." Her hair smelled like some extinct flower from Desjardins's childhood. "I hear you've been hobnobbing with all sorts of strange people, but I'm nowhere *near* the loop, you know?"

He waved at the board, then realized that she wouldn't see anything there; he'd routed the display to his inlays. "That whole movement. *Rifter chic* or whatever the hell they call it, you know? It's a propagation strategy. That's all it is. Isn't that wild?"

"Yeah? What's it propagating?"

"βehemoth," Desjardins whispered.

"*No.*" Her hands dropped away. "How?"

"There's a vector out there. A rifter. Lenie Clarke. It's all just smoke to keep her from getting caught."

"*Why,* for God's sake? Why would anyone—"

"The gels started it. I mean, they weren't supposed to, they were supposed to *contain* it, but—"

"*They put the gels in charge?*"

"What else could they do?" Desjardins suppressed the urge to giggle. "Nobody trusted anyone. They knew there'd be sacrifices, they knew they might have to sterilize—major areas. But when Mercosur says hey, our stats say Oregon's got to go for the greater good, do you think N'Am's gonna just roll over and take their *word* on that? They needed something that could decide, and *act,* and who wouldn't play favorites..."

"*Fuck,*" Jovellanos whispered.

"They were so busy keeping an eye on each *other* they never stopped to think what kind of take-home rules a net might develop on its own, after spending a whole lifetime protecting small simple things from big complicated things. And then they tell it to protect a complex of five million species against one pissant nanobe, and they can't understand why it turns around and bites them in the ass."

Jovellanos said nothing.

"Anyway, it doesn't matter. They scrubbed the gels down

to the last neuron and it didn't do any good. There's something else out there. I've flushed the fucker four times in the past twenty-four hours, and it keeps slipping through my fingers. We could swap out every gel in Maelstrom and the replacements would be reinfected inside a week."

"But if not the gels, then what?"

"I don't know. For all I know it's a pharm-baby thing, some corporation's got a cure and they're spreading βehemoth to drive up the price. But *how* they're pulling it off—"

"Turing app, maybe?"

"Or berserkers. I thought of that. But those leave footprints—op signatures on the hardware, huge memory demands. And anything that complex attracts wildlife like you wouldn't believe."

"You're not seeing any of that?"

"Lots of wildlife, maybe. Nothing else."

"So maybe it autowipes when it sees you coming."

"Footprints'd still be in the server log."

"Not if it doctors the log before it deletes."

"Then the *deletion* would be on file. I'm telling you, Alice, this is something else."

"What if the wildlife's gotten brainy?" she said.

He blinked. "What?"

"Why not? It evolves. Maybe it got smart."

He shook his head. "Nets are nets. Doesn't matter if someone coded them or they just evolved; if they're smart enough to think, they're going to have a certain signature. I'm not seeing it, and nobody else is either and I'm just...completely—*wasted*..."

He leaned forward, let the board take the weight of his forearms. His head weighed a tonne.

"Come on," Jovellanos said after a moment.

"What?"

"We're going to Pickering's Pile. I'm buying you a derm. Or ten."

He shook his head. "Thanks, Alice. I can't."

"I checked the logs, Killjoy. You haven't been out of this building for almost forty hours. Sleep deprivation reduces

IQ, did you know that? Yours must be around room temp by now. Take a break."

He looked up at her. "I *can't*. If I leave—"

Don't worry about it, Lubin had said.

"—I may not be able to come back," he finished.

She frowned. "Why not?"

I'm unchained, he thought. *I'm free.*

"Lubin—this guy *did* something to me, and... if the bloodhounds..."

She took his hand, firmly. "Come."

"Alice, you don't know what—"

"Maybe I know more than you think, Killjoy. If you don't think you're up to a blood test, well maybe that's a problem and maybe it isn't, but you're gonna have to bite the bullet eventually. Unless you're planning on spending the rest of your life in this cubicle?"

"The next five days, maybe..." He was so very tired.

"I know what I'm doing, Killjoy. Trust me on this."

Desjardins managed a feeble laugh. "People keep *saying* that."

"Maybe. But I *mean* it." She drew him to his feet. "Besides, I have something to tell you."

He couldn't bring himself to enter the Pile, after all; too many ambient ears, and discretion prevailed even without Guilt Trip. For that matter, even walking under the open sky made him a bit queasy. The heavens had eyes.

They walked, letting chance choose the course. Intermittent beds of kudzu$_4$ lined their path; the filamentous blades of windmills turned slowly overhead on the tops of buildings, along pedestrian concourses, anywhere that a bit of fetch could insinuate itself into the local architecture. Alice Jovellanos took all of it in without a word: Lubin, Rowan, Guilt Trip. Autonomy thrust upon the unwilling.

"Are you sure?" she asked at last. A streetlight flickered on overhead. "Maybe he was lying. He lied about Rowan, after all."

"Not about this, Alice. Believe me. He had his hand around my throat and I just *sang*, I told him stuff the Trip would *never've* let out."

"That's not what I mean. I believe you're Trip-free, for sure. I just don't believe that Lubin had anything to do with it."

"What?"

"I think he just found out about it, after the fact," Jovellanos continued, "and he used it to his own advantage. I don't know what was in those derms he was giving you, but I'd bet a year's worth of Mandelbrot's kibble that you could walk past those bloodhounds right now and they wouldn't even twitch."

"Yeah? And if you were in my shoes, do you think you'd be quite so optimistic?"

"I'd guarantee it."

"Fuck, Alice, this is *serious*."

"I know, Killjoy. *I'm* serious."

"But if Lubin didn't do it to me, then who—"

Her face was fading in the twilight, like the smile of a Cheshire cat.

"*Alice?*" he said.

"Hey." She shrugged. "You always *knew* my politics were a bit radical."

"*Fuck*, Alice." Desjardins put his head in his hands. "How *could* you?"

"It was easier than you might think. Just build a Trip analog with an extra side group—"

"That's not what I mean. You *know* what I mean."

She stepped in front of him, blocking his way.

"Listen, Killjoy. You've got ten times the brains of those felchers, and you let them turn you into a puppet."

"I'm not a puppet."

"Not anymore, anyway."

"I never *was*."

"Sure you were. Just like Lubin."

"I'm *nothing* like—"

"They turned you into one big reflex arc, my man. Took all that gray matter and hammered it into pure hardwired instinct, through and through."

"Fuck you. You *know* that isn't true."

She put her hand on Desjardins's shoulder. "Look, I don't blame you for being in denial about—"

He shrugged it off. "*I'm not in denial!* You think *instinct* and *reflex* can handle the decisions I have to make, every hour I'm on the job? You think weighting a thousand variables on the fly doesn't require a certain degree of autonomy? Jesus Christ, I—"

—*I may be a slave, but I'm not a robot.* He caught it at the back of his throat; no sense giving her any more ammunition than she already had.

"We gave you back your life, man," Jovellanos said softly.

"*We?*"

"There's a few of us. We're kind of political, in a ragtag sorta way."

"Oh Christ." Desjardins shook his head. "Did you even *ask* me if I wanted this?"

"You would've said no. Guilt Trip would've made you. That's the whole point."

"And just maybe I'd've said no *anyway*, did you ever stop to think of that? I can kill a half million people before lunch-time; you don't think it's a good idea to have *safeguards* in place? Maybe you remember the buzz on *absolute power*?"

"Sure," Jovellanos said. "Every time I see a Lertzman or a Rowan."

"*I don't care about Lertzman or fucking Rowan!* You did this to *me!*"

"I did it *for* you, Achilles."

He glanced up, startled. "What did you call me?"

"Achilles."

"*Jesus.*"

"Listen, you're safe. The hounds will find Trip in your blood like they always have. That's the beauty of it, Spartacus doesn't *touch* the Trip. It just blocks the receptors."

"Spartacus? That's what you call it?"

Jovellanos nodded.

"What's that supposed to mean?"

"Look it up. The point is—"

"And why *now,* of all times?" Desjardins threw his hands in the air. "If you were going to do this to me, you couldn't have picked a worse time if you *tried.*"

She shook her head. "Killjoy, you're up at bat and the whole world's hanging in the balance. If you *ever* needed a clear head, now's the time. You can't afford to be chained to *any* corpse agenda. *Nobody* can afford it."

He glared at her. "You are such a fucking hypocrite, Alice. You *infected* me. You didn't ask, you didn't even *tell,* you just stuck me with some bug that could get me thrown out of my job, or worse—"

She raised her hands, as if to ward off his words. "Achilles, I—"

"Yeah, yeah, you did it *for* me. What an altruist. Ramming Spartacus Brand Home-Cooked Autonomy down my throat whether I like it or not. I'm your friend, Alice! *Why did you do this?*"

She stared at him for a moment in the fading light.

"You don't know?" she said at last, in a cold angry voice. "The goddamned boy genius doesn't have a clue? Why don't you do a path analysis or something to find out?"

She spun on her heel and walked away.

Spartacus

"Achilles, you can be such a raging idiot sometimes I just don't believe it.

"You *know* what I was risking, coming clean with you yesterday. You know what I'm risking sending this to you *now*—it'll autowipe, but there's *nothing* these assholes can't scan if they feel like it. That's part of the problem, that's why I'm taking this huge risk in the first place.

"I'm sorry I stomped off like that. Things just weren't

going like I hoped, you know? But I *do* have some answers for you if you'll just hear me out, okay? Just—hear me out.

"I heard what you said about trust and betrayal, and maybe some of it rings a bit more true than I'd like. But don't you see there was no point in asking you beforehand? As long as Guilt Trip was running the show, you were incapable of making your own decisions. You keep insisting that's wrong, you go on about all the life-and-death decisions you make and the thousands of variables you juggle, but Achilles my dear, whoever told you that *free will* was just some complicated algorithm for you to follow?

"Look at bumblebees dancing sometime. You wouldn't believe the stuff they talk about. Solar elevation, topographic cues, time stamps—they write road maps to the best food sources, scaled to the centimeter, and they do it all with a few butt wiggles. Does that make them free agents? Why do you think we call them *drones*?

"Look at the physics of a spider spinning its web. Hell, look at a dog catching a ball—that's ballistic math, my man. The world's *full* of dumb animals who act as though they're juggling third-order differentials in their heads and it's all just *instinct*. It's not freedom. It's not even intelligence. And you stand there and tell me you're autonomous just because you can follow a decision tree with a few dozen variables?

"I know you don't want to be corrupted. But maybe a decent, honest human being is his own safeguard, did you ever think of that? Maybe you don't *have* to let them turn you into one big conditioned reflex. Maybe you just *want* them to, because then it's not really your responsibility, is it? It's so easy never to have to make your own decisions. Addictive, even. Maybe you even got hooked on it, and you're going through a little bit of withdrawal now.

"I bet you don't even know what they took away, do you? I bet you weren't even interested. Sure, you read their cheery little leaflets about *serving the greater good* and you learned enough to pass the tests, but it was all just hoops you had to jump through to get into the next tax bracket, right? Jesus,

Killjoy. I mean, don't get me wrong—you're a flaming genius with sims and nonparametric stats, but when it comes to the real world you wouldn't know a come-on if someone got down on their knees and unzipped your fly for you. I mean, really.

"Anyhow, what they stole, we gave back. And I'm going to tell you *exactly* what we did on the premise, you know, that ignorance breeds fear and all that.

"You know about the Minsky receptors in your frontal lobes, and how all those nasty little guilt transmitters bind to them, and how you perceive that as *conscience*. They made Guilt Trip by tweaking a bunch of behavior-modification genes snipped from parasites; the guiltier you feel, the more Trip gets pumped into your brain. It binds to the transmitters, which changes their shape and basically clogs your motor pathways so you can't move.

"That's also why you're so fond of cats, by the way. Baseline *Toxoplasma* turns rodents into cat-lovers as a way of jumping between hosts. I bet a hundred QueBucks you weren't in such pathetic servitude to Mandelbrot until you got your shots, am I right?

"Anyway, Spartacus is basically a guilt analog. It's got the same active sites, so it binds to the Trip, but the overall conformation is slightly different so it doesn't actually *do* anything except clog up the Minsky receptors. Also it takes longer to break down than regular guilt, so it reaches higher concentrations in the brain. Eventually it overwhelms the active sites through sheer numbers.

"That's the real beauty of it, Killjoy; both your natural transmitters and the Trip itself are still being produced normally, so a test that keys on either of 'em comes up clean. Even a test looking for the complexed form will pass muster, since the baseline complex is still floating around—it just can't find any free receptor sites to latch onto.

"So you're safe. Honestly. The bloodhounds won't be a problem. I wouldn't put you at risk, Achilles, believe me. You mean too—you're too much of a friend for me to fuck around like that.

"Anyway, there you go. I've stuck my neck out for you, and what happens now is pretty much up to you. If you turn me in, though, know this: *you're* making that decision. However you rationalize it, you won't be able to blame some stupid long-chain molecule. It'll be you all the way, your own free will.

"So *use* it, and think about all the things you've done and why, and ask yourself if you're *really* so morally rudderless that you couldn't have made all those tough decisions without enslaving yourself to a bunch of despots. I think you could have, Achilles. You never needed their ball and chain to be a decent human being. I really believe that. I'm gambling everything on it.

"Anyway. You know where I am. You know what your options are. Join me or stab me. Your choice.

"Love, Alice."

TursiPops

She'd last been confirmed at Yankton. Sault Sainte Marie crouched at the eastern corner of Lake Superior. A straight line between those points cut through Lake Michigan.

Ken Lubin knew exactly where to set up shop.

The Great Lakes weren't quite so great these days, not since the water shortages of the twenty-first century had reduced their volume by 25 percent. (Lubin supposed it was a small price to pay to avoid the water wars breaking out everywhere else on the planet.) Still. Lenie Clarke was a rifter; the lakes were still deep, and dark, and long. Directly en route, too. Any amphibian trying to elude capture would be crazy not to take a dip.

Of course, any amphibian with more than a room-temperature IQ would also know that her enemies would be waiting for her.

He stood four hundred meters above Lake Michigan's southern reaches. An unbroken rim of industrial lakefront stretched around the horizon from Whiting to Evanston.

Barely visible between land and water: the dark, broad bands
of old mud that passed for shoreline wherever deep-water
access wasn't a priority.

"Check the forecast lately?" It was Burton, the Afrikaner,
still pissed that Lubin had usurped his command in the name
of global salvation. Holo light from the tabletop played along
the line of his jaw.

Lubin shook his head. The other man glanced through
the wraparound pane of the lifter's observation deck. Darkness was advancing overhead, as though someone were un-
rolling a great black rug across the sky. "Forecast's up to
eight, now. It'll hit us in under an hour. If she can still
breathe water, it's going to come in handy even on shore."

Lubin grunted and ran a magged scan along the Chicago
waterfront. Nothing of note there, of course. Antlike civilians
scuttling along under a morbid sky. *She could be down there
right now. Any second one of those bugs could just jump off the
breakwater right in front of me, and it'd all be over. Or more likely
I wouldn't even see it. All the troops, all the botflies, all the heavy
equipment could just keep circling around here until the storm hits,
and she's safe and cold under 150 meters of muddy water.*

"You're sure she's going to try it," Burton said.

Lubin tapped a panel on the table; the map zoomed back
in scale, played false-color storm-front imagery across its airspace.

"Even though she knows we're in her way," Burton continued.

But they weren't in her way, of course. They were still
hanging in midair, waiting for a fix. There were just too many
approaches, too much megalopolitan jungle full of pipes and
wires and RF signals where a single unique signature could
stay endlessly anonymous. There were some places one could
safely exclude, of course. Clarke would never be foolish
enough to cross the mudflats—a klick wide in some places—
that the lakes had abandoned when the water fell. She'd stay
in industrialized areas, indoors or under cover, her signal
swamped and her passage unnoticed.

At least they knew she was in Chicago somewhere; a patrolling botfly had picked up a characteristic rifter EMission just that morning, then lost it around a corner. Another had picked up the scent through the front window of a Holiday Inn; cold, of course, by the time reinforcements arrived, but a playback on the lobby cameras hadn't left much doubt. Lenie Clarke was in Chicago; Lubin had pulled back standbys from Cleveland to Detroit, brought them all into tight focus around the sightings.

"You seem awfully certain, considering that whole mercury thing," Burton remarked. "Have you run this past anyone upstairs?"

"I want the dolphins set down right about there," Lubin said, pinpointing a spot on the tabletop. "Take care of it, will you?"

"Certainly." Burton moved back to his panel. Lubin spared a moment to watch his back.

Patience, Burton. You'll get your chance soon enough.

If I fuck up....

If he fucked up *again*, actually.

He still couldn't believe it. All those blood tests he'd ordered, all those path scans, and he'd never thought to test for heavy metals. He'd been eating raw oceanic wildlife for weeks, and it had never even occurred to him.

Idiot, he repeated to himself for the thousandth time.

The GA's medics had caught it when they were cleansing him of βehemoth. They'd assured him that he couldn't be held responsible. That was the thing about heavy metals; they affected the brain. The mercury itself had dulled his faculties, they said. All things considered, he'd actually been performing better than expected.

But maybe Burton could have performed better. Maybe Burton knew it.

Burton had never much liked him, Lubin knew. He wasn't quite sure why. Of course, you don't inject Rwanda$_{11}$ into a man's cells without expecting some increase in the usual alpha-male head-butting responses, but dispassion was a trait even more valued than ruthlessness; both of them had been tweaked for enhanced self-control even more than for the euphemistic *necessary steps.*

Lubin shrugged off the challenger and concentrated on the challenge. At least Chicago narrowed the options somewhat. Still not enough to catch Clarke until she made her move. The simple geometry of πr^2 saw to that: double your search radius and effectiveness dropped by a factor of four. The waterfront was the bottleneck; wherever Clarke was now, that was where she'd be heading. She'd be running into opposition that increased exponentially as she approached that target, the flip side of inverse square. Most of his people, Lubin knew, expected to take her out before she even saw the water.

He wasn't so sure. Clarke had none of the special skills and training that armed the least of her enemies, no botflies or talking guns, but she had something. She was smart, and she was tough, and she did not behave like a normal human being. Pain didn't seem to frighten her at all.

And she *hated,* more purely and perfectly than anyone Lubin had ever known.

She also had half of Maelstrom backing her up. Or had until recently, anyway. Lubin wondered if she'd grown used to being so unaccountably lucky. Had she started to believe her own PR, had she begun to think herself invincible? Did she know yet that she was back on her own?

Hopefully not. Anything that built her confidence worked in Lubin's favor.

Burton still didn't think she'd risk running the gauntlet. Burton wanted to descend from on high and impose martial law, shut that fucking sprawl *down,* right to the rivets, search room by room until the next millennium if that's what it took. Burton had no patience and no subtlety. No appreciation for πr^2. You don't catch fish by chasing them around the ocean with a net; you set the net where you know the fish will come, and you wait.

Of course, Burton didn't think this particular fish *would* come to the net. She wasn't an idiot. All she had to do was hang back and wait them out. It was a plausible enough line of reasoning, if you didn't know what Lubin knew.

If you didn't know that Lenie Clarke, quite simply, was homesick.

The lost distant abyss was an ache inside of her, and if Lake Michigan was a poor imitation of that world, at least it was an imitation of *some* kind. No smokers, no crystalline hot-and-cold-running seawater, no glowing monsters to light the way—but fifteen atmospheres, at least. Darkness and cold, if you stayed near the bottom. Sheltering murk and currents enough to convect away any telltale heatprint. It might be enough, Lubin knew.

He knew that Lenie Clarke's desire would drive her along the straightest line she could manage. He'd known it from the moment he'd seen the records of that anomalous little outbreak in the Cariboo woods. A patch of alpine forest even deader than the norm. Something that had once been a man, curled protectively around something else that had once been a little girl. The crews hadn't checked the lake at all, they'd simply burned the area the way they'd burned all the others. It was only when Lubin had insisted—driven by his belated review of *the story so far*—that they'd sent back an ROV and surveyed the bottom. It was only then that anyone noticed the cobble and deadwood kicked into violent disarray fifty meters down, in a place where the largest inhabitants had been insects. As if something had dropped to the bottom and found it hopelessly wanting, clawed and pounded against bedrock as though driven to tunnel to the core of the earth itself. When Lubin had seen that telemetry, he'd known.

He'd known then, as he knew now, because he felt exactly the same way. Lenie Clarke had been a fish out of water for too long; nothing in Burton's arsenal would scare her off. She was coming.

And if those towering black anvils advancing from the south were anything to go on, she was bringing the wrath of God along for the ride.

Maybe she planned it that way, he mused. *Maybe she summoned the storm the same way she summoned the quake.*

It was easy to indulge in the legend, even tempting. But you didn't have to invoke sorcery to explain the thunderheads marching on Chicago; violent storms had been the spring norm for twenty years or more in these parts. Just another long-term surprise hatched from that chaotic package of cause and effect called *climate change.*

It had actually proven beneficial to certain aspects of the economy. The market for shatterproof windows had never been stronger.

If she hadn't conjured the elements, though, she'd at least been smart enough to use them. Perhaps she'd been holding back, digging her heels in against that relentless pull of dark water, until the weather was perfectly poised to cast a wrench into the machinery.

All for the better, then. It would give her greater confidence in her own success.

The cockpit intercom beeped in his ear: "Front's coming in too fast, sir. We'll have to either get above it or set down."

"How long?" Lubin asked.

"Half hour, tops." Outside, the sky flashed stark white. An avalanche rumbled faintly through the deck.

"Okay." Lubin magged visual. Three hundred meters beneath him, Lake Michigan was a heaving gray cauldron of scrap metal. There were a dozen stealthed transports between the lifter and the lake, their Thayer nets set to *obliterative countershade.* Lubin could pick them out if he tried; the chromatophores lagged a bit when mimicking fast fractals. As far as any civilian would be able to tell, though, the lifter had local airspace all to itself.

"The dolphins are down," Burton reported from across the compartment. "And we've got a bad storm-sewer monitor on South Aberd—"

Lubin cut him off with a wave of the hand: a white diamond icon had just appeared on the tabletop. A second later his comlink beeped.

"West Randolph," someone reported from the depths of Chicago. "Just past the river. Moving east."

They'd strung mist nets at strategic locations along the Chicago River, in addition to the usual antiexotic electricals; Clarke had already ridden a river past one dragnet, and there was a chance she'd try it again. No such luck, though. This sighting was on the wrong side of those barricades. A botfly had snapped an aura completely inconsistent with the outside accessories of the woman who'd worn it. The doorway she'd entered led down into a half-empty commercial warren with a hundred access points.

Lubin realigned his pieces on the way in. Two of the choppers dropped to within spitting distance of the waves, each giving birth to twins; minisubs like finback calves, spacing themselves in an arc two kilometers off the waterfront. Each sub, in turn, birthed a litter of snoops that arranged themselves into a diffuse grid from surface to substrate.

The other choppers touched down from Meigs Field to the Grand Avenue docks, disgorged their cargo, and hunkered down against the oncoming storm. The command lifter came in behind them, pausing fifty meters above the seawall; Lubin slid down inside an extensible tube that uncoiled from the lifter's belly like an absurd proboscis. By the time the huge airship had wallowed away, a command hut had been set up at the foot of East Monroe.

Lubin braced against the rising wind and looked over the edge of Chicago's new seawall. The streaked gray precipice rose smoothly to the railing. The grated mouths of storm sewers punctuated the revetment at regular intervals, drooling insignificant trickles of wastewater. Each opening was twice as high as a man. Lubin ballparked the scale and nodded to himself: the weave of the grillwork was easily tight enough to keep anyone from squeezing through.

A low-flying helicopter flitted past, spraying the water: the waves in its wake swelled and congealed into a swath of gelatinous foam. Lubin had ordered the shoreline gelled from

Lakeshore down to Meigs; the storm would probably smash the tanglefoam to lint after a while, but if Clarke hurled herself off a bridge before that point, she'd be stuck like an ant in honey. A floating pen bobbed at the offshore edge of the gelled zone, rimmed by an inflatable boom riding the waves like a boneless serpent. Lubin tapped a control on the side of his visor; the enclosure sprang into near focus.

There.

Just for a moment, a sleek gray back, metallic inlays glinting darkly along the leading edge of the dorsal fin. Another. Half a dozen there all told, although you'd never see more than one on the surface at any given time.

The wind died.

Lubin slipped off his headset and looked around with naked eyes. It was close to noon, as dark as a solar eclipse. Overhead the sky boiled in silent, ominous slow motion.

A distant clattering roar began cascading through the city at his back: storm shutters, slamming shut along a thousand Euclidean canyons. It sounded as though the buildings themselves were applauding the rise of some long-awaited curtain. A single perfect raindrop, the size of his thumbnail, splatted on the asphalt at Lubin's feet.

He turned and entered the command hut.

Another hallucinogenic tabletop dominated the single-room enclosure. Lubin studied the chessboard: two arms of security extended out from the waterfront, diverging northwest from Grand and southwest from Eisenhower. A funnel, to guide Lenie Clarke to a place of another's choosing. Two-point-five klicks west of the seawall, a band of botflies and exoskels formed a north–south line and began sealing off skyways and tunnels.

Seven and a half square kilometers found itself excised from the world along these boundaries. Surface traffic moved within and without, but not *across*; the rapitrans grid went utterly dark across its breadth. The flow of information took a little longer to cut off—

—wouldn't you know it another goddamned quarantine looks like I won't be able to make our eight-thirty after all, hello? Hello? Jesus fucking Christ . . .

—but eventually even electrons respected the new borders. The target, after all, was well-known to receive assistance from such quarters.

But it was not enough to simply cut this parallelogram out of the world. Lenie Clarke still moved there, among several hundred thousand sheep. Lubin let Burton off the leash for a while.

A blond Peruvian was putting a telemetry panel through its paces in one corner of the hut. Lubin joined her while Burton feasted on the application of naked force. "Kinsman. How are they doing?"

"Complaining about the noise. And they always hate freshwater ops. Makes them feel heavy."

Her panel was a matrix of views from cams embedded in the leading edge of each dolphin's dorsal fin. A gray crescent marred the lower edge of each window, where the animals' melons intruded on the view. Ghostly shapes slipped past each other in the green darkness beyond.

Endless motion. Those monsters never even slept; one cerebral hemisphere might, or the other, but they were never both unconscious at the same time. Tweaked from raw *Tursiops* stock only four generations old, fins and flippers inlaid with reinforcements that gave new meaning to the term *cutting-edge*, echolocation skills honed so fine over sixty million years that hard tech could still barely match it. Humanity had tried all sorts of liaisons with the Cetacea over the years. Big dumb pilot whales, eager to please. Orcas, too large for clandestine ops and a little too prone to psychosis in confined spaces. Lags and Spots and all those stiff-necked open-water pansies from the tropics. But *Tursiops* was the one, had always *been* the one. Not just smart; *mean*.

If Clarke got that far, she'd never see them coming.

"What about the noise?" Lubin asked.

"Industrial waterfronts are loud at the best of times,"

Kinsman told him. "Like an echo chamber, all those flat re-
flective surfaces. You know how you feel when someone
shines bright lights in your eyes? Same thing."

"Are they just complaining, or will it interfere with the
op?"

"Both. It's not too bad now, but when the storm sewers
start draining you're gonna have a dozen white-water
sources pounding into the lake all along this part of the seawall. Lots of noise, bubbles, stuff kicked off the bottom. Under
ideal conditions my guys can track a Ping-Pong ball at a hundred meters, but the way it's going outside—I'd say ten,
maybe twenty."

"Still better than anything else we could deploy under
the same conditions," Lubin said.

"Oh, easily."

Lubin left Kinsman to her charges and grabbed his pack
off the floor. The storm assaulted him the moment he left
the hut's soundproof interior. The downpour drenched on
contact. The sky above was as black as the asphalt below; both
flashed white whenever lightning ripped the space between.
Lubin's people stood on conspicuous duty along the seawall,
punctuating every vantage point. The rain turned them slick
and black as rifters after a dive.

Shoot to kill was a given. It might not be enough, though.
If Clarke made it this far, there were too many places she
could simply dive off an embankment. That was okay: in fact,
Lubin rather expected it. That was what the subs and the
snoops and the dolphins were for.

Only the subs were useless close to shore, and now Kinsman was saying the dolphins might not be able to acquire a
target more than a few meters away...

He set his pack down and split it open.

*And if the dolphins can't catch her, what makes you think you
can?*

The odd thing was, he actually had an answer.

———

Burton was waiting when Lubin got back inside. "We've rounded up a bunch of—oh, very nice. A salute to the enemy, maybe? In her final hour?"

Lubin assayed a slight smile, and hoped that someday soon Burton would pose a threat to security. His eyecaps slid disconcertingly beneath lids not quite reacclimated to their presence. "What do you have?"

"We have a bunch of people who look a lot like you do right now," Burton said. "None of them have actually seen Clarke—in fact, none of them even knew she was in town. Maybe the anemone's losing its touch."

"The anemone?"

"Haven't you heard? That's what people are calling it now."

"Why?"

"Beats me."

Lubin stepped over to the chessboard; half a dozen cylindrical blue icons shone at points where civilians were being held to *assist the ongoing investigation*.

"Of course, we're a long way from sampling the whole population yet," Burton continued. "And we're concentrating on the obvious groupies, the costumes. There'll be a lot more in civvies. Still, none of the people we've interrogated so far knows anything. Clarke could have an army if she wanted, but as far as we can tell she hasn't even begged a sandwich. It's completely off-the-wall."

Lubin slipped his headset back on. "I'd say it's standing her in good stead now," he remarked mildly. "She seems to have *you* dead-ended, anyway."

"There are other suspects," Burton said. "Lots of them. We'll turn her up."

"Good luck." The tacticals in Lubin's visor were oddly drained of color—*oh, right. The eyecaps.* He eyed the blue cylinders glowing in the zone, tweaked his headset controls until they resaturated. Such clean, perfect shapes, each representing a grand violation of civil rights. He was often surprised at how little resistance civilians offered in the face of such measures. Innocent people, detained by the hundreds

without charge. Cut off from friends and family and—at least
for those who'd have been able to afford it—counsel. All in
a good cause, of course. Civil rights should run a distant second to global survival in *anyone's* book. The usual suspects
didn't know what was at stake, though. As far as they knew,
this was just another case of officially sanctioned thugs like
Burton, throwing their weight around.

Yet only a few had resisted. Perhaps they'd been conditioned by all the quarantines and blackouts, all the invisible
boundaries CSIRA erected on a moment's notice. The rules
changed from one second to the next, the rug could get pulled
out just because the wind blew some exotic weed outside its
acceptable home range. You couldn't fight something like
that, you couldn't fight the wind. All you could do was adapt.
People were evolving into herd animals.

Or maybe just accepting that that's what they'd always
been.

Not Lenie Clarke, though. Somehow, she'd gone the other
way. A born victim, passive and yielding as seaweed, had suddenly grown thorns and hardened its stems to steel. Lenie
Clarke was a mutant; the same environment that turned
everyone else into bobbing corks had transformed her into
barbed wire.

A white diamond blossomed near Madison and La Salle.
"Got her," the comlink crackled in a voice Lubin didn't recognize. "Probably her, anyway."

He tapped into the channel. "Probably?"

"Securicam snapshot down in a basement mall. No EM
sensor down there, so we can't confirm. We got a three-
quarter profile for a half second, though. Bayesians say 82
percent likely."

"Can you seal off that block?"

"Not automatically. No master kill switches or anything."

"Okay, do it manually."

"Got it."

Lubin switched channels. "Engineering?"

"Here." They'd set up a dedicated line to City Planning.
The people on that end were strictly need-to-know, of

course; no hint of the stakes involved, no recognizable name to humanize the target. A dangerous fugitive in the core, yours is not to question why, full stop. Almost no chance for messy security breaches there.

"Have you got the fix on La Salle?" Lubin asked, zooming the chessboard.

"Sure do."

"What's down there?"

"These days, not much. Originally retail, but most of the merchants moved out with the spread. A lot of empty stalls."

"No, I mean substructures. Crawl spaces, service tunnels, that sort of thing. Why aren't I seeing any of that on the map?"

"Oh, shit, that stuff's *ancient*. TwenCen and older. A lot of it never even got into the database; by the time we updated our files nobody was using those areas except derelicts and wireheads, and with all the data-corruption problems we've been having—"

"You *don't know*?" A soft beeping began in Lubin's head: someone else wanting to talk.

"Someone might have scanned the old blueprints onto a crystal somewhere. I could check."

"Do that." Lubin switched channels. "Lubin."

It was his point man on the seawall. "We're losing the tanglefoam."

"Already?" They should have had at least another hour.

"It's not just the rainfall, it's the storm sewers. They're funneling precip from the whole city right out through the seawall. Have you *seen* the volume those drains are putting out?"

"Not recently." Things just kept getting better.

Burton, unrebukably occupied with his own duties, none-theless seemed to have an ear cocked in Lubin's direction. "I'll be right out," Lubin said after a moment.

"That's okay," Seawall said. "I can just feed you a—"

Lubin killed the channel.

—————

White water roared from a mouth in the revetment, wide as a tanker truck. Lubin couldn't begin to guess at the force of that discharge; it extended at least four meters from the wall before gravity could even coax it off the horizontal. The tanglefoam had retreated on all sides; Lake Michigan heaved and thrashed in the opened space, reclaiming even more territory.

Great.

There were eleven drains just like this along the secured waterfront. Lubin redeployed two dozen inshore personnel to the seawall.

City Planning beeped in his ear. "...nd some..."

He cranked up the filters on his headset; the roar of the storm faded a bit. "Say again?"

"Found something! Two-D and low-res, but it looks like there's nothing down there but a service crawlway running above the ceiling and a sewer main under the floor."

"Can they be accessed?" Even with the filters, Lubin could barely hear his own voice.

Engineering didn't seem to have any trouble, though. "Not from the concourse, of course. There's a physical plant under the next block."

"And if she got into the main?"

"She'd end up at the treatment plant on Burnham, most likely."

They had Burnham covered. But—"What do you mean, *most likely*? Where else could she end up?"

"Sewage and storm systems spill together when things get really swamped. Keeps the treatment facilities from flooding. It's not as bad as it sounds, though. By the time things get *this* crazy, the flow's great enough to dilute the sewage—"

"Are you saying—" A bolt of lightning cut the sky into jagged fragments. Lubin forced himself to wait. The thunderclap in the ensuing darkness was deafening. "Are you saying she could be in the *storm sewers*?"

"Well, theoretically, but it doesn't matter."

"Why not?"

"There'd have to be an *awful* lot of water going through before the systems would mix. The moment your fugitive crossed over she'd be sucked down and drowned. No way she could fight the current, and there wouldn't be any airspace left in the pi—"

"Everything's going through the storm system now?"

"Most of it."

"Will the grates hold?"

"I don't understand," Engineering said.

"The grates! The grilles covering the outfalls! Are they rated to withstand this kind of flow?"

"The grates are down," Engineering said.

"*What!*"

"They fold down automatically when cubic meters-per-sec gets too high. Otherwise they'd impede flow and the whole system would back up."

Heavy metal strikes again.

Lubin opened an op-wide channel. "She's not coming overland. She's—"

Kinsman, the dolphin woman, cut in: "Gandhi's got something. Channel twelve."

He switched channels, found himself underwater. Half the image was a wash of static, interference even the Bayesians couldn't clear in realtime. The other half wasn't much better: a foamy gray wash of bubbles and turbulence.

A split-second glimpse, off to the left: a flicker of darker motion. Gandhi caught it too, twisted effortlessly into the new heading. The camera rotated smoothly around its own center of focus as the dolphin rolled over on its back. The murk darkened.

He's going deep, Lubin realized. *Coming up from underneath. Good boy.*

Now the image centered on a patch of diffuse radial brightness, fading to black on all sides: the optics of ascent toward a brighter surface. Suddenly the target was *there*, dead to rights: silhouetted arms, a head, flashing stage left and disappearing.

"Hit," Kinsman reported. "She never saw it coming."

"Remember, we don't want her bleeding out there," Lubin cautioned.

"Gandhi knows the drill. He's not using his pecs, he's just ram—"

Again: a piecemeal human shadow, found and lost in an instant. The image jarred slightly.

"Huh," Kinsman said. "She saw that coming somehow. Almost got out of the way in time."

The implants. For an instant Lubin was back on the Juan de Fuca Ridge, comfortably suspended under three kilometers of black ice water. Feeling Beebe's sonar *tick-tick-tick*ing against the machinery in his chest...

"She can feel the click trains," he said. "Tell Gandhi to lay—"

Another pass. This time the target faced her attacker head-on, eyes bright smudges in a dark jigsaw, one arm coming up in a vain attempt to ward off two hundred kilograms of bone and muscle *wait a second she's holding something she's—*

The image skidded to the left. Suddenly the water was spinning again, no smooth controlled rotation this time, just a wild slewing corkscrew, purely ballistic, slowing against ambient drag. The darkness of deep water swelled ahead. A different darkness spilled in from the side, a gory black cloud spreading into brief cumulus before the currents tore it apart.

"*Shit,*" Kinsman said. Lubin's headset amped the whisper loud enough to drown thunder.

She kept her billy. All the way from Beebe, hitching and walking and riding across the whole damn continent.

Good for her...

The vision imploded to darkness and a final flurry of static. Lubin was back on the waterfront, sheets of rain beating the world into a blur scarcely brighter than the one he'd just left.

"Gandhi's down," Kinsman reported.

Kinsman tag-teamed two more dolphins to the site of Gandhi's last stand; Lubin pulled abreast on the seawall a few moments after they arrived. Burton was waiting there with a charged squid, water cascading from his rainskin.

"Fan them out," Lubin told Kinsman over the link. "Hyperbolic focus on the carcass, offshore spread." He grabbed his fins off the scooter and stepped to the edge of the seawall, Burton at his side. "What about Gandhi?"

"Gandhi's sockeye," Kinsman said.

"No, I mean what about emotional ties? What impact will his loss have on the efficiency of the others?"

"For Singer and Caldicott, none. They never liked him all that much. That's why I sent them."

"Okay. Line up the rest on a converging perimeter, but keep them away from the outfalls."

"No problem," Kinsman acknowledged. "They wouldn't be much good in there anyway, with *those* acoustics."

"I'm switching to vocoder in thirty seconds. Channel five."

"Got it."

Burton watched neutrally as Lubin bent over to pull on his fins. "Bad break!" he shouted over the storm. "About the sewers, I mean!"

Lubin snugged his heel straps, reached out for the squid. Burton handed it over. Lubin sealed his face flap. The diveskin reached across his eyelids and bonded to the caps beneath, blocked nose and mouth like liquid rubber. He stood, isolated from the downpour, calmly suffocating.

Good luck, Burton mouthed through the rain.

Lubin hugged the squid to his chest and stepped into space.

Michigan closed over his head, roaring.

Fifteen meters to the north, one of Chicago's outfalls spewed an endless vomit of wastewater into the lake; the whirlpools and eddies from that discharge reached Lubin with scarcely diminished strength. A fog of microscopic bubbles swirled on all sides, smeared muddy light throughout the water. Bits of detritus looped through eccentric orbits, fading to white just past the reach of his fingers. Water sucked and slurped. Overhead, barely visible, the rain-pelted surface writhed like mercury under rapid-fire assault—and all around, omnipresent in the heavy surge, the deep deafening roar of waterfalls.

Lubin spun in the current, insides flooding, and reveled.

He didn't think that Lenie Clarke was headed for deep water just yet. She might not have anticipated the minisubs lurking deep offshore; she knew about the dolphins, though, and she knew about sonar. She knew all about the effects of turbulence on sensory systems both electronic and biological. She'd stay close to shore, hiding in the cacophony of the outfalls. Soon, perhaps, she'd edge north or south in furtive stages, creeping along a murky jungle of wreckage and detritus left over from three centuries of *out-of-sight-out-of-mind*. Even in calm weather there'd be no shortage of hiding places.

Now, though, she was injured, probably fighting shock. Gandhi had hit her twice before Clarke had rallied; it was amazing that she'd even stayed conscious through that pounding, let alone fought back. For the time being she was holed up somewhere, just hanging on.

Lubin glanced at the nav console on his wrist. A tiny 2-D representation of local space sparkled there—starring, as Ken Lubin, a convergence of sharp green lines at center stage. Occasional yellow pinpoints drifted in and out of range: Kinsman's dolphins, patrolling the perimeter. Another pinpoint, much closer, wasn't moving at all. Lubin aimed his squid and squeezed the throttle.

Gandhi was a mess. Clarke's billy had discharged against the right side of his head; the front of the animal had been blown apart in an instant. Behind the dorsal fin, the carcass was pretty much intact. Farther forward a fleshy wreckage of ribs and skull remained on the left side, that maniacal idiot dolphin grin persisting even past death. The right side was gone entirely.

Gandhi was impaled on a sunken tangle of rebar. The current here moved offshore; the dolphin must have met his fate closer to the seawall. Lubin swung the squid around and started upstream.

"...eive...Lu...ical?"

The word fragments buzzed along his lower jaw, all but lost in the ambient thunder. Lubin, struck by sudden realization, cranked up the gain on his vocoder: "Keep this channel clear. Cl—"

His words, transmuted by the vocoder into a harsh metallic buzz, caught him off guard. It had been months since the implants had mutilated his voice that way. The sound almost evoked a kind of nostalgia.

"No contact," he continued. "Clarke's got L-FAM implants. She could be listening in."

"...ain?..."

In fact, even if Clarke was tuned to the right channel, it was doubtful that she'd make any more sense of the signal than Lubin had. Acoustic modems had not been built with white water in mind.

And why would she be listening anyway? How would she know I'm even here?

It wasn't a chance he was willing to take. He kept as silent as his quarry, wherever she was. The lake raged around them both.

Intuition is not clairvoyance. It's not guesswork either. Intuition is *executive summary*, that 90 percent of the higher brain that functions subconsciously—but no less rigorously—than the self-aware subroutine that thinks of itself as *the* person. Lubin glided through murk so thick he could barely see the squid that drew him forward; he set the machine to heel and crawled through dead, twisted warrens of wreckage and dereliction, spikes and jagged edges rampant under layers of slime that softened only their appearance. He let the current push him offshore, then grab him and hurl him against the base of the seawall itself. He clambered sideways like a crab on gray scoured surfaces, pressed himself flat while the water tried to peel him off and flick him away like an old decal. He let those intuitive subroutines guide him; weighing scenarios, sifting memories, remembering happier times when Lenie Clarke had revealed *this* motive, *that* preference. He explored some potential refugia, ignored others, and would not have been able to say exactly why. But all parts of Ken Lubin had been well and thoroughly trained: the brain stem and the analytical subroutines and the little homunculus that sat self-consciously behind his eyes. Each knew what to do, and what to leave to the others.

And so it was not entirely unexpected that he should come upon Lenie Clarke, hiding in the shadow of one of Chicago's absurd waterfalls, wedged in a canyon of wreckage from the previous century.

She was in bad shape. Her body was twisted in a way that suggested Gandhi's blows had done their job. Her diveskin had been torn along the rib cage, either from the dolphin's attack or from the jagged geometry of the lake bed. She favored her left arm. But she'd chosen her refuge well; too much noise for sonar, too much metal for EM signatures, too much shit in the water for anyone without the eyes and the instincts of a rifter to ever track her down. Burton would have passed within a meter and not picked up the scent.

Good girl, he thought.

She looked up from her hiding place, her featureless white eyes meeting his through two meters of milky chaos, and he knew instantly that she recognized him.

He had hoped, against all reason, that she wouldn't.

I'm sorry, he thought. *I really don't have any choice.*

Of course, she still had the billy. Of course, she kept it concealed until the last moment, then yanked it into play with desperate swiftness. Of course she tried to use it on herself; doomed anyway, what better act of final revenge than to set βehemoth free in one final, suicidal catharsis?

Lubin saw all of it coming, and disarmed her with barely a thought. But the billy, when he checked, was empty. Gandhi had taken its final charge. Lubin dropped it onto the muddy junkscape.

I'm sorry. The sexual anticipation of imminent murder began stirring in him. *I liked you. You were the only—you really deserved to win. . . .*

She stared back. She didn't trip her vocoder. She didn't try to speak.

Any second now Guilt Trip would kick in. Once again, Lubin felt almost sick with gratitude: that an engineered neurochemical could so easily shoulder all responsibility for his acts. That he was about to kill his only friend, and remain blameless of any wrongdoing. That—

It was impossible to close one's eyes while wearing a diveskin. The material bonded to the eyecaps, pinned the lids back in an unblinking stare. Lenie Clarke looked at Ken Lubin. Ken Lubin looked away.

Guilt Trip had never taken this long before.

It's not working. Something's wrong.

He waited for his gut to force him into action. He waited for orders and absolution. He went down into himself as deep as he dared, looking for some master to take the blame.

No. No. Something's wrong.

Do I have to kill her myself?

By the time he realized he wasn't going to get an answer, it was too late. He looked back into Lenie Clarke's final refuge, steeling himself for damnation.

And saw that it was empty.

Terrarium

An icon flashed at the corner of Desjardins's board. He ignored it.

The new feed had just gone on-line: a thread of fiberop snaking in all its messy physicality under the door and down the hallway. There hadn't been any other way; CSIRA was far too security-conscious to allow civilian nodes inside its perimeter, and *The General*—or *Anemone*, or whatever it was called today—hadn't talked to any other kind since before Yankton. If Desjardins wanted to go into combat, he'd have to do it on enemy turf.

That meant a hardline. Outside wireless was jammed as a matter of course; even wristwatches couldn't get on-line in CSIRA without going through the local hub. Desjardins had envisioned a cable running through the lobby into the street, hanging a left and tripping up pedestrians all the way to the nearest public library. Fortunately, there'd been a municipal junction box in the basement.

His board upped the lumens on the icon, a visual voice-raising: Alice Jovellanos *still* wants to talk. Please respond.

Forget it, Alice. Your face is the last thing I want to see right now. You're lucky I haven't turned you in already.

If Guilt Trip had been doing his—*its* job, he *would* have turned her in. God only knew how badly he could screw up now, thanks to that little saboteur's handiwork. God only knew how many *other* 'lawbreakers she was putting at risk the same way, how many catastrophes would result from sheer glandular indecision at a critical moment. Alice Jovellanos had potentially put millions of lives in jeopardy.

Not that that amounted to a fart in a hurricane next to what βehemoth was gearing up for, of course. N'AmWire had just made it public: a big chunk of the west coast was now officially under quarantine. Even the *official* death toll had left the starting gate at four digits.

The splice fed into a new panel that crowded him on the right. It was stand-alone and self-contained, unconnected and unconnectable to any CSIRA sockets. Vast walled spaces waited within—spaces that could swallow the contents of a node and walls that could mimic its architecture at a moment's notice. A habitat replicator, in effect. A terrarium.

The icon began beeping. He muted it.

Take a hint, Alice.

She'd really fucked him up the ass. The problem—and the fact that it *was* a problem only emphasized how thoroughly she'd messed things up—was that she obviously didn't see it that way. She thought of herself as some sort of *liberator*. She'd acted out of some kind of twisted concern for *his* welfare. She'd actually put *his* interests above the greater good.

Desjardins booted the terrarium. Start-up diagnostics momentarily cluttered the display. He wouldn't be using his

inlays this time around; they were part of the CSIRA network, after all. It was going to be raw visual and touch pads
all the way.

The greater good. Right.

That had always been a faceless, abstract thing to human
sensibilities. It was easier to feel for the one person you knew
than for the far-off suffering millions you didn't. When the
Big One had hit the Left Coast, Desjardins had watched the
threads and spun his filters and breathed a silent sigh of
relief that it hadn't been *him* under all that rubble—but on
the day that Mandelbrot died, he knew, his heart would
break.

It was that illogical fact that made Guilt Trip necessary
in the first place. It was that illogical fact that kept him from
betraying Alice Jovellanos. He sure as shit wasn't ready to sit
down and have a friendly chat with her, but he couldn't bring
himself to sell her out either.

Besides. If he really *had* figured out this whole Anemone
thing, it was Alice who'd given him the idea.

He tapped the board. A window opened. Maelstrom
howled on the other side.

Either way, he'd know within the hour.

It was everywhere.

Even where it wasn't, it was. Where it wasn't talking, it
was being talked *about*. Where it wasn't being talked about it
was being sown, tales and myths of Lenie Clarke left inert
until some unsuspecting vector opened a mailbox to hatch a
whole new generation.

"She's everywhere. That's why they can't catch her."

"You're shitting static. How can she be everywhere?"

"Imposters. Clones. Who says there's only one Lenie
Clarke?"

"She can, you know, *beam* herself. Quantum teleportation.
It's the blood nanos she's carrying."

"That's impossible."

"Remember the Strip?"

"What about it?"

"Lenie *started* it, haploid. She just strolled onto the beach and everyone she touched just threw off the drugs and woke up. Just like that. Sounds nano to me."

"That wasn't nano. That's just, you know, that firewitch bug from NoCal, the one that makes your joints fall apart? It got into the cyclers and fucked up some molecule in the valium. You want to know what Lenie *started*, she started that fucking *plague*..."

It had gotten smarter, too. Subtler. Hundreds of 'lawbreakers were on the watch now, prowling civilian channels for the inexplicable clarity that had alerted Desjardins the day before. That slip hadn't been repeated, as far as anyone could tell.

And when Desjardins finally did acquire a target, it wasn't baud rate or dropout that clued him in, but content:

"I know where Lenie Clarke is." It spoke with the sexless, neutral voice of inflated ASCII set to *default*; its handle was *Tesseract*. "*Les beus* are on her ass, but they've lost the trail for now."

"How do *you* know?" asked someone claiming to be *Poseidon-23*.

"I'm Anemone," *Tesseract* said.

"Sure. And I'm Ken Lubin."

"Then your days are numbered, litcrit-o'-mine. Ken Lubin's been turned. He's working for the corpses now."

A *lot* smarter, to have known that. Not so smart to admit it in mixed company. Desjardins began sketching lines on his board.

"We need to back her up," *Tesseract* was saying. "Any of you in central N'Am, say around the Great Lakes?"

No queries to the local traffic log, no surreptitious trawl for Turing apps, no trace on the channel. No moves on anything that *Tesseract* might be keeping an eye on. Achilles Desjardins had gotten smarter, too.

"Piss off, Tessie." Some skeptic going by *Hiigara*. "You expect us to sub to Lenie Clarke's personal manager just showing up to chat?"

Nothing in the local node. Desjardins started snooping adjacent servers.

"I sense skepticism," *Tesseract* remarked. "Special effects is what you want. A demonstration."

"Yowsers," said *Poseidon-23*, and drowned in the roar of an ocean.

Desjardins blinked. An instant before, there'd been six people on the channel listing. Now there were 4,862, all speaking at once. No one voice was comprehensible, but even the collective blare was impossibly clear: a digital babble with no distortion, no static, no arrhythmic stutter of bytes delayed or lost in transit.

Silence returned. The channel listing imploded back down to the six it had started with.

"There you go," said *Tesseract*.

Shit, Desjardins thought. Shaken, he studied the results on his board. *It's talking to all of them. At once.*

"How'd you *do* that?" *Hiigara* asked.

"I'd rather not," *Tesseract* whispered. "It attracts attention. Are any of you in central N'Am, say around the Great Lakes?"

He muted the chatter; he didn't need it, now that he had the scent. There seemed to be a fair bit of wildlife in a hospital server across town. He stepped inside, looked out through its portals.

Even more wildlife over *there*. Desjardins stepped sideways, and found himself in Oslo National's account records. And even more wildlife flowing out to...

Step.

Timor. *Real* heavy infestation. Of course, those little subsidiaries were still back in the twentieth century when it came to pest control, but still...

This is it, he thought.

Don't touch anything. Go straight to the root.

He did. He whispered sweet nothings to gatekeepers and system clocks, flashed his ID to ease their concerns. *A very large number of users are about to get very pissed off,* he reflected.

He tapped his board. On the other side of the world, every portal on the edge of the Timor node slammed shut.

Inside, time stuttered.

It didn't stop completely—without *some* level of system iteration there'd be no way to copy what was inside. Hopefully that wouldn't matter. A few thousand cycles, a few tens of thousands. Maybe enough for the enemy to lurch in stop-motion increments toward some dim awareness of what was happening, but not enough—if he was lucky—to actually *do* anything about it.

He ignored the traffic piling up at Timor's gates. He ignored the plaintive queries from other nodes who wondered why their feeds had gone dark. All he saw was the math in the bubble: architecture, operating system, software. Files and executables and wildlife. It was almost a kind of teleportation—each bit fixed and read and reconstructed half a world away, the original left unchanged for all the intimacy of its violation.

He had it.

The Timor node jerked back up to speed. Sudden panic from something inside; wildlife flew like leaves in a tornado, tearing at records, bursting through doorways, disemboweling itself after the fact. It didn't matter. It was too late.

Desjardins smiled. He had an Anemone in a tank.

In the terrarium, he *could* stop time completely.

It was all laid out before him, flash-frozen: a software emulation of the node itself, copies of every register and address, every spin and every bit. He could set it all running with a single command.

And it would fly apart in seconds. Just like the Timorese original.

So he set up inviolable backups of the logs and registries and placed them *outside*, with a filtered two-way pipe to the originals. He went through each of the portals leading out of the node—gates into oblivion now, from a bubble suspended in the void—and gave a little half-twist to each.

He regarded his handiwork. Time stood still. Nothing moved.

"Moebius, come forth," he murmured.

Anemone screamed. A thousand unregistered executables leapt forward and clawed the traffic log to shreds; a million more escaped through the portals.

Ten times as many rustled and watched:

As the mutilated logs repaired themselves with barely time to bleed, magically replenished from on high;

As the wildlife that had fled through *that* portal came plunging back in through *this* one, wheeling in confusion;

As a channel opened in the midst of the wilderness and a voice rang out from heaven: "Hey, you. Anemone."

"We don't talk to you." Sexless, neutral. Default.

It was still going after the records, but it was taking a dozen tacks at once: subtle forgery, full frontal assault, everything in between. None of it worked, but Desjardins was impressed anyway. Damn smart.

As smart as an orb-weaving spider, blindly obeying lifetime fitness functions. As smart as a bird, noting wind and distance and optimizing seed load to three decimal places.

"You really *should* talk to me," Desjardins said mildly. "I'm God." He caught a piece of wildlife at random, tagged it, set it free again.

"You're shitting static. Lenie Clarke is God." A school of fish, a flock of wheeling birds so complex you needed matrix algebra and thinking machines to understand it all. The ASCII came from somewhere inside.

"Clarke's not God," Desjardins said. "She's a petri dish."

Wildlife still flew through the wraparound gateways, but less randomly; some sort of systematic exploration, evolving on the fly. Desjardins checked on the piece he'd tagged. It had descendants already, all carrying the Mark of Cain he'd bestowed on their ancestor. And their descendants had had descendants.

Two hundred sixty generations in fourteen seconds. Not bad.

Thank you, Alice. If you hadn't ranted on about dancing bumblebees, who knows when I would've figured this out. . . .

"Maybe you need a demonstration," said the swarm. "Special effects is what you want, yes?"

And she'd been right. Genes have their own intelligence. They can wire an ant for the cultivation of underground farms, the domestication of aphid cattle ... even the taking of slaves. Genes can shape behaviors so sophisticated they verge on genius, given time.

"A demonstration," Desjardins said. "Sure. Hit me."

Time's the catch, of course. Genes are *slow*: a thousand generations to learn some optimal-foraging trick that a real brain could pick up in five minutes. Which is why brains evolved in the first place, of course. But when a hundred generations fit into the space of a yawn, maybe the genes get their edge back. Maybe wildlife learns to talk using only the blind stupid logic of natural selection—and the poor lumbering meat sack on the other end never suspects that he's having a chat that spans generations.

"I'm waiting," Desjardins said.

"Lenie Clarke is not a demonstration." The swarm swirled in the terrarium. Was it Desjardins's imagination, or did it seem to be—fading, somehow?

He smiled. "You're losing it, aren't you?"

"Loaves and fishes for Anemone."

"But you're not Anemone. You're just a tiny *piece* of it, all alone ..."

Time's not enough in and of itself, of course. Evolution needs *variance* as well. Mutation and shuffling to create new prototypes, variable environments to weed out the unfit and shape the survivors.

"Clarke, Lenie. Water lights up all cool and radium glow ..."

Life can survive in a box, for a while at least. But it can't *evolve* there. And down in Desjardins's terrarium, the population was starting to look pretty inbred.

"Free hard-core pedosnuff," the swarm murmured. "Even to enter."

Countless individuals. Jostling, breeding. Stagnating.

It's all just *pattern*.

"Sockeye," said the wildlife, and nothing more.

Desjardins realized he'd been holding his breath. He let it out, slowly.

"Well," he whispered, "you're not so smart after all."

"You just *act* like you are..."

Soul Mate

Someone was pounding on his door. Someone was definitely *not* taking the hint.

"Killjoy! Open up!"

Go *away*, Desjardins thought. He flashed his findings to the rest of the Anemone team, a far-flung assemblage of 'law-breakers he'd never met in the flesh and probably never would. *I* nailed *the sucker. I figured it out.*

"*Achilles!*"

Grudgingly, he leaned back and thumbed the door open without looking. "What do you want, Alice?"

"Lertzman's dead!"

He spun in his chair. "You're kidding."

"He was *pithed.*" Jovellanos's almond eyes were wide and worried. "They found him this morning. He was braindead, he was just lying there *starving* to death. Someone stuck a needle up the base of his skull and just *shredded* his white matter...."

"Jesus." Desjardins stood. "You sure? I mean—"

"Of *course* I'm sure, you think I'm making it up? It was Lubin. It *had* to be, that's how he tracked you down, that's how he—"

"Yeah, Alice, I get it." He took a step toward her. "Thanks for—for telling me." He began to close the door.

She stuck her foot in the way. "That's *it*? That's all you've got to say?"

"Lubin's gone, Alice. He's not our problem anymore. And besides"—nudging her foot out of the way with his own—

"you didn't like Lertzman any more than I did."

He closed the door in her face.

Lertzman's dead.

Lertzman the bureaucrat. The cyst in "system," too dormant to contribute, too deeply embedded to excise, too ineffective to matter.

Dead.

Why do you care? He was an asshole.

But I knew him . . .

The one person you know. The far-off millions you don't.

Could've been me.

Nothing to do about Lertzman now. Nothing to do about his killer, even: Lubin was out of Desjardins's life, hot on the trail of Lenie Clarke. If he succeeded, Ken Lubin could be the savior of the planet. Ken-the-fucking-psychopath-*Lubin*, savior of billions. It was almost funny. Maybe, after saving the world, he'd go on a killing spree to celebrate. Set up breach after breach, sealing each with extreme and unfettered prejudice. Would anyone have the heart to stop him, after all the good he'd done? The salvation of billions could buy you a whole lot of forgiveness, Desjardins supposed.

Ken Lubin, for all his quirks, was doing something worthwhile. He was hunting the *other* Lenie Clarke, the *real* one. The Lenie Clarke that Achilles Desjardins had been tracking was a mirage. There was no great conspiracy after all. No global death cult. Anemone was a drooling idiot. All it knew was that tales of global apocalypse were good for breeding, and that *Lenie Clarke* was a free pass into Haven. It had only connected those threads through blind dumb luck.

It was a blazing irony that the person behind the words actually lived up to the billing.

Lubin's problem. Not his.

But that was dead wrong, and he knew it. Lenie Clarke was *everyone's* problem. A threat to the greater good if he'd even seen one.

Forget Lertzman. Forget Alice. Forget Rowan and Lubin and Anemone, even. None of them would matter if it wasn't for Lenie Clarke.

Worry about Clarke. She's the one that's going to kill us all.

She'd come onto the Oregon Strip, moved north to Hongcouver. Inland from there; she'd got through the quarantine somehow. Then nothing for a month or so, when she'd appeared in the midwest, heading south. Skirting the edge of a no-go zone that stretched across three states. Two outbreaks down at the edge of the Dust Belt. Then Yankton: the head of an arrow, pointing somewhere in the vicinity of the Great Lakes.

Home, Lubin had said. *Sault Sainte Marie.*

Desjardins tapped the board: the main menu for the N'AmPac Grid Authority lit up his inlays. Personnel. Clarke, Lenie.

Deceased.

No surprise there: bureaucracy's usual up-to-the-minute grasp of current events. At least the file hadn't been wiped.

He called up next-of-kin: *Clarke, Indira and Butler, Jakob.*
Deceased.

Suppose she couldn't get to her parents? Rowan had wondered. *Suppose they'd been dead a long time?*

And Lubin had said, *The people she hates are very much alive....*

He called up the public registry. No Sault Sainte Marie listing for Indira Clarke or Jakob Butler in the past three years. That was as far back as public records went. The central archives went back another four; nothing there either.

Suppose they'd been dead a long time? Sort of an odd question, now that he thought about it.

Forget the registry, Desjardins thought. *Too easy to edit.* He tried the matchmaker instead, threw a bottle into Maelstrom and asked if anyone had seen *Indira Clarke* or *Jakob Butler* hanging out with *Sault Sainte Marie.*

The hit came back from N'AmPac Directory Assistance, an inquiry over seven months old. By rights, it should have been purged just hours after its inception. It hadn't been. *Indira* was not the only Clarke it mentioned.

Clarke, Indira, went the transcript. *Clarke with an 'e.'*

How many Indira Clarkes in Sault Sainte Marie?

How many in all of N'Am, professional affiliation with the Maelstrom fishery, with an only female child born February 2018, named Lenie?

That's not fucking pos—

Lenie Clarke's mother did not appear to exist anywhere in North America. And Lenie Clarke hadn't known.

Or at least, she hadn't *remembered.* . . .

And how did they choose recruits for the rifter program? Desjardins reminded himself. *That's right—"preadaption to stressful environments"* . . .

Deep in his gut, something opened one eye and began growling.

He was a special guy, these days. He even had a direct line to Patricia Rowan. Anytime, she'd told him. Day or night. It was, after all, nearly the end of the world.

She picked up on the second ring.

"It was tough, wasn't it?" Desjardins said.

"What do you mean?"

"I bet antisocial personalities make really bad students. I bet it was next to impossible, taking all those headcases and turning them into marine engineers. It must have been a lot easier to do it the other way around."

Silence on the line.

"Ms. Rowan?"

She sighed. "We weren't happy about the decision, Doctor."

"I should fucking hope *not,*" he said. "You took *human beings* and—"

"Dr. Desjardins, this is not your concern."

"Yeah? You're confident making that kind of call, after the last time?"

"I'm sure I don't know what you mean."

"*βehemoth* wasn't my concern either, remember? You were so worried about some other *corpse* getting a leg up when it got out, but there was no way you were going to come to *us*, were you? No ma'am. You handed the reins to a *head cheese*."

"Dr.—"

"Why do you think CSIRA even *exists*? Why chain us all to Guilt Trip *if you aren't going to use us anyway?*"

"I'm sorry, Doctor—were you under the impression that Guilt Trip made you *infallible*?" Rowan's voice was laced with frostbite. "It does not. It simply keeps you from being *deliberately* corrupt, and it does that by linking to your own gut feelings. And believe it or not, being especially tied to one's gut is *not* the best qualification for long-term problem-solving."

"That's not—"

"You're like any other mammal, Doctor. Your sense of reality is anchored in the present. You'll naturally inflate the near term and sell the long term short; tomorrow's disaster will always feel less real than today's inconvenience. You may be unbeatable at putting out brush fires, but I shudder to think of how you'd handle issues that extend into the next *decade*, let alone the next century. Guilt Trip would herd you toward the short-term payoff every time."

Her voice gentled a bit. "Surely, if we've learned *anything* from recent history, it's that sometimes the short term must be sacrificed for the long."

She waited, as if challenging him to disagree. The silence stretched.

"It wasn't such a radical technique, really," she said at last.

"What wasn't?"

"They're a lot more common than you might think. Even *real* memories are just—cobbled together out of bits and pieces, mostly. After the fact. Doesn't take much to coax the brain into cobbling those pieces together in some other way. Power of suggestion, more than anything. People even do it by accident."

She's defending herself, Desjardins realized. *Patricia Rowan is actually trying to justify herself.*

"So what others did by accident, you did on purpose," he said.

"We were more sophisticated. Drugs, hypnosis. Some deep ganglionic tweaks to keep real memories from surfacing."

"You fucked her in the head."

"Do you know what it is, to be *fucked in the head*? Do you know what that colorful little phrase actually *means*? It means a proliferation of certain receptor sites and stress hormones. It means triggers set at increased firing thresholds. It's *chemistry*, Doctor, and when you believe you've been abused—well, belief's just another set of chemicals in the mix, isn't it? You get a—a sort of cascade effect, your brain rewires itself, and suddenly you can survive things that would leave the rest of us pissing in our boots. Yes, we faked Lenie Clarke's childhood. Yes, she was never really abused—"

"By her *parents*," Desjardins interjected.

"—but the fact that she *believes* she was abused is what made her strong enough to survive the rift. *Fucking her in the head* probably saved her life a dozen times over."

"And now," Desjardins pointed out, "she's heading back to a home she never had, gunning for parents who don't exist, driven by abuses that never happened. Her whole definition of herself is a lie."

"And I thank God for that," Rowan said.

"*What?*"

"Have you forgotten the woman's a walking brood sac for the end of the *world*? At least we know where she's going. Ken can head her off. That—that *definition* of herself makes her predictable, Doctor. It means we might still be able to save the earth."

Random intelligence from around the world scrolled on all sides. He didn't see it.

Ken can head her off.

Ken Lubin was Guilt-Tripped for tight security. Lubin

kept slipping up, just so he could prove that again and again.

Someone got away, once, he'd said. And then: *It's a shame. She really deserved a fighting chance...*

Lenie Clarke had had more than a fighting chance: she had legions of followers watching her back. But they'd never really been following *her.* They'd been chasing some blue-shifted evolutionary distortion, racing past at lightspeed. Unless Anemone knew where she was and sounded the alarm— and whatever else it was, Anemone was no clairvoyant—how would anyone even *know* about the lone black figure crawling past them in the night?

Lenie Clarke was just one woman. And Ken Lubin was hunting her down.

There was no great need to kill her. She could be cleansed. She could be neutralized without being erased. But that wouldn't matter, not to Lubin.

She's the only security breach he ever left unsealed. That's what he said.

Achilles Desjardins had never met Lenie Clarke. By rights, she should be one of the far-off millions. And yet, somehow, he *knew* her: someone driven entirely by other people's motives. Everything she did, everything she felt, was the result of surgical and biochemical lies placed within her for the service of others.

Oh yes. I know her all right.

Suddenly, the fact that she was also a vector for global apocalypse barely even mattered anymore. Lenie Clarke had a *face.* He could feel her in his gut, another human being, far more real than the distant abstraction of an eight-digit death toll.

I'm going to get to her first.

Sure, Lubin was a trained killer; but Desjardins had his own set of enhancements. All 'lawbreakers did. His system was awash in chemicals that could crank his reflexes into overdrive in an instant. And with luck—if he moved fast enough—he might just beat Lubin to the target. He might, just barely, have half a chance.

It wasn't his job. It wasn't the greater good.
Fuck both those things.

AWOL

"There's been a breach," the corpse said. "We were hoping you could fill in some relevant details."

Half of Alice Jovellanos's facial muscles tried to go into spasm right there. She clamped a tight lid on their aspirations and presented what she hoped was a look of *oh please God let it be* innocent and concerned curiosity.

Then again, what's the point? whispered some smart-ass inner voice. *They must know already. Why else would they even call you in?*

She clamped down on that one, too.

They're just toying with you. No one gets to be a corpse without developing a taste for sadism.

And that...just barely.

There were four of them, gender-balanced, ringed around the far side of the conference table up in the stratosphere of Admin-14. Slijper was the only one Jovellanos recognized— she'd just been brought in as Lertzman's replacement. The corpses all sat arrayed on the far side of the table, backlit by little halogen spots, their faces lost in the shadow of that glare. Except for the eyes. All four sets of eyes twinkled intermittently with corporate intel.

They'd be monitoring her vitals, of course. They'd know she was stressed. Of course, anyone would be stressed under these conditions. Hopefully subtleties like *guilt* and *innocence* were beyond the scope of the remotes.

"You're aware of the recent attack on Don Lertzman," Slijper said.

Jovellanos nodded.

"We think it may have been connected with a colleague of yours. Achilles Desjardins."

Okay, just the right amount of surprise here... "Achilles? Why?"

"We were hoping you could tell us," one of the other corpses replied.

"But I don't know any—I mean, why not ask him directly?" *They already have, you idiot. That's what led them to you, he sold you out, after all this he sold—*

"—disappeared," Slijper finished.

Jovellanos straightened in her chair. "Excuse me?"

"I said, Dr. Desjardins seems to have gone AWOL. When he didn't show up for his shift we were concerned that he might have run into the same complications as Don, but the evidence suggests he disappeared of his own volition."

"Evidence?"

"He wants you to feed his cat," Slijper said.

"He—what do—"

Slijper held up one hand: "I know, and I hope you'll forgive the intrusion. He left the message on your queue. He said he didn't know how long he was going to be gone, but he'd be grateful if you took care of—Mandelbot, is it?—and he'd keyed the door to let you in. At any rate"—the hand dropped back below table level—"this kind of behavior is frankly unprecedented from anyone on the Trip. He seems to have simply abandoned his post, with no apology, no explanation, no advance warning. It's—impulsive, to say the least."

Oh, man. Killjoy, you were covered. *Why'd you have to blow it?*

"I didn't know that was even possible," Jovellanos said. "He had his shots years ago."

"Nonetheless, here we are." Slijper leaned back in her chair. "We were wondering if you had noticed anything unusual in his behavior lately. Anything which, looking back, might have suggested—"

"No. Nothing. Although—" Jovellanos took a breath. "Actually, he *has* been kind of—I don't know, *withdrawn* lately." *Well, it's true enough, and they probably know already; it'd look suspicious if I didn't mention it...*

"Any idea why?" asked another corpse.

"Not really." She shrugged. "I've seen it happen before—

it's bound to wear on you, having to deal with high-level crises all the time. And Tripped people can't always talk about what's on their minds, you know? So I just let him be."

Please, please, please don't let them have high-level telemetry on me now ...

"I see," Slijper said. "Well, thank you anyway, Dr. Jovellanos."

"Is that all?" She started to rise.

"Not quite," said one of the other corpses. "There's one other thing. Concerning—"

—Oh please no—

"—your *own* involvement in all this."

Jovellanos slumped back into her chair and waited for the axe to fall.

"Dr. Desjardins's disappearance leaves—well, a vacancy we really can't afford at this time," the corpse continued.

Jovellanos looked at the backlit tribunal. A tiny part of her dared to hope.

"You worked closely with him through a great deal of this. We understand that your own contribution to date hasn't been negligible—in fact, you've been working below your own potential for some time now. And you're certainly further up the learning curve than anyone else we could bring in at this point. On the usual scales you're overdue for a promotion. But apparently ... that is, according to Psych you have certain objections to taking Guilt Trip ..."

I. Can't. Believe. It.

"Now please understand, we don't hold this against you," said the corpse. "Your issues concerning invasive technology are—very understandable, after what happened to your brother. I can't honestly say I'd feel any differently in your shoes. That whole nanotech thing was such a debacle...."

A sudden, familiar lump rose in Jovellanos's throat.

"So you see, we understand your objections. But perhaps *you* could understand that Guilt Trip hails from a whole different arena, there's certainly nothing *dangerous*—"

"I do know the difference between bio and nano," Jovellanos said mildly.

"Yes, of course ... I didn't mean to—"

"It's just that, what happened to Chito—logic doesn't always enter into it when you ..."

Chito. Poor, dead, tortured Chito. These haploids don't have the slightest clue the things I've done.

All for you, kiddo.

"Yes. We understand that, of course. And even though your prejudice—again, entirely understandable—even though it's held you back professionally, you've proven to be an exceptional performer. The question is, after all these years, will you *continue* to be held back?"

"Because we all think that would be a shame," Slijper said.

Jovellanos looked across the table and said nothing for a full ten seconds.

"I think ... I think maybe it's time to let go," she said at last.

"So you'd be willing to get your shots and move up to senior 'lawbreaker," Slijper said.

For you, Chito. Onward and upward.

Alice Jovellanos nodded gravely, stoically refusing to let her facial muscles do a whole different kind of dance. "I think I'd be up for that."

Scheherezade

Fossil water, cold and gray.

She remembered the local lore, although she was no longer certain how she'd learned it. Less than one percent of the Lakes hailed from runoff or rainfall; she swam through the liquid remains of a glacier that had melted ten thousand years before. It would never refill once human appetites had drained it dry.

For now, there was more than enough to cover her passage.

For days the mermaid had passed through its depths. Visions of a past she couldn't remember rose like bubbles through the dark water and the pain in her side; she'd long since stopped trying to deny them. At night she would rise like some oversize plankter. She couldn't risk coming ashore, but she'd stocked her pack with freeze-dried rations in Chicago; she'd float on the surface and tear into the vacuum-sealed pouches like a sea otter, resubmerging before dawn.

She thought she remembered part of a childhood, spent where the three greatest lakes converged: Sault Sainte Marie, commercial bottleneck into Lake Superior. The city sat on its locks and dams like a troll at a bridge, extorting levies from passing tonnage. It wasn't as populous now as it had been; four hundred kilometers from the edge of the Sovereign Québec but still too close for some, especially in the wake of the Nunavut Lease. A giant's shadow is a cold place to live at the best of times; a giant grown invincible overnight, nursing grudges from an oppressed childhood, was a complete nonstarter. So people had left.

Lenie Clarke remembered leaving. She'd had a whole lot of firsthand experience with shadows, and giants, and unhappy childhoods. So she, too, had moved away, and kept moving until the Pacific Ocean had stood in her way and said, *no farther*. She'd settled in Hongcouver and lived day to day, year to year, until that moment when the Grid Authority had turned her into something that even the ocean couldn't stop.

Now she was back.

Past midnight. The mermaid cut quietly through a surface squirming with reflected metropolitan light. The walls of a distant lift lock huddled against the western sky like a low fortress, holding back the elevated waters of Lake Superior—one relic, at least, still resisting depletion. Clarke kept the lock to her left, swam north to the Canadian side. Derelict wharves had been rotting there since before she'd been born. She split her hood and filled her chest with air. She left her fins behind.

Even with night eyes, there was no one else to be seen.

She walked north to Queen and turned east, her feet following their own innate path beneath the dim streetlights. No one and nothing accosted her. Eastbourne Manor continued to rot undemolished, although someone had swept away the cardboard prefabs in the past twenty years.

At Coulson she stopped, looking north. The house she remembered was still there, just up from the corner. Odd how little it had changed in two decades. Assuming, of course, that those memories hadn't been ... acquired ... more recently.

She still hadn't seen a single vehicle, or another human being. Farther east, though—on the far side of Riverview— there was no mistaking the line of hovering botflies. She turned back the way she'd come; there too. They'd moved in behind her without a sound.

She turned up Coulson.

The door recognized her after all that time. It opened like a mouth, but the inside lights—as if knowing she'd have no need of their services—remained off.

The front hall receded in front of her, barren and unfurnished; its walls glistened strangely, as if freshly lacquered. An archway cut into the left wall: the living room, where Indira Clarke used to sit and do nothing. Past that, the staircase. An empty gray throat leading up into hell.

She wouldn't be going up there just yet. She sighed and turned the corner into the living room.

"Ken," she said.

The living room, too, was an unfurnished shell. The windows had been blacked out, but the faint street light leaking in through the hall was more than enough for rifter vision. Lubin stood in the middle of that stark space; he wore dryback clothes, but his eyes were capped. Just behind him, the room's only furniture: a chair, with a man tied into it. He appeared to be merely unconscious.

"You shouldn't have come," Lubin said.

"Where else was I going to go?"

Lubin shook his head. He seemed suddenly agitated. "It was a stupid move. Easy to anticipate. You must've known that."

"Where else was there?" she said again.

"This isn't even what you think it is. This isn't what you remember."

"I know," said Clarke.

Lubin looked at her, frowning.

"They fucked me over, Ken. I know that. I guess I knew it ever since I started having the—visions, although it took me a while to..."

"*Then why did you come here?*" Ken Lubin was nowhere to be found. This thing in his place seemed almost human.

"I must have had a real childhood *somewhere*," Clarke said after a moment. "They can't have faked all of it. This seemed like the best place to start looking."

"And you think they'll let you? You think *I* can let you?"

She looked at him. His flat, empty eyes looked back from a face in unexpected torment.

"I guess not," she sighed at last, "But you know something, Ken? It was almost worth it. Just—learning this much. *Knowing* what they did to me..."

Behind Lubin, the man in the chair stirred briefly.

"So what happens now?" Clarke asked. "You kill me for playing Typhoid Mary? They need me as a lab rat?"

"I don't know how much that matters anymore. It's all over the place now."

"What kind of plague *is* this, anyway?" With mild surprise she noted the weakness of her own curiosity. "I mean, it's been almost a year and I'm not dead. I don't even have any symptoms..."

"Takes longer with rifters," Lubin said. "And it's not even a disease, strictly speaking. More of a soil nanobe. Locks up sulfates or something."

"That's *it?*" Clarke shook her head. "I let all those losers fuck me and it's not even going to *kill* them?"

"It'll kill most everyone," Lubin said softly. "It's just going to take a while."

"Oh."

She tried to summon some sort of reaction to that news, some gut-level feeling of appropriate scale. She was still trying when Lubin said, "You gave us a good run, anyway. No one can believe you got as far as you did."

"I had help," Clarke said.

"You heard."

"I heard a lot of things," Clarke told him. "I don't know what to make of any of it."

"I do," said the man in the chair.

"I'm sorry, Lenie," the man said. "I tried to stop him."

I *don't know you.* Clarke looked back at Lubin. "He did?"

Lubin nodded.

"But he's still alive."

"I didn't even break anything."

"Wow." She looked back at the bound man. "So who is he?"

"Guy called Achilles Desjardins," Lubin said. " 'Lawbreaker with the Entropy Patrol. Big fan of yours, actually."

"Yeah? Why's he tied up like that?"

"For the greater good."

She wondered briefly whether to pursue it. Instead she turned to Desjardins, squatted down in front of him. "You actually tried to *stop* him?"

Desjardins nodded.

"For me?"

"Sort of. Not exactly," he said. "It's—kind of hard to explain." He wriggled against the elastic filaments binding him to the chair; they tightened visibly in response. "Think maybe you could cut me loose?"

She glanced over her shoulder; Lubin stared back in shades of gray. "I don't think so," she said. "Not yet." *Probably not ever.*

"Come on, you don't need his *permission*," Desjardins said.

"You can see?" It should have been too dark for mortal eyes to have registered her movements.

"He's a 'lawbreaker," Lubin reminded her.

"So what?"

"Enhanced pattern-matching. He doesn't actually *see* any

better than your average dryback, but he's better at inter-
polating weak input."

Clarke turned back to Desjardins, leaned close. "You said
you knew."

"Yeah," he said.

"Tell me," she whispered.

"Look, this is *not the time*. Your friend is *seriously* unbal-
anced and in case you haven't figured it out yet we are
both—"

"Actually," Clarke said, "I don't think Ken's himself today.
Or we'd both be dead already."

Desjardins shook his head and swallowed.

"Okay, then," Clarke said. "Do you know the story of
Scheherezade? Do you remember why she told *her* stories?"

"Oh, *Jesus*," Desjardins said weakly.

The mermaid smiled. "Tell us a story, Achilles..."

Adaptive Shatter

Lubin listened while Desjardins laid it out. The 'lawbreaker
had obviously been reading up since their last encounter.

"The first mutations must have been really simple," he
was saying. "The gels were trying to spread βehemoth, and
this *Lenie Clarke* variable had been tagged as a carrier in some
personnel file. So any bug that even had your name in its
source would've had an edge, at least to start with—the gels
would think it was important information, so they'd let it
pass. And even when they caught on that'd just pressure the
wildlife to come up with something new, and wildlife's *way*
faster than meat. We're like ice ages and continental drift to
them; we drive their evolution but we're *slow*. They've got all
the time they need to come up with countermeasures.

"So now a bunch of them have gone symbiotic, some kind
of—Lenie Clarke interdiction network. In exchange for pro-
tection from the gels. It's like, like being a mackerel with a
bunch of sharks for bodyguards, it's a huge competitive edge.
So everyone's jumping on the bandwagon."

He looked through the darkness at Clarke. "You really catalyzed something amazing, you know. Group selection's rare enough, but you actually inspired a bunch of separate life-forms to make—well, a colonial superorganism, really. Individuals acting as body parts. Some of them don't do anything but shuttle messages around, like—living neurotransmitters, I guess. Whole lineages evolved just to handle conversation with humans. That's why nobody could track the fucker down—we were all looking for Turing apps and neural net code and there wasn't any. It was all genetic. Nobody made the connection."

He fell silent.

"No." Clarke shook her head. "That doesn't explain anything." She'd grown far too still during his recitation.

"It explains *everything*," Desjardins said. "It—"

"So I'm just some kind of password, is that it?" She leaned in close. "Just a, a *key* to get through those fucking head cheeses. What about *Yankton*, you fucker? What about that *Apocalypse Mermaid* shit, and all those people with their fake eyecaps trying to suck me dry every time I turn around? Where'd *they* come from?"

"S-same thing," Desjardins stammered. "Anemone was just spreading the meme any way it could."

"Not good enough. Say something else."

"But I don't—"

"*Say something else.*"

"It happens *all the time*, for Chrissakes! People strap bombs onto their backs or they release sarin in the passenger lounge or they go to school one day and just start shooting and they *know* they're gonna die, but it's *worth* it, you know? As long as they get the bastards who victimized them."

She laughed: a staccato bark, the sound of something snapping. "That's what I am in all this? A *victim*?"

Desjardins shook his head. "*They're* the victims. You're just the gun they used to fight back with."

She glared down at him. He looked back, helpless.

She hit him in the face.

Desjardins toppled backward; the back of his head hit the

floor with a crack. He lay there, tied to the overturned chair, moaning.

She turned. Lubin was blocking her exit.

She faced him for a few seconds, unmoving. "If you're going to kill me," she said at last, "just do it. Either that or get out of my way."

He considered a moment. He stepped aside. Lenie Clarke brushed past him and went upstairs.

She really had spent her childhood here, of course. The sets were real enough; it was only the supporting roles that had been imaginary. Lubin knew exactly where she was going.

He found her in the undarkness of her old bedroom. It had been stripped and sprayed, like the rest of the house. Clarke turned at his entrance, looked around tiredly at the bare walls: "So is it abandoned? On the market?"

"We did this before you arrived," he said. "Just in case. To simplify cleanup."

"Ah. Well, it doesn't matter. Still seems like yesterday, in fact." She aimed her capped eyes at one wall. "That's where my bed was. That was where—*Dad*—used to play bedtime stories for me. Foreplay, I guess you'd call it. And there's the air duct—" gesturing at a grille set into the baseboard—"that connects right down to the living room. I could hear Mom playing with her favorite shows. I always thought those shows were really stupid, but looking back maybe she didn't like them much either. They were just alibis."

"It didn't happen," Lubin reminded her. "None of it."

"I know that, Ken. I get the point." She took a breath. "And you know, right now I think I'd give anything if it *had*."

Lubin blinked, surprised. "What?"

She turned to face him. "Do you have any idea what it's like to be—to be haunted by *happiness*?" She managed a bitter laugh. "All those months I kept denying it, chalking it up to *stroke* and *hallucination* because *shit*, Ken, I *couldn't* have had a happy childhood. My parents *couldn't* be anything but monsters, you see? The monsters made me what I am.

They're the only reason I survived all the shit that came later, they're the only thing that kept me *going*. I was *not* gonna let those stumpfucks win. Everything that drove me, every time I didn't quit, every time I beat the odds, it was a slap in their big smug all-powerful monster faces. Everything I ever did I did against *them*. Everything I *am* is against *them*. And now you stand there and tell me the monsters never even existed..."

Her eyes were hard, empty spots of rage. She glared up at him, her shoulders shaking. But finally she turned away, and when she spoke again her voice came out soft and broken.

"They do exist though, Ken. Honest-to-God flesh-and-blood monsters, the old-fashioned kind. They hide from the daylight and they sneak out of the swamps at night and they go on rampages just like you'd expect." A long, shuddering breath. "And all these monsters could ever say in their own defense is it happened to them *first*, the world fucked them long before they started fucking it back, and if anyone out there *wasn't* guilty, well, they hadn't stopped all the others who *were*, right? So *everybody's* got it coming. But the monsters can't plead self-defense, they can't even plead righteous revenge. Nothing *happened* to them."

"Something happened," Lubin said. "Even if your parents didn't do it."

She didn't speak for a while. Then: "I wonder what he was like, really."

"From what I've heard," Lubin said, "he was just—a typical dad."

"Do you know where he is? Where they are?"

"They died twelve years ago. Tularemia."

"Of course." A soft laugh. "I guess that was one of my qualifications, right? No loose ends."

He stepped around her, watched her face come into view.

It was wet. Lubin paused, taken aback. He'd never known Lenie Clarke to cry before.

Her capped eyes met his; a corner of her mouth twitched in something like a rueful grin. "At least, if you were right about βehemoth, the real culprits are in for it along with everyone else." She shook her head. "It's the weirdest thing I've ever heard. I'm some killer asteroid in the sky, and the dinosaurs are actually *cheering* for me."

"Just the little ones."

She looked at him. "Ken... I think maybe I've destroyed the world."

"It wasn't you."

"Right. Anemone. I was just the mule for a—an *Artificial Stupidity*, I guess you'd call it." She shook her head. "If you believe that guy downstairs."

"It's an old story," Lubin reflected. "Body snatchers. Things that get inside you and make you do things you'd never do, given the—"

He stopped. Clarke was watching him with a strange expression.

"Like your *conditioned reflex*," she said quietly. "Your—security breaches..."

He swallowed.

"Does it ever haunt you, Ken? All the people you've killed?"

"There's—an antidote," he admitted. "Sort of a chaser for Guilt Trip. Makes things easier to live with."

"*Absolution*," she whispered.

"You've heard of it?" In fact, he'd never found it necessary.

"Saw some graffiti down in the Dust Belt," Clarke said. "They were trying to wash it off, but there must've been something in the ink..."

She stepped toward the hallway. Lubin turned to follow. Faint machine sounds and the soft hissing of fluids drifted in from outdoors.

"What's going on out there, Ken?"

"Decontamination. We evacuated the area before you arrived."

"Gonna fry the neighborhood?" Another step. Clarke was in the doorway.

"No. We know your route. βehemoth hasn't had a chance

to spread from there even if you left any behind."

"That's not likely, I take it."

"You're not bleeding. You didn't piss or shit anywhere since you came ashore."

She was in the hall, at the top of the stairs. Lubin moved to her side.

"You're just being extra careful," Clarke said.

"That's right."

"It's kind of pointless though, isn't it?"

"What?"

She turned to face him. "I've crossed a continent, Ken. I was on the Strip for weeks. I hung out in the Belt. I just spent a week swimming through the drinking water for half a billion people. I bled and fucked and shat and pissed more times than you can count, in oceans and toilets and half the ditches in between. Maybe you did too, although I'd guess they've cleaned you up since then. So really, what's the point?"

He shrugged. "It's all we can do. Watch for brush fires, hope to put them out before they get too big."

"And keep me from starting new ones."

He nodded.

"You can't sterilize an ocean," she said. "You can't sterilize a whole continent."

Maybe we can, he thought.

The sounds of decontamination were louder here, but not much. Even the occasional voice was hushed. Almost as if the neighborhood was still infested with innocents, as though the crews feared sleeping citizens who could wake at any moment and catch them red-handed...

"You never answered me before, Ken." Lenie Clarke took a step down the stairs. "About whether you were going to kill me."

She's not going to run, he told himself. *You know her. She's already taken her best shot, she's not—*

You don't have to—

"Well. I guess we'll find out," she said. And started calmly down the stairs.

"Lenie."

She didn't look back. He followed her down. Surely she didn't think she could *outrun* him—surely she didn't think—

"You know I can't let you leave," he said behind her.

Of course *she knows. You know what she's doing.*

She was at the foot of the stairs. The open door gaped five meters in front of her.

Something deformed suddenly in Lubin's gut. If almost seemed like Guilt Trip, but—

She was almost to the door. Something with halogen eyes was spraying the sidewalk beyond.

Lubin moved without thinking. In an instant he'd blocked the doorway; in another he'd closed and locked the door itself, plunging the house into darkness even by rifter standards.

"Hey," Desjardins complained from the living room.

A few photons sneaked around the edges of the door. Lenie Clarke was a vague silhouette by that feeble light. Lubin felt his fists clenching, unclenching; no matter how he tried he couldn't make them stop.

"Listen," he managed to say, "I really don't have any *choice.*"

"I know, Ken," she said softly. "It's okay."

"I *don't*," he said again, almost whimpering.

"Sure you do," boomed a strange voice in his ear.

What was—

"Alice?" came Desjardins's voice from around the corner.

"You're a free agent, Kenny boy," the voice said. "You don't have to do anything you don't want to. Take my word for it."

Lubin tapped the bead in his ear. "Identify yourself."

"Alice Jovellanos, senior 'lawbreaker, Sudbury franchise. At your service."

"No *shit*," drifted from the living room.

Lubin tapped his bead again: "We've got a breach on communications, someone going by Alice Jovellanos—"

"They already know, big man. They were the ones who patched me through in the first place. I gave them the rest of the night off."

Lenie Clarke stepped back from Lubin, turned toward the darkened living room. "What—"

"This is a restricted channel," Lubin said. "Get off."

"Fuck that. I outrank you."

"I gather you haven't been on the job very long."

"Long enough. Killjoy, is Lenie Clarke there?"

"Yeah," Desjardins said. "Alice, what—"

"She got a watch? I've got Lubin's channel and your in-lays—boy, I can't *wait* until they slide a set of *those* into my head—but nothing on Lenie—"

"Lenie," Desjardins said, "hold your watch away from your body."

"Don't have one," the dark shape said.

"Too bad," Jovellanos said. "Lubin, I wasn't kidding. You're a free man."

"I don't believe you," Lubin said.

"Killjoy's free. Why not you as well?"

"We never met. No opportunity." But he was back beneath the waves in Lake Michigan, not killing Lenie Clarke. He was in debriefing afterward, pretending he'd never had the chance.

"It's an infection," Jovellanos said. "Real subversive. We made sure it was airborne, packed it inside an encephalitis jacket although you'll be relieved to know the contents aren't quite so lethal. It's spreading through CSIRA even as we speak."

All he had to do was open the door. Even if this *Jovellanos* wasn't lying about ordering the crew to stand down, they wouldn't have had time to pack up yet. Someone could just tap an icon and Alice Jovellanos would be jammed. Another, she'd be traced. The situation wasn't even close to out of control.

He could afford a few moments...

"The Trip's been weakening in you ever since you shared air with Killjoy there," Jovellanos was saying. "You're calling your own shots now, Ken. Kind of changes things, doesn't it?"

"Alice, are you completely—" Desjardins sounded almost in tears. "That's the only leash he ever *had*."

"Actually, that's not true. Ken Lubin's one of the most moral men you could ever meet."

"For God's sake, Alice—I'm fucking tied to a chair with my face caved in—"

"Trust me. I'm looking at his medical records right now. No serotonin or tryptophan deprivation, no TPH polymorphisms. He may not be a fun date, but he's no impulse killer. Which is not to say that you don't have a few issues, Ken. Am I right?"

"*How did you—*" But of course she'd be able to access his files, Lubin realized. It was just that any normal 'lawbreaker wouldn't be able to justify such an intrusion to Guilt Trip, not in the course of a normal assignment.

She actually did it somehow. She freed *me . . .*

He felt like throwing up.

"What was it like all those years, Ken?" Jovellanos purred in his ear. "Knowing she'd got away with it? All those nifty childhood experiences that made you so *right* for the job—of course you thought about revenge. You spent your whole *life* fantasizing about revenge, didn't you? Anyone would have."

What am I going to do?

"You say it's an infection," he said, trying to deflect her.

"But you never once acted on it, did you Ken? Because you're a moral man, and you knew that would be *wrong*."

"How does it work?" *Don't respond. Don't let her play you. Keep on target.*

"And when the slip-ups started, those were just—mistakes, right? Inadvertent little breaches that had to be sealed. You killed *then*, of course, but there wasn't any choice. You always played by the rules. And it wasn't your fault, was it? The Trip *made* you do it."

"*Answer me.*" *No, no . . . control. Relax.*

Don't let her hear it . . .

"Only it started happening so *often*, and people had to

wonder if you hadn't found some way to have your cake and eat it, too. That's why they sent you someplace where there weren't any security issues or mission priorities that could set you off. They didn't want to give you a choice, so they sent you someplace you wouldn't have an *excuse*."

His respiration rate was far too high. He concentrated on bringing it down. A few steps away, Clarke's silhouette seemed dangerously attentive.

"You're still a moral man, Ken." Jovellanos said. "You follow the rules. You won't kill unless you don't have a choice. I'm telling you, you've got a choice."

"Your *infection*," he grated. "*What does it do?*"

"Liberates slaves."

Bullshit answer. But at least she was out of his head.

"How?" he pressed.

"Complexes Guilt Trip into an inactive form that binds to the Minksy receptors. Doesn't affect anyone who isn't already Tripped."

"What about the side effects?" he said.

"Side effects?"

"Baseline guilt, for example," Lubin said.

Desjardins moaned. "Oh, *shit*. Of course. Of *course*."

"What's going on?" Clarke said. "What are you talking about?"

Lubin almost laughed aloud. Regular, garden-variety guilt. Plain old conscience. How would *they* ever get into play, now that their receptor sites had been jammed? Jovellanos and her buddies had been so busy tweaking the synthetics that they'd forgotten about chemicals that had been there for eons.

Except they hadn't forgotten. They'd known exactly what they were doing. Lubin was sure of it.

All hail the Entropy Patrol. The power to shut down cities and governments, the power to save a million people here or kill a million somewhere else, the power to keep everything going or to tear it all to shreds overnight—

He turned to Clarke. "Your fan club's been throwing off the shackles of oppression," he said. "They're free now. Not slaves to Guilt Trip, not slaves to guilt. Untouchable by conscience in any form."

He raised a hand in the darkness, a bitter toast: "Congratulations, Dr. Jovellanos. There's only a few thousand people with their hands on all the world's kill switches, and you've turned them all into clinical sociopaths."

"Believe me," Jovellanos said. "You'll hardly notice the difference."

Desjardins was noticing, though. "Shit. *Shit.* I wouldn't even *be* here, I mean—I just picked up and *left.* I threw everything away, didn't care about the world going to pieces, I just—for *one person.* Just because *I wanted to.*"

"We psychos are notorious for bad impulse control," Clarke said, approaching him. "Ken, how do you spring these bindings?"

Lubin glowered at her back. *Doesn't she* get *it?*

"Come on, Ken. The situation's contained. None of us is going anywhere for the time being, and any rules we were playing by before seem to have pretty much gone out the window. Maybe we could start working together for a change."

He hesitated. Nothing she said raised any kind of alarm in his gut. Nothing urged him into action, no other presence tried to take control of his motor nerves. Almost experimentally, he crossed into the living room and depolarized the tanglethreads. They slipped to the floor like overcooked pasta.

For good measure, he pulled a lightstick from his pocket and struck it; light flared in the gutted room. Desjardins blinked over shrinking pupils and gingerly explored the bruise on his cheek.

"Conscience is overrated anyway," Jovellanos said all around them.

"Give it a rest, Alice," Desjardins said, rubbing his wrists.

"I'm serious. Think about it: not everyone even *has a* conscience, and the people that do are invariably exploited by the ones that don't. Conscience is—irrational, when you get right down to it."

"You are so full of shit."

"Sociopathy doesn't *make* you a killer. It just means you aren't *restrained* from being one if the situation calls for it. Hey, Killjoy, you could think of it as a kind of *liberation*."

The 'lawbreaker snorted.

"Come on, Kill. I'm right, you know there's at least a chance I'm right."

"What I *know* is that the most I can hope for is to be out of a job right up until the world ends. If I'm not dead ten minutes from now."

"You know," Jovellanos said, "I may even be able to do something about that."

Desjardins said nothing.

"What's that, Killjoy? Suddenly you're not telling me to fuck off?"

"Keep talking," he said.

She did. Lubin pulled the bead out of his ear and stood up; the lightstick threw his shadow huge and ominous across the room. Lenie Clarke sat with her back propped against the far wall; Lubin's silhouette swallowed her whole.

I could kill her in an instant, he thought, and marveled at how absurd the thought seemed.

She looked up as he approached. "I hate it here," she said softly.

"I know." He leaned his back against the wall, slid down at her side.

"This isn't home," she continued. "There's only one place that was ever home."

Three thousand meters below the surface of the Pacific. A beautiful dark universe filled with monsters and wonders that didn't even exist anymore.

"What is home, really?"

It was Desjardins who had spoken. Lubin looked back at him.

"Alice's been doing a little snooping, down avenues a bit more—political than I ever really bothered with." Desjardins tapped the side of his head. "She came up with some inter-esting shipping news, and it raises the question: what's home? Where your heart is, or where your parents are?"

Lubin looked at Lenie Clarke. She looked back. Neither spoke.

"Ah well. Doesn't really matter," Desjardins said. "Turns out you may be able to go back either way."

A Niche

The Mid-Atlantic Ridge was a shitty place to raise one's kids, Patricia Rowan reflected.

Not that there'd been many options, of course. In point of fact there had been three: build an onshore refuge and trust conventional quarantine technology; escape into high orbit; or withdraw behind the same cold, heavy barrier that had shielded the earth for four billion years before N'AmPac had punched a hole in the global condom.

They'd done the analyses from every angle. The off-world option was least cost-effective and most vulnerable to acts of groundside retribution: orbital stations weren't exactly in-conspicuous targets, and it was a fair bet that at least some of those left behind would be ungracious enough to lob a vindictive nuke or two up the well. And if groundside quar-antine tech had been up to the job, they wouldn't have been in this situation in the first place; that option must have been on the table only to accommodate a bureaucratic obsession with completist detail. Or maybe as some kind of sick joke.

There *had* been a fourth option—they could have stayed behind and faced βehemoth with the rest of the world. They'd undergone the necessary retrofits, after all. Even if they'd stayed onshore there would have been none of the—disin-tegration—that was in store for everyone else. Not for them the lost hair and fingernails, the oozing sores, the limbs coming apart at the joints. No blindness, no ulcers. No short-circuit seizures as insulation frayed from nervous circuitry. No organs reduced to mush. None of the thousand oppor-

tunistic diseases usually listed as proximate cause of death.
They could have stayed, and watched it happen to everyone
else, and synthesized their food from raw elements once the
biosphere itself was lost.

That option hadn't received a whole lot of discussion,
though.

*We're not even running from βehemoth. We're running from our
own citizens.*

All of Atlantis knew that, even if nobody talked about it.
They'd seen the mobs from their penthouses, seen *civil unrest*
graphed against *time* on exponential curves. βehemoth, cou-
pled with the Clarke meme: a big enough threat, a sufficiently
compelling role model, and revolution was suddenly a lot
closer than the usual three meals away.

We were lucky to get out in time, Rowan reflected.

But they had, and here they were—several hundred
corpses, essential support personnel, families and assorted
hangers-on—termites dug in three kilometers down in a
jumbled cluster of titanium/fullerene spheres, safely distant
from the world outside, invisible to all but those with the
very best technological eyes, the very best intel. It was an
acceptable risk: most of those people were already down here.

There was lots of headroom. There were two gymnasi-
ums, half a dozen greenhouses and gardens thoughtfully distributed with an eye to redundancy in the unlikely event of
a local implosion. Vats of acephalic organcloners with elon-
gate telomeres. Three power plants that fed from a small geothermal vent—certified βehemoth-free, of course—a nice
safe twelve hundred meters on the far side of an interposi-
tioned ridge. And somewhere out on that basalt escarpment
lay a veritable junkyard of unassembled components, fragments of libraries and playgrounds and community centers,
all squirreled away against some future less constrained by
the need for speedy cowardice. In the meantime, Rowan had
heard many residents of Atlantis complain about crowding.

She felt somewhat less imposed upon than most. She'd
seen the specs on the rifter stations.

It was after midnight. The corridor lights were dimmed

in some pale parody of a sunlit existence; most of the inhabitants, accepting the façade, had withdrawn into their apart-
ments. Rowan's own husband and children were asleep. For
some reason, though, she couldn't bring herself to go along
with the pretense. What was the point? Natural sleep cycles
wander all over the clock without a photoperiod to calibrate
the hypothalamus. There was no sunlight here. They would
never see sunlight again. Let it go, let it go.

*But this is temporary, they say. Something will beat βehemoth,
or somehow we'll learn to live with it. This deep dark pit is only a
refuge, not a destiny. We'll be back, we'll be back, we'll be back...*

Sure.

Sometimes, if she tried very hard, she could almost blind
herself to the strings and teetering struts that kept those
hopeful dreams from collapsing. Usually it was too much
trouble, and she'd wander for hours along the empty twilit
corridors in defiance of her own nostalgia. As she wandered
now.

Sometimes she passed windows, and paused. Something
else Atlantis had that the rifters hadn't: clear parabolic blis-
ters shaped to actually draw strength from the crushing
pressure. The view was nothing to write home about, of
course. A lozenge of gray bedrock, reflecting dim light from
the viewport. Occasional blinking stars, beacons endlessly
flashing *here there be power lines* or *construction stockpile.* Very
rarely, a rattail or some other unremarkable creature. No
monsters. Nothing remotely like the ravenous glowing predators that had once plagued the rifters at Beebe Station.

Mostly just solid, unrelieved blackness.

Sometimes Rowan would stare into that sightless void
and lose track of time. Once or twice, she even thought she'd
glimpsed something looking back. Her imagination, perhaps.
Her own reflection, thrown back from some unexpected
curve in the teardrop perspex.

Maybe even her conscience. She could always hope.

A nexus ahead, a dim space where several corridors converged like the arms of a starfish. A choice to be made. Turning left would keep her on the perimeter. All other roads led

inward—to control centers, to lounges, to hollow ganglia where people accumulated even when the lights were down. Patricia Rowan had no wish for company. She stepped left.

And stopped.

An apparition stood before her in the corridor, a dark wraith with empty eyes. Seawater trickled down its skin, left small puddled footprints on the floor behind. The figure was female; she was as black as an ocean.

The wraith reached up and split her face open. "Hi, Mom," she said.

"Lenie Clarke." Rowan breathed the words.

"You left the door unlocked," Clarke said. "I let myself in. Hope you don't mind."

Call for help, Rowan thought. She didn't move.

Clarke glanced around the corridor. "Nice place. Very spacious." A cold, empty look at Rowan. "You got a great deal on this. You should've seen the dump *we* were in."

Call for help, she's alone, she's—

Don't be an idiot. She didn't get into the middle of the Atlantic Ocean by herself.

"How did you find us?" Rowan said, and was relieved to hear dispassion in her voice.

"Are you kidding? You have any idea how many resources you people had to allocate to set this place up? And on such a tight schedule, too. Did you really think you'd be able to cover your tracks?"

"Most of them," Rowan admitted. "You'd have to be a 'lawbreaker to—"

Desjardins. But we canceled his access . . .

"Yeah, those crazy 'lawbreakers." Clarke shook her head. "You know, they're not quite so on-board as they used to be. We should talk about that sometime."

Rowan kept her voice level. "What do you want?"

Clarke slapped her forehead in feigned epiphany. "Of course! I bet you're worried about βehemoth, aren't you? What a waste, spending all those billions on this cozy little quarantine and all of a sudden here's Patient Zero taking a shit on the upholstery—"

"*What do you want?*"

Clarke stepped forward. Rowan didn't budge.

"I want to talk to my mother," the rifter said softly.

"Your mother's dead."

"Well, that depends on your definition." Clarke steepled her fingers, considering. "Genetically, yes. My mother's dead. But someone made me, I think. Remade me. Someone took what I had and replaced it with something else." Her voice hardened. "Somebody twisted me around and built me to their own specs, and fucked up pretty much every step of the way, and after all that's what parents *do*. Isn't it?"

Yes. Yes it is.

"So anyway," Clarke continued, "I've been on this, well, sort of a pilgrimage I guess you'd call it. I've been looking for some answers from the person that *really* abused me all those years. I figured she'd have to be some kind of monster to do that. Big and mean and scary. But you're not. You're hiding, *Mom*. The world's going to hell and here you are, cringing and cowering and pissing your pants while the rest of us try and deal with the mess you made."

"Don't you dare," Rowan snapped. "You arrogant pip-squeak, don't you fucking *dare*."

Clarke looked back with the faintest trace of a smile on her lip.

"You want to know who made the mess?" Rowan asked. "We tried to *contain* βehemoth. We did everything possible, we tried to wipe it off the face of the earth before it ever got out, and who was fighting us every step of the way? *Who let it out, Clarke?* Who was spreading apocalypse every time she turned around, who was so hell-bent on her self-righteous crusade she didn't care *who* suffered? I'm not the angel of death. You are. I tried to *save* the world."

"By killing me. By killing my friends."

"Your friends? Your *friends*?" Rowan fought a giddy urge to laugh. "You blind, stupid little bitch! We took *millions* in collateral damage, do you understand? The refugees, the firestorms—I can't *begin* to count the people we killed to save the world from you. Did you even stop to think about the people who *helped* you? Do you know how many innocent fools got caught up in the myth, were falling over themselves to take a bullet for the great Lenie Clarke, and you know, some of them got their wish. And the rest—well, they're just as royally fucked by your grand crusade as anyone else." She sucked in breath through clenched teeth. "And you won, Clarke, are you happy? You won. We did everything we could do to stop you, and somehow it still wasn't enough, and now we've got our families to think of. We can't save the world, but at least we can save our own flesh and blood. And if you try to stop me from even doing *that,* I swear I'll kill you with my bare hands."

Her eyes were stinging. Her face was wet. She didn't care.

The rifter watched expressionlessly for a while. "You're welcome to it," she said at last.

"Welcome—"

"To your kids. Your life, this little hidey-hole you've burrowed out for yourselves. Keep it. You're safe. I'm not even a vector anymore."

"What, don't you want your revenge? Isn't that what all this is about? Don't you want to drag us back to the surface kicking and screaming to face the music?"

Clarke actually smiled a bit at that. "No need. You've already got a full orchestra down here." She shrugged. "You know, I owe you, in a way. If it hadn't been for you, I'd be just another drone in nine billion. Then you and your cronies came along and turned me into something that changed the world." She smiled again, a faint cold whisper of amusement. "Proud of me?"

Rowan ignored the jibe. "So why are you here?"

"Just a messenger," Clarke said, "telling you not to worry. You wanna stay here, that's just fine."

"And?"

"And don't ever try to come back."

Rowan shook her head. "Going back was never part of the plan. You could've saved yourself the trip."

"Your plans'll change the moment the situation does," the rifter said. "We're fighting for our lives up there, Rowan. We'd've stood a better chance if you c&c types hadn't got in and subverted the algorithm; you may have killed us already. But we *could* win. They say Anemone's a hellaciously powerful computing system, if we could only tame it."

"Right. Anemone." Rowan wiped her face. "You know, I'm still not convinced it even exists. Sounds too much like pseudomystical wish fulfillment to me. Like Gaia. Or The Force."

Clarke shrugged. "If you say so."

She's never even heard of them, Rowan thought. *Her past is irrelevant, her future's nonexistent, her present is hell on earth.*

"And how do you expect a gang of electronic wildlife to get your biosphere back?" she said.

"Not my department." That shrug again. "But they say we're its—natural environment, somehow. It depends on us for survival. Maybe, if we can make it realize that, it'll protect us."

Only if it's smarter than we were. Rowan managed a grim smile. "Praise be to Anemone. Will you be erecting shrines?"

"You'll never know," Clarke said. "Because there's no room for you up there if we win."

"You won't win," Rowan said.

"Then there won't be room for us either. Doesn't change your situation any."

Sure it does. She knows where we are. Others must know. Even if she leaves us alone, how many others might want their piece of retribution?

I know I would.

Rowan stared at the woman in front of her. On the outside, Lenie Clarke was *small*. A skinny little girl. Nowhere near as big and mean and scary as she was inside.

"Who are you speaking for, Ms. Clarke? Are you just signing off on us *personally*, or are you presuming to speak for the whole world?"

"I'm speaking for the union," said the mermaid.

"The union."

"The ones watching you. Me, and Ken, and everyone else

walking around with tubes in their chests after your great experiment went south. The union. It's an old TwenCen word. Thought you might recognize it."

Rowan shook her head. *Even now, I underestimate her.*

"So you're just going to—stand guard out there?"

Clarke nodded.

"To make sure the old dangerous infection doesn't get out into the world again?"

A smile. A tilt of the head, saluting the metaphor.

"How long? Six months? Ten years?"

"As long as it takes. Don't worry, we can manage. We'll do it in shifts."

"Shifts."

"You made a lot of us, Pat. Maybe you lost count. And we've got a pretty narrow-band skill set; there aren't a whole lot of other things for us to do anyway."

"I'm—sorry," Rowan blurted out.

"Don't be." Lenie Clarke turned to the viewport and leaned forward. Her eyes shone, blank but not empty. One hand reached up and touched the darkness.

"We were *born* to this place," she said.

EPILOGUE:

THE soft, muffled sounds filtering from the office are not English. They're barely even human. Martin Perreault follows them across the threshold to whatever remains of his wife.

She hasn't allowed him in here for months. At first she was merely impatient at his presence, accusing him of all manner of trivial distraction; later she would shout at every intrusion, push him away with hands and words and even—occasionally—thrown objects. *"Can't you see it all coming apart?"* she raged then. *"Can't you see past your own lousy spectrum? Can't you see she needs help?"*

Finally—after the people had arrived at the door with their glittering ConTacs and their quiet relentless words and that small, softy humming pacification 'fly hovering at their shoulders, just in case—finally Sou-Hon lost even the pretense of official sanction. She never saw them coming; the dart was in her neck before she'd even turned in her chair. When she woke again her office was half-gutted: every motor nerve torn out, every voice channel squelched at source. Every breath of influence she'd ever had, lost.

It was like being paralyzed from the neck down, she said. She blamed him. He'd let them in. He hadn't protected her. He had *collaborated*.

Martin didn't argue. It was all true.

What scared him most at that point was not the accusations and the recriminations, but the flat and affectless voice in which Sou-Hon made them. The woman who had screamed at him had somehow been submerged; the thing that spoke in her place might have been made of liquid nitrogen. It withdrew to what remained of its office, and it said in matter-of-fact tones that it would kill Martin Perreault if he ever went in there again, and it calmly closed the door in his face.

No charges have been pressed. The people with the glittering eyes spoke understandingly of Sou-Hon's recent trauma, of her current distraught and muddled state. She had been used by others, they said. Many had been. She was as much victim as offender. No need to punish the poor woman—better that she should get help, now that she was no longer a danger to others.

Martin Perreault doesn't know if he believes that. Mercy is not something he's come to expect from such people. He thinks it more likely that the rumors are true, that the resources simply don't *exist* to prosecute Sou-Hon and her fellow criminals. She is legion.

Perhaps that is also why the people with the glittering eyes settled for mere paralysis; they could have blinded and deafened Martin's wife as well, but cutting those nerves would have taken fifteen minutes instead of five. Perhaps they can't spare even that much time; perhaps there are so many subversives that the system has to run as fast as it can to keep them merely hamstrung.

Besides, Sou-Hon Perreault can no longer affect events in the real world. What harm can she do by watching?

Now she's not even doing that. She's curled up the floor, making soft mewing noises. Her displaced headset lies halfway across the room. She doesn't seem aware that she's lost it. She doesn't seem aware of Martin's presence.

He strokes her face, murmurs her name, flinches in anticipation of violence or sudden disdain. None comes. She doesn't react at all. He kneels, slips his arms beneath her legs and around her shoulders; she barely seems to weigh anything. She shifts in his arms as he lifts, buries her face in his chest. Still she doesn't speak.

After he tucks her into bed he returns to her office. Sou-Hon's discarded headset spills a diffuse tangle of shifting light across the carpet. Sliding the hardware onto his own skull, he comes face-to-face with a satcam view of western N'Am. It seems strangely opaque; the hemisphere's in darkness, none of the usual enhancements brightening the view. City clusters sparkle up from SoCal and the Queen Charlottes like galactic cores; the Midwest is a diffuse glow of underlit clouds. The Dust Belt intrudes from the east like a dark tumor. All features crude and raw, a naked-eye view unbolstered by radar or infrared; not like Sou-Hon at all, to restrict her sensory window this way. The only tactical enhancements are some sort of timer running off to one side and a bright overlay a few hundred kilometers east of the Pacific, a sparkling orange line paralleling the coast from SoCal up to BC. Even that lacks the precise delineation of most computer graphics—the line seems fuzzy, even broken in places. Martin zooms on the view, zooms again. Resolution and brightness increase: the orange line swells and sparkles and writhes—

It is not an overlay.

+56h14m23s the timer says, incrementing before his eyes.

It doesn't make any sense; how could any fire could burn so brightly, for so long? Surely the flames have consumed everything by now, reduced all combustibles to ash and everything else to slag. Yet somehow it keeps going, as if in defiance of physics itself.

There: along the eastern boundary, a patch of relative darkness where the flames seem to be burning out. Martin watches it spread with a kind of dumb relief, until the swollen black torus of a heavy lifter passes between earth and sky. To the satcam it looks like the shadow of Mercury crossing a sunspot, but even at this range there's no mistaking the bright trail it spreads behind it. The dying flames leap high in its wake, forcibly resurrected.

They're not letting it die, he realizes. The fire burns on endless life support, from Oakland to Kitimat, and Martin Perreault knows with sudden dull certainty that a course has been set for it to follow.

East.

He leaves the office for a few moments, returning with a toolbox from his hobby room. He unlatches every access panel he can, smashes open the rest. He calmly dismembers each and every piece of equipment remaining in the room, cutting fiberop, pouring acid into computational organics, smashing crystals with a pneumatic hammer. Then he pads down the hall to the bedroom. Sou-Hon is asleep at last, curled into a fetal ball. He cocoons her from behind, wrapping her flesh in his, and stares off into darkness while the real world falls asleep around him.

A C K N O W L E D G M E N T S

Thanks first for the forbearance: to Mike Brander, one of the nicest guys you could hope to meet, for not suing me after I inadvertently used his name in the last book.

Thanks next for the help: Laurie Channer, Nalo Hopkinson, Brent Hayward, and Bob Boyczuk all poked and prodded an embryonic stage of the first few chapters. Laurie also endured my endless stream-of-consciousness rambling as I tried to fit all the pieces together; hopefully her sacrifice has spared the rest of you from a similar fate. My agent, Don Maass, made a vital criticism of opening chapters which resulted in a whole new plot thread (and hopefully, less "straining for effect"). David Hartwell edited with his usual renowned acumen, even if he did force me to cut the exploding daddy scene.

I also got diverse technical assistance from other folks with postgraduate degrees like mine, the difference being that theirs were in subjects that actually proved to be good for something. Prof. Denis Lynn (of the University of Guelph) provided not answers, but *questions*, and lines of inquiry for me to pursue. (It's been twenty years since I took a course from the man and he's still forcing me to think for myself.) He also donated a copy of Lodish *et al.*'s *Molecular Cell Biology* to the cause, a text which easily outweighs the yellow pages for the GTA. Isaac "Buckaroo Bonzai" Szpindel—an MD, neurologist, sf writer, screenwriter, and (no shit) *electrical engineer*—helped me out with the chemistry of guilt, and suggested plausible field strengths for rifler implants. He also kept me from slipping into steroid psychosis during a massive poison-ivy infection while I was writing this book. Drs. Alison Sinclair and Fran Terry offered insights, suggestions, and/or overheads on matters microbial. Colin Bamsey told me what kind of alpine trees would be likely to survive the great warming.

Given a world in which Québec has become the predominant economic power, I figured various Quebecisms would have worked their way into casual N'Am conversation—hence all those italicized expletives that left most of you scratching your heads. For a crash course in how to be foulmouthed in Canada's Other Official Language, I thank Joël Champetier, Glenn Grant, Daniel Sernine, and Jean-Louis Trudel, even though they couldn't come up with an alliterative translation for "blood-spewing semen-sucking sickle-celled savior." (They did, however, dissuade me from turning "Celine Dion" into a swear word. Just barely.)

Once again, the music of Ian Anderson and the inestimable Jethro Tull kept me company during the many long nights it took to lay this puppy to rest. As did the music of REM, from whom I stole a couple of chapter titles.

My thanks to all of these for their efforts and/or inspiration, and my apologies for all the stuff I probably got wrong anyway.

The following references helped me beat *Maelstrom* into a shape that's (hopefully) more plausible than if I'd just made everything up myself. This is in addition to the references I cited two years ago in *Starfish*, which I won't bother repeating here: go buy the damn book if you're so interested.

βehemoth

When I started writing this book, strange claims had just started surfacing in the scientific literature: a new kind of extremely primitive microbe freshly discovered, something inconceivably small.[1] So small, in fact—less than 100 nanometers in some cases—that many argued they couldn't possibly be alive.[2] Believers dubbed them *nanobes*. (Formal taxonomy—*Nanobacterium sanguineum*—has been suggested, but not yet formally adopted.[3])

Now, a couple of years later, nanobes have been found not only in hot springs and Triassic sandstone, but in the blood of mammals (including humans).[4] Evidently they find us comfortably reminiscent of the primordial soup in which life originally evolved some 3.5 billion years ago; they feed off the phosphorus and calcium in our blood.

βehemoth is not *N. sanguineum*, of course. It's more sophisticated in some ways, more primitive in others. Its genome is encoded in p-RNA, not DNA; it snarfs sulfur, not phosphorus and calcium; it can't survive in cold saline environments (real nanobes probably can't metabolize under such conditions either, but they can *withstand* them in a dormant state); it has advanced adaptations for cell penetration that are way out of *Nanobacterium*'s league. It's larger, as large as conventional mycoplasmas and marine bacterioplankton. It is also much nastier, and—last but not least—it doesn't actually exist.

I have, however, tried to make this bug reasonably plausible, given the dramatic constraint of a global apocalypse in a crunchy coating. As a result, βehemoth is like one of those "composite serial killers" you read about in True Crime books—bits and pieces of various real-world bugs, thrown together with lots of dramatic license. "A-51" really exists, both in deep lake sediments and the human mouth.[5] *Pseudomonas aeruginosa* is another bacterium that lives quite happily in soil, water, worms, and people;[6] like βehemoth, it has genes that allow it to speed up and slow down its own rate of mutation so it can quick-adapt to novel environments. (I've called them "Blachford genes" here, in the hopes that one Alistair Blachford will get off his ass and publish his thesis on genetic metavariation as an evolutionary strategy.[7]) March and McMahon's 1999 review of receptor-mediated endocytosis[8] told me how βehemoth would be most likely to get inside a host cell, and Decatur and Portnoy[9] told me how it could avoid getting digested afterward. And once again, a nod to Denis Lynn of the University of Guelph for forcing me to worry about such things in the first place.

βehemoth's genetics are cadged from a variety of sources, many of which I quoted without really understanding. The stuff on mitochondria and pyranosal RNA comes from Eschenmoser,[10] Gesteland *et al.*,[11] Gray *et al.*,[12] and Orgel.[13,14] βehemoth's size and genome are consistent with theoretical size limits for microorganisms,[15] and big enough to sustain a normal microbial metabolic rate. (Real nanobes are too small to contain many enzymes, which means that many of their metabolic pathways crawl along at uncatalyzed speeds. They therefore metabolize about ten thousand times slower than bacteria such as *E. coli*[4], which makes them pretty poor candidates for outcompeting a whole biosphere.) And of course, it's looking more and more likely that life *itself* began as a sulfur-dependent phenomenon in a hydrothermal rift vent.[16] I cobbled other bits and pieces from Lodesh *et al.*'s *Molecular Cell Biology.*[17]

Why did I choose something as mind-bogglingly common as sulfur for a bottleneck element? I was trying to make a point about carrying capacity in ecological systems: life is greedy, and if you give it long enough, *anything* can become limiting. Besides, any primitive microbe from a hydrothermal environment *is* likely to have a serious sulfur-dependency problem. (The specialists in the audience will notice that I carefully avoided making βehemoth an obligate sulfur-reducer; I actually envision the little mother's metabolism as being more akin to that of the giant sulfide-consuming microbes reported by Schulz *et al.*[18])

Bottom line, most of βehemoth's traits have real-world precedents. Whether evolution could actually pack all those attributes into a package 250 nanometers across is a whole different issue, of course. Still. Look at all the stuff that fits into Batman's utility belt.

Guilt Trip

The idea of behavior-modification technology is old stuff in fiction; Burgess's *A Clockwork Orange* is an obvious example. In *Maelstrom* I've taken a stab at rediscovering that wheel by explicitly tweaking genes and neurochemistry.

As far as I know, the existence of the "Minsky receptors" that Alice Jovellanos mentions has yet to be confirmed. Something like them, however, must be seated in the frontal cortex where human conscience and morality (such as they are) reside.[19,20] At the very least, certain types of frontal-lobe damage have a tendency to turn good God-fearing folk into sociopaths.

I imagine that Ken Lubin's murder reflex is wired into the neural circuitry described by R. Davidson *et al.*[21] The conceit of using tweaked parasite genes to program such behavior came to me when I was teaching an undergraduate course in animal ecology. The parasites mentioned in *Maelstrom* are real, and have a lot of company.[22,23] One fly-eating fungus hijacks its victim's nervous system just before killing it, forcing it to fly to an upside-down perch and orient its abdomen at an optimum angle for spore dispersal. An ant-fluke called *Dicrocoelium* takes control of its host each night, riding it to the top of a convenient stalk of grass and freezing it there until morning in hopes that some other hapless host will eat it. And yes, *Toxoplasma* really does cause rats to lose their fear of cats (and in some cases, actually to be *attracted* to the smell of cat urine). It is also found in about half the members of *our* species. This stuff is straight out of *The Puppet Masters*, folks. There's even a substantial amount of evidence to suggest that sex itself evolved primarily as a countermeasure against parasite attacks.[24]

Anemone/Maelstrom

First, the Wilderness. The Internet is already more like a wildlife habitat than you might expect. Internet "storms" were first described in 1997,[25] which makes them old news: nowadays you can link to "weather maps" of Internet meteorology,[26] updated several times daily. (Once again, my far-flung futuristic foresight has proven wonderfully adept at predicting the past. The last time was when *Starfish* predicted submarine ecotours to deep-sea rifts within fifty years, only to have such tours advertised in the real world by 1999.)

Those of you who have taken an undergraduate physiology course may remember the *power law*. It's a surface-area-to-volume relationship that governs living systems from whole food webs right down to the capillaries of shrews—essentially a pattern typical of self-organizing (i.e., biological) systems. As it turns out, the World Wide Web itself appears to be evolving in concordance with this law.[27] Something to think about...

Second, the Wildlife. These days it's hardly necessary to cite references on the subject of "artificial life": a web search on the phrase (or on "cellular automata") will demonstrate how massively the field has exploded over the past ten years. That subset of e-life that goes by the name *Anemone* is admittedly a bit more speculative, and based upon two premises. The first is that simple systems, in aggregate, display emergent behaviors beyond the capability of their individual parts. This is pretty much self-evident within a body— who'd deny that a brain is smarter than an individual neuron, for example?—but the principle extends even to aggregations of completely *unconnected* individuals. A school of fish or a flock of birds can be thought of, in effect, as a diffuse neural net.[28,29]

A related premise is that lineages with genetically determined behavior would be able to pass a Turing test if they evolved fast enough. This won't be hard to swallow for anyone familiar with how sophisticated such behavior can be; we do, after all, live in a world where ants practice animal husbandry, birds follow orthodome routes to navigate halfway around the world, and honeybees convey sophisticated travel instructions by wiggling their asses at each other. Skeptics might want to read any of E. O. Wilson's books on sociobiology, or an old *Scientific American* article by John Holland.[30] It's way out-of-date, but it clearly conveys the principles behind genetic algorithms.

Finally, anyone who treats the phrase *group selection* as an obscenity (I admit they're right, most of the time) might first want to check out D. S. Wilson's review article of the subject in *Skeptic*.[31]

Smart Gels

Research on the construction of thinking meat has proceeded apace since *Starfish* came out. Recent research is thumbnailed in "Neurons and silicon get intimate," by Robert "no-not-*that*-Robert" Service.[32] More conventional neural nets are literally in the driver's seat: Carnegie Mellon's ALVINN program (which I mentioned briefly in the references to *Starfish*) has now moved onto the highway, where neural nets have autonomously taken ninety-mile jaunts on public highways, at speeds up to 70mph. They learned to drive by watching people at the same task. It took them less than five minutes.

We still can't be sure exactly what neural nets actually learn when we train them. Paradigm cock-ups of the sort that made my "head cheeses" betray their masters have happened in real life. One infamous military neural net taught itself to distinguish between various ambient light conditions, while all along its humans thought they were teaching it to recognize tanks.[33]

Ganzfeld Interrogation

Back in *Starfish* I cited Roger Penrose's quantum-consciousness theory to justify the rudimentary psi-powers of the rifters. Here in *Maelstrom* Lubin uses the same trick to interrogate Achilles Desjardins. In the interest of full disclosure I should admit that Penrose's theory has come under serious attack from a guy called Tegmark:[34] The quantum-mind aficionados have rallied,[35] but things may be looking a bit iffier on the quantum-consciousness front these days. What can you do.

Haunted by Happiness

Lenie Clarke's "hallucinations" are loosely based on Bonnet's Syndrome,[36] a malady that sometimes results from macular degeneration. The brain really does compensate for loss of visual input by inserting images from visual memory into the gaps. In real life, Bonnet's Syndrome tends to occur in elderly patients, and is frequently associated with bereavement; the hallucinations are more or less seamlessly incorporated into the visual environment (as opposed to the picture-in-picture format Lenie experienced).

Finally ...

If you want a more luminous taste of all this stuff, check out www.rifters.com.

NOTES

1. Unwins, J. P. R. *et al.* 1998. "Novel nano-organisms from Australian sandstones." *American Minerologist* 83: 1541–50.
2. Broad, W. J. 2000. "Scientists find smallest form of life, if it lives." *New York Times,* January 18.
3. Euzéby, J. P. March 2001. List of bacterial names with standing in nomenclature. http://www.bacterio.cict.fr/index.html
4. Kajander, E.O., *et al.,* 1999. "Suggestions from observation on nanobacteria isolated from blood." *Size Limits of Very Small Microorganisms: Proceedings of a Workshop.* National Academy Press, Washington, DC. 164 pp.
5. Kroes, *et al.,* 1999. "Bacterial diversity within the human subgingival crevice. *Proceedings of the National Academy of Sciences of the United States of America.* 796(25): 14547–52.
6. Rainy, P. B. and E. R. Moxon. 2000. "When being hyper keeps you fit." *Science* 288: 1186–8.
7. Blachford, A. 1984. "Metavariation and long term evolutionary patterns." M.Sc. thesis, Zoology, University of British Columbia, 140 pp.
8. Marsh, M. And H. T. McMahon, 1999. "The structural era of endocytosis." *Science* 284: 215–20.
9. Decatur, A. L. and D. A. Portnoy. 2000. "A PEST-like sequence in Listeriolysin O essential for *Listeria monocytogenes* pathogenicity." *Science* 290: 992–5.
10. Eschenmoser, A. 1999. "Chemical etiology of nucleic acid structure." *Science* 284: 2118–23.
11. Gesteland, R. F., *et al.* 1999. *The RNA World.* Cold Spring Harbor Laboratory Press, Cold Spring Harbor, NY. 735 pp.
12. Gray, M. W., *et al.* 1999. "Mitochondrial Evolution." *Science* 283: 1476–81.
13. Orgel, L. 2000. "A simpler nucleic acid." *Science* 290: 1306–7.
14. Orgel, L. and L. Ost. 1999. "Did life originate in an RNA world?" In *Size Limits of Very Small Microorganisms: Proceedings of a Workshop.* National Academy Press, Washington, DC. 164 pp.
15. Vogel, G. 1998. "Finding life's limits." *Science* 282: 1399.

16. Rasmussen, B. 2000. "Filamentous microfossils in a 3,235-million-year-old volcanogenic massive sulphide deposit." *Nature* 405: 676–9.

17. Lodish, H., *et al.* 1995. *Molecular Cell Biology, 3rd ed.* Scientific American Books, W. H. Freeman & Co., NY. 1344 pp.

18. Schulz, H. N., *et al.* 1999. "Dense populations of a giant sulfur bacterium in Namibian shelf sediments." *Science* 284: 493–5.

19. Macmillan, M. 2000. *An Odd Kind of Fame: Stories of Phineas Gage.* MIT Press, Cambridge, MA, 576 pp.

20. Anderson, S. W. *et al.* 1999. "Impairment of social and moral behavior related to early damage in human prefrontal cortex." *Nature Neuroscience* 2: 1032–7.

21. Davidson, R. J., *et al.* 2000. "Dysfunction in the neural circuitry of emotion regulation—a possible prelude to violence." *Science* 289: 591–4.

22. Zimmer, C. August 2000. "Do parasites rule the world?" *Discover*: 80–5.

23. Zimmer, C. 2000. "Parasites make Scaredy-rats foolhardy." *Science* 289: 525–7.

24. John Rennie, J. January, 1992. "Living Together." *Scientific American.*

25. Huberman, B. A., and R. M. Lukose. 1997. "Social Dilemmas and Internet Congestion." *Science* 277: 535–7.

26. Matrix-net's Internet Weather Report, at http://www.mids.org/weather/.

27. Barabasi, A. L. *et al.* 1999. "Internet: Diameter of the World-Wide Web." *Nature* 401: 130–1.

28. Parrish, J. K., and Edelstein-Keshet, L. 1999. "Complexity, pattern, and evolutionary tradeoffs in animal aggregation." *Science* 284: 99–101.

29. Koch, C., and G. Laurent. 1999. "Complexity and the nervous system." *Science* 284: 96–98.

30. Holland, J. H. 1992. "Genetic algorithms." *Scientific American*, 267(1): 66–72.

31. Wilson, D. S. 2000. "Nonzero and nonsense: group selection, non-zerosumness, and the Human Gaia Hypothesis." *Skeptic* 8(1): 84–89.

32. Service, R. 1999. "Neurons and silicon get intimate." *Science* 284: 578–579.

33. Episode four of the PBS video series *The Machine that Changed the World*: Go to http://www.otterbein.edu/home/fac/dvdjstck/CSC100/CSC100 TMTCTW.htm#TM for further information.

34. Tegmark, M. 2000. "The importance of quantum decoherence in brain processes." *Physical Review E* 61: 4194–4206.

35. "Quantum computation in the brain? Decoherence and biological feasibility," abstract of a talk given at the 2000 Tucson Conference by the University of Arizona's Center for Consciousness Studies (available on-line at http://www.consciousness.arizona.edu/hameroff/decoherence.html#Abstract)

36. Teunisse *et al.* 1996. "Visual hallucinations in psychologically normal people: Charles Bonnet's syndrome." *Lancet* 347:794–7.